THE SABRE'S EDGE

Also by Allan Mallinson

A CLOSE RUN THING

HONORABLE COMPANY

A REGIMENTAL AFFAIR

A CALL TO ARMS

THE SABRE'S EDGE

ALLAN MALLINSON

THE OVERLOOK PRESS
Woodstock & New York

First published in the United States in 2004 by
The Overlook Press, Peter Mayer Publishers, Inc.
Woodstock & New York

WOODSTOCK:
One Overlook Drive
Woodstock, NY 12498
www.overlookpress.com
[for individual orders, bulk and special sales, contact our Woodstock office]

NEW YORK:
141 Wooster Street
New York, NY 10012

Library of Congress Cataloging-in-Publication Data

Mallinson, Allan.
The sabre's edge / Allan Mallinson.
p. cm.

1. Great Britain. Army. Cavalry—Fiction. 2. Hervey, Matthew
(Fictitious character)—Fiction. 3. British—Burma—Fiction.
4. British—India—Fiction. 5. Great Britain—History, Military—19th century—
Fiction. 6. Calcutta (India)—Fiction. 7. Rangoon (Burman)—Fiction. I. Title.
PR6063.A36615 S23 2004   823'.914 22   2004043477

Manufactured in the United States of America
FIRST EDITION
ISBN 1-58567-533-4
1 3 5 7 9 8 6 4 2

To

Skinner's Horse

raised 23 February 1803

FOREWORD

In his enigmatic memoir *Bengal Lancer*, Francis Yeats-Brown recounts how the Honourable East India Company received its licence to trade in Bengal. The Mughal overlord, the Emperor Shah Jehan, who built the Taj Mahal, had a daughter, Jehanara – 'modest and beautiful'. One day Jehanara's maid upset an oil lamp in the palace, and in trying to save her the princess scorched herself about the face and hands. Shah Jehan, distraught, sent word for the best physicians in the empire to come to Agra. One Gabriel Broughton, surgeon of the Company's factory at Surat, arrived quickly and, though hampered by the etiquette of purdah (he was only allowed to feel his patient's pulse from behind a curtain), he not only healed Jehanara but also saved her legendary beauty. As reward, he would take nothing for himself, but asked that a charter be given to the Company to trade in Bengal. 'These are the threads of *karma* that go to the making of ant-heaps and Empires,' writes Yeats-Brown: 'a clumsy slave girl, a kind princess, and an altruistic doctor who asked for the charter on which the British built Calcutta.'

When the Mughal hegemony began to weaken, in the middle of the eighteenth century, Bengal broke away from Delhi's rule, along with

Sind, Oudh and Gujerat, and the Company found itself increasingly drawn into the power politics of the successors to the empire. Fortunately there were Robert Clive, Warren Hastings and a great many others of their kind to advance British interests, and by the third decade of the next century John Company was the predominant power in the whole of India.

But there were always challengers, within and without, and the sepoys of the armies of the presidencies of Bombay, Madras and – above all – Bengal, together with the handful of British (King's) regiments for which the Company paid, found themselves from time to time campaigning hard. However, in India the climate and disease claimed many more lives than did the tulwar, the jezail or the jingal – in the war that begins my story, nineteen men out of the legions of twenties who died.

But dead men's boots meant promotion for the lucky ones who survived. That was the soldier's silver lining in the clouds of war . . . In addition to those I have thanked in previous books, and in whose debt I remain, I would add this time Major Patrick Beresford, regimental secretary of the King's Royal Hussars (and their Winchester museum's curator), Sally Brown of the British Library, Liza Verity of the National Maritime Museum and Christopher Calkins of the Petersburg National Battlefield. I must likewise acknowledge my debt over some years now to Dr Anne-Mary Hills, whose long study of Nelson's pathology, and of his navy's medicine, she has unstintingly shared with me. My thanks are also due to Dr Michael Crumplin, surgeon, whose knowledge of surgical practice in Wellington's army is, I suspect, unrivalled. I am, as ever, full of appreciation for Chris Collingwood, whose jacket paintings show a deep knowledge of the minutiae of uniforms and equipment, and whose skill in composition and drawing so vividly sets the scene for my cavalry tales.

On the reverse of the jacket of this, the fifth of Matthew Hervey's adventures, there are two sowars in the distinctive yellow kurtas of Skinner's Horse, better known to the world, perhaps, as the 1st Bengal Lancers. This glorious regiment was raised on 23 February 1803. To them, in admiration, I dedicate *The Sabre's Edge*.

And Israel smote him with the edge of the sword, and possessed his land from Arnon unto Jabbok, even unto the children of Ammon; for the border of the children of Ammon was strong.

The Fourth Book of *Moses*,
called *Numbers*

THE BAY OF BENGAL
1823

' The Commander-in-Chief can hardly persuade himself, that if we place our frontier in even a tolerable state of defence, any very serious attempt will be made by the Burmans to pass it: but should he be mistaken in this opinion, he is inclined to hope that our military operations on the eastern frontier will be confined to their expulsion from our territories, and to the re-establishment of those states along our line of frontier which have been overrun and conquered by the Burmese. Any military attempt beyond this, upon the internal dominions of the King of Ava, he is inclined to deprecate; as instead of armies, fortresses, and cities, he is led to believe we should find nothing but jungle, pestilence and famine.'

The Adjutant-General of the Presidency's Army, to the
Government of Bengal, 24 November 1823

PART ONE

JUNGLE, PESTILENCE AND FAMINE

CHAPTER ONE

THE WOODEN WALLS

The Rangoon River, noon, 11 May 1824

'Sile-e-ence!'

The gun-deck of His Majesty's Ship *Liffey* at once fell still. The big fourth rate had furled sail, dropped anchor and beat to quarters, and her first lieutenant would have the gun crews silent to hear the captain's next order.

Astern of *Liffey* were the sloops of war *Larne*, *Slaney* and *Sophie*, their guns likewise run out and trained ashore. And astern of these, with great pyramids of white sail still set, was the rest of the British flotilla – close on a hundred men-of-war and transports, sailing slowly with the tide up the broad, brown Rangoon river.

The stockades at the water's edge were silent too. Like the gun crews aboard the warships, the Burman soldiers crouched behind their wooden walls, but teak-built walls, not oak. With their spears and ancient muskets, they had no doubt that the white-faced barbarians would pay for their effrontery in sailing up the river without acknowledging the supreme authority of King Bagyidaw, Lord of the White and All Other Elephants.

On *Liffey*'s quarterdeck, Commodore Laughton Peto turned to

Major-General Sir Archibald Campbell, general officer commanding the Burmese Expeditionary Force. 'Well, Sir Archibald?'

'They have had their time, Peto.'

But the commodore required a more emphatic order. Firing first
on an almost defenceless town was not a decision to be entered
lightly. 'You wish me to commence firing, sir?'

Before the general could reply, the shore battery erupted in
smoke and flame. Two or three heavy shot whistled harmlessly
through *Liffey*'s rigging.

The general was obliged, but amazed. His flotilla had violated
the sacred waters of the Kingdom of Ava: but in such force that
could not be resisted. He, Sir Archibald Campbell KCB, veteran
of the Peninsula, had offered suitable terms of surrender. By all the
usages of war the Burmans should have accepted at once.

'Presumption, and folly,' he declared, snapping closed his
telescope. 'Commence firing!'

Peto nodded to his first lieutenant. 'Commence firing.'

The lieutenant raised a speaking trumpet to his lips. 'Fire!'

Hervey started. The roar of cannon was like nothing since
Waterloo – fourteen twenty-four-pounders firing as one, nearly the
weight of shot that the whole of the horse artillery could dispose
that day along the ridge of Mont St-Jean. He gripped the taffrail
as if he would be shaken off his feet. But before the smoke rolled
back over the quarterdeck, he just managed to glimpse the
destruction that the broadside had wrought – the guns in the shore
battery toppled and the great teak doors of the stockade beaten
down.

There was another broadside, this time from *Larne*, and even
closer to the bank. Not as heavy as *Liffey*'s, but almost as
destructive, it battered down yet more of the stockade, the nine-
pound shot from the guns on her upper deck firing high and
sending showers of bricks and tiles from the buildings within.
Hervey did not think the business could take much longer.

Now *Slaney*'s and *Sophie*'s guns were bearing on the walls, and
soon too were those of the East Indiamen-of-war astern of them,
so that there was a drumroll of fire as the crews worked their
pieces like demons.

No, the Burmans could not take a pounding like this for much
longer. No one could.

Campbell agreed. He turned to the little knot of staff officers behind him. 'How our work might have been easier in Spain, eh, gentlemen, had we been able to sail our artillery about so!'

And had the enemy been so obliging as to call a pile of logs a fortress, said Hervey to himself.

Major Seagrass, the general's military secretary, turned to his temporary assistant. 'Where are these war boats of yours, Hervey?'

Hervey nodded. He had warned of them, albeit from limited experience, and the flotilla was taking particular precautions against surprise. 'It seems our luck is great indeed. And the Burmans', too, for those boys yonder are bruising for a fusillade.' He indicated the lines of red at the gunwales of the transports, private men and sepoys alike in their thick serge, muskets trained ready to repel the war boats. The attack would be a swift, swarming affair if it did come.

The general judged it the moment. 'Signal the landing!'

A midshipman had the signal-flag run up in a matter of seconds. There was cheering from the transports, audible enough even with the crashing broadsides. Soon boats were being swung out and lowered, or hauled alongside by their tow lines, and redcoats began descending to them.

As they began pulling for the bank, fire erupted once more from the battery. *Liffey* answered at once, and there was no more firing from the stockade.

The landing parties scrambled from the boats and raced for the breaches. They exchanged not a shot, and soon there was more cheering as the Union flag rose above the shore battery. Campbell saw his success, called off the bombardment and ordered the rest of his force to follow. In half an hour two brigades were ashore, with still not a musket discharged by either side. Later the general would learn that not a man of his had been so much as grazed, and he would remark again on the address with which battle could be made with artillery such as he had.

He turned now to the little group of officers on *Liffey*'s quarterdeck. 'Well,' he said, with a most satisfied smile, his thick red side-whiskers glistening with sweat in the clammy heat of the season before the monsoon. 'Let's be about it. We have a great need of beef and water, and it is there ashore for the taking. My boat, please, Commodore Peto!'

Captain Matthew Hervey had watched many an infantry action in his dozen and more years' service, but always from the saddle. The quarterdeck of one of His Majesty's ships was undoubtedly a more elevated vantage point, and perhaps preferable in that respect, but it was no less frustrating a place for an officer to be when there was hot work to be done with the enemy. But then the only reason he was able to observe the action at all was that he had a friend at court – or, more exactly, on the supreme council of the presidency of Bengal – who had arranged that he join the expedition on General Campbell's staff, the general being clearly of a mind that there was no place for cavalry on this campaign. Indeed, the general had planned his operations certain that everything would be accomplished by his infantry – King's and Company's – with the sole support of the guns of the Royal Navy, and without any transport but that which floated, or supply other than obtained locally. It was, by any reckoning, an admirably economical expedition.

Hervey's regiment, His Majesty's 6th Light Dragoons, had been scattered about Bengal on countless trifling errands these past three years, frustrating to officers and men alike. They had hoped to be employed against this impertinent King of Ava, who threatened the Honourable Company's domain, insulted the Crown and boasted of his invincibility, but it seemed that nowhere on the eastern frontier were their services required. Especially not in this *coup de force*, by which it was calculated that the Burman king would at once capitulate. No, their value to the Company – which, after all, paid the Crown handsomely for their services in India – lay in their ability to be fast about Hindoostan in the event of trouble. The commander-in-chief would not easily be persuaded, therefore, to tie down a single troop of King's cavalry that constituted his meagre reserve. And so, with the prospect of further months of tedium before him, any diversion had seemed attractive to Hervey – even as assistant to an officer who himself had little to do. But it had truly been an unexpected delight to learn that his revered friend Peto had the naval command.

Not that in other terms Hervey had been ill content with the years since Chittagong. Chittagong had been an affair, indeed, of real cavalry daring, if through country wholly unsuited to the arm.

'And we shall shock them': that had been his intention. And how they *had*, cavalry and guns appearing from the forest like chinthes, routing the Burman invaders and burning their war boats. Yes, he had hazarded all, and the Sixth's reputation in Calcutta had been made. And he had watched his troop's star continue to rise afterwards. He had taken real pleasure in advancing several of his men, though he had had occasion more often to shed a tear when the fever or some such had claimed one of them (the regiment's corner of the cemetery in the Calcutta lines now held the bones of more dragoons than any single troop could muster). Above all, however, the regiment was at ease with itself. That was their colonel's doing. Sir Ivo Lankester may have been an extract, but he had his late brother's blood in his veins, and never did the Sixth have a finer officer than Sir Edward Lankester until they had had to bury him at Waterloo. And the regiment was no less handy for being at ease, for Sir Ivo managed somehow to have the best of them, always, without recourse to any more rebuke than he might for an inattentive hound. It was said that he had only to look pained for the hardest of sweats to feel shame, and only to smile for the same to believe they were as good as chosen men. He had returned to England for his long leave two months before, and he had done so with utter confidence: the major, Eustace Joynson, for whom sick headaches and endless returns had been the miserable order of the day under the previous colonel, was now modestly self-assured. Sir Ivo knew that Joynson would always err on the side of kindness, and that since the troop captains and lieutenants, and the non-commissioned officers, were all sound enough, a right judgement would be reached in those things that mattered most. One of those judgements had, indeed, been to permit Hervey his attachment to the general's staff.

Despite having almost nothing to do, Hervey had from the outset found the appointment fascinating, for it allowed him a seat at the general's conferences, albeit in an entirely attendant capacity. He had thus been privy to the plan of campaign throughout almost its entire evolution. It was, like all good plans, in essence simple. The Governor-General, Lord Amherst, was of the opinion that it would be necessary only to occupy Rangoon, the country's great trading port, for the King of Ava to lose courage and ask for terms, and that the Burman people, in their condition of effective

7

slavery to King Bagyidaw, would welcome the British as liberators. Thereafter it would be an easy enough business to sail the four hundred miles or so up the Irawadi to Ava itself and take it – opposed or otherwise. Even the timing was propitious, for the rainy season was soon to begin, and the river would thereby be navigable to Commodore Peto's flotilla. Furthermore, since this was to be a maritime, indeed a riverain, expedition, there would be no need to embark the transport required to maintain the army. It was altogether a very thrifty way of making war, and General Campbell was justly pleased with the speedy accomplishment of the first part of his design. Pleased and relieved, for he had provisioned his force only for the crossing of the Bay of Bengal, and there had been delays. Now he had the better part of eleven thousand mouths to feed, and the sooner they were ashore the sooner they could begin buying beef – and water.

Hervey beckoned to his coverman to get into the cutter before him. Besides the sailors at the oars, they were the only occupants of the general's two boats not wearing red. They settled towards the bow and Hervey took off his shako, then mopped his forehead and fastened closed the front of his tunic. 'Did you see anything of the cannonade?'

'No sir,' said Lance-Corporal Wainwright, grimacing. 'I was helping bring shot. My ears are still ringing.'

'Mine too,' said Hervey, looking at his watch. It was not yet one o'clock.

'Pull!' called the midshipman, and a dozen oars began ploughing the flat brown water of the Rangoon river.

In not many minutes they were grounding on the shallow slope of the bank in front of what remained of the great teak gates of the stockade – no need even for wet feet. Tidy files of redcoats, King's and Company's alike, marched ahead of them with sloped arms as if at a field day. Hervey jumped from the boat wondering if his misgivings had been wholly unfounded after all. Eyre Somervile's misgivings, rather, for it had been his friend at court who had voiced them first. His own doubts could be only those concerning the military arrangements, although in truth these he found worrying enough.

Somervile had been convinced that the greatest peril lay in King

Bagyidaw's self-delusion. The third in council of the Bengal presidency had his own sources of information in Ava, which told him that the king was surrounded by sycophants and believed all their blandishments about the invincibility of the Burman soldier. Indeed, Somervile had learned that the king had not even been told of Hervey's spoiling raid at the headwaters of the Chittagong river three years before; that, instead, the king believed it had been the hand of Nature that had laid a torch to his boats, for no barbarian could set foot on Avan soil without the authority of the Lord of the White and All Other Elephants. And anyway, did not he, Bagyidaw, have the greatest of generals – Maha Bundula – to pit against an impertinent invader?

Eyre Somervile was therefore of the decided opinion that the fall of Rangoon would merely presage a long and arduous campaign. And he was by no means convinced, either, that the Burman people would welcome the invader as a liberator. Why, indeed, should they, if they too believed that Maha Bundula would throw him back into the Bay of Bengal whence he had come? And if that were to happen, death would follow automatically for anyone who had in the least part aided the invader. Eyre Somervile, after years of study, and years of practical business, did not believe for one minute that a single Burman would risk his neck in the Company's cause.

But this landing at Rangoon was so easy, the resistance so lacking in spirit, that perhaps, thought Hervey, Somervile had given too much credence to his admittedly well-placed agents. There were things he must see for himself, and quickly. 'If you have no direct need of me, sir,' he said to his principal, as matter-of-fact as he could, 'I should like to make a reconnaissance of the town.'

'Of course, Hervey, of course,' replied Major Seagrass, distracted. General Campbell's military secretary had somehow contrived to be the only member of the staff to get his feet wet, and was trying to rid his boots of water. 'There'll be scarce enough for one of us to do till the headquarters are open.'

Hervey had used the military term to describe his intended survey of the town, and it was certainly the case that he had a military purpose to his perambulation, but in truth he was just as curious to see the sights of the fabled seaport of the Burmans. By all accounts some of its temples were singular. 'Very well, then, sir.

9

I shall report back by sunset at the latest.' He saluted and made away before Seagrass could have second thoughts.

Corporal Wainwright unclipped his carbine and took a cartridge from his crossbelt pouch. He bit off the end, tapped a little powder into the priming pan, then poured the remainder down the barrel, dropped in the ball from between his teeth and rammed it home with the swivel rod.

Hervey noted with satisfaction that it was done in mere seconds.

'Just in case, sir,' said Wainwright, feeling it necessary to explain the precaution even with so many redcoats abroad.

Hervey smiled grimly. 'Don't be too sure that you'll draw the charge, Corporal Wainwright. The Burmans may have fled, but I doubt they'll count themselves beaten.'

There were so many infantrymen about the streets, however. Even if the Burmans counter-attacked, Hervey thought they must be repulsed before they could get a footing on the stockades. But in fleeing before the bombardment, they had made a good job of leaving little for the comfort of the invader. House after house was empty of portables, the heavier furniture was broken up, and Hervey was further disquietened by the evident system with which it had been accomplished. It spoke of a discipline that might be turned to good effect against an invader. It was evidence, certainly, that Calcutta's assumption of cooperation was wholly ill-conceived. As he made his way past groups of infantrymen waiting for the serjeants to allocate a billet (at least they would have a roof over their heads when the rains came), Hervey began to fear the worst – that the rice stores and granaries had been emptied too, and the cattle driven into the jungle.

He tramped the town for an hour. It proved an unlovely place, with few buildings of any solidity and aspect, even the official ones. In the wake of the redcoats he saw not a house whose doors or windows remained barred, but neither did he see a man with any-thing more valuable in his hands than an iron cooking pot or a pan. Here and there a Buddhist shrine would impress, as much by the gilded contrast with its surroundings as by any true merit, and from time to time he would catch sight of the soaring pagoda of Shwedagon a league or so to the north, rising above the squat meanness like St Paul's above the rookeries of the City.

'I would lay odds that yonder place will be a regular hornet's nest,' said Hervey to Wainwright as they climbed a wall to get a better view. 'I'll warrant that's where they've bolted with the treasury.'

There was shooting still, sporadic shots from the redcoats searching the streets. But it did not trouble him. He knew they were aimed not at the enemy but at obstinate locks. It had been the same every time they had captured a place in Spain. It took a while, always, for the officers to regain order – hot blood, the exhilaration of being alive after the fight, the prospect of a bit of gold, the certainty of finding something to slake a thirst. That was all it was, but it could be brute enough when it ran unchecked for too long. At least he would not see the worst of it today, for there had been no fighting to hot the blood, no long march beforehand. Only the wretched, clammy heat of the day.

They pressed on. Several much smaller pagodas bore the signs of the infantry's passing.

'Ah, this looks worthier,' said Hervey, stopping at one of them. 'As resplendent, I'd say, as any of the shrines around Calcutta. Except, of course, it's all sham.' He prodded at the gold leaf with his sabre. 'In Calcutta it would be marble instead of this teak, and the inlay wouldn't be glass. Evidently our red-coated friends thought little of it.'

The pillaging seemed to have consisted in dashing all the lattices to the floor and then being disappointed to find that the imagined rubies and emeralds became so many cheap shards. Hervey sighed to himself. He'd seen a lot worse – the Prussians, for one (after Waterloo they had been thoroughly wanton in their destruction). But knocking down even gaudy pagodas was hardly the way to win the hearts of the Burman people, let alone their active support. And support was what General Campbell's plan of campaign depended on. He just hoped the officers would have their men in hand soon.

'But solid enough, sir,' said Wainwright, having made his own assessment of the structure. He pointed to the roof. 'Look at that.' An iron shot from one of the broadsides was embedded in a joist. It had not fully penetrated but had somehow caused the wood to splinter on the inside. Hervey had heard Peto speak of the especial danger in teak-built men-of-war. Unlike oak, Peto said, a teak splinter invariably meant a septic wound. He had been most insistent on it, most insistent that while the Indies might be a place of sickness for the soldier, the sailor faced his trials too.

Many would be the trials in this campaign, right enough. Hervey sheathed his sabre and took off his shako. 'You know, Corporal Wainwright, it is one thing to enter the roads of a seaport and bombard the town – many a captain's done that. But it's quite another to sail upstream for all of five hundred miles when the degree of resistance is uncertain.'

Corporal Wainwright had been a dragoon for nearly five years and had worn a chevron for two of them. Hervey held him in particular regard, not least because he was recruited from his own town, but more so because of his thoroughgoing decency and unwavering sense of duty. He reminded him of Serjeant Strange, yet without that fine NCO's somewhat chilly piety. Hervey had made him his covering corporal at the first opportunity.

'Well, it couldn't be less resistance than here, sir.'

It was true that the defenders of Rangoon had been scarcely worth the name so far, but was the town defensible against so powerful a cannonade as that which Peto's ships had delivered at point-blank range? Hervey sat down on the pagoda steps and loosened his collar. 'But what does the disappearance of every living soul, and all their chattels and livestock, bode?'

Corporal Wainwright had not been on campaign. He had tramped through the jungle three years before with Hervey's troop to fire the Burman war boats, but that was a mere raid, scarcely comparable in military organization with the scale of this expedition. This indeed was war. Nevertheless, he could make a fair estimate. 'One way or another, sir, we're going to be here longer than we thought.'

Hervey nodded. He knew from Peninsula days that General Campbell could make battle, but he had no idea if he could make war. What he had seen so far – not least the delays even in getting to Rangoon – was not auspicious. 'Well, Corporal Wainwright,' he said, taking a draw on his canteen. 'I think that it is a show of resistance and we might expect more. I think the battalions had better get this place into a state of defence quickly, lest the Burmans counter-attack. Our men-of-war wouldn't be able to support them. It may well be why the Burmans abandoned the town.'

As if in response to Hervey's assessment, redcoats of His Majesty's 38th Foot now came doubling past. Except that things weren't quite right.

Hervey sprang up. 'Come on, Corporal Wainwright. There's the glint of gold in those eyes.'

More men rushed by, without NCOs, almost knocking Wainwright to the ground.

'Or liquor, sir.'

'Either way it'll be trouble.'

They drew their sabres. Wainwright lashed out with the flat of his to check the barging of another gaggle, this time from the Thirteenth. 'Hold hard! Don't you see the officer?' he bawled.

They took off after the Thirty-eighth, Hervey cursing.

The narrow ways between the houses were soon choked with men, some without their muskets. Then it was impossible to go any further. Wainwright clambered onto the roof of one of the more solid-looking houses to try to see ahead. He was down again as quickly, bringing a shower of tiles with him and a foul string of abuse from the infantrymen below. 'Drink, sir. They're tossing bottles of it out of a warehouse. There must be two hundred men there, at least.'

'Well, we can't do anything of ourselves. Where are their NCOs?' Hervey turned and began pushing his way past men still homing on the irregular issue. 'Always the same,' he snarled, using his own sabre freely to force his way through. 'And these not even Irish!'

Down one of the side streets they found a picket of the Forty-first in good order. The corporal came to attention.

'Where is your officer?' asked Hervey, raising his sword to acknowledge.

'The colonel is only just in there, sir,' replied the man in a pronounced Welsh accent, indicating an official-looking building with a high-canted roof. 'The picket officer 'as just been round, sir.'

Hervey nodded and sheathed his sword, then made for the battalion's headquarters.

The Forty-first's colours were hanging from a window, with a sentry close to. 'I am Captain Hervey, of General Campbell's staff. I should like to speak to your colonel.' Hervey touched his shako in reply to the private man's butt salute.

'Sir!' The sentry turned and went inside.

Hervey shook his head. Between the Forty-first and the Thirty-eighth, and for that matter the Thirteenth, there was nothing to choose as a rule. They were all steady on parade: he had seen it with his own eyes in Calcutta. But once the NCOs had lost their hold—

The adjutant came out, hatless. 'Captain Hervey!' He made a small, brisk bow. 'The colonel is with the brigade-major. May I assist you?'

'There's a riot towards the north gates,' began Hervey, indicating the general direction. 'The Thirteenth and the Thirty-eighth, two companies and more arriving, and no sign of their officers. They've found a drink store.'

The adjutant did not hesitate. 'Serjeant-major!'

Out came the shortest regimental serjeant-major Hervey had ever seen, shorter even than Private Johnson. 'Yessah!'

'There's a riot of the other two battalions. Summon the picket.'

'Sah!'

'I'll have the reserve company under arms at once, Captain Hervey. But the picket – a stitch in time.'

Hervey was not certain he understood. 'I don't think a picket will be—'

The RSM reappeared. His eyes blazed as he struck the palm of his hand with the silver knob of his cane. 'Right, sah!'

The picket – a dozen men – were already falling in.

The RSM was impatient for the off. Twenty years in a red coat told him that indiscipline was contagious, and he was not about to have his Welshmen tempted from military virtue by intemperate roughs from other regiments. 'Follow me, Corporal Jones. Double march!'

Hervey had no choice but to take the lead.

A curious sight they made, a captain and a lance-corporal of light dragoons doubling through the alleyways of Rangoon with a dozen red-coated infantrymen in file behind them, muskets at the high port and the diminutive RSM at their head. But the stitch was not in time enough to prevent the drink from doing its worst. When they reached the warehouse there was hardly a man on his feet, and those that were staggered hatless and without their muskets.

14

'Lord, deliver us,' said the RSM, holding up his cane to halt the picket. 'What in the name of God have they got inside them?' He seized a canteen from the hand of one of the capering privates and sniffed it. 'Brandy!' He poured what little remained to the ground.

The Thirteenth's private objected very foully. Corporal Jones stepped forward and felled him with a butt stroke to the chest.

'Stand up, you men!' bellowed the RSM, jabbing his cane here and there. 'Officer present!'

They were too far gone. They neither knew nor cared about their delinquence. 'Right!' growled the RSM. 'If that's the way it is to be. Picket, fix bayonets!'

Hervey had a moment's doubt, but there seemed no alternative. More men were appearing with every minute, all in search of their 'dues'.

The RSM began pushing through the mob of redcoats, shouting orders, cursing, lashing out with his cane, while to his left and right a single file of bayonets marched ready to do the worst if anyone should resist with more than abuse. Hervey, and Corporal Wainwright with his sabre drawn, followed as best they could.

They reached the source of the intoxication for the cost of a mere three further men succumbing to the musket's butt. The point of the bayonet had only been threatened, and the RSM had still not drawn his sword. Hervey marvelled at the man's self-possession and resolve. By his reckoning there were the best part of three hundred soldiers about the streets in abject disorder, yet the RSM seemed no more perturbed than if he were stepping between two brawlers in a barrack room. 'Right, Corporal Jones, two men on the doors, then get inside and clear them out!'

'Sir!' shouted the corporal, turning to look at the picket. 'Morgan and Jones-Seven-seven – on the doors. The rest of you, inside with me!'

'Of all the things them Burmans took, sir, and they have to leave brandy behind!' said the RSM, rapping his hand again with the cane.

Hervey shook his head. 'I shouldn't be surprised if they left it for the purpose, sar'nt-major. It's halted more men than their muskets have.'

'That is true, sir. A European merchant, do you suppose?'

'Probably. He's doubtless taken to the jungle with the rest of them. I hope he had more sense than to try to guard his stock.'

It took fifteen minutes to secure the warehouse, and another thirty to have the comatose occupants carried out, the RSM pressing disappointed new arrivals to the task. Only then did officers and NCOs from the offending regiments begin arriving. It seemed that this was not the only brandy warehouse, though Hervey was past caring what had detained them. One of the lieutenants told him plaintively that liquor had gone about the ranks faster than he'd ever seen. Hervey could believe it. It was no excuse, but it happened when the taut discipline of going into action was suddenly let down, when NCOs, their eyes on other things for the moment, lost their firm grip of the ranks. It was no more than a horse let off the bit surprising its rider with a nap. Except here it was getting on for a whole battalion off the bit.

Hervey saw smoke rising above the rooftops beyond the warehouse. He thought the redcoats better left to their own, and set off instead with Corporal Wainwright to investigate the source.

They felt the heat even before they saw the flames. Hervey, now alarmed, began running to see what had taken hold. Almost every building he'd seen was made of wood, and the streets were so narrow there would be nothing to check the spread of the fire. A few sepoys were doing their ineffectual best, but there was yet no organized attempt.

'Shall I get the RSM again, sir?' asked Wainwright, seeing the sepoys willing but without means.

Hervey saw a havildar, and then a lieutenant. 'No, I think the native battalion will have to cope. Better return to General Campbell's headquarters and report. I'll warrant he'll have no notion how perilous things are in this part of the town.'

It took a long time to reach headquarters. The streets and alleyways were a press of men, some fully under discipline, some imperfectly, some not at all. Smoke kept barring progress, and from time to time flames, for the fire was spreading aloft and others had been started as carelessly as the first. When Hervey finally arrived at his destination, the customs house close by the main gates, and begged leave to report, he found the general in a deal of agitation and his face the colour of his red side-whiskers.

'What in God's name is going on?' Campbell spluttered, staring at the smoke now filling the sky over the northern part of the city. 'What are the brigadiers about?'

Hervey told him as much as he knew.

The general looked fit to burst.

However, his staff colonel appeared with news that relief was at hand. 'Sir, I have just learned that Commodore Peto, seeing the fires, has ordered ashore as many of his and the other ships' men as possible to our assistance.'

Hervey allowed himself a smile at the thought of the choice words with which Peto would have given his opinion of affairs on land. But it was Peto through and through – as prompt to take action as any man in the service.

General Campbell turned to his colonel. 'Get me the brigadiers,' he rasped. 'By the sound of things we stand close to being burnt out, and the Burmans could put half the brigades to the sword if they'd a mind!'

Not for the first time did Hervey find himself making unfavourable comparisons between the wooden world and the ranks of red. And he had no doubt that Peto was at this very moment doing likewise.

CHAPTER TWO

AGAINST THE TIDE

That evening

Flowerdew poured two glasses of Madeira. He offered the silver tray first to Hervey and then to his captain before Peto dismissed him with his customary nod.

'Well, a damned sorry start to a campaign!' said the commodore when his steward had gone. 'Half the men ashore drunk and incapable of standing to their posts, and all the signs of a country as hostile as any other that's invaded.'

'Hardly *half* the men, Peto!'

'I grant you the native troops may be in good order, but I've a thousand hands and marines ashore doing others' duty. There'll be no relief for those in the guard boats tonight.'

'It's certainly dark enough for the Burmans to get alongside,' agreed Hervey.

'It's not the war boats that trouble me but fire boats. The tide's still running out. They could run them down all too easily, and it'll be the best part of tomorrow before we have the boom finished.'

Hervey grimaced. There was no doubting the havoc that fire boats would wreak, for a topman could very nearly climb from

18

ship to ship. 'The general's sent pickets for a mile upstream. They ought to be able to raise the alarm, at least.'

Peto took another sip of his Madeira. 'We must believe it. But I am already uneasy about what Campbell intends next. I assume the native provision will remain elusive but that he will march on Ava nevertheless. In which case how does he expect me to supply him, with both banks of the river in hostile hands? How may I risk a merchantman up or down without escorts? And I have not the ships.'

Hervey thought Peto uncommonly downcast. After all, here was the man who, but six or seven years ago, had sailed the frigate *Nisus* up the Godavari until there was nothing beneath her keel, and had then dismounted her guns and sent them in boats to the aid of his friend. 'You have the ships to force the river to Ava, though, have you not?'

'Four hundred miles, Hervey; four hundred! And I have but one steamer. Just imagine it.'

Hervey could. Memories of the Peninsula had not faded with the years. 'I don't suppose it would be any easier to stretch a line of communication here than the French found in Spain. And there, at least to begin with, the people supported them.'

Peto nodded. 'There should have been warning enough in what was learned these twenty years past in Holland. Folly to embark on an expedition in the hope of a country turning its coat.'

'But now we are come, I don't see that the general has any choice but to go to Ava.'

Peto refilled their glasses and shook his head. 'Nor I. But as soon as the Burmans learn what we're about, they're bound to bring back every last man from Arakan and Assam. There'd be the very devil of a job fighting through them all. Campbell's only course is to make lightning work of the advance. Do you see any prospect of that?'

Hervey frowned. 'It has been an inauspicious beginning, let us say. But in fairness, these are early days.'

'We wasted enough of them at Andaman looking for beef and water. I've never heard of an army that marched without provisions before.'

'You know,' began Hervey, measuring what he had to say as if not completely certain of it himself, 'Eyre Somervile told me the commander-in-chief and the Governor-General had disagreed very profoundly over the campaign.'

'I had not heard, but then why should I? I've met with Paget only once, and that was to present my compliments. The Governor-General I have never set eyes on.'

Hervey looked surprised. This was their first opportunity for intimacy since the expedition had got under way, and he had imagined Peto might have had at least some say in events. 'It seems the reason for our expecting the populace to rise is that Lord Amherst had intelligence from Ava to the effect that King Bagyidaw would at once lose heart if we took Rangoon. It would appear that Bagyidaw knows all too well that his officials so oppress the people they would see us as come to lift their yoke, so to speak.'

'Perhaps they believe their yoke is easy compared with what a foreigner might bring on them. What was Paget's opinion?'

'General Paget was convinced that operations should be directed principally towards securing Chittagong. He believed the Burmans were best punished then by striking from the sea.'

'It doesn't seem to amount to any great difference as far as we are concerned at this moment.' There was a distinct note of disdain in Peto's voice. 'I do despair of our great men at times. They show so little propensity to think a matter through. They seem always to think it somehow sufficient for the navy to put ashore redcoats, and that by that very act there will be fearful trembling at the heart of the enemy's enterprise. I blame Pitt – he was forever breaking windows with guineas.'

Hervey merely raised his eyebrows (Peto knew his mind in these matters without need of words). 'I should say that it is, too, Somervile's opinion. And he, I think, sees the whole very well.'

Peto shook his head despairingly. 'So it seems we have embarked on a strategy which may already be turning turtle.' He rose to fetch a chart from the table, then sat down again and began peering at it. 'We descend upon Ava from the sea, so to speak, because we cannot do so from land. And we bring no provisions or transport with us because, consequent on the taking of Rangoon, the populace will not only desist from interfering with our progress upstream but supply us with all our material needs as my ships take the army to gain its object.'

Hervey raised his eyebrows again. The course of Peto's logic was evident.

'Rangoon is burned and the populace driven off, and the Irawadi will need clearing with the bayonet to enable my ships to reach Ava. I count that a major reverse in design.'

Hervey could only nod.

'And of course, to give us every facility in the venture, the expedition is timed so that the rains which begin any day will swell the Irawadi to enable my ships to make easy progress.' Peto laid down the map, shaking his head and looking as sad as he was angry. 'You and I know those same rains will fix the army here in Rangoon. The country'll be turned to swamp. I'll warrant even Amherst would want to rethink his stratagem if he were to think through these little matters.' He smiled, but wryly. 'I concede, however, that these are early days still!'

Hervey found himself in an unusual position: he was a mere observer of events. However, all his instincts demanded still that he took his commander's view. And that required that he forgo too much criticism and look for advantage instead. 'Let us see what the day brings. Rain will at least make the country equally impassable to the Burmans.'

'You must hope so,' said Peto. He sipped his Madeira in a way that spoke to Hervey of the chalk-and-cheese difference in their fighting milieus. 'But I shall want the general to take the offensive upstream tomorrow, for we have to have all the Burman boats burned within a league. I cannot sit here beyond another day. You may take that message ashore with you, if you will.'

'It might be best if you were to impress it upon Campbell in person.'

Peto shook his head again. 'No. I'll not go ashore when there's the threat of fire boats. I'll see him early in the morning and we can agree on what support I can lend him. I take it he'll want the rest of the divisions landed?'

'I'm sure of it.' Hervey made to rise.

Peto rose with him and clapped a hand on his arm. 'I'm sorry you will not stay longer. It is very good to see you, though I could wish for better circumstances.'

Hervey smiled. 'Ours are not professions that would prosper in better circumstances!'

'Indeed, no. And I had at one time thought I should never get a command again once Bonaparte was put in his box.'

'Should we not still be saying "God rest his soul" then?'

Peto returned the smile. 'Perhaps. It will be an unquiet one otherwise, for sure.'

'Thank you for my dinner. I have a premonition of its being the last of any substance or quality for some time.'

'Not if you can find reason to come aboard *my* ship, I assure you!'

Flowerdew brought Hervey his cape.

'By the way,' said Peto, his smile turning wry again. 'I did not say how very active and smart your corporal seems. A considerable improvement on your Private Johnson.'

Hervey remembered the first time his groom had presented himself to Peto's ship, almost ten years ago. No one would have declared him a model of military bearing. 'I could not bring the two of them, and Johnson's place is properly with the chargers. But I suspect I shall miss his resource.'

Peto came on deck just before dawn. The officer of the watch touched his hat but said nothing. It was not his place to extend even a greeting without invitation, and had he been sure of which side the commodore wished to stand, he would have quitted his place at once to take the other. Peto looked quickly about, searched the heavens to see what they revealed of the coming rains, then went to the starboard rail. There was the faintest glow in the sky above the jungle. The sight was not new to him, but he was fascinated still. In another ten minutes the sun would rise, and the creatures of the earth would begin the drama of another day, unseen – unseen but noisy. And here in the Indies there was no leisurely beginning, as in temperate parts; no lengthy overture in which to settle to the change to come. It was night, and then it was day, at full throat. Peto watched, wondering. He thought for a moment of the sunrise in his native Norfolk, of the times as a boy he had slipped out of his father's vicarage to run the mile or so to watch the sun come up over the grey waters of the North Sea. He had been so many years in His Majesty's navy; could he ever imagine himself on land again? He shivered, though the air was warm enough. It was not the thought of the land itself so much as the want of companionship there, for his family were few and he had never taken a wife. Indeed, he had scarcely been in the habit of speaking to a woman beyond what was necessary for courtesy – except perhaps Hervey's sister.

He had spoken of Elizabeth with Hervey at dinner. Not much, for their preoccupations had been the here and now, but he had praised her, calling her a woman of spirit and discernment; to which Hervey had replied that she was greatly more than that, worthy though the description was. She had devoted herself wholly to familial duties, not least indeed the care of her own niece, her brother's child. She made sacrifices that were humbling to contemplate.

And Peto had been moved to hear it, as well as, in truth, disheartened by the degree of nobility it spoke of.

He looked over his shoulder towards the stockaded town. It was dark now where last night it had been ablaze. Fires by night always looked worse than they were. He turned to the officer of the watch. 'Has there been gunfire at all?'

He asked so abruptly that the lieutenant half stammered his answer. 'None that I have heard these past two hours, sir. And there was none reported on my relieving Mr Afflick.'

Peto made no reply, merely turning back to watch the eastern sky. So Hervey had had a peaceful night too. Maybe these *were* early days after all. Maybe the populace had taken to the forest in fear for their lives, and would return as soon as the invaders showed themselves benevolent. Maybe the Burman soldiers had no fight in them when it came to facing regular troops. Maybe they had fled the ranks. Peto sighed. There were altogether too many 'maybes'.

Hervey too was awake. In the early hours, General Campbell had given orders for the 89th Foot to be landed and to make ready for a sortie from the stockades at first light. The general had not been idle. He had applied his mind to the situation his brigadiers had reported, and had become convinced that the Shwedagon pagoda was the rallying point for the Burman 'defenders'. Major Seagrass had not objected when Hervey had asked if he might accompany the Eighty-ninth, and so he now stood, with Corporal Wainwright, next to the two ensigns carrying the regiment's cased colours, waiting for the gates at the northern end of the stockade to be swung open. He was not greatly apprehensive, for like the Eighty-ninth he was only too glad to be unconfined at last. On the other hand he was at a loss to know why the general had not ordered a reconnaissance during the night. It was but normal practice after all. Someone had said the reason was that the fires would have lit up anyone moving outside the stockade. But the flames had been doused by three o'clock, and the pagoda was little more than a league distant.

The commanding officer's orders had been straightforward. The battalion would advance in column of route by companies, the light leading, and in double time for the first mile or until contact with the enemy was made (in the cool of the dawn doubling would be no hardship). On meeting the enemy's pickets, the light company would deploy to skirmish and the others in column of companies would take the position with the bayonet.

The men looked eager, even on a breakfast of biscuit and rum. Corporal Wainwright had spoken to several of them as they formed up: it seemed there were many Irish, that some had fought on the Niagara frontier a decade before, but for the most part the battalion had not been shot over.

'I have never marched in a regular advance by infantry,' said Hervey, looking about him at the novel order.

'I don't think I care for it much in truth, sir,' replied Corporal Wainwright, unclipping the carbine from his crossbelt. 'You can't see anything in these ranks, just the man in front.'

It was true, although in the dark there was little enough to see beyond the man in front. 'Yes,' said Hervey, drawing on his gloves. 'From a horse there's a good view of things. And a troop of them now would be worth their while. That is for sure.'

The great gates at last swung open. Commanding voices front and rear animated the ranks. 'Company, atte-e-nshun!'

'Trail arms!'

Hervey took up his sabre scabbard.

'Company will advance. By the front, double march!'

The battalion company in front set off as one – an impressive feat, thought Hervey, since breaking off at the trot was always a ragged affair with cavalry.

'Colour party, double march!' barked the senior ensign.

The two ensigns and their serjeant-escorts took off in step with Number One Company, colours now uncased and at the slope, the commanding officer and serjeant-major to a flank, and Hervey and Wainwright to the rear.

Hervey found it surprisingly easy to keep time. Serjeants called out continuously and with such authority that to break step would have required a marked will. He had not marched to a serjeant's command since joining the depot troop as a new-minted cornet straight from school. There was something of a comfort in it: no need at all to think. But that was the purpose of drill, was it not, to make a man act as if he were a machine, oblivious to all else? And Hervey for one was pleased to be relieved of the need to think too much this morning. He had slept little. There had been a continual coming and going at General Campbell's headquarters during the night, and at one stage there had been a general alarm, with reports that Burman soldiers were observed creeping up on the stockade from the west. But it had proved false. And then there had been another alarm when one of the bamboo cottages near the headquarters had burst into flame, for no reason that the sentries could see. It had been past four o'clock, by his reckoning, when he had at last fallen into a good sleep, only to be woken by Corporal Wainwright at five with tea and a bowl of hot shaving water – exactly as Private Johnson had instructed.

After five minutes the companies changed to quick time, and sloped arms – prudently, thought Hervey, for the eastern sky was now lightening. He had walked these paths before, so to speak: the affair at the river, three years ago. How determined he had been to time the moment of the attack perfectly with the appearance of the sun above the jungle canopy. Almost a ritual, it had been, like the sun rising at the stone circle on the great plain at home in Wiltshire.

It was curious how marching freed the mind to wander. How many hours more would they have to wait in Wiltshire before this same sun rose on them? And how did it rise on his daughter? Did it fall directly on her, or did it light her room only indirectly? Did she wake to see it? Did she fear the dark when it was gone? How strange not to know the answers to such simple questions. But it had been five years, almost, since last he had seen her. Her first letter he carried in the pouch of his crossbelt, along with

Henrietta's likeness, though he had taken neither from their oilskin in a year.

The sky was heavier than that day at the river. There was rain to come; they all knew it. But when? He looked back towards the town. A pall of smoke hung over the greater part of it, and, mean as the place was, he thought it as sorry a sight as at Badajoz or Vittoria, or any other of the Spanish towns that had fallen prey to the revels of the drunken soldiery in their celebration of victory. The Duke of Wellington had cursed the army often enough – the Sixth not excepted – for being too drunk to follow up victory. And usually the men had resented it; officers too. They had had to make long, wearying marches; they had had to fight desperately; they had lost friends; they thought they had earned their rowdy ease.

Not since Waterloo had Hervey been surrounded by so many redcoats, and even that day he was first amidst his own regiment (and at the very end in their van). It felt different from being in ranks of blue. Yet their common bond was discipline, the prime requirement of an army, for without it no other quality was guaranteed. Could it really be the lash that guaranteed these men's good order? Were the Eighty-ninth, and for that matter every other battalion of infantry of the Line, so different from his own?

The Sixth abhorred the lash. They had abhorred it since before he had joined. They took it as a point of pride that a dragoon was animated by something more noble than fear of a flogging. But the duke had always supported the lash, and his judgement had been long in the forming, and tested in the worst circumstances. He held that without it all the lesser punishments could not have effect. 'Who would bear to be billed up but for the fear of a stronger punishment?' Hervey had once heard him say. 'He would knock down the sentry and walk out!' And had he not heard many a man in the old light division say that Crauford had flogged them through the mountains to Vigo, and that had he not done so they would never have got there? But how far would men acknowledge that the lash kept them alive when the going became desperate? And did General Campbell have the determination to see the expedition through to Ava, as 'Black Bob' Crauford had seen the retreat through Galicia?

'Company will break into double time; double march!'

*

In another five minutes there was but a half-mile to go, and it was light enough to make out Shwedagon's soaring dome. Hervey thought it unlikely that the Burmans would have abandoned it unless they had no intention at all of fighting.

'It's like piss-proud Pat of a Sunday morning,' came a voice from the ranks behind.

A welter of reproach followed from an NCO.

'D'ye think there'll be much gold, Serjeant?' came another voice.

'Stick to the drink, Mick. You won't have to carry it as far!'

'He can't hold on to either for long!' came yet another voice from the ranks.

Hervey smiled. The banter was not so very different from the Sixth's, though he did not doubt the capacity for riot in the Eighty-ninth's wild Irish ranks. It was as well that its NCOs brooked no disorder.

There was a shot. Then half a dozen others. A couple of hundred yards ahead? It was difficult to tell. Hervey felt the momentum check just a fraction. Then came the shouting – *quick time!* – and the companies breaking from the double march. Serjeants barked out the step – left, right, left, right; pick it *up!* The ensigns raised the colours. The commanding officer took off for the front of the column. Runners began coming and going. The thrill of action flashed through the ranks like a quickmatch. It would have been the same in the Sixth, thought Hervey – but perhaps more so here, for the ranks were tighter-packed, the men shoulder to shoulder rather than knee to knee.

'Skirmishers out!'

He heard the order ripple along the column. And then a bugle. He didn't recognize the call, supposing it must be for the light company. If *they* were deploying, it couldn't be many minutes before the battalion companies did the same.

'Number One Company, *halt!* Company will incline left; left *incline!* Company will form right, at the halt; right *form!*'

It took less than a minute for Number One Company to change from column of route to face front in two ranks, and with no more seeming effort than if they had been on parade. And this in spite of the semi-darkness and the broken ground.

'With ball cartridge, load!'

27

The best part of a hundred men reached as one into black leather pouches to take out a greased paper cartridge. They bit off the end, poured a little of the powder into the pan of the musket-lock, closed it, emptied the remainder down the barrel, spat in the one-ounce ball of iron, pushed in the paper tube and rammed it home with a clattering noise like a mill full of flying shuttles. Then up came the East India-pattern muskets to the port. Even after so many years Hervey found himself awed by the drill. Rough men, these; unlettered for the most part, the sweepings of the gutters. Yet they worked like the well-turned mechanism of a fine watch. He could feel the swagger in the drill, the pride and confidence in what each man was about, as if he were saying there was no one better at this – no company better, no battalion better; and certainly no army. The 89th Foot, well to the left of the Line, had no royal lace to distinguish the regiment, only green facings like many another; but the 89th (Prince of Wales' Irish) counted themselves second to none, and neither Burman nor monsoon would stop them getting to Ava if that was the general's command. It would have been the same too had the battalion been the 90th Foot, or the 91st. Indeed it would have mattered not what number was worn on the pewter buttons or the blackened 'trotters' – except to the men who wore them. Hervey smiled to himself: the drill would be the same anywhere along the Line, and the spirit no less so.

'Company will fix bayonets; fix . . . *bayonets*!'

More clattering, then sudden silence.

''Shun!'

Number One Company stood stiffly at attention. No man dared move a muscle lest it bring the withering rebuke of an NCO. It was a moment that could not long hold. Neither was it meant to; it was just the captain's final check before the off that he had his men in hand, as a dragoon might bring his horse up sharp onto the bit before pressing him forward to a gallop.

'Company, should-e-e-r *arms*!'

The line seemed to sway, eager to be on with it, though not a foot moved.

'Po-o-rt *arms*! By the right, quick march!'

It would be full light in not many minutes. Hervey strained to see their objective as they struck off, but too many shakos stood in his way. There had been no more firing. It didn't surprise him: the shots came from the outposts, for sure. They'd done their job: raise the alarm, then fall back. He wondered how many cannon the Burmans had, and how close they'd let the battalion come before putting the slow matches to the touch-holes. But he didn't suppose there was a man afraid, nor even for a moment anxious. As soon as the Burmans fired, the battalion would give them a volley and be in on them with the bayonet before they could reload. A ball might take a head off, and grape might tear through flesh and bone, but there was nothing anyone could do about it, so there was no point in having a care of it.

But there was no thunder of cannon, nor rattle of musketry. Only the sudden command, 'At the double!' And then they were running again, faster this time, not quite charging speed he imagined, but definitely faster. Still he could not see where they were doubling to, only the dome of the pagoda itself a couple of hundred yards away. In no time they had closed the distance without another shot, and officers and NCOs were shouting orders for sections and half-sections to follow. Up the steps to the pagoda itself, or to either side of its balustrades, or to beat out the cover to right or left, or to search the shrines that lined the great maidan at the bottom of the steps. They went at it like harriers into kale.

Hervey saw relief and disappointment in equal measure in the faces around him. The Prince of Wales' Irish did not load with ball cartridge here except to discharge it at a live target; they had discharged shot enough at practice ones these several past years. But at least there were not the screams of fallen comrades to heed. Could there be such contradictory feelings in any other craft? For his part, Hervey had no particular desire to blood his sabre again, nor to discharge the pistol that was lodged in his belt. His only thought was what this peculiar absence of resistance portended.

He came upon the commanding officer, a man not much older than he, who wore an expression of both determination and perplexity.

'What in God's name is going on, Hervey?'

They had first met at Vittoria, a dozen years before, when each man's sword had been red, for there had been no doubt what they were meant to be doing *that* day. 'I cannot say, Colonel. But there seem to be only two possibilities.'

29

'Indeed,' sighed the Eighty-ninth's man, ramming home his sword in its scabbard. 'And I wonder how long we shall have to wait to discover which it's to be. There's a degree of confusion so far that I haven't seen since Corunna.'

The captain of the light company came up and asked for orders, to which the colonel replied that his men should beat towards the jungle's edge.

It was exactly as Hervey would have done. 'I fancy the answer will only be found in there, sir,' he said as the captain made off. 'I think sooner or later the general shall have to send patrols some way into the forest to see if the Burmans make a stand or no.'

'Ay,' sighed the colonel. 'And it won't be easy. But first Campbell had better strike upstream, for if the Burmans mount any sort of attack along the river we'll be at sixes and sevens. And fire boats'll be giving yonder commodore a deal to think about, too, I'll warrant.'

'Sir,' was all Hervey thought it necessary to say, for they were but Commodore Peto's own strictures of the night before.

'Well, this place has the makings of a decent billet, at least,' said the colonel, beckoning over his adjutant. 'Come, Merrick. Let us have a look inside that pagoda before Alltoft's men do it any great injury.'

Hervey smiled again. Here was the dry humour of one who sat permanently atop a powder keg, an officer whose easy victory might yet turn to ruin at the hands of the same men who had delivered him the prize. And Shwedagon was a place where riot even on a small scale would not do – a religious site of prominence, of some grandeur indeed. The general would certainly want to see it in one piece. No doubt the colonel was half disbelieving in his good fortune in not having had the battalion ashore when the brandy was flowing. Hervey wondered how the Eighty-ninth's discipline would hold now they were no longer in close order. How active were the subalterns? How true were the corporals? Once, in Spain, he had seen an entire company fire its muskets at the windows of an empty palace rather than draw the charges; the smashing of every pane seemed to give satisfaction to men denied a shot at the French. And gilded carvings and finials were an awfully tempting target.

Now there was more shouting. 'Pres-e-e-ent *arms*!'

30

Hervey looked about to see what the sudden fuss was, and saw General Campbell coming up with Colonel Macbean, commander of the Madras brigade.

The general looked pleased. And well he might, thought Hervey. Yesterday had been one of mixed honours, at best, and this morning's work was a model of method and celerity by comparison.

General Campbell raised his hat to the saluting muskets. 'The guns will be up with you within the hour, Ireson,' he said, eyes twinkling, his red whiskers as bright as his coat. 'This without doubt is the key to Rangoon. Hold on to the pagoda, Ireson, and any attack on the town must falter.'

'Very good, General,' said Colonel Ireson, sounding matter-of-fact.

The colonel's luck was indeed great, thought Hervey. What any man would do to be in a position of the first importance, though he wondered why the Burmans must attack from the north through Shwedagon. But he had not seen a good map and he supposed the general had.

The general had certainly not seen *him* until that moment. 'Ah, Hervey! What brings you here?'

'Major Seagrass had no need of me, General.'

'And you had a mind to see how infantry work! Well you might, sir; well you might. I imagine this campaign shall go down as the first to be made without benefit of cavalry!'

Hervey checked himself. 'Indeed, sir?' The general's novelty knew no bounds. It was already a most singular campaign having no transport or supply.

'Yes indeed. Audacity and the bayonet, Hervey. That is what this campaign is about.'

The general slapped his neck, but the mosquito evaded his hand. It would be the first of many to do so.

An hour later it was raining. The rain fell not in drops, or even in torrents, but as a single sheet of water, so that it was impossible to see more than a dozen yards, and only then with a great distortion. Hervey did not think he had seen anything like it. Neither was it how the monsoon was supposed to begin. But for once the poor redcoats, the infantrymen of the Line and the sepoys, on whom alternately rain fell and fierce sun beat, were dry, for the shrines that surrounded the pagoda of Schwedagon afforded cover for all. Cooking fires blazed inside – teak burned very satisfactorily – and there was skilly and tea in every belly before the hands of Hervey's watch showed nine. Sharing a canteen with the men in whose billet he had taken cover might have seemed an unlikely pleasure for him, but it was almost like being in the Peninsula again. He stood a little apart, with Corporal Wainwright, trying to make out the language of their gestures and method – as strange to him at times as the accents in which they spoke. As flesh and blood they could not, in truth, be so very different from the Sixth, but they were men who drilled as a body, whose military utility was solely as part of that body. They marched as a body, took aim as a body and they fired in volleys. They did exactly as they were told, when they were told. He could certainly admire them for it. He had seen enough red-breasted lines stand rock-like in the face of Bonaparte's columns, and he had seen those lines go forward with the same unshakeable resolve. His dragoons were different. At his best, each was his own man, who used sabre and carbine as he himself judged fit, yet who knew how to combine with others to multiply the effect. Was a man better suited to the one method drawn to the bringers of a particular regiment by some unknown process perhaps? Or was it only drill that made them different? Hervey wondered.

It could not be other than drill, surely, for the recruiting process was haphazard to say the least. He had only to look at Corporal Wainwright to be reminded of quite how haphazard. Wainwright would not have been in uniform at all had not he, Hervey, and Serjeant Collins gone that day to Warminster Common to search for the odd lad who had sunk to where he could sink no further – who was more likely than a husbandman or mechanical to be tempted by the King's shilling. It could only be the process of drill that made a soldier what he was; the drill and how it was imparted. And on this latter the difference was plain enough to him, for he had already noted how awkward these men seemed at being spoken to directly, addressing their remarks in return to Corporal Wainwright. No doubt it was necessary in drilling men to volley and manoeuvre as one body, but it must be deuced awkward never being able to speak directly to a man.

By the time the downpour had eased, a full hour later, Hervey had concluded that of the seven private men, five of whom were from Dublin and thereabouts, four might take to being dragoons with very little effort – supposing, of course, they showed a modicum of aptitude for the saddle – and that of the other three, two were inveterate 'machine men', happy only when their every action was preceded by a word of command from the corporal, while the other was quite probably unsuited even to his present position, so sullen was he that Hervey imagined the serjeant's pike a regular prompter. However, much as he admired the Eighty-ninth's drill that morning, and the relish with which they had gone to the expected fight, he would admit to missing E Troop with its cheery, sometimes outspoken, dragoons. Whatever General Campbell might say now about the utility of cavalry, Hervey was certain he would feel the want of them before the month was out.

As the rain had become little more than a drizzle, he stood up and went to the door of their shelter. He could now see the river again. Pulling upstream were a dozen boats filled with marines and men from the Calcutta brigade, not yet 'blooded' in this curious inaction. He had helped write their orders the night before: they were off to do what he and his dragoons could have done in a fraction of the time and with far less effort. If only those who had conceived this adventure had allowed the possibility of action over land rather than solely from water! He had heard it said in Calcutta that horses could not pass over such terrain. How could anyone doubt that, where a man could go in this country, there for the most part could a horse? Nor, indeed, that when the monsoon turned the country to nothing but swamp there would be no passage for beast *or* man.

Hervey thought of hailing the boats. It would be diverting to join them, for there was nothing to do here but watch the Eighty-ninth put the place in a state of defence. But he reluctantly concluded that it was time he reported himself back to Campbell's military secretary. He was sure there would be nothing for him to do – nothing, at least, of the slightest consequence – but if he exhausted Major Seagrass's indulgence too soon it would be so much the harder to get leave for when the infantry made a determined foray. He slapped his neck with left and right hand in rapid succession, but too late to prevent the bites, and he cursed. It was worse than the fleas in the lousiest billets in Spain.

CHAPTER THREE

THE POINT OF THE BAYONET

Four days later

Hervey slipped into the room where Major-General Sir Archibald Campbell was about to hold his council. It was not very large – enough for a couple of dozen people – and the lamps and candles were making the otherwise coolest time of the day hot. Hervey wondered what could be the imperative for calling the conference three hours before dawn. He supposed he would have heard of any alarm, so the general must have intelligence new come by; or else he had resolved on something that he had been privately turning over for days.

The two brigadiers rose as the general entered, and with them the dozen or so officers on the headquarters staff. Sir Archibald Campbell nodded – all sat – and then he nodded once more, to his quartermaster-general, who pulled loose the knot that held furled a sheet on the wall. Down rolled a hand-drawn sketch of the stockaded port and the Rangoon river to the extent of some two leagues to the north. At the furthest point of the river, on the eastern bank, there was a red circle.

'Gentlemen,' began the general briskly, seizing the bayonet on the table beside the wall and tapping the map with it. 'In the five and one-half days since we hove to in the river yonder' (he inclined his head to indicate the direction), 'our circumstances have changed so decidedly that I am obliged to conceive a wholly new plan of campaign.'

Hervey, as every man in the room, was all attention. He was hardly surprised to hear the assessment, only that it had been the best part of a week in the making. And he was as much relieved as he was surprised to hear it stated so candidly. There had never been any doubting Major-General Sir Archibald Campbell as a fighting officer. Word was that he had been given the exacting command of a Portuguese brigade in the Peninsula because of his impressive physique and offensive spirit, and because the duke himself knew at first hand of his youthful exploits in Mysore. But fearless and spirited fighting was one thing; the design of a campaign – the decision *how* to fight – was quite another. And the design of a campaign was not something to which General Campbell had had any apprenticeship.

'Or perhaps, gentlemen, I should say that it is necessary to recognize that our circumstances are not as were earlier imagined. It is evident that the Burman people are either too afeard to rally to us, or have no heart to do so. We are therefore in want of supplies from Calcutta, and any expedition to Ava will be through hostile territory. Indeed, it will need to be *supplied* through hostile territory.'

Every man in Rangoon must be of the same opinion, thought Hervey. Indeed, Peto had told him yesterday that the sloops he had sent to reconnoitre the mouths of the Irawadi had reported the channels running close in to numerous forts. But at least now they might proceed openly on the presumption of Burman hostility. They might even be allowed to butcher the few cattle that remained. Immunity from the slaughterman's axe had been one thing five days ago, but there was scant reason now to let the troops starve so that sacred cattle could live.

'It is also evident,' continued General Campbell, his voice slowing a little as if to emphasize the importance of what was to follow, 'that the enemy have built themselves stockaded forts upriver, and that thence they are in a position to assail us at will, by land and, what is more, by river, and not least is the renewed threat of fire boats.'

Hervey wondered which might be the general's inference, for there were two that he and Peto had drawn. Would he require to hold Rangoon as a base for operations against the interior, or did he intend to abandon the port since its capture was evidently not the calamity the Governor-General had anticipated? Although, in fairness, there had scarcely been time for the news to shake Ava.

The general brandished the bayonet again. 'And so, gentlemen, our first object is to destroy the Burman capacity for the offensive.'

The declaration of the objective and the jabbing of the bayonet had an immediate effect. There was such a hubbub that the sentry posted outside peered round the door.

The general raised his other hand, and there was silence again. 'Today, therefore, we make a beginning. Colonel McCreagh, you will seize the stockaded village of Kemmendine, *here*.' He stabbed at the red circle on the map. 'And I wish the assault to be given to my own regiment, the Thirty-eighth.'

Colonel McCreagh simply nodded. There was no need of questions: it would be boat work and the bayonet.

'Colonel Macbean, I wish the Madras brigade to ascertain where to the west of Rangoon the enemy are encamped, and what their intentions are.' The general pointed vaguely at the left of the map, where the forest was represented by pictures of trees of very English appearance.

Hervey hoped that no one imagined it would be like taking a walk in an English park. He had memories enough of the jungle, and he counted that he had been very lucky in his adventures.

'Very well, General,' replied Colonel Macbean. There was no need of questions in this either, for the colonel saw it much like searching for the needle in the bottle of hay.

'And now the matter of supply.'

The general's voice did not falter, but Hervey thought he detected a note less assured. It beggared belief that within hours of the start of England's first war since Waterloo (as Campbell had grandly announced it to his officers in Calcutta), the regiments had been placed on half rations and sentries set to guard the water butts. In the decade since that battle had every hard-learned lesson been forgotten?

'Gentlemen, as I speak, the Royal Navy is taking in hand the unsatisfactory state of affairs in which we find ourselves.

They shall provision the expedition direct from Bengal.'

There was much nodding of heads, and murmurs of 'Hear, hear'. Hervey smiled to himself. The navy would have to keep them alive in the old way. It were better, without doubt, that the extended 'exterior lines' were afloat rather than on land – even on a river whose banks were not free of the enemy – but he couldn't help wondering if it would end in the old way, like Walcheren and Corunna.

There followed detail that would much occupy the staff in the days to come, and then the general stood up again. 'I shall have a word in private with the brigadiers,' he said, laying the bayonet at rest on the table. 'For the remainder, you may dismiss to your duties . . . except for Captain Hervey, if you please.'

Major Seagrass eyed his deputy curiously. And well he might, thought Hervey, for he himself could not imagine why the general had singled him out. Poor Seagrass: he was not enjoying this expedition one bit, and now he was looking in distinctly poor spirits – an ague coming on, perhaps?

When the room was empty but for those bidden to stay, which also included the general's chief of staff, the quartermaster-general, Hervey stepped forward and stood at attention.

'Take a seat, Hervey,' said General Campbell, evidently finding the room rather too close and opening the collar of his jacket.

Hervey found himself admiring the tartan lining of the lapels, evidently the general's own, for it was well known that he had commanded an English regiment. There was no doubting it: Campbell had the crack. In battle, men followed officers like him.

'Captain Hervey?'

'General?'

'You appeared distracted.'

'My regrets, sir.'

The general frowned, but benignly. 'Gentlemen, Captain Hervey is the only man in the division to have any experience of fighting the Burmans. You may find his counsel of assistance, therefore.'

Hervey stood up.

'No, no; sit at ease, Hervey. Give the brigadiers time to reflect. But in any case, you shall place yourself at their disposal as they contemplate their plans.'

'Very good, General.' He turned to the brigadiers. 'At your service, gentlemen.'

Neither McCreagh nor Macbean looked to him as though they would be eager to engage that experience.

'Is there anything you would say here and now?' asked the general.

Hervey wished he had a few minutes to marshal his thoughts. Before Waterloo, by a happy accident of the chase, he had found himself riding beside the Duke of Wellington, who had asked him what he thought Bonaparte's design would be. There had been no alternative but to answer at once and he had done so, to the duke's approbation. But that was with the carefree confidence of youth – and the assurance that the duke was merely sporting with him. 'Sir, my experience of the Burmans is very limited, and I am not sure what general principles may be drawn from it. I should say that they are not fighters as good as the Sirmooris or Rajpoots. They can be deadly enough when at close quarters, but I observed they were reluctant to close with us. I judge, however, that they would be ferocious adversaries in the way of the Spanish *guerrilleros*. And I know, by accounts I have a regard for, that they are most active in stockading and entrenching.'

'This much reluctance to close we have witnessed already, I should say,' said the general, looking at the brigadiers.

They nodded.

Hervey nodded too. 'But I say again, sir, they have a reputation in developing an assault, akin to how we would go about a siege. They are prodigious builders of these stockades, and they dig holes in which their men conceal themselves very cunningly. They can advance upon a position very surely.'

'Is this how we shall find them in the jungle?' asked Colonel Macbean.

'I cannot say for certain, Colonel, but I would suppose that would be their practice. And if you should find them so, then it would indicate they are intent on fighting.'

The nodding of heads said the logic was sound.

Hervey felt encouraged to develop his appreciation further. 'But I must add,' he began, and with a distinct note of caution, 'I believe the Burman may be in want above all of generalship. There is, perhaps, no telling how much better would their fighting men

38

be if led well. And they do have one general, at least, of repute—'

'Maha Bundula,' said General Campbell.

Hervey nodded. It was the first time the general had given any intimation of prior knowledge. 'Just so, sir.'

'He is by all accounts in Assam,' said the quartermaster-general.

Hervey was encouraged. Here indeed was evidence that the expedition was not entirely blind to the significance of what the enemy might do.

'Then we must hope he is tempted here,' said Campbell, most emphatically. 'The defeat of their best general would indeed be the likeliest way to bring about a surrender.'

Hervey raised his eyebrows before he could stop himself. Why Campbell supposed he was the superior of Mahu Bundula he could not imagine, especially with the evidence of the past two weeks before them. Yet he could still admire the gallant confidence. It might yet get them to Ava. But he greatly feared the cost.

'Is there anything else, Hervey?'

'No, sir. I shall try to recall those details which might be of help, and communicate them directly with the brigadiers.'

'Very well, gentlemen,' concluded the general, picking up the bayonet once more. 'Let's be about it. But make no mistake. We shall be sitting out the best part of the rainy season here, and it will be far from pleasant.'

In his quarters, a well-made brick affair which had been the rice store of the *myosá* – the 'town-eater' – the official whose duty it was to extort the most revenue he could from the citizens of Rangoon, Hervey sat down to a breakfast of biscuit and coffee. At least here, though, he was free of the plague of mosquitoes. And plague they had become. He had bought a good quantity of oil of citronella in Calcutta, which he burned in the lamps on the table and by his bed, and no mosquito seemed inclined to linger. But he knew now he would have to calculate very carefully the rate at which he could use it. 'Far from pleasant,' the general had said. They were, to all intents and purposes, besieged in Rangoon, if not exactly by the Burmans – yet – then certainly by the monsoon. How long would it be before the siege was lifted, or they themselves broke it? The rains would continue until the end of September, and during that time there would be nothing to stop

Burman reinforcements coming south by river. Meanwhile, the sick rate in Rangoon – even once the Royal Navy had begun provisioning them – would rise, for the air would soon be corrupted by swamp and stagnant water.

He had written at length to Eyre Somervile the evening before, and now he would have to write a postscript. He calculated that operations could not begin in earnest before October at the earliest, for until they were able to clear the forts the flotilla could not navigate the Irawadi. And so the Burmans would attack first, being in the position of greater strength. The only thing Campbell could do was keep making spoiling attacks to disrupt the preparations. But they would be costly. Hervey was certain nothing would be decided before November. The citronella would be long used up, but by then it would be the least of his cares.

Corporal Wainwright came in. 'I'm sorry I could find nothing better than biscuit, sir,' he said, tucking his shako under his arm.

'I doubt even Johnson could find better,' said Hervey, frowning and motioning to the other chair. 'And *he* would not scruple to forage in the general's own kitchen!'

'I heard the Eighty-ninth had beef last night, sir.'

'Indeed?'

'A regular ox-roast I heard it was.'

Hervey was sure there had been no rescinding order. 'Corporal Wainwright, I cannot imagine the officers would allow—'

'All the officers were dining together – a regimental day, or something.'

Hervey smiled. 'But not on beef.'

'I should imagine not, sir.'

'Mm. Well, if you have half a chance of buying any then take it. I'd be pleased to part with a fair few rupees for a plate of something other than maggoty biscuit.'

'Sir.' Wainwright tried not to smile; they had been under pain of the lash not so much as to lay hands on a beast up until now. 'The word is we're to go after them, by the way, sir – the Burmans.'

'And it is right, which is why you found me already about at reveille. I was copying orders for two hours.' He pushed away the remains of the biscuit porridge. 'The Madras brigade's to beat into the jungle to find where they have gone. The other brigade's to attack upstream and clear the stockades.'

Wainwright looked pleased. 'Do we go with them, sir?'

'We do, I hope. I shall want you to go to the Thirty-eighth and find out when they are to begin. They have orders to take a stockade about two leagues north. I intend going with them, but I'll first have to ask leave of Major Seagrass.'

In the event, the interview with the military secretary proved an unusual exchange. By nine o'clock it was raining again, a steady downpour of the type that cruelly tested the builder's art. The *myosá* had built his rice store well, and Hervey remained dry while others in more exalted positions found themselves dodging leaks and inundations. Major Seagrass was abed complaining of cramps and a sore head when Hervey reported to him. His quarters were almost adjacent to the general's, but water dripped with the regularity of a ticking clock onto the floor near his head, and mosquitoes hovered like wasps about a fallen plum on an English summer's day.

Hervey assumed at once that Seagrass's indisposition would rule out his own hopes of slipping away from the headquarters to join the Thirty-eighth, but he was surprised to find instead that the major did not in the least object – although his manner of reasoning was startling. 'Go on, Hervey,' he moaned, hardly opening his eyes. 'You may as well be killed in the cannon's mouth as sickening and dying in this place!'

Hervey was appalled at the self-pity. Could a man sicken quite so quickly? He looked down at the plump outline of the military secretary concealed beneath the grey blanket, and he sighed. How was it that men were appointed to commands and to the staff who were so manifestly incapable? There was another way of looking at it, of course; and perhaps he ought not to be quite so contemptuous of Seagrass's words, for the major knew as well as he that sickening was not a soldier's business. Perhaps he was only lamenting his disability. In any case, Hervey himself had no intention of either sickening or succumbing to the cannon's roar. He took his leave, summoned Major Seagrass's servant to his quarters and sent him back with a phial of citronella.

Hervey cursed himself and everything as he hastened to buckle on his sword and bind his pistols with oilskin. It was barely an hour since reveille, but the Thirty-eighth had been quicker off the mark than he fancied even his own troop would have been. *Liffey*'s boats were already on the water and pulling through the deluge as if it were nothing but a spring shower. He ought to have known it, he muttered, fastening closed his lapels: men who had been cooped up for so long would be off at their quarry like hounds on to a hare.

The door flew open. 'Sir, the Thirty-eighth—'

'Yes, Corporal Wainwright. I've just seen for myself. Are you ready?'

'Ay, sir.'

They ran all the way to the river, slipping and sliding in the mud, drenched within a couple of minutes. Corporal Wainwright began hailing the boats. There was no one else about in that rain, so their object must have been plain enough, and it was not long before a cutter began pulling towards them.

The boats were packed with the Thirty-eighth's biggest men, the grenadier company, and there was scarcely space for one more, let alone two. But the grenadiers looked happy enough that an officer in another uniform – from the staff indeed – thought their enterprise worthy.

The grenadier captain was welcoming. 'It would not do for a dragoon to be overtaken by foot,' he said, smiling and holding out his hand. 'I am Richard Birch, sir.'

'Matthew Hervey, sir. And very pleased to join your ranks, though I fear my coat a little conspicuous in so much red.'

'I should worry not, Captain Hervey, for I have no doubt we shall all look the same within minutes of scrambling ashore.'

Seeing the colour of the grenadiers' belts, Hervey could only smile ruefully; the white pipeclay had run off onto their jackets and trousers, and even the red dye was not holding fast. 'I freely confess that your alacrity took me by surprise, though. It was but a few hours ago that the general gave the brigadier his orders.'

Captain Birch smiled. 'The colonel has had a company under arms since we landed. It was my good fortune that it was the grenadiers' turn for duty today.'

Hervey nodded. Even so, he thought, it was smart work.

'The rest of the battalion will follow. Our intention is to test the strength of the stockade and to try to take it by surprise.' Captain

Birch had to raise his voice against the beating rain and the sailors' oar work, and his resolve seemed all the stronger thereby.

Hervey had no doubt that Birch's company would carry all but the most determined resistance before them – if they could make headway enough to reach their objective: so strong was the current that the sailors were red in the face despite the cooling drench. If ever they had need of the steamship to give them a tow it was now, but Commodore Peto had said he would not risk *Diana* until he was sure the banks were clear of cannon, and the river of fire boats.

Captain Birch's little flotilla was not without resource, however. The naval officer in command, one of *Liffey*'s lieutenants, had as good an eye for water as Hervey prided himself he had for ground. As they reached the point of the big bend that hid Rangoon from further observation upstream (and, as Hervey observed, vice versa), and where the oars could shift no more water in that swollen flow, he signalled for the boats to turn full about and for hands to pull hard for the slack water by the left bank.

It was done in less than a minute, and very neatly thought Hervey – quicker, for sure, than trying to row broadside across the stream, as *he* would have attempted. The crews now put the boats about again and struck off with a will, for there was an obvious danger in going for the slacker water – too close to the bank, easy prey to musketry no matter how ill-aimed.

It was a tense quarter of an hour before the lieutenant was able to lead the boats to the middle of the river again, but there was no sign of life on either bank except for a solitary zebu that watched them pass, mournful looking.

'Can we make room in the boat for him on the way back, Corporal?' came a voice from the bows.

Captain Birch replied. 'It will be yours if we take the stockade!'

There were cheers. Hervey smiled to himself. A beef dinner – not a promise that would excite men ordinarily to great feats of arms. But such was the miserable fare to which the expedition had been reduced that a pile of gold was worth nothing compared with boiled meat. He turned his cloak collar up once more against the rain.

'Pull hard now, lads; pull hard!' Though the lieutenant's voice carried easily to the other three boats, there was just something in his tone that *coaxed* the extra from his sailors rather than commanded it. It promised them something if they did pull hard rather than threaten if they did not. In truth, they needed little encouragement. Months confined, cruising the Bay of Bengal, and now the prospect of action. It would take more than the monsoon and the Rangoon river in spate to damp their ardour.

After half an hour's pulling hard, the boats swung closer to the right bank to clear a thick knot of mangrove that reached into the river like a giant's arm. And then their first sight of the enemy, or rather his work – a hundred yards distant on the opposite bank.

'Still a mile to go by my reckoning, at least,' said Captain Birch. 'An outpost do you think?'

Hervey had no more prior intelligence than Birch. 'I think it best to work on that assumption. It's not a thing to have at your backs as you go for Kemmendine – or, for that matter, in front of you as you come back.'

'My view precisely.' Birch cupped his hands to be heard above the fall of water. 'Mr Wilkinson!'

The lieutenant brought his boat within easier hailing distance, and without once losing the stroke.

'I want to put half the company ashore to assault yonder fort,' called Birch, gesturing with his pistol. 'The rest I would have Mr Ash work upstream to assault the Kemmendine stockade. We can go at it from two sides at once. But maintain a contact.'

Both officers signalled their understanding, and put their boats for the bank.

Out scrambled the grenadiers like ants swarming from a nest, with Hervey and Wainwright almost knocked over in the rush. There were no orders, no forming-up, just a headlong rush with the bayonet.

Shots rang out from the fort. At a hundred yards the musketry was well wide, though one ball sent a man's shako flying.

It continued as grenadiers splashed through the sodden padi, and still no nearer the mark. Hervey could hear the whizz of balls high above, or see the odd one spatter in front. He was surprised the Burmans stood their ground at all, for they could neither volley nor snipe.

Now they were under the bamboo walls, breathless. 'Up, up, get *up!*' shouted the corporals as grenadiers clambered onto each other's shoulders: the Burmans were only ten feet above them, and the redcoats wanted but a fingerhold to claim first blood.

But the Burmans wouldn't wait for them to gain the top. They leapt from the parapet and ran for the gate for all they were worth. The stockade was no longer a fort but a pen.

Over the parapet came the Thirty-eighth, wild-eyed and baying like hounds on to their fox.

The gate wouldn't open, and then not wide enough. And then the press of Burmans was so great that it jammed closed again, trapping three dozen of them, perhaps four.

Hervey picked himself up after half tumbling from the wall.

The grenadiers' yelling was truly terrible. The Burmans turned to receive them on their spears, but they had never faced English bayonets before.

The ferocity astonished even Hervey. Two dozen of them fell to the point of steel in a handful of seconds, a single man sometimes to three and more bayonets. The rest would have fallen the same had not the gates been suddenly wrenched from their hinges, terror-stricken Burmans throwing down spear and musket and fleeing through the ooze in bare feet twice as fast as boots could follow. They were lucky that the rain kept lead from following, too.

Hervey looked at the heap of dead, a sight he was spared as a rule since the horse took him and his dragoons on from their slaughter. The Burman soldier looked the same in death as any other: untidy, unsuccessful. He felt nothing for them. Had they stayed at their posts and fought they might at least have repulsed the first headlong attack. Was that not what they were paid to do? Perhaps Calcutta was right: perhaps there *was* no fight in the Burman army.

'Good work this, eh, Hervey?' called Captain Birch from outside the gates. He bent to wipe his sword on a Burman coat.

'Very good work indeed. But I wonder they were not more determined. You might have lost a fair few men had they stood their ground.'

'Perhaps,' said Birch, returning his sword. 'But in this rain they would not have been able to reload, and we'd have pushed them from that wall in no time. See the size of these men compared with mine.'

Hervey did. The grenadiers were picked men. It had been many years since the biggest soldiers in a battalion had been mustered together to throw the grenade, but the custom of putting the biggest men in the same company remained – quite evidently so in the Thirty-eighth. He nodded. 'But I doubt we shall be so fortunate every time. I can but admire the ardour of your men, though,' he added quickly, not wanting to belittle it in the slightest.

Captain Birch turned to his ensign. 'Have them form up in column of route, if you please.' And then to Hervey. 'Shall you come with us?'

'Indeed I shall.'

'Good. We all know of your exploits in Chittagong.'

Hervey was gratified, if surprised. He made no reply.

He did not speak for the best part of one full hour. They marched the while, first through mud so gummy that it pulled boots from feet at every step, and then through forest that from the outside looked deceptively like an English wood.

'No, no; it's too much,' said Captain Birch, coming to a stand-still in the middle of a particularly dense tangle of *byaik*.

'I've never seen thicker,' agreed Hervey.

'We'd better make for the river and re-embark. We've lost enough time – and surprise, too.'

Hervey could but agree again. 'The shots may not have carried that far in this rain, but the runaways will have. They're bound to know a way through this.'

Captain Birch cursed.

Hervey sympathized. An approach march through difficult country for an attack from an unexpected direction was an admirable undertaking, much to be preferred to a frontal assault from the direction they were expected. But, as he had heard say often enough, the business of war was merely the art of the possible, and passage of this verdure was not possible in the time they had.

'At least this rain's to our advantage,' said Birch, signalling the change of march with his hand to those behind.

Hervey smiled. Here was an infantryman who knew his job: a

man who preferred a soaking to the skin in order that it might soak the powder of his enemy too.

'Pull hard again, my lads; pull hard!' called *Liffey*'s lieutenant as they struck off.

'I'm grateful to you, sir,' said Captain Birch, who had decided to place himself in his barge as they re-embarked. The rain had not eased in the slightest; he turned up the collar of his cloak again. 'You kept a good contact. Did you see aught of the fugitives bolting the stockade?'

'We did indeed, sir! Your lieutenant was all for putting ashore to give chase, but they sped so there was little chance of taking any. I fancy they're hiding in that wilderness and won't come out for a week.'

'And *I* fancy they're already half-way to Kemmendine to raise the alarm. What say you, Hervey?'

Hervey was trying to secure the bib of his jacket, having pulled off a couple of buttons while scrambling into the cutter. 'We must pray they're not like the Thirty-eighth, Birch, but proceed as if they are.'

'Well said. And very wise. I think we'd better take their measure this next time before hurling ourselves at the walls. Anyway, we're number enough to give them a fright.'

Hervey was relieved. It saved him the trouble of telling a man his job. A bayonet rush may have overawed the stockade, but Kemmendine would be different. A show of discipline and steady bearing, and all in red, might do better. It would at least preserve a good many of them, for he could not quite believe that Kemmendine had as little fight in it as the place they'd just sent packing. 'And we shall shock them!'

'Ay, indeed, Hervey. Naught shall make us rue!'

'I recall when last I said that, just as we were about to attack a Burman camp. We thought ourselves very bold.'

'You were.'

'It was a comfortable affair compared with this.'

'You would count yourself happier in the saddle, I suppose?'

Hervey smiled. 'Does it seem ill that I would?'

'Not at all. The cobbler is better at his last. I wonder you've exchanged a dry billet at all for this.'

Hervey clapped a hand on Birch's shoulder. 'Oh, don't mistake me; I would not miss this for all the tea in China, even if I mayn't be dry-shod.'

Birch offered him his brandy flask.

'What is your intention then?' asked Hervey, taking a most restorative swig.

'It is not easy to say without seeing the object, but I shall land out of musketry range and then advance with skirmishers. I think the navy might feint beyond. You never know: we might yet bolt them as we did before.'

'It will be a famous business if you do,' said Hervey, taking another draw on the flask. 'That and to put a torch to the place.'

The reason they were making now for Kemmendine was Peto's fear of fire boats, for it was no hindrance to progress if the general struck for the Irawadi. That said, if Campbell could not proceed for a month or so – and in this weather Hervey thought it nigh impossible – then it would not do to have the village become a fortress from which Maha Bundula's men might sortie. The general himself believed that the same weather would also hold up the Burmans, but Hervey had reasoned that they would be moving on interior lines and might therefore do so much swifter. And he knew enough of Maha Bundula's reputation to know that he would march where others could not. Captain Birch's work today might well be an affair on which the expedition turned. He had better let him know it.

How those sailors pulled on the oars! Hervey marvelled at their skill and strength – like the free hands that propelled the triremes of ancient Greece faster than could the galley-slaves of their enemies. The rain had stopped, quite suddenly, revealing how warm was the morning – and how soon could the mosquitoes set about them again, so that in a little while both red- and bluejacket alike would have welcomed back the rain in whatever measure. And, of course, the rain dispersed the miasma, the mist that brought the fevers. Hervey, having lowered his collar and unfastened his cloak, quickly reversed the decision with the first bites at his neck. He was lucky to have his hands free for it, unlike the oarsmen.

'There's the place,' exclaimed Captain Birch suddenly,

double-checking his map. 'It's good and flat, and Kemmendine just around the bend ahead. We land there.'

Hervey searched with his telescope. It was an excellent place to disembark. Boats could beach and the grenadiers jump to dry land, if that description was at all apt. ''Ware pickets, though, Birch. It's altogether too likely a place.'

'It may be so, Hervey, but we're beggars in choice.' He hailed his ensign in the boat alongside. 'Secure a footing, Kerr!'

Ensign Kerr, looking half the years of any man in his boat, saluted and put the cutter at once for the shoal.

'Pull!' bellowed the mate: he would have it run well up the bank.

Out scrambled the grenadiers as the boat stuck fast, a full ten feet of keel out of the water. At once a fusillade opened on them.

Musket balls struck the clinker side. A grenadier crumpled clutching his stomach. One dropped to his knees, his hip shot away. Another fell backwards into the water with a ball in his throat.

'Lie down!' shouted Ensign Kerr.

They did so willingly, even in so much mud, while Kerr himself stood brazenly looking for the source of the musketry.

Another volley. White smoke billowed from a thicket not a hundred yards away.

Bad soldiers, tutted Kerr. No target for the volley and all to lose by giving away the position. The bayonet should dislodge them easy enough!

But no – his eyes deceived him. It was no haphazard cover in which the musketeers hid, but bamboo walls as before, only this time most artfully, *cunningly*, concealed. He looked up and down the bank. There was no other place to land to advantage.

'Stand up, men!'

As soon as fire was opened, Captain Birch had signalled for the other boats to row for the bank, covered from view by abundant mangrove. 'We'll just have to hack through,' he called to Hervey, gesturing at the tangle that overhung the river.

Both were now standing in the stern trying to get a clearer picture of Kerr's skirmish.

'Not two dozen muskets by the sound of it,' said Hervey. 'Your man might yet do it on his own.'

That indeed was Ensign Kerr's intention. 'Fix bayonets! On guard!'

He would waste no time trying to load – certainly not to have so many of them misfire with damp powder. And the clattering of bayonets locking home was a fine sound!

'Advance!'

Captain Birch gasped at the audacity. 'Make after them!' he bellowed. 'Pull hard!'

They fairly raced through the slack water of the bank, but there wasn't the same room to get the boats run up the shoal.

'Out! Out!' roared Birch, leaping from the stern into water knee-deep, followed by Hervey and Corporal Wainwright.

The silting was so bad it took the greatest effort to make the five yards to the bank. 'All right, sir?' asked Wainwright as they crawled out.

'Ay, just,' said Hervey, sliding back a second time before getting to grips with a firm-rooted clump of rushes to pull himself free of the silt. 'I'd forgotten how much easier it is on four legs.'

Captain Birch was only a stride ahead of them, and Ensign Kerr's picket was half-way to the stockade. 'Come on you grenadiers, form line!' he bellowed.

But his voice could barely be heard above those of the NCOs, all of whom had the same idea.

'Right *marker*!' a corporal was screaming, his hand raised.

A line started to take shape, in double rank – if not as on parade, then no very great distance from it.

Birch doubled to the front and centre. He would have regularity. 'Company will fix bayonets. Fix . . . *bayonets*!'

Hervey, coming up beside him, drew his sabre.

Behind him came the rattle of a full five dozen blades being rammed home.

'Company, on guard!'

Up came the muskets, bayonets thrust out to impale the luckless souls who stood in their way.

'Company will advance, by the centre, quick *march*!'

The stockade had fallen silent. The going was heavy but Ensign Kerr's dozen grenadiers had kept admirable dressing. They had but twenty yards to go.

Kerr raised his sword. 'Double march!'

A ragged volley greeted them. A ball struck the hilt of Kerr's sword, knocking it from his hand. Another struck him in the groin

50

so that he staggered left and right, then fell to his knees, his mouth open.

The line wavered.

The serjeant, his face a picture of horror, shouted for them to keep going as he rushed to the ensign.

'No, no. That's not the way,' groaned Captain Birch, seeing plainly the loss of momentum. He pointed his sword at the fort. 'Company, *double march!*'

It was not what he'd wanted to do – not to blow them all by doubling through this mud. They'd need every bit of breath to scale the walls. But he couldn't have the picket faltering.

Hervey saw it too. These Burmans were a deal more resolute than the others. If they could volley as fast as British infantry they had less than half a minute to get to the lee of the stockade.

It was as well the defenders were more resolute than capable, for the mud clung to the grenadiers' feet as if demons were trying to pull them into hell. Never did Hervey think himself so powerless.

He could scarcely get his breath as they made the walls. The others looked no better, and some much worse. Furious musketry from above felled two corporals and enveloped the walls in smoke. A ball struck a grenadier full in the mouth. He ran back towards the river squealing like a stuck pig until another ball sent him sprawling in the mud, choking his way to a merciful death.

Hervey crouched watching as two grenadiers holding a musket between them put their shoulders to the wall.

A third, a big Irishman, jumped onto it. 'By Jasus I'll not spare one of them!' he cursed as they heaved him up full stretch.

Hervey could only marvel at their strength – and then at the Irishman's raw fight as he withstood the rain of blows to his head and hands. He got a footing on the parapet and at once the defenders shrank back, but another rushed him with a spear, and the point sank deep in his chest. The Irishman seized the man's head with both hands and they fell to the ground as one.

Hervey drew his pistol to despatch the executioner, but the grenadiers beat him to it.

There was no shortage of volunteers for the escalade. The lieutenant himself, not long out of his teens, was now hauling himself up, his sword in his mouth like a pirate boarding a prize.

Where were the ladders, wondered Hervey? Why were they

going against stockades without so much as a grapple and line?

'Will you be going, sir?' called another of the grenadiers, as if they were asking if he intended taking a walk.

'Me first, sir,' said Corporal Wainwright, his foot on the musket in an instant.

Up it went before Hervey could protest. Wainwright, a jockey-weight compared with the grenadiers, was almost flung over the parapet.

He rolled forward in a neat somersault and sprang to his feet facing the way he had come, sabre already in hand. A clumsy lunge from a spearman was met by a parry and then a terrible slice which parted the spear, and the hand gripping it, from its wielder. Another two spearman backed away at once. 'Clear, sir!' he called.

Hervey clambered up the same way seconds later, by which time Wainwright had accounted for the reluctant supports. He looked at his covering-corporal's handiwork, and nodded: he could not have done it neater himself – perhaps not even as neat.

Left and right, all along the parapet, there were grenadiers duelling with Burmans. Theirs was not so neat work – the jabbing bayonet, the boot, the butt end. There were few shots, a pistol here or there. It was the brute strength of beef-fed redcoats and good steel that were carrying the day, although the grenadiers had had precious little beef this month.

The parapet was now treacherous, running as much with blood as rain. Hervey nearly lost his footing as he made for a down-ladder.

Wainwright was first to the ground, sabre up challenging any who would contest his entry. But there were none that would. Those who could get away from the parapet were making for the back of the stockade, some of them crawling with fearful wounds and a trail of blood. The grenadiers pouring over the wall were looking for retribution, and these men now obliged them. With each point driven into Burman flesh they avenged their comrades – a very personal slaughter, this. Hervey was only glad of the anger that could whip men up to escalade high walls with no other wherewithal than the determination to do so. Ferocious, savage; not a pretty sight, but the proper way, no question. And then get the men back in hand so that blind rage did not lead them to their own destruction. Where *was* Captain Birch?

Hervey soon learned. The serjeant-major was a colossus even among the giants of the grenadier company, and Captain Birch lay across his shoulder like a rag doll. 'Have you seen Mr Napier, sir?' he asked, coolly, seeing the fight was all but over.

'No, Sar'nt-major, I haven't,' replied Hervey, dismayed at the lifeless form of the company commander. 'Is the captain dead?'

'Sir. He took a ball in the throat just as he was broaching the wall.'

'Very well, Sar'nt-major. Will you have his orderly attend him, and come with me if you please. We must put the stockade in a state of defence at once.' Hervey did not imagine a counter-attack was likely, but that did not remove his obligation to take measures to repel one.

'Ay, sir. But let me just lay the captain aside decently first.'

Hervey hurried to the back of the stockade. 'Close the gates!' he shouted to two grenadiers.

They seemed uncomprehending.

He cursed, saw a corporal, gave him the same instruction, and at once the gates were pushed shut.

Up came the serjeant-major again. 'Set them shakos straight!' he bellowed at two men on the parapet.

Hervey could hear Armstrong in that command. It was remarkable how quickly a wound began healing in a regiment: that need to carry on, the notion of next-for-duty, and all. Where *was* the lieutenant?

Lieutenant Napier had given chase. He now returned with a look of thunder. He saw Hervey and shook his head. 'They've bolted, damn them. They beat us to the jungle by a minute, no more, but it's so thick—'

'I'm afraid Captain Birch is killed,' said Hervey.

Napier's thunder was stilled. He had already seen the ensign's death with his own eyes. He looked about the stockade and saw redcoats lying wounded; he knew there were more outside. 'How many, Sar'nt-major?'

'We can muster fifty sir, thereabout.'

That was a lot for the surgeon, or for the chaplain to say words over; a heavy butcher's bill indeed. The lieutenant set his teeth. 'See if we can torch this place, Sar'nt-major. Then we get our wounded back to the boats, and the dead too, and then press on

53

for Kemmendine.' He checked himself, turning to Hervey. 'If you approve, sir.'

'Carry on, Mr Napier,' said Hervey grimly.

The lieutenant nodded.

The serjeant-major saluted. 'Serjeant Craggs, bearers! Serjeant Walker, find everything you can that will light – Burmans included!'

Hervey took the lieutenant to one side. 'Do you judge that you will be in a position to take Kemmendine?' he asked, the doubt more than apparent in his voice.

The lieutenant looked as if the question had never crossed his mind. 'Those are our orders, sir.'

'But I asked you if you considered that you had the strength to execute them.'

Still the lieutenant was incomprehending. 'The Thirty-eighth do not balk at trials, sir, however great.'

Hervey was becoming irritated. 'I do not doubt it. But to expend more life in a *hopeless* venture is base. More than that, however, it would be hazardous for the expedition as a whole. If you fail to take Kemmendine then the enemy will be emboldened. The essential thing while we stand on the defensive at Rangoon is not to have a setback in combat with them.'

'That is as may be, sir, but the Thirty-eighth were given orders to—'

'And *I* am now giving you an order to remain here until the rest of your battalion arrives!'

The lieutenant visibly braced himself. 'Very well, sir, but I must ask for the order in writing.'

'You may have it in any form you wish, Mr Napier. But I counsel you not to protest too much in front of your troops. They have fought bravely and it is no dishonour to them that they retire now.'

Corporal Wainwright listened intently to the exchange. He had seen his captain, sword in hand, display enough courage for a dozen men; yet countermanding a general's orders must require a different courage from the everyday kind. He wondered at it, took careful note, and hoped fervently that his captain was right as well as brave.

CHAPTER FOUR

THE SORTIE

Two days later

Hervey picked up a pencil. Pen and ink was no good. The paper was damp and the ink spread, so that even his carefully formed letters became indistinct in a matter of seconds. Damp paper, damp powder, damp biscuit – mouldy, even – on which they now subsisted, damp leather inside which men's feet chafed, the sores then suppurating: it was as inauspicious a beginning to a campaign as ever he had known. Indeed, it was more than inauspicious: it was ignominy in the making. Four hundred miles still to their object – Ava – and here they struggled through the delta's mud to attack stockades with only bayonets and the breasts of brave men. Hervey was ashamed, and not a little angry.

Rangoon,
17 May 1824

My dear Somervile,
I am very afraid that your strictures regarding the assumptions on which this war is prosecuted appear already to have been most sadly

prescient. We made a landing here but one week ago against opposi-
tion unworthy of mention, but the populace has not risen in our
support. Indeed, the native people are nowhere to be seen, and with
them, we may suppose, are all the provisions and transport upon which
the supply of the army was to be found. There are some cattle here-
about, but the order that they be unmolested remains, and therefore our
soldiers starve that the sacred cows might live. The rains have come – in
such torrents as I could scarce describe – and the river is now swollen in
the manner required, but Peto's flotilla is unable to make progress until
the supply is ordered and the gun forts all about – of which nothing was
known hitherto – are reduced.

Two days ago I attended the Grenadier Company of the 38th,
which is Campbell's own regiment, in two most gallant attacks upon
stockades upstream of here. Their Captain was killed, and the
ensign too, and they lost one in three of the Company, but they were
all for assaulting a third and stronger fort until I ordered them to
await reinforcement by the battalion companies, which, in the event,
did not show because of some alarm here. The fighting spirit of the
men is admirable, but I have a fear that it will be frittered away in
ill conceived assaults – the Company had not even ladders for the
escalade – and, perhaps the more so, by sickness, which is already
rife.

Major Seagrass is dead of a fever, and I am thereby now General
Campbell's military secretary. There is little for me to do, however,
and yesterday when I gave my opinion of the parlous state into
which we were lapsing (my cause was in respect of the mounting
sick lists), Campbell became so angered that I am still unaware if it
were on account of his despair at our situation or with my candour,
though in this connection I must say that I do not believe he has a
true grasp of our peril. I see none of the energy for which he had
reputation in Spain, nor any faithful imagination of the scale of the
undertaking. I pray most fervently that I am wrong in this assess-
ment, but . . .

There was the sound of spurs outside and then a knock. The door
opened and into Hervey's quarters stepped one of General
Campbell's ADCs, well-scrubbed, hat under arm and sword
hitched high on his belt. 'Sir, the general would speak with you; at
once, if you please, sir.'

'Very well,' said Hervey, rising. 'Do you know in what connection?'

'I am afraid I do not, sir. The general has spent much of the morning in conference with his brigadiers.'

Hervey placed the letter to Somervile in the pocket of his writing case, gathered up his sword and shako, and left his quarters certain that he was to hear another paragraph of sorry testimony for inclusion in the letter.

The general's door was open. Hervey knocked and stood to attention.

'Come in, Captain Hervey; come in.'

General Campbell looked tired. Or was it worry? Hervey had received no word from him after handing the quartermaster-general a report on the Thirty-eighth's endeavours. He was unsure even if he had read it, for there had been nothing but routine orders from Campbell's office in days. Neither had there been any sort of conference; Peto had fumed about it when they had dined together the evening before. 'Good morning, General,' said Hervey, a shade warily.

'Sit down, sit down.'

It was curious, thought Hervey, how the general repeated his bidding. He did it not infrequently, of late especially. Was it a mere affliction of the nerves, like blinking or twitching, or did it reveal an uncertainty? Since the general could not doubt that any order would be obeyed, it could only be that he tried to overcome his reluctance to give the order by repeating it for his own hearing. Yet in such small matters as entering a room and taking a chair, what could there be by way of difficulty? Except, perhaps, that the general intended saying something disagreeable.

Surely not? Surely a major-general would not rebuke a captain direct when there were others to whom he might so easily delegate the unpleasant task. Hervey took off his shako and sat in a rush-seat chair in front of the general's writing table.

'I did not say that I approved of your conduct the other day – on the river, I mean.'

Hervey was perplexed. The fact was indisputable, but the words suggested one thing and the manner of their delivery another. Was this a statement of disapproval or not? The general did indeed seem weary. 'No, sir.'

'I *did* approve, most decidedly. We can have no frittering-away of our troops, especially not our best ones. We shall need every man.'

Hervey nodded. He would once have said 'Thank you' to a sign of approval, but now he saw no occasion for thanks.

'I have intelligence that Kemmendine shall be the base from which the Burmans will launch their attacks on us. It is in all likelihood in a strong state of fortification already.'

Hervey nodded again, wondering what these remarks portended.

'Your observations on the Burman manner of fighting would appear most apt. It would seem they are advancing on us by degrees through the jungle, digging and throwing up their damned stockades with each day.'

Hervey frowned. 'That is exactly the manner in which I understand them to fight, General. But I must say that it is not by my observation as much as by study of what others have written before.'

The general waved a hand dismissively. 'Yes, yes, but it was you who wrote the memorandum. *That* is what I meant. And now you've been inside one of these damned bamboo forts of theirs, you'll have other notions of how to deal with them, no doubt.'

Hervey was about to say that he considered any attack without artillery to be iniquitous, when the general pronounced his intention to deal with the encroaching threat. 'I shall attack at once – tomorrow. I shall take them utterly by surprise.'

Hervey, certainly, was surprised. Indeed, he was as intrigued by the notion as he was by the general's purpose in summoning him.

'You think ill of my design, then, Captain Hervey?'

Hervey would once have been flattered by such an enquiry. Now he felt only anger for the reply he would have to make, for it hardly seemed a design at all – more a statement of hope. 'I should not advise it, sir.'

The general looked taken aback; whether by the sentiment or by its plain expression, Hervey could not tell. Nor, indeed, was he in the slightest degree concerned.

The general frowned. 'How so?'

Again, Hervey would once have measured his words; now he paused but a moment. 'The jungle is the Burman's habitude, General. It is where they would choose to fight us. To fight them there we should have an approach through very trappy growth, and could scarce keep formation. Or, if we were in column, it would be the very devil to deploy, especially if there were skirmishers concealed. And in all this it would seem to me utterly impossible to achieve the slightest degree of surprise.'

General Campbell looked astonished. 'That is not the opinion of my brigadiers.'

'They must answer for themselves, General,' replied Hervey confidently. 'With respect, sir, you asked me for my opinion.'

The general made no reply for the moment. He might at other times have been angry, but now he was thoroughly baffled. He might be new-come to India, but he had fought here long ago, and in Mysore, and it was 'the India rule' that a prompt attack confounded the enemy. Was that not, indeed, the duke's own tactic at Assaye? It had certainly been their method at Seringapatam. 'Then what would be your course?'

Hervey imagined the answer was obvious. He managed nevertheless to hide his dismay. 'Let them expend their effort in coming to us. Fight them in the open, or at the forest's edge, not when they're behind their walls. We might borrow some of the navy's artillery, too.'

'I don't care for the notion of waiting,' replied Campbell, shaking his head very decidedly.

'I am not suggesting we sit idly, sir. There is much to be done by way of outposts and patrols, and harassing. The thing is this: the Burmans must come to us if they are to seek any decision. They have no alternative. In which case we can make their work devilish unpleasant.'

The general sighed, loud and rather peevishly, then lapsed into silence.

After what seemed an age, Hervey judged his attendance no longer required. He replaced his shako, saluted and left for his quarters without a word.

He was not long there when the same ADC announced that General Campbell would see him again. Hervey put down the pencil once more and returned to the headquarter office, unsure this time whether he would hear testimony for inclusion in his letter of denunciation, or another outburst of anger (Campbell was

59

hardly likely to reproach him for not seeking formal permission to dismiss?).

In truth, he did not much care what was the reason. Indeed, there was almost an air of truculence about Captain Hervey as he opened the general's door.

'You make a lot of sense, Hervey,' said Campbell, briskly. 'A lot of sense. I have decided to attack the Burmans when they reach the forest edge. But I shall not sit idly until then. We must have very active outpost work – patrols and the like – day and night. Put the Burmans on edge, deny 'em sleep. And I've decided to lead an attack myself on one of these stockades. Tomorrow. Can't abide sitting here another minute!'

Hervey was cheered; also gratified by the general's confidences, if uncertain as to their cause. 'Shall you want me to accompany you, sir?'

Campbell looked rather surprised. 'If you would like to, yes. But don't trouble yourself if there are other duties to be about.'

Hervey took his leave, formally this time. He returned to his quarters and resumed his letter-writing mystified in no small degree by the affair.

At long length he finished the deposition, with its postscript on the general's new intentions, and signed it wearily. He laid down his pencil, then he picked it up again, adding after his signature, 'We must, however, allow that the general is a gallant man.'

In the afternoon, there being no duties to detain him, Hervey went aboard *Liffey* to dine.

Peto's mood had changed; he was no longer merely exasperated. Flowerdew had to give him wide berth as he circled with the decanter, the commodore's gesticulations becoming more and more extravagant. 'Half my ships ply to Calcutta like packets, now, and the rest all but careened here. And the crews sicken: Marryat hasn't an officer or warrant officer fit for duty, and he's had ten men die already. I'm sending *Larne* to sea for better air. In a month I'll have no ships in fighting trim at this rate.' He waved the decanter away, and then waved it back again. 'Dammee, this is no longer just a business of the Company's sovereignty. The honour of the Service is at stake!'

Hervey sipped at his glass of hock, chilled very tolerably by its immersion for several days in the river. He could understand his friend's dismay, for this was His Majesty's navy's first trial since— 'But the two are in consonance, surely? Ava is the object, is it not?'

Peto subsided but frowned severely. 'Only up to a point, Hervey. The Company will have safeguarded its position by defeating the Burmans' design. All they have to do is stop his offensives in Arakan and force a treaty. You know full well it was the commander-in-chief's opinion that we should have stood solely on the defensive. Whereas the Royal Navy shot its way into Rangoon and cannot now move but out the way it came!'

'Ay, but unless Bagyidaw is deposed there'll be no end of alarms,' countered Hervey, shaking his head and reflecting the commodore's frown. 'Someone shall have to go to Ava. Of that there's no doubt.'

Peto beckoned his steward to serve their dinner. 'And what if he should delay so long as to be then unable to clear the Irawadi? It would be *my* ships that are seen to turn.'

Hervey blanched. 'Are you suggesting we abandon it? How will that serve the honour of the navy?'

'I am suggesting no such thing. I am suggesting that the commander-in-chief will break off the campaign here when the attacks on the borders of the Company's territory have been repulsed. And we shall have to steal away from this place without a shot – like thieves in the night.'

Hervey looked doubtful. 'That is if the Governor-General is of the same mind as the commander-in-chief.'

Peto huffed. 'Amherst has the mind of a nincompoop, as we have ample evidence.'

'What would be *your* design?'

'To reduce the garrison here to what is required only to repulse an attack. What would that be? A brigade? No more, surely? And then to take off the remainder at once to force the Irawadi. Rangoon will draw in the Burmans from far and wide, and that we should take advantage of. But there's no profit in sitting here the while with so many, and all my ships tied up supporting them. And for that matter, every day our numbers dwindling.'

'I grant you we might force the Irawadi. But without the strength to garrison it, the lines of communication would be at the Burmans' mercy. This general, Maha Bundula – he would see it at once.'

Peto looked put out. 'I thought you might have allowed that I would see the same!'

Hervey frowned. 'I don't comprehend, Peto.'

'All these transports and escorts now plying back and forth across the Bay of Bengal: all they're doing is feeding the garrison here. Cut the garrison by two-thirds and there'd be no need of external supply. I could land half my own stores. It would see them through any siege. And the ships released thereby could keep open the Irawadi.'

Hervey pondered the notion as Flowerdew laid a plate of fish on the table. 'Have you shared this opinion with the general?'

'I have sent him a memorandum, just before you came.'

Hervey wondered how it would be received. The fall of Ava was not essential to the general's reputation. All that was necessary was for him to hold Rangoon. It was not his fault that the Burmans hadn't flocked to his support. If the commander-in-chief wished him to take Ava against such opposition, then he would have to supply him with the means to do so. And yet, the taking of Ava in such very trying circumstances – against the odds – would surely be his making? 'He intends awaiting a general attack for a week or so. He will certainly want the support of your guns. And tomorrow he is going to lead an assault on one of the stockades.'

'And do you go with him?'

'Yes. He intends that I should write the despatch.'

'I've a mind to come with you, but I've called my captains aboard.'

Hervey smiled. 'There'll be more opportunities, I assure you. The general is determined to have the garrison as active as possible while he waits.'

Peto helped his guest to a fair portion of fish. 'Bekti. The best you'll ever taste. Caught this morning and brought upriver by *Diana*. What a boon she is.'

Hervey had seen steam on water before, first in a boat no bigger than *Liffey*'s cutter on the Blackwater river in Ireland, and then the barge that had towed their transports steadily upstream on the St Lawrence, six winters ago. But nothing like *Diana*. *Diana* was a gunship, her ports painted Nelson-style, and her smokestack half as high as *Liffey*'s mainmast. 'The baby figure of things to come, do you think?'

'Of some things, perhaps. But *Diana* could never stand off in a fight. A twelve-pounder would smash her paddles to pieces. I can't risk her in the van too long if the river narrows and the forts get her range.'

Hervey tried his fish. 'I don't know whether it's because I've not had a spoonful of anything half-decent in a week, but this I agree is uncommonly good.'

Peto looked pleased. He drained his glass and let Flowerdew refill it. Then he leaned back in his chair. 'Let us speak of agreeable things for a time. I never told you my news, did I? It is signed and sealed and I had a note of it only yesterday.'

Hervey indulged his friend by laying down his fork and sitting back to receive the evidently happy intelligence.

'I have bought an estate near my father's living.'

'An estate, indeed,' said Hervey, as impressed as he was surprised.

'Nothing on any grand scale. And the house shall need attention. But it has a good park, and is but a short drive from the sea.'

Hervey wondered why a man who so much disdained being ashore should take such a course. 'Do you plan going on half pay?'

'It will come to it, Hervey; it will come to it. I have a tidy sum invested in Berry's cellars, and another in two-per-cents, but I have a notion of something a shade more . . . substantial.'

Hervey smiled. 'Then you are not contemplating matrimony?'

Peto raised his glass and took a very urbane sip. 'A man in his right mind who *contemplates* matrimony will never embark upon it, Hervey. In any case, a house has no need of a mistress – only a keeper.'

Hervey said nothing.

Peto realized the import. 'Oh, my dear fellow: I am so dreadfully sorry. I—'

Hervey smiled and shook his head. 'Think nothing of it. I'll take another glass of your hock, and drink to your arrangements in Norfolk.'

Peto cursed himself for being the fool.

Corporal Wainwright came to Hervey's quarters before first light with a canteen of tea, and returned shortly afterwards with hot water. Their exchanges were few.

'It's raining, sir.'

Hervey wondered at the need of this news, supposing that the hammering on the roof was the same that had been for the last fortnight.

'And the guard says it's been raining all night, sir.'

This much was perhaps of some moment, since the going would clearly be of the heaviest, perhaps even preventing the general from taking the field piece. Hervey sighed to himself at the thought of another affair of the bayonet. The wretched infantry – no better served now by the Board of Ordnance than if they had been with Marlborough a century past. For ten years – more – he, Hervey, had had a carbine that would fire in the worst of weather, yet the Ordnance showed not the least sign of interest. The notion of a percussion cap when a piece of flint would do seemed to the board an affront to economy. And little wonder if its members were as fat-headed as Campbell.

Hervey sighed again as he drank the sweet tea in satisfying gulps. Perseverance – that was the soldier's virtue. It was both duty and consolation. 'Corporal Wainwright, I give you leave to remain here and keep things dry.'

'And I decline it, sir, if you please. Thanking you for the consideration, that is, sir.'

Hervey smiled. 'It was not entirely for your welfare, Corporal Wainwright. I had a thought to my own comfort on return!'

'I'll engage one of the sepoys, sir.'

Hervey smiled again as he rose to his toilet. 'It's not what I said it would be, Corporal Wainwright, is it? Hardly the dashing campaign, with gold to fill the pockets.'

Corporal Wainwright pulled the thatch from Hervey's boots and began to rub up the blacking while Hervey began lathering his shaving brush. 'I don't hold with stealing, sir, and it seems to me, from what I've heard, that that's all it amounts to half the time. Prize money's a different thing. But plundering a place is no better than thieving.'

'Your sensibility does you credit, Corporal Wainwright. The duke himself would applaud it.' Hervey spoke his words carefully, but only because he had regard to the razor's edge.

'Pistols sir? I'm taking mine.'

'I suppose so. It is conceivable the rain will cease.'

'What I should like to know, sir, is how rain stays up in the sky before it begins to fall.'

Hervey held the razor still. 'You know, I have never given it a thought. Nor, indeed, do I recall anyone else doing so. I suppose there is an answer.' He resumed his shaving.

'I'll bind the oilskin extra-tight, sir. Wherever this rain's coming from, there doesn't look to be any shortage.'

In a few minutes more, Hervey was finished. He dressed quickly, thinking the while of the rain question. 'The rain is in the clouds. That much is obvious.'

Yet that was only a very partial answer (consistent with his knowledge of natural history). The rain outside descended as a solid sheet of water the noise on the roof was, if anything, louder than when he woke – yet how did it rise to the height of the clouds in the first place, and then stay aloft?

'Steam. Steam *rises*,' he said, pulling on his boots. 'That *Diana* works that way, I think.'

Corporal Wainwright said nothing, content instead to listen to the emerging theory.

'A great deal of this rain must have begun as steam.'

But then why should it now fall as rain? And where did all the steam come from in the first instance?

'For the rest I must ask Commodore Peto. The weather is his business. For us it is just weather, I fear.' He fastened closed his tunic. It had become a poor affair with a daily soaking this past month.

Wainwright took away the bowl of water.

Hervey looked out, observed the downpour and put off his visit to the latrines until after breakfast.

He sat down at his desk-cum-table still turning over the rain question in his mind. Peto would surely know a great deal more – all there was to know, probably. But what opportunity he would have to pose his query in the coming weeks, he couldn't tell. The commodore had declared he would be taking *Liffey* and two of the brigs out to blow good sea air through her decks and give the hands practice with canvas again.

Wainwright was soon back with Hervey's breakfast – excellent coffee (he had been careful to lay in a store of that before leaving Calcutta) and a very indifferent gruel. Hervey thanked his luck for the supper of bekti the night before, and for the lump of salt pork that Peto had pressed on him to bring ashore. It would be their ration today, for the salt beef had now gone, and it was biscuit only again.

In half an hour the bugle summoned him – 'general parade'. He put on his shako, fastened his swordbelt and drew on his gloves. He looked at the pistols, wondering. He picked up both and pushed them into his belt: if the rain did stop, he'd feel undressed without them. He wished he'd brought his carbine, but it had seemed the last thing he would need when he joined the general's staff in Calcutta.

The sortie paraded outside the north gate. They were six companies, three British and three native, together with two field pieces – a six-pounder and a howitzer – some five hundred men in all, and another fifty dhoolie-bearers. They gave an impression of unity by their red coats, except for the artillerymen, who wore blue, but close to they were rather more disparate than a Calcutta inspecting officer would have been used to. It was but a fortnight since the landing, and already some of the troops had a ragged appearance which spoke of their exertions and the flimsiness of their uniforms, as well as the lack of supply. For the most part, the trousers were white, summer pattern, but heavily patched, and the sepoy companies had abandoned their boots. Some of the officers wore forage caps. The general, indeed, wore one. Hervey would have been appalled had he not witnessed all that had gone before: an officer of the Sixth never wore a forage cap but in the lines. That it should have come to this in one month beggared belief.

There was no doubting the effect as a whole, however. In close order, and from a distance, these men looked like a solid red wall. They would stand, come what may. And their muskets – they would know how to handle them, for sure. Five rounds in the minute at their best – how could the Burmans match or bear it? The trouble was, the best volleying was only possible with dry powder.

General Campbell was rapt in conversation with the sortie's lieutenant-colonel, a short, stocky man whose voice was said to be the loudest in the expedition. Hervey studied the general carefully.

He had not fully appreciated his height before, for he seemed now to stand taller than any man on parade. Without doubt, Sir Archibald Campbell had the crack and physique to convince a subordinate of his competence; Hervey pushed all his doubting thoughts to the back of his mind.

Would Campbell address the sortie? The rain hammered so loud it would be pointless but for a few men in the front rank. So they would just turn into column of route and march off down the track into the forest. Poor infantry – trudge, trudge, trudge, a mouthful of black powder biting the cartridge, a minute of rushing blood in a bayonet charge, and then . . .

Then it was the same for all of them – kill or be killed. The soldier's life was nearest Nature – lowly, nasty, brutish, and all too frequently short.

It was, of course, why they made comrades of one another so quickly. Everyone knew that. Hervey had seen it in his first week at the depot squadron, and he supposed it was why, perhaps, decent society could sometimes hail the soldier, for all his licentiousness. The quality certainly liked an officer in his regimentals. He wondered if they ever imagined them as they appeared this morning, however – sodden, tattered, grubby. Or what they looked like when rent with grape, ball, or the point of iron and steel.

It was strange he should think now of Henrietta. Now, when things stood at their most brutish. But Henrietta had had a good imagination of the truth, for all her feigning otherwise. Not so Lady Katherine Greville. Hervey did not suppose *she* had ever thought of it, let alone was capable of imagining it. Regimentals were not for this. They were for the delighting of her and those like her – a mark of potency rather than aught else. He did not suppose it, indeed; he knew it. Her letters told him as explicitly as she had implied the day they had ridden together in Hyde Park. That was four, nearly five years ago, and still she wrote. He wrote too, not exactly by return, but with sufficient despatch to keep the correspondence lively. It flattered him. She might have her pick of officers in London – and no doubt did – and yet she penned him letters. He smiled to himself, now, at her questions. Did he wish to be an ADC? Did he wish for an appointment at the Horse Guards? If he would not return soon to London, did he wish a place on the commander-in-chief's staff, or even the Governor-General's? There was not much, it seemed, that Lieutenant-General Sir Peregrine Greville could not arrange if his wife were to ask him.

'Sir?'

Hervey turned.

'I asked if you still don't want your cape, sir,' said Corporal Wainwright, water running down his shako oilskin as if it were an ornamental fountain. 'I can fetch it quick enough.'

Hervey shook his head. 'No. I think we're beyond all help in rain like this. It'll be sodden in minutes and then a dead weight. Why don't you take yours though?'

'No, sir. It'll be just as sodden. And I'd as soon kick off these boots.' He smiled.

Hervey smiled back. Corporal Wainwright had been wearing shoes when first he had seen him on Warminster Common, though the rest of the inhabitants of that sink had been barefoot. 'Easier going in the approach, I grant you, but just wait till you get a bamboo splinter!'

Words of command now rippled through the ranks, like dominoes toppling. Back up to attention came the companies; they shouldered arms, moved to the right in column of route, then struck off to the dull thud of soggy-skinned drums and watery fifes – a cheery enough display for the general, thought Hervey, even if the sepoys did look distinctly ill-used to marching in torrents of rain. The King's men, he didn't doubt, would have marched in many times worse, and some of them in the Peninsula, where the rain could fall as a stinging hail of ice rather than as a warm drench. Poor, wretched infantry – the regiments of foot – and their feet often as not cold and wet. The cavalryman knew privation, and worked the harder for having a horse to look after as well as himself, but his feet bore nothing like the punishment of the infantryman's.

'Nice tune, sir,' chirped Corporal Wainwright as he picked up the step.

'Yes,' said Hervey, in a vague way.

'Don't you recognize it, sir?'

'No?' Corporal Wainwright obviously thought it of significance. 'The rain it fell for forty days!'

'Of course,' he said, smiling – black humour, the soldier's

privilege. 'But I'm afraid the drum-major is excessively an optimist. The rains will be an affair of months, I fear.'

They were not set off more than half an hour, and only a short distance into the jungle, when the first shots were fired. In this rain they defied belief. Hervey could not conceive how any powder might be dry enough, especially in Burman hands.

There was at once a great cheer and the leading men went at the pickets with the bayonet. It was over in a minute. Hervey saw nothing.

The column halted and the general pushed his way to the front, Hervey with him. They found a half-finished stockade built directly across the track and extending the length of a cricket pitch each side into the forest, empty of all but redcoats, and half a dozen Burman musketeers too slow on their feet. General Campbell peered at the bodies, as if they might reveal something of the campaign before him. 'Pull the place down!' he snapped. 'Press on, Colonel Keen!'

They left a sepoy company to the work, and the column trudged on into jungle made increasingly dark by the heavy skies. In another half-hour they passed three more stockades just as hastily abandoned, and then not a sign of the enemy in five miles of swamp and thicket until the artillerymen were too exhausted to pull their guns any further.

'In God's name get the sepoys to the ropes!' cursed the general.

Hervey despaired. He had taken gallopers into the jungle – two-pounders dismantled, and carried by packhorses. But guns like these . . . it would not serve. 'Sir, I believe the effort may not be worth it. And when it comes to withdrawing, we could never afford to abandon them.'

'I agree, General,' said Colonel Keen.

Campbell looked vexed. He wanted to blow in a stockade and tell the Burmans there was nowhere safe for them. But he had brought the wrong guns and he knew it. The Madras artillery's commander had told him so last night. 'Very well. The sepoy company will remain guarding them until we return.'

There were no packhorses, of course. Not one. Indeed, there was not a single animal in the entire expeditionary force. But this was to be an entirely novel campaign, one that did not observe the normal usages of war. Hervey seethed. Who *were* these officers who would undertake a campaign without a few ready horses?

The next two miles were done much quicker without the guns. They did not find the enemy, however, nor any sign of him, and in an hour the column emerged from the forest into green padi fields six inches deep in water.

Colonel Keen halted the column to allow the general to come forward.

'What do you make of it, Colonel?' asked Campbell, sounding confident still.

The colonel had the advantage of two minutes' survey through his telescope, but even so there was not much he could tell him. 'I feel the want of a map very sorely, General. I suppose yonder village is fortified, or at least has some hasty stockading erected, for they must have known of our approach these several hours.'

General Campbell now surveyed the ground for himself.

The village lay half a mile ahead astride the track by which they had come. Without a map it was impossible to tell if it ran through the village and beyond, in which case the village commanded further advance, or whether it ended there. Colonel Keen thought the question apposite since, he reasoned, the Burmans would be bound to defend the former whereas they would probably have abandoned the latter.

The general nodded to the logic, but either way he would have the place. 'And if I find so much as a loophole in yonder buildings I'll raze the entire village.'

Colonel Keen folded his telescope. 'Column of companies, I think, General?'

'If you please.'

The colonel turned to his adjutant. 'Column of companies if you please, Mr Broderick.'

While this evolution was taking place, which required the sortie to advance a good hundred yards to make manoeuvre room, and for the companies to extend left and right for about fifty into the padi, Hervey climbed to the lower branch of a sal tree and began his own survey. To the right of the village, perhaps a little closer than to the forest's edge, was water – one of the delta's many creeks, he supposed. To the left, and beyond, the same distance, was jungle. He strained to make out something of the village, but the cloud and the rain made it impossible to tell whether there was any stockading. There was certainly no sign of life. He looked at his watch: a little past midday. They could not advance much further without spending the night in the forest. And there were the guns to think of.

The companies struck off at a good pace, splashing through the muddy rice as if skylarking on a beach. Hervey climbed down and pushed his way along the track to where the general marched with the Thirty-eighth's lieutenant-colonel, just to the rear of the leading company. He fell in behind the adjutant, counting himself lucky to have his feet out of the padi. It was only then that he observed how effective was a general's cocked hat in a downpour. Campbell had his pulled over his ears, and water ran down the points 'fore and aft' clear of both face and neck. Strange, the things one noticed at times such as these, he mused.

'View halloo!'

Hervey woke instantly. Where? What? He couldn't see beyond the shakos of the company in front.

'Skirmishers out!' he heard the lieutenant-colonel order.

Men from the light company began doubling past on both flanks to form a skirmishing line. How would they load in this weather?

'Smart work!' said the general.

Hervey could now see the Burmans forming up on either side of the village – with officers on horseback. He prayed there would be no cavalry, however inexpert. They would have the advantage, for sure, even in this going.

'Curse this padi!' It was taking forever to make headway. Hervey glanced left and right: the lines were uneven, and they were having to mark time in the middle, the men on the flanks up to their knees in water, mud sucking at every stride. He thought it bordered on the reckless. If there were cavalry behind the village they could be onto flanks in an instant. He began unbinding one of his pistols, but he had little expectation of its serviceability. He cursed again. A pistol which misfired, perforce at short range, was worse than useless. He began rebinding. He would trust to the sabre, as the infantry would trust to the bayonet.

At a hundred paces musketry broke out from in front of the village, left and right. Hervey could scarce believe it. Just as at

71

Kemmendine the Burmans had concealed their stockades in *byaik* little more than shoulder high, *and* kept their powder dry. But again they'd fired too soon and not a ball struck home.

The skirmishers held their fire: theirs was to discourage any who would stand in the open.

Coolly, as if at a field day, the general took in the business before him. 'One company, if you please, Colonel,' he said, matter-of-fact. 'Remainder to stand fast in reserve lest those there begin to advance.' He pointed at the Burmans drawn up either side of the village.

It was promptly done. Eight dozen bayonets in two ranks inclined right and quickened almost to double time, Campbell following.

Hervey was hard-pressed to keep pace.

The musketry increased, but it was ragged and had no more effect than before.

The ground now fell away – three feet, perhaps more. Down the slope to the bamboo walls ran the company – eight-foot walls, not five.

There were shots from the left – hopelessly too far again – as Hervey and the general raced to catch them up. He couldn't understand how the Burman fire discipline could be so poor when their other skills were so admirable.

The general glanced left, marked the smoke, then drew his sword and sprinted the last dozen yards to the fort.

The Thirty-eighth were already atop the walls. Hervey glimpsed the bayonets at work – bloody, vengeful work.

The general climbed on a corporal's shoulders and heaved himself up. Hervey and the ADCs followed as best they could. Hervey lost his footing on the wet bamboo several times until Corporal Wainwright leaned out and got hold of his crossbelt.

But it was over by the time they were up. Five minutes' work, at most, to turn the fort into a slaughterhouse as bad as he'd seen. There were dozens of dead piled against the gates, and as many more scattered about the stockade in ones and twos where they had stood and fought or cowered and craved mercy, both in vain.

General Campbell, sword still drawn, but unbloody, at once ordered out the company to assault the second stockade. Hervey, standing on the parapet, glanced back at the other three companies formed up ready, their colonel in front, and wondered at the general's impetuosity. Was it that he was happy at last, knowing exactly what he was about – the simple certainty of fighting, and with his old corps? He might almost be seeking a glorious death. He made work for his covermen, for sure.

'Two ranks! Get fell in!' The serjeant-major blew his whistle fiercely and waved his sword. 'That was nothing! Look sharp, damn you!'

The voice of the Black Country made Hervey think of Ezra Barrow: dragoon to captain – what would *he* make of it? He would not have volunteered for it, that was certain. 'Never volunteer for anything' was a maxim Barrow had long lived by. And it had evidently served him well. Hervey might almost envy him at this moment, undoubtedly taking his pleasure in an afternoon's repose.

At last the company was fell in to the serjeant-major's satisfaction. They were scarcely depleted, for all the ferocity of the first assault, though every man was as gory as a surgeon's mate. No matter, the rain would wash them clean. But by their look, Hervey wondered if it was what they would want.

The general now threw over all restraint and placed himself in front of the line. He waved his sword at the objective, two hundred yards ahead. 'Once more, the Thirty-eighth! Let 'em have *Brummagem!*'

There was a great cheer.

Poor Colonel Keen, sighed Hervey. The general was a captain again and nothing would stop him.

He took post on the right of the front rank, along with the ADCs, with Corporal Wainwright beside him. It would be the closest he had come to a bayonet charge – just as he'd wanted. He could already feel the strength of a line of well-drilled men elbow to elbow, 'the touch of cloth', even blue with red. If only the enemy were not behind a palisade! But no, he needn't worry: the bamboo walls would delay them, not stop them, surely? These men's blood was hotted: they would take the place by escalade again, and the Burmans would once more rue their lot.

But the second stockade was not as easy as the first. The walls were no higher, and the defenders no greater, but the Burmans held their fire and then stuck at it just that bit longer. The first volley came at about seventy yards – some lucky hits, enough to shock – then another at fifty which felled several men including a serjeant.

'Charge!'

The general's voice was louder than the rain and the firing combined, and the cheering louder still as the right-flank company of His Majesty's 38th Foot, under their erstwhile colonel, ran slipping and sliding to the wooden walls.

This time the defenders would not be bolted. They held their ground and kept up a steady fire even as the first redcoats were scrambling up the palisade.

The second rank began desperately unwrapping their flintlocks to engage them. Few managed to fire.

The Burmans had the advantage and the will this time, and the fallen red coats began to show.

But little by little – it seemed an age yet could not have been more than minutes – red began to preponderate atop the palisade. It defied reason, for they could not be gaining it by fire. Hervey himself had fired both his pistols, and the rounds were wide. No, it was not fire that let the redcoats escalade the fort.

He got a shoulder again from a thickset private – 'Yow mun gow, sir; me leg's shot through.' This time he reached the parapet while there was still fighting. 'Where's the general?'

'I can't see 'im, sir,' said Wainwright, looking either side of the wall.

'Christ!' It wasn't his business to guard him, but—

An ear-splitting roar and the whizz of shrapnel – smoke rolled across the stockade floor and hid all for an instant.

Hervey leapt from the parapet and dashed for the gun. A dozen redcoats beat him by a mile. A dozen more lay full of iron.

He saw his man though, spear couched, hesitant but standing his ground. Up went the sabre as he ran in, Wainwright with him.

He didn't feel the ball strike. He only saw the lights dancing in the sky as he fell. And then the shadow of Corporal Wainwright over him, saying something he couldn't hear.

CHAPTER FIVE

THE SURGEON'S BLADE

That evening

The sight of a horse, even a lone horse, made the sentries at Rangoon's gates rush to their posts, and the inlying picket stand to. A horse was at best the bearer of a Burman who wished to treaty; at worst it bore the forerunner of a Burman army.

'Shall I take a shot at 'im, sir?' called the picket-corporal to his officer.

The lieutenant strained to make out the target. Two hundred yards: he could not determine who sat astride, and he was as certain that his corporal, for all his reputation as a hawk eye, could strike neither horse nor rider at that range with a common musket. And with the extra windage of the French balls they'd been issued with he'd have no more chance at half the range. He looked for reassurance towards the field piece in the mouth of the gate – the gunners were already ramming home shell. 'No. Let him come on some more.'

The guard company now stood to, hastily, dressing in two ranks.

Their captain scaled the ladder to the palisade to see for himself.

He raised his telescope; a hundred yards the rider had closed to.

The lieutenant rued his own want of so useful an instrument.

'*Two* men, Torrance – one leading. They're not wearing red, but they're not niggers either.' He turned and hailed his ensign. 'Out, Wilks, and give a hand!'

They brought Hervey to the surgeon in a dhoolie. Corporal Wainwright, every muscle weary, stayed with him despite the serjeant's entreaties to fall out and take his ease. The horse, exhausted too, and lame, was led away by a corporal – fresh meat at last, joked the men.

The hospital occupied the town-eater's collecting house – and every building around it, now. Men lay everywhere, barely tended. The place stank worse than Calcutta when the Hooghly was on the turn.

'Out you go, Corporal,' said the surgeon. He had come at once, tired and red-smeared from his ministrations with the bleeding stick.

'I'd rather stay, if you don't mind, sir.'

'I *do* mind. You're no use to me in here.'

Hervey lay unconscious. The assistants were already cutting away the left sleeve of his coat. Corporal Wainwright did not move.

'Oh very well,' grumbled the surgeon. 'But be out of my way. You both reek of rum.'

Corporal Wainwright stepped back, allowing the surgeon and his assistants full play at the table. One of them held a lantern up close to Hervey's shoulder.

'Too late,' said the surgeon.

Corporal Wainwright's jaw dropped.

'It'll have to come off. It looks like a ball in there. The shoulder will be a deal too smashed, and putrefaction too far advanced.' He sounded as tired as he was certain.

'Sir, with respect, sir,' pleaded Wainwright, stepping forward. 'Captain Hervey couldn't draw his sword and hold the reins with but one arm.'

The surgeon spun round. 'Damn your impudence, Corporal! I've a mind to have the guard throw you out! Another word and I'll have that stripe from your arm.' He turned back to his assistants. 'The saw, please!'

Corporal Wainwright did not flinch. 'Sir, you *must* try and save Captain Hervey's arm!'

The surgeon went purple. 'Throw 'im out!'

Corporal Wainwright drew his sword and pulled the pistol from his belt. The assistants fell back. 'I'll take the captain with me then, sir.'

'You damned fool,' spluttered the surgeon. 'This is gross insubordination – *worse*. The arm's got to be amputated, and quickly, otherwise it will gangrenate.'

Wainwright sheathed his sword.

'Sensible fellow,' said the surgeon, nodding. 'Now why not wait outside?'

Wainwright levelled the pistol again.

No one moved a muscle.

He stepped forward, crouched slightly, beckoned an assistant to help, and took Hervey over his shoulder. He stood full upright in one movement, with a strength that awed the watchers, and walked out of the hospital.

He walked past orderlies too alarmed by the fierce eyes and the pistol to stop him. Indeed, so compelling was Wainwright's bearing that soon there were sepoys supporting him.

At the river he found more allies, this time in blue. 'It's Captain Hervey, sir,' he called to one of *Liffey*'s officers in an approaching gig.

Liffey's officer of the watch had also been observing from the quarterdeck. 'Fetch the captain,' he snapped at a midshipman. 'And the surgeon. I think it's Hervey.'

Peto came at once with Surgeon Ritchie, both of them fresh-scrubbed and dressed for dinner. 'Hervey, you say?' The edge to the tone was obvious. Peto leaned well out as the boat bore alongside.

'I believe so, sir,' said the lieutenant. 'And his—'

'Great heavens,' exclaimed Peto, springing back from the rail. 'Mr Ritchie, your best work; your best work please!' He rushed to the gangway. 'Two marines – leave your muskets!'

The sentries at the foot of the companionways grounded arms and followed the captain down.

'Sir, Captain Hervey's shot, sir, in the shoulder,' said Corporal Wainwright, as Peto bounded down the gangway. 'The army surgeon wanted to take his arm off, sir.'

Peto pulled back the cloak to see for himself. He grimaced when he saw how much blood there was. The whole of the buff bib was red-brown. 'A hammock, there!' he shouted to the lieutenant, who had already anticipated the need.

Another marine scuttled down the gangway with it.

'Bear him up gently, men,' said Peto, more a plea than an order. 'Gently as you can.'

Seamen and marines began lifting him into the hammock.

'My cabin, if you please, Ritchie,' he called to the surgeon.

Surgeon Ritchie raised his hand to acknowledge and sent the loblolly boys sprinting to the cockpit for his instruments and the medical chest.

The marines, red in the face and sweating like pigs, bore Hervey up gently. Two more came to the job as they reached the main deck.

'I'll have your table, if you will, sir,' said the surgeon, as Peto came back on deck.

'Ay, of course, of course,' replied Peto absently. He pushed past, calling for his steward. Together they began clearing the table of its silver and fine china.

'Save the tablecloth, sir, if you please,' called the surgeon. 'Sit Captain Hervey upright,' he said to the marines. 'Support him with the cloth until I know what we're about.'

Back came his assistants.

'Lay it all out here and give me the sharpest knife!'

Corporal Wainwright's stomach heaved. 'Sir, I—'

'One way or another the coat will have to come off, Corporal,' said Ritchie, moving candles closer.

Corporal Wainwright's relief was palpable.

'A bowl of hot water and some brandy, if you will, Flowerdew.'

To anyone who observed the preliminaries of the two surgeons – the army's and *Liffey*'s – the reason for the crew's high opinion of theirs would have been clear. Whereas, ashore, the man had worked in Stygian gloom, though there was no obvious cause to, and his prognosis was made after the most cursory of visual examinations, Surgeon Ritchie made full use of the evening sunlight that streamed through the stern windows – and his magnifying glass.

His prognosis, however, tended to the same. 'Not good, I'm afraid. Lint, please.'

An assistant rummaged in a haversack.

'*Clean* lint. Let's not have any more stink than needs be.'

Hervey opened his eyes.

'Capital, my dear friend!' said a delighted Peto. 'You're in good hands, now.'

Hervey appeared not to register where he was or even who was there.

'An ill-timed recovery, I'm afraid, my dear sir,' muttered the surgeon, pouring brandy on the lint and wiping away some of the blood caked about the wound.

Hervey's head rolled.

Peto peered over the surgeon's shoulder at Hervey's. 'He reeks of rum, Ritchie,' he said, shaking his head. 'Little wonder he nods.'

Ritchie threw the lint to the floor.

'Hold hard there, my old friend!' Peto called, as if to a deaf man, which, to all intents and purposes, Hervey was.

'How much rum has he drunk, Corporal?' asked Ritchie.

'Only a very little, sir,' replied Wainwright, standing to attention by a bulkhead. 'I poured the most of it into Captain Hervey's shoulder, sir.'

Ritchie turned and looked at him before more rubbing with new lint. 'And why, pray, did you do that?'

'I know Lord Nelson's body was preserved in brandy, sir. I thought it could help Captain Hervey.'

'You did, did you? Well, it can't have done too much harm, though it might have been better had you poured it all down his throat.' He took off his coat and pulled up his shirtsleeves. 'A digital examination, then, now the wound's exposed proper.'

Peto screwed up his eyes, the better to see the work, although it anticipated the flinch too.

Ritchie inserted a finger – the right index – with the utmost care, but the pain was so great that Hervey let out a cry and at once passed out.

'Good,' said Ritchie. 'Much the best way,' as he continued probing.

Peto grimaced, but more in anticipation of what Ritchie might say. Wainwright stood stock-still, at attention. He could do no more now than trust.

'There's been prodigious bleeding,' said Ritchie after a while.

'But no disruption of the glenoid cavity. No bone splinters either. And I believe I may feel the ball.' He withdrew his finger and wiped it on some lint, taking good care to observe Hervey's breathing as he did so.

The marines shifted their weight a little.

'Keep him proper upright, and hold his head back, one of you,' said Ritchie, wiping the sweat from his brow with his left arm. 'Probe-point bistoury, please, Magan.'

One of the assistants handed him the curved knife.

'Corporal, be aware that I might be doing your captain no favour in this. I may remove the ball, but if the shoulder is more damaged than I surmise it would be better that I disarticulate the limb now.'

Corporal Wainwright nodded. 'Sir.'

'Stand easy, man,' said Peto, kindly.

'But first there'll be more blood,' warned Ritchie, wiping his forehead again. 'Turn him round a wee bit more to the light.'

The marines turned him carefully with the linen sling.

'First I have to enlarge the wound.' He dipped the bistoury in the hot water. 'Curious thing how the patient afterwards says he felt the cold blade. Nelson did. Might as well make things as comfortable as possible.' He wiped the bistoury on his sleeve then deftly elongated the wound two ways, pulling the flesh apart either side with the thumb and finger of his left hand while he probed for the ball with the knifepoint.

Blood began to run copiously again. The assistants dabbed at it with lint.

'Forceps.'

Magan handed them to him and took the bistoury. Ritchie, as he had done with the knife, warmed the bullet-extracting forceps before putting them to the flesh.

Peto began silently to pray, although he was not a praying man. Wainwright *was* a praying man; he had scarcely ceased praying since first lifting Hervey into the saddle.

'Hold him hard. I don't want a struggle,' growled Ritchie as he pulled aside the flesh again and inserted the forceps.

But Hervey was in too deep a syncope to know how the instrument probed.

*

In the end it was done quickly. Out came forceps and ball in less than a minute. Ritchie examined the missile for signs of having struck bone. Then, satisfied, he tossed it to Corporal Wainwright. 'Your captain may want to see the intruder.'

'Sir. Will that mean he'll be well now, sir?'

Ritchie was already back to work with magnifying glass and the smaller forceps. 'I dare say so.' He tutted, picking out particles of blue serge from the wound. 'Lord, but this cloth's bitty. More light, there! A candle or two.'

It was Peto who obliged him quickest.

'But no braid, though, it seems,' said Ritchie in a tone of some relief, and peering even closer. 'Well, he's as good a chance as any. I'll suture now, Magan. Keep him steady, my lads. Good work.'

'And then to my cot,' said Peto, nodding with the greatest appearance of approval. 'Well done, Mr Ritchie. Well done, sir!'

'I could do no better, Captain. But your praise may be premature. It will be two weeks, perhaps three, before we see the laudable pus – the exuviae of the sickness. Only then can we say the arm is saved. What he needs now is to rest, and to be still. I'll bleed him tomorrow.'

PART TWO

HOME TRUTHS

CHAPTER SIX

CAMP FOLLOWERS

Calcutta, four months later

The girl ran a finger down the neat line of the scar. Hervey felt no pain. Quite the opposite, for her touch was always delicate and accompanied by the gentlest of kisses. He sighed with the pleasure of their intimacy. 'You had better go, Neeta. Manu will be here shortly, and you know how you dislike him.'

The girl hissed. 'I do not know why you keep him as your bearer when you have so good a servant as Mr Johnson!'

Hervey smiled. 'Manu is a good bearer too. And he does Johnson's bidding willingly.'

The girl rose from the bed, tied a lungi about her, then sat at Hervey's dressing table and took one of his brushes to her long black hair, as Henrietta used to do.

What a solace she was – companion these past two years, and nurse these last two months. Yet how dismayed he had been when first she had come to Calcutta looking for him. Chittagong had seemed so far behind. He rose, put on his dressing gown, then took her shoulders, watching in the mirror as she brushed – so very like Henrietta, and yet in appearance so different. It was all very safe, therefore. But he broke the rules. A bibi did not visit; she was but a 'sleeping-dictionary'. He kissed the top of her head, then went outside.

It was a quiet afternoon in the lines, even allowing for the usual retreat to the shade and the punkah, although the worst of the south-west monsoon's clammy heat was long past. There were a few mounted men about the cantonment, but no hawkers, no rumble of wheels. The Company was at war with Ava, but the war was so far distant that the seat of government was undisturbed.

It had no right to be. Hervey had seen the effects of that detachment, men dying for want of the staples of war. And if the Calcutta quality, and the clerks and the merchants, really knew how badly went things they would be busy burying their silver and taking passage home. Not that the war would ever come to this. Ava might boast of marching into Bengal, and her great general, Maha Bundula, might lead the army, but the Burmans could never prevail against redcoats. In the end, he believed there was no one who could, for however ill he was served, a redcoat – a *King*'s redcoat – fought with the ferocious conviction of his own superiority. That was why so many of them died: they did not accept defeat, because redcoats were never defeated. Too many people had traded on that simple notion in years past. They did so now with the army in the east.

Hervey wondered how many of those good companions he had known in Rangoon had since been stilled by the enemy's shot or the fever. He scarcely dared think of how Peto was faring, for he knew that gallant man would be everywhere his sailors faced danger, be it the enemy or the country. There would be so many widows' letters, or to other kin. And none of them would say that such and such a good servant of the King had died because other servants of the King had been careless of his life. But, in the end, the merchants of the Honourable Company would not need to bury their silver. The Burmans were no martial race. Their armies had been formed neither by the British, the Moghuls nor the French. Indeed, by what right did they begin a fight they could not win?

But it would be some time. Yesterday, Eyre Somervile had come, as he had every day since Hervey's return weak with fever, and the news from the east had been as dispiriting as might have been.

General Campbell's force had fewer than three thousand effectives, and the flotilla was in a poor way too, with whole crews laid low by remittent fevers – even the bigger ships (*Larne* was so incapacitated she had had to be replaced by *Arachne*). There had been some successes, but Campbell was besieged still, by Nature and the Burmans. And now there was speculation that Maha Bundula himself, at the head of his army of Arakan, twice the strength of anything Campbell could muster, might soon be marching through the Irawadi's delta.

Well, he must put it all out of his mind. Today he was to dine with Somervile and Emma for the first time since leaving for Rangoon; Ledley, the regimental surgeon, had at last pronounced him fit (Hervey had pronounced himself fit more than a week ago). It was near six o'clock and his bearer would soon be here to supervise the team of bhistis who filled his bath with hot water. The surgeon had been most explicit in his warning against any chill, for he was advised that the fever was born of the malaria of the Rangoon marshes and could recur at any time, perhaps even in severer form.

Hervey took care to put on a good lawn shirt when he had bathed, and a linen coat, for as soon as the sun set he would otherwise feel the cool of the evening keenly. He took up his brushes and smiled as he picked the strands of black hair from them. One evening soon he would dine with his bibi here – whatever the rules said. But she dared not return this evening. He would go instead to her at the bibi khana beyond the civil lines towards the Chitpore road, where the rich Bengali merchants lived. It was a comfortable and private place. He liked it there. He was pleased he kept her properly.

Emma Somervile greeted him with a kiss to the lips. 'I never doubted you would be restored,' she said, smiling. 'But it has been many weeks, and you looked so fevered when last we visited.'

Hervey took a glass of champagne from the khitmagar and sat, as she bade him, beside her.

'Eyre will be here presently. There is an express boy come.'

'He is much occupied, I think. It must be the hardest thing to be so at odds with the Governor-General.'

Emma raised an eyebrow. 'It wears him more than I could have imagined. Oh, I do not mean the disagreements themselves, but the dismay at seeing so much going wrong when he had counselled against it from the start. And still Lord Amherst is not inclined to listen.'

Hervey frowned. 'There's a certain sort of man who would rather exhaust all his stock than admit to a wrong course and take a new one at half the cost. I fear there's many a grave that will be testimony to our Governor-General's obduracy. I'm only glad there are men such as Eyre who will expose the folly of it.'

Moments later Eyre Somervile entered the room with a look half triumphant and half exasperated. He dispensed with formal greetings. '*This* is just as I had expected – *worse*.' He waved a letter at them. 'Maha Bundula is now in Ava. Bagyidaw's recalled Prince Tharrawaddy and Bundula is to have command of the army they've been assembling these past three months.'

'Do you have any notion how large?' asked Hervey.

'Thirty thousand – over and above the same number back from Arakan.' Somervile consulted the letter again. 'Also, three hundred jingals, the Cassay Horse from Manipur – about a thousand of them – artillery on elephant-back . . .'

'What is a jingal?' asked Emma.

'A gun,' replied Hervey, turning to her. 'Very light – the ball weighs less than a pound – but they tote them anywhere. And very destructive they are too.'

'Campbell will be thrown out of Rangoon in very short order indeed,' added her husband.

'How do you come by the intelligence, Eyre?'

Somervile seemed rapt in thought.

'Eyre?'

'I'm sorry, my dear. I was thinking how much time we had, for the report says that Bundula boasted to Tharrawaddy he would feast in Rangoon in eight days. He could not, of course – not from the time of making the boast. The distance is too great in the best of weather. I suspect he meant eight days after once besieging the place.'

Emma stayed her questions for the time being.

Hervey looked uncertain. 'Unless, that is, Bundula were to engage Campbell piecemeal.'

'That is against the best precepts, is it not?'

'As a rule, but there would be advantage in bringing pressure to bear gently on Rangoon, for Campbell's so weakened that he might seek terms—'

Emma looked shocked. 'Do you mean to say that General Campbell could surrender?'

Hervey shook his head. 'I think it the last thing he would do. But Maha Bundula might not. The Burmans do not have a very high opinion of the Company.'

'Well,' said Somervile, making to turn. 'I must send to the commander-in-chief and to Amherst. They will surely now wish to reinforce Campbell's garrison. That, or order its withdrawal. You will excuse me for the moment.'

Hervey sat down again, taking a second glass of champagne.

'Do *you* know the source of his intelligence, Matthew?' asked Emma. 'Is it the same as before?'

'I imagine so,' he replied, cautiously. Somervile's best intelligence had come thence, and he knew of no other capable of yielding such precise and valuable information. Not the girl herself – she had merely been the cause for the boundless gratitude of a father whose abducted daughter had been returned unsullied, an unexpected prize from Hervey's action against the war boats on the Chittagong three years before. But Somervile had played up Hervey's chivalry in the jungled hill tracts to great purpose – like Rama and Sita, he had described her rescue. Indeed, he considered himself to be an intriguer of the first water on account of it. And so a favourite of King Bagyidaw's had become a most willing collaborator with the Company. 'And very good intelligence it is, too. Though I fear that neither Campbell nor the commander-in-chief can make the best of it.'

'How do you mean?'

'I don't know what plans Paget has in hand to reinforce Rangoon, but if there are none it is almost certainly too late to do so. And what will Campbell do when he learns that an army twenty times his strength is bearing down on him? He has the flotilla's guns, of course, but they might not be in a position to intervene decisively. If he is so reduced in numbers through sickness as we hear, then he would be best advised to quit the place, to use the ships to take off his force before it is utterly destroyed.'

'He is not likely to do that, surely? You yourself said as much.'

'I said he would not surrender. But he was with Moore at Corunna. And so was Paget for that matter. He has seen good precedent, therefore.'

Emma suddenly looked worried. 'Matthew, what if the intelligence is false?'

Hervey raised his eyebrows, and nodded. 'Just so. It is highly favourable to the Burmans, that is for sure. And for that reason it must be regarded circumspectly. Campbell's quitting Rangoon on a false report would be a most sorry business indeed.'

'You will warn Eyre of this, Matthew?'

'He will not need my warning, but, yes, I will speak my mind.'

Emma was relieved. She had felt the perturbation of the past year very keenly. Lord Amherst had set his face very decidedly against her husband's opinion. Somervile was a relatively junior member of the presidency council, although he was the acknowledged authority on the country powers and their neighbours. But he was an interventionist. Or rather, he advocated military action to obtain conditions favourable to the Company; the action itself – as in the case of Ava – did not have to take the form of an offensive. And so he found himself frequently in contention with the Governor-General, who thought him contrary, one minute seeming to urge boldness in meddling in native affairs, and in the next seeming to recoil from it. Somervile confided much in his wife, but she knew he did not tell all. That was too often apparent in his countenance and disposition.

'What about the regiment, Matthew,' said Emma abruptly, if brightly. 'I've not seen much of them since Sir Ivo left for England.'

Hervey was pleased to oblige her, for although he could not give the best of reports, or the fullest, he would rather be speaking of the regiment now than contemplating the mournful situation in Rangoon. 'I think they are well. But there's little for them to do save guards and drill, says Serjeant-Major Armstrong. And I'm not sure Eustace Joynson is happy with the regiment's reins entirely in his hands.'

'How long shall he have them?'

'A full twelve months, less the two already gone.'

'I do wish it were not so long. We are in need of society here, and Lady Lankester will be a welcome increase. Do you know anything of her?'

'Her people are from Hertfordshire, Lankester's seat. Her father is Sir Delaval Rumsey. I have not met her but it is said she is a very handsome woman.'

'I knew Sir Delaval at one time,' said Emma, just as brightly as before. 'Rather, I knew Lady Rumsey. She was a kindly woman, and herself quite a beauty, and a wit too.'

'Then we should all be content. Did I say that poor Joynson is having trouble with his daughter again?'

'Indeed?'

'According to my lieutenant. Seems she's been a deal too way-ward since first we arrived. The attentions of so many officers have sorely tested her senses, it would seem. I'm sure Joynson would wish you would take her in hand.'

Emma raised her eyebrows. 'I should not say it, but I have observed many times how it is the plainer girls whose senses are the least apt for testing.'

Hervey frowned again, but more playfully. 'Frances Joynson is not so *very* plain, Emma.'

Emma frowned, but more determinedly. 'I rather fancy that that is an acclimated opinion, Matthew.'

Hervey thought it indelicate, and unsafe, to proceed.

'In any case, her reputation has not been remarked on in the drawing rooms yet, so her behaviour cannot be so very bad.' Emma sipped at her champagne. 'Your name has been spoken of, however, Matthew.'

'Oh yes?' He intended to sound only the merest degree interested . . . curious.

'Lately, at the general's.'

Hervey simply raised an eyebrow and took another sip at his champagne.

'I fancy by the time Sir Ivo's bride is brought here it will be the talk of *every* drawing room.'

Hervey put his glass down, scarcely troubling now to hide his real sentiments. 'Emma, what is the matter with Calcutta? In Madras—'

'She visits, Matthew. That is what is the matter. And do not be angry with me because I tell you.'

He sighed. 'I am not angry with you, Emma. When I first came to India, almost ten years ago, things were . . . I am just astonished at so much canting.'

Emma would not be drawn. 'And another thing, Matthew. You have refused all society with Bishop Heber.'

Hervey frowned impatiently and held out his glass to the khitmagar. 'Please do not think I include Heber in my strictures, Emma. He is a good man from all I hear. But I do not feel the need of a bishop's society.'

'He only presses his claim on your acquaintance because your Mr Keble wrote to him.'

'Mr Keble presumes a deal too much.'

'Oh, Matthew!'

She touched a nerve, but he was not minded to give in. 'I sometimes think that Mr Keble believes the prospect from his parsonage window is the only one in the world.'

She frowned again. 'And you have seen so much more of the world!'

'Yes; I have.'

Emma sighed deeply. Had she not known him better it might have been a sigh of despair. Instead it was the mildly rebuking but tolerant sigh that his sister might have breathed. 'Then I should be careful not to see excess of it, Matthew.'

Eyre Somervile returned, to Hervey's relief. 'Well, it is done. I have sent my opinion to both Amherst and Paget. Doubtless they'll think it unreliable. But nothing I've sent them to date has been other than borne out by events. Paget's no fool. He may be a little too ready to defer to Amherst, but he's no fool.'

'You are perfectly certain of your intelligence?' Hervey held his gaze until an answer came.

Somervile inclined his head very slightly. 'There is, of course, the possibility that it was sent to me with but one object. In which case I might well precipitate an evacuation of Rangoon for no reason. That is what you allude to, I imagine? This I have laid out in my memoranda to Amherst and Paget. The veracity of the report is unknowable, unless some corroboration is received, but the *possibility* of it is certain, and in consequence the peril of Campbell's force. One way or another, it is imperative to act. *That* is the material point.'

Hervey glanced at Emma, and smiled. 'Somervile, for once I do not fret at not marching towards the sound of the guns. I fear it will be a wretched business either way. Campbell is a brave man, but I give it as my opinion that he has no place in command of a campaign such as this. And I for one am done with such men.'

Emma looked startled, but her husband had heard this opinion often enough these past two months. 'My dear,' he said, half smiling and taking a glass from the khitmagar. 'You must know that we have a dinner companion of very refractory military disposition. I do have a notion that he believes all between him and the Duke of Wellington to be but deadwood.'

Hervey frowned. But as things stood, he felt little inclination to deny it.

'Come, let us eat, then,' said Somervile, content in the knowledge that there was no more a man in his position could do for the moment. 'I would hear of how things are with the regiment.'

Emma rose.

Hervey followed, though not so nimbly as once he might. 'Does it matter very much how things are? Whatever course Campbell chooses, there's no place for cavalry in it.'

'Hah!' Somervile stepped aside to let Emma lead them to the dining room. 'You make the same mistake as those in council who seem capable of looking in only one direction at a time. In India, Hervey, as you must surely know, one must be Janus-like with regard to whence the next blow shall come. Let me tell you what has been happening among the country powers while our eyes have been diverted eastwards . . .'

Next morning, Hervey rode out for the first time since returning to Calcutta. Private Johnson had brought Gilbert to his bungalow just before dawn, as Hervey took his *chota hazree* – sweet tea and figs. He had never, as a rule, taken anything but tea before morning exercise, even in the cold season, but he had felt weaker than he supposed he would on rising. He cursed the time it was taking for him to regain his full strength. The shoulder had, to all appearances, knitted together well enough, but the fever had left him like a woman in the first gravid months – dizzy, puking, listless. It had come and gone, and each time seemed worse, but in the last weeks he had felt himself recovering his proper spirits with each day. It

93

was just the mornings, now, that reminded him there was still a course to run.

'Is tha sure tha's all right, sir?' enquired Johnson, watching him, curious.

Gilbert's manners were not as he would have wanted, and Hervey seemed unable to stop the jogging.

'To tell the truth, Johnson, I'd as soon be listening to one of the chaplain's sermons.'

'*That* bad, sir.'

'Perhaps not. But it can't go on.' He tried once more to sit easy, to persuade the gelding to get off its toes, but it made no difference. 'What have you been doing with him all these months?'

'Swap 'orses, sir?'

'Don't be impertinent.'

Johnson smiled. Ten years they had been together now – more, almost eleven – longer than any officer and groom in the Sixth, or in memory indeed. He had no pleasure in his captain's infirmity, but he could at least take satisfaction in the tables being turned just a little. ''As tha 'eard t'RSM's to be wed?'

The dodge worked. Hervey looked astonished. 'You would as well persuade me that the sar'nt-major is to take the cloth.' He flicked his long schooling whip at Gilbert's quarters in mounting exasperation.

There was little reason why he should believe it. Mr Lincoln had been regimental serjeant-major for fifteen years. It was generally imagined that he was the senior in the whole of the cavalry. Why should he suddenly feel the need of a wife? Except that Johnson's canteen intelligence was almost invariably accurate . . .

'I'd put any money on it, sir.'

'Who is she?' demanded Hervey, sounding almost vexed.

'Widder o' one o' t'Footy's quartermasters.'

Hervey, for all his nausea and discomposure, managed an approving smile. 'She must be a redoubtable woman. How is it known? Has there been any announcement?'

Johnson became circumspect; there were canteen confidences to safeguard. 'Mr Lincoln saw Major Joynson yesterday an' asked 'is leave to marry.'

Hervey smiled again. A clerk with an ear to the door, and a thirst to be quenched by selling tattle in the wet canteen. Things hadn't changed. Not that Johnson would have paid for his information. Hervey had learned long ago that Johnson received word from many a source because the canteen attributed to him considerable powers of prophecy and intercession. 'What a tamasha that will be, then. And colonel and RSM wed in the same year.' Then he frowned. 'Oh, I do hope this doesn't mean Mr Lincoln intends his discharge.'

It was a curious thing, and Hervey knew as well as the next man, and better than most, that 'new blood' was as necessary in the officers and senior ranks of a cavalry regiment as it was in its horses. And yet with Mr Lincoln it was different. It was scarcely conceivable that there could be any want in the performance of his duties, and his grey hairs served only to add distinction to his appearance. In any case, the RSM would yield to no one in the jumping lane at the end of a field day. To many, indeed, Mr Lincoln *was* the regiment. No one in the Sixth had served longer, though his actual record of service, with its attestation date, had been conveniently lost years ago.

'I bet that's not what Serjeant-Major Deedes thinks,' said Johnson, screwing up his face.

That was the problem. There could only be the one crown, and for as long as the admirable Lincoln wore it above his stripes no other could. Deedes was next in seniority, and had been for five years or more, and behind him were others wondering if the crown would ever be theirs to wear before they were obliged to leave the colours. One of those, indeed, was Armstrong. Hervey had never given it much thought before. Could he imagine Geordie Armstrong filling Lincoln's boots? It was pointless his making any comparison, for so different were the two men. Except, perhaps, that Armstrong's formation had been at Lincoln's hands as much as anyone's.

There was, of course, one man who would by now have been the acknowledged heir. Serjeant Strange could have worn the crown, a worthy successor in every respect, except that by now another regiment might have made a claim on him, or even a field commission might have come his way. It was nigh on ten years ago, in a corner of the battlefield at Waterloo, that Strange had demonstrated his singular worth – and had lost his life doing so. Hervey still thought about that day, and his own part in Strange's fall. He asked himself the same questions, and the answers were always as uncertain.

'Still, dead men's boots are a sight easier to come by 'ere than at 'ome,' chirped Johnson. He did not actually nod to the garrison cemetery, and its growing regimental plot, but the timing of their passing could not have been more apt.

'For heaven's sake, Johnson, have a little compassion!'

Johnson mistook Hervey's meaning. 'Sorry sir, I didn't mean as I thought *tha* were—'

'Oh, thank you. You'll be sure to let me know when the canteen shortens the odds on *my* getting to the end of this posting, won't you?'

Johnson looked only very slightly abashed.

'Come then,' said Hervey, sighing. 'Let's shorten the reins instead and see what we can do.'

Gilbert broke into a trot a fraction before the aids applied, leaving Hervey to curse his own lack of handiness as well as his horse's. It was going to be a long business, this getting back to condition.

When they returned to the bungalow the best part of an hour later, for he had wanted to ride right out of the lines onto the plain, Hervey slid from the saddle in better spirits and health, and said that he would attend morning stables. Then he went inside for *hazree* and an hour with his pen. There was correspondence long overdue and he meant to make a start today, just as he intended taking back the charge of his troop.

On his desk were five letters. Two were from Horningsham, one from Elizabeth, the other from his father. They had been written a fortnight apart but had arrived together. That from his father contained the same warm paternal sentiment as that sent to Shrewsbury when first he had gone up, on his fourteenth birthday. Indeed, it was in essence the same letter, except for a line or two on diocesan affairs (which hitherto Archdeacon Hervey had rarely mentioned) and the news that his monograph on Archbishop Laud was at last nearing completion.

The letter from Elizabeth was not greatly longer but contained altogether more information – about the village, their part of Wiltshire, the country as a whole (garnered, she admitted, from the newspapers), about their parents and relatives, and last, but at greatest length, about his daughter. Georgiana was six months older than when Elizabeth had last written, and it seemed she was a favourite at both Longleat and the vicarage. She showed all the signs of a fine intelligence, was able to read, and she could sit a pony well. She laughed a great deal. It was a letter to reassure an absent father that he should have no concerns for the well-being of his child. And yet this agreeable report had the effect of making Hervey want to be with his daughter as keenly as would an unhappy one, for Georgiana was Henrietta's offspring.

He laid the letter to one side. It would be as difficult to begin a reply to his sister's as to his father's, if for wholly different reasons. He picked up the third, from John Keble. He imagined it written with that same prospect before the writer against which he had inveighed the evening before at the Somerviles. It was a letter composed in a Gloucestershire curate's house, an untroubled place where dreams could be dreamed, a letter full of rebuttals of this divine and that, with a lengthy description of the work he was jointly embarked on with Hervey's father – a charge to the clergy of the archdeaconry of Sarum. There was the startling revelation that Keble had been asked if he would go to the West Indies, as archdeacon of Barbados no less; and the wholly unsurprising addendum that he had declined. The letter concluded with an evidently pained enquiry into whether or not Hervey had yet had occasion to discourse with Bishop Heber, it being more than a year since that prelate had been enthroned. It was, indeed, so worthy a letter that Hervey felt it required a peculiar state of grace before any response could be attempted. He laid it down and picked up the fourth.

He already knew its contents. Yet even as he began rereading a third or fourth time, it had its effect. The hand was the freest of the four, the sentiment likewise. What it was to have a female of the likes of Lady Katherine Greville bestowing her time on him. How diverting seemed the gossip that had formerly repulsed him so. How fondly, now, he remembered their brief company, and her uninhibited pleasure in it – and how lame his own response had been. But it had been different then – too close to events, his mind encumbered by all sorts of notions and doubts. Things were not the same now. India, for all her heat, had moistened that dried-up

97

interior of his. First she had given him back his very being as a soldier. It did not matter that in reality the affair of the head-waters of the Karnaphuli had been unhonoured by Calcutta, or that the campaign he had so recently left in a dhoolie was the re-creation of that muddle in the Low Countries a quarter of a century before. India was a stage on which the soldier could expound his art, learn stratagems and devices unheard of at home, and above all might have that most prized thing – the true exercise of command. Yes, Hervey was angry with Major-General Sir Archibald Campbell and the campaign in Ava; but it and the other diversions of this singular country made him feel as alive as ever he could remember.

He took a sheet of paper from the drawer and picked up his pen. Perhaps as little as a year ago he would have begun his replies in the strict order of filial duty, then sibling love, then respectfulness for the cloth, and then . . . But this morning he began, 'Dear Lady Katherine'. An hour or so later, having written rather more than usual to this wife of an absentee husband, and likewise having returned her teasing and toying in fuller measure, he put on cantonment dress – the looser-fitting cotton jacket that the Sixth had adopted soon after arriving, with light cotton overalls and forage cap – and walked to the regimental headquarters to report himself back at duty.

Major Joynson heard him through the open door of his office and came at once into the adjutant's room to add his salutation. 'And a word with you as soon as you are done here,' he added, in a manner that Hervey could not quite determine as encouraging or otherwise.

He wanted to appear neither apprehensive nor indifferent, and so after ten minutes with the adjutant, in which he was apprised of the comings and goings of his troop, and its defaulters, Hervey signed the orders book and then repaired to the major's office.

Since the death of his wife, an invalid to laudanum, and the military demise of Lord Towcester, Eustace Joynson had grown steadily in stature and affection in the regiment. His reputation for painstaking administration had always been high, but the demands made on him by his late wife had sapped his vigour, and Towcester's martinet command had all but eviscerated him. Now, the sick headaches that had removed him from duty with

98

monotonous regularity had all but gone, and he enjoyed many a mess night where before he had found them a sore trial. However, he did not feel himself entirely a match for the decision before him now. And there were none, perhaps, who would blame him, for the decision was one of the utmost importance to every man in the Sixth.

'Hervey, close the door and take a seat. Have you had coffee? Would you like a little Madeira? No? Perhaps a shade early. I never do, not before eleven. Have you heard that Mr Lincoln's to marry?'

Hervey sat in a tub-chair that creaked with the slightest move of a muscle. 'I have. Joyous news.'

'You think so? Possibly, I suppose . . . yes.'

'Is there some objection to the lady?'

'Oh no. No, indeed not. She is a very respectable woman; very highly regarded by the light infantry's colonel. Lincoln's calling on him this very morning.'

'Then why do you sound uncertain?'

'Because Marsh is to send in his papers. Says he wants to spend his declining days in Ipswich rather than be quartermaster here.'

'Singular!'

Joynson smiled. 'A man who prefers Ipswich to Calcutta might rightly be said to have begun his decline already. I could not say that even the worst of the stink here would drive me to such a decision.'

Hervey nodded, returning the smile, a sort of mock grimace. 'Ipswich. Indeed no.'

'But you will imagine that there must be a replacement quartermaster.'

'And a replacement for the replacement.'

'Exactly so. I am excessively pleased that Lincoln shall join us at last in the mess. Indeed, it is long overdue. But the pleasure is dulled by the thought of having to determine his own succession.'

The word was well chosen. Lincoln's had been a long reign by any standard. Hervey wondered what the RSM himself thought of relinquishing the crown. 'It should be Deedes, by rights. Is there any serious objection? It has always been seniority tempered by rejection.'

Joynson took off his glasses and polished them with a silk cloth. 'I've been disappointed with Deedes these past twelve months.

There's a want of vigour. I dare say that he'll make no mistakes, but if we're to have him for any time then I fear he'll begin to drop the bit. Rose thinks so too.'

Hervey raised an eyebrow. 'Deuced tricky superseding Deedes. He'll fall right away and become a malcontent, no doubt. And the rest of his mess will be ill at ease if they perceive no very good reason for it. Who is next in seniority? Harrison?'

'Telfer.'

'Oh dear.'

'Precisely. Who would *you* want?'

'Hairsine.'

'Exactly.'

Hervey frowned. 'They've all been too long in the rank, even Hairsine. In that respect the war brought them on too quickly. I can remember Hairsine the night we had word of the surrender, at Toulouse. He was orderly serjeant-major. It was *ten years* ago.'

'Deedes's time will be up in a couple of years in the normal course of things. And Harrison's not much later. I suppose we could take a chance on him, and Hairsine could bide his time a while longer.'

'There'll be more talk of dead men's boots. But it wouldn't do any more harm, I suppose. What would Sir Ivo want to do?'

'Strange to say, we never spoke of it. Marsh looked the last man to give up so cosy a billet as quartermaster.'

Hervey supposed it an apt description of quartermaster in a station such as Calcutta. 'Can he not be persuaded to remain in post a little longer?'

Joynson shook his head. 'He's determined to leave by October – to have the spring in Ipswich, he says. And in any case, all we should have is six months of jockeying and wagering and heaven knows what else. All very unedifying. No, it's a decision I shall have to take myself, and be content with the notion that it will not be possible to make the right one.'

Hervey smiled again. Joynson knew his pack. The only decision that had the remotest possibility of being acknowledged the right one was that made by the commanding officer himself. The major might carry the horn this season, but he was not the master. 'Anything else?'

Joynson hesitated. 'Are you sure you won't have some Madeira?'

'Thank you, no. In truth, I think my gut ought still to be listed sick at present.'

'I list mine sick one week in every month, and feel the better for it. Coffee then?'

'Yes, coffee.'

Joynson called for his bearer to bring two cups. 'What do you make of Barrow?'

It seemed a strange turn in the conversation. Hervey looked wary.

'If he has any he could call a friend it would be you, I think,' said Joynson, polishing his glasses again.

'I think it would be fairer to the three of us if you first said why you asked, sir,' replied Hervey. 'Especially since I have been absent for the best part of the year.' And he always tried that much harder with Barrow, for Barrow was an officer from the ranks – the ranks of another regiment, indeed – and Hervey had not cared for him to begin with. Not that Barrow had seemed to want to help himself in terms of popularity with his new-found fellow officers.

Joynson nodded. 'You're right. It may come to nothing. Let's hope so. But I've had word – it doesn't matter where from; it's not the regiment – that he's on the take with his remount fund.'

Hervey smiled. 'I saw some of his remounts this morning. How he's managed to find that quality *and* take a backhand glass I can't imagine!'

'I thought that too only yesterday when his troop paraded for escort. However, the accusation comes from one of the dealers, it seems.'

'What are you going to do?'

'I don't know. I was only apprised of it yesterday. The next board of officers isn't for another six months. I can't very well roist his accounts about meanwhile without good cause. We can't jump to every bazaar-wallah who complains of *backshee*. I'm inclined to have the dealer arrested if he won't make a proper deposition.'

'What do you want me to do?'

Joynson looked uncertain. 'Could you think it of Barrow?'

'Why should I think it any more or any less of Barrow than of the others?'

'You know very well why.'

101

'So Barrow's coming from the ranks puts him more in the way of temptation?'

'Don't sport with me, Hervey. If it were Hugh Rose we'd never hear the charge out.'

Hervey frowned. 'I think that if we are making private means the touchstone then we would be obliged to enquire whether Rose's fortune had disappeared.'

'You are not being of much assistance.'

The bearer brought their coffee. Hervey took his and began stirring the strong black liquid. 'I'll keep an ear cocked,' he said when the man had gone.

'Thank you.' The major took his coffee and heaped sugar into the cup.

Hervey thought he would try to end the line of questioning. 'How is Frances? I haven't seen her in months.' He meant it not unkindly. No regimental officer could be an island when it came to domestic troubles, and it was as well to know if there were any vexations in that respect.

Joynson sighed, heavily. 'I have been on the point of speaking to the colonel of the Thirteenth, and several of the Company's, many times these past six months. I feel they have as much responsibility in allowing her to expose herself in so frequent a way. I am very happy that she has such diversions as these levees and balls, but . . .'

Hervey nodded.

'She sorely misses a mother. She always has.'

Hervey felt the footsteps over his grave.

'Are you quite well, Hervey?' asked Joynson, narrowing his eyes.

'Of course, sir. Perfectly well. Very well indeed.'

Poor Joynson. His nickname had been 'Daddy' for the short time he had had a troop in the Peninsula. He had his weaknesses, and he knew them, but in intention he had served his country as well as anyone, and he had a true attachment to his regiment. Hervey thought it most unjust that his standing should be risked by a silly daughter.

'I think it would be ill to deny her any society properly ordered. Perhaps she might attach herself to some matron here?' It was as well as he could manage, for he had little enough experience to draw on.

They sat awhile, talking of how things were going in the east, and of what the regiment might do in the autumn by way of field days. At length Hervey rose to take his leave so as to catch his troop at morning stables.

'Very well, Hervey,' said Joynson, a little brighter. 'It's good to have you back again. Come and dine with us soon.'

'I should like that, sir. Thank you.' He put on his forage cap, saluted, then left the regimental headquarters pondering the peculiar trust that Joynson had shown. He liked the intimacy of the personal confidences, even if they had momentarily reminded him of his own situation. And in respect of the succession of serjeant-majors, it was good to be assured periodically of one's own stake in the regiment.

E Troop's stables stood at the end of the single line of back-to-back standing stalls that stretched for three hundred yards beyond the regimental maidan. They were brick-built and whitewashed, with a good thatch and khus-khus tatties that extended from the joists to about the chest height of a dragoon. In the summer, therefore, the troop-horses stood in shade, and the doused tatties and punkahs provided some relief in the otherwise still, oven-hot air, while in the monsoon season and the winter the animals were protected from rain and wind, be it hot or cold. At the end of each troop block was the stabling for the officers' chargers, six loose boxes in line with a separate store for saddlery and tackling.

At nine o'clock of a morning at this time of year, early October, the lines were all activity. The rains were receding, and the regiment had begun its cool-weather routine. Horses had been fed two hours before and the dragoons had breakfasted. It was a hearty meal, a dragoon's breakfast, just right for a morning's work: half a pound of bread, the same of beef, and plenty of coffee. Hervey wondered if he would be able to keep such a meal down ever again. But a dragoon needed his beef for such a morning – the fetching and carrying, the brushing and strapping, for there was only so much the native grass-cutters were allowed to do. The men clattered about the brick-laid floor in their clogs and stable dress like workers in a cotton mill, but ten times as lively. At nine-thirty the trumpeter would sound 'boot and saddle', and the serjeants would check every last buckle and strap. And many a hapless dragoon who had thought the shine on his leather more than adequate as he polished by lamplight would find that the Indian sun was a merciless revealer of insufficiency. And then he might think for a moment, but only a moment, that he might prefer other employment.

For the time being, however, they were still at work with brush and curry-comb. It was just that bit easier while horses had their summer coats, but there was sweat on every dragoon's brow nevertheless. It was not a time for shouted commands, rather of careful observance of standing orders and the accumulated experience of the corporals. Above all it was not a time for officers. It was the serjeant-major's hour. It was he, and his trusted NCOs, who turned out the troop to perfection – both horses and men. Then the officers led them in the practice of war, real or imagined. And the serjeant-major did not expect supervision.

Hervey's appearance in the lines this morning was therefore doubly unusual. He had not even sent word to Myles Vanneck, his lieutenant, that he was reporting himself fit for duty, and there was at once a buzz as the news passed from stall to stall. The dragoons nearest the end stood to attention as others gawped or tried to steal a look. Hervey felt as if he were some ghost. 'Carry on, Harkness,' he said, nodding and smiling as he began walking the line of stalls.

Private Harkness, the broadest of shoulders making his trooper look short-backed, returned the smile confidently.

Another dragoon came to attention as Hervey reached his stall. 'Carry on, Hicks. How is your leg now?'

Private Hicks turned red. His leg had been mended for all of three years, but still his nickname in the troop was Giles, 'the cripple'. 'Very good, sir, thank you, sir.'

The next man had neither brush nor comb in his hand, and he therefore saluted.

Hervey smiled again. Beneath the watering cap were thick black curls, unmistakable. 'Good morning, French. What is the news from Wales?'

'Agreeable, I think, sir. My father has taken another living, and my brother is to be ordained too.' The voice was not perhaps so differently cast from the other recruits' as first it had seemed on joining; but it was still the voice of a man of some education.

The ringing of spurs made Hervey turn.

'Good morning, sor!'

Hervey smiled the more – an indulgent sort of smile. 'Corporal McCarthy!'

'It's good to see you on your feet again, sor. And back in time for all the drill, too.'

'Indeed, indeed.' Yes, he had timed his return well – as if he had had any say in it.

'Go and fetch the sar'nt-major, Rudd,' said McCarthy, addressing the next stall.

Hervey looked across keenly; he had not noticed Private Rudd, and he watched with satisfaction as he doubled away, for he had saved the boy from a cloying mother and the dubious occupation of milliner. Rudd ought to be corporal soon: if only there were more *places*.

He carried on down the line, Corporal McCarthy by his side. 'How is your section then, on the whole?'

'Well, sor; *very* well. Not a horse lame nor a man sick.'

Hervey nodded appreciatively. It was as well at the beginning of what they called here the unhealthy season.

Next he stopped by Private Needham's stall. Needham's hair almost covered the stub of his right ear, but the old wound was vivid enough. Hervey recalled the bloody sight when the Burman tulwar had sliced the flesh away. Needham stood to attention now with brush and comb clasped in each hand by his side, as fit as the day Hervey had enlisted him on Warminster Common, but he did not smile.

'Good morning, Needham. How is your mare?'

Hervey chose well. Needham and his mare were ever closer by the day. 'She's doing a treat, sir. She won best turnout last week.'

'A credit to you,' said Hervey, nodding approval. And he would say no more for the time being, for they had buried Needham's best friend, Private Spreadbury, barely a week ago, and there were now but two of the original 'Warminster pals' left.

How well the pals had served him, thought Hervey. That day, five years ago, when he had defied all his instincts and gone to Warminster Common to look for recruits – it had repaid his efforts no end. Indeed, would he be alive this day had he not done so? For Wainwright was first of the pals. He smiled at the thought of what the King's shilling could buy – and what the King's uniform could do for a man in return. He hoped he would live long enough to see four chevrons on Wainwright's sleeve.

'Good morning, Captain Hervey sir!'

The voice filled the stables. There was no need for Hervey to turn to see whose it was. 'Good morning, Sar'nt-Major!' he replied, as cheerily as he had been hailed.

'Not a horse off the road, sir, nor a man neither.'

Troop Serjeant-Major Armstrong, collier-turned-cavalryman – the only horse he had seen before enlisting was pulling a coal tub; but what a source of strength, always, was that voice of the Tyne. Hervey's thoughts were at once of Sahagun, Corunna, Albuhera, and a dozen other places where Armstrong's voice had done its work: cursing, checking, cajoling. To his mind, Armstrong *was* the Sixth, as much as was Lincoln (and, God rest his soul, as Strange had been). Without him the regiment could surely never be the same – or as good?

'Corporal McCarthy tells me so. Very good husbandry, Sar'nt-Major.' It was, perhaps, fortunate that Hervey was enquiring this day and not a week before. That the last man sick, poor Spreadbury, had died was not something to be reflected in the day's parade state. In their five or so years in Calcutta E Troop had lost eighteen men to the agues and fevers that plagued the cantonments every season. And before he had left for Rangoon the sick rate had been three men in ten. The other troops had fared no better, but that was little consolation to mess mates – nor to Hervey and Armstrong whose concern it was to maintain a decent muster. But no men sick this morning – not a bad way to begin command again.

'The vet'in'ry's round the other side, sir, if you want me to tell him you're here. Just doing his rounds, that is. No problems.'

'Just say not to leave before I'm able to have a word.'

Armstrong nodded to Rudd, who cut away smartly.

They advanced another stall. 'A new face, I perceive.'

The dragoon stood at attention, as Needham before him, with brush and curry-comb in either hand. But his look was a touch anxious rather than melancholy.

'Private Toyne, sir,' said Armstrong. 'Joined last month.'

Hervey looked him up and down – a well-made youth,

fresh-faced and clean. 'Where are you from, Toyne?'

'Appleby, sir,' in a voice not unlike the serjeant-major's.

But Hervey was none the wiser.

'Westmorland, sir,' explained Armstrong. Long years had taught him that officers spoke of counties, not places.

Hervey knew there were hills in Westmorland, but that was about all. 'What brought you to the Sixth then?'

'My cousin is in the Fifty-fifth, sir, and 'e took me to enlist. But I said I wanted to work with 'orses, and so the Fifty-fifth let me change.'

'Did they, indeed? That was very generous of them.' And most unusual, too. No doubt the recruiting serjeant had sworn blind that the Fifty-fifth were mounted on the best bloods – and more besides if it would secure another man.

'Well, sir, I had to pay a bit of money.'

'A recruit *buying* into the cavalry. Now there's a thing!'

Toyne would not understand the humour just yet, but Armstrong smiled pityingly. 'There's not much for company but sheep up there, sir. He's made a good start, though. Sits well.'

Hervey nodded to show his appreciation. 'You worked with horses in Appleby then?'

'Yes sir. I used to help with the fair, sir.'

'Fair?'

'Yes sir. There's an 'orse fair twice a year. People comes from all over to buy.'

Hervey nodded again. 'Well, I'm pleased to have you in my troop. Carry on.'

Toyne turned as red as Hicks had done.

'A good 'un,' said Armstrong, voice lowered, as they stepped off. 'A real liking for horses. He'll make a good groom in his turn.'

Hervey took note. It was difficult not to when a man had parted with money in order to be with horses.

At the other stalls it was reunion rather than introduction – and sometimes banter. Hervey, his spirits already lifted, was content, for here were a confident troop, who thought themselves a cut above the others since the affair at the river three years before. None of the other troops had so much as chased a dacoit, let alone bloodied a sabre, and a man who had not cut or thrust – or even

107

fired carbine or pistol in anger – could hardly think himself a proper dragoon. For sure, it was the veterans of Waterloo who were honoured above all others in the wet canteen. Not with exaggerated reverence, but with the nodding respect that they had seen something never to be seen again, and were therefore possessed of certain insights and certain rights. And sometimes an E Troop man who had overreached himself in the canteen on the business of fighting would be brought up sharply by a Waterloo hand and reminded that the affair at the river, sharp though it had been, could never compare with that day in June. But an E Troop man stood in the veterans' respect nevertheless.

It was no longer true perhaps that the army divided into two parts – those who had been at Waterloo and those who had not – but the army was just as divided in its opinion of the future. It was true, certainly, that no officer believed in his heart there would be a battle the like of Waterloo again; never so many men in the field at once, never so great a number of guns. And – worst of all for those of Hervey's calling – never again so many cavalry manoeuvring to decisive effect. No, not even in India. What, therefore, would be their fate? Was it to be as mere spectators, from afar even, as in Burma – a pretty corps of escorts, in uniforms more and more elaborate and less and less serviceable? Or would they just become a corps of skirmishers, little better than Pandours and Croats?

Hervey had his opinions. They were formed in the Peninsula, confirmed at Waterloo and proven often enough these past three years. Perhaps he would write of them – write a book – as Peto had suggested. Many would sneer at his doing so of course, but he didn't care; not any longer.

'Good morning, Captain Hervey,' said the veterinary surgeon.

'Ah, David – good morning.'

David Sledge was the only officer habitually called by his Christian name, from colonel to cornet. The veterinary surgeon stood in a curious position regarding rank and seniority, and the Sixth had come to an admirable working arrangement.

'You wanted to see me?'

'No, not especially. Only to say that I am returned to duty. I gather I have a fit troop?'

Armstrong took his leave. There were things he would attend to with Serjeant Collins: 'Them gram-grinders, sir. Still not sized off.'

Hervey nodded, then turned to Sledge again. 'It says a good deal for Armstrong, that parade state.'

'Yes, very satisfactory,' said Sledge, checking his pocketbook. 'Not a cough nor a warm leg in the stables these past six weeks. And I take my hat off to Brennan too.'

Hervey had long been convinced that E Troop had the best farrier. And so much steadier was Brennan these days with a fellow countryman in McCarthy to share tobacco and grog with (and a fellow with stripes to boot). 'I shall tell him. But he's had light work in respect of numbers, I see – a good dozen short. Do you know what are the remount arrangements?'

The purchase of remounts was not the business of the veterinary surgeon, but he had an obvious interest. 'Nothing's coming from the Company studs this year, apparently, so it's all down to dealers. When you're ready to look I'll come with you if you'd like. We've kept the lines free of infection all year and I shouldn't want anything brought in on approval.'

Hervey smiled. 'David, I should value your opinion on more than just the animal's health. But not for a day or so, I think – unless you say others will be looking too. I'll ask the RM as well.'

Sledge looked pained. 'Broad's not been in best sorts of late. Ledley's had to dose him a good deal.'

'Fever?'

Sledge still looked pained. 'N-o-o.'

'Well, I hope whatever is the cause he will not be indisposed long. I've seen no better man with remounts.'

'I shall be seeing him later. I will pass on your regard.'

Hervey scowled. 'Come, David; you are not telling me all.'

Sledge looked relieved. 'To be explicit, it's a case for mercury and nitrate.'

'Oh God,' groaned Hervey. 'But what of *Annie* Broad? Has she gone home or something?'

Sledge raised his eyebrows. 'I should ask Rose.'

'What?'

'Been drawing his yard there, it seems. Better not speak of it here.'

Hervey shook his head slowly. 'Is it much talked about?'

'What – the mercury or Rose?'

'Both.'

'Neither generally, but the mercury's out in the ranks, I think. The Rose business Broad himself told me. But not here, Hervey. Can you come to my dispense later?'

Hervey finished his tour of the horse lines alone, then went to the troop office, where he found Myles Vanneck and his new cornet, Green.

'Good morning, Hervey!' said Vanneck, and with evident pleasure – even though his captain's return meant he would no longer have charge of things.

Hervey had found it easy leaving the troop in his lieutenant's hands. It was, after all, what was intended by the name of that rank. But in Myles Vanneck he had especial trust, as much as he had known in Seton Canning, even. Vanneck had been with the Sixth scarcely five years, but he had taken to command with the greatest of ease – the same ease, indeed, as that of his elder brother in the Eighteenth, whom Hervey had known in the Peninsula. And Vanneck had been lucky, too, for the means to buy a lieutenancy when the time came had been but a trifle to him at 'India rates', though when it was his turn for a captaincy the regiment would, for sure, be back in England and he would thereby have to pay well over price. Not that that should present the Honourable Myles Vanneck with too much difficulty, however: Lord Huntingfield's sons did not go in want of anything. And it was one of the reasons that Hervey so liked him, for he could easily have bought into a home regiment and enjoyed the pleasures of London or Brighton rather than the dust and heat, and the doubtful society of Calcutta. And, of course, the young *Cornet* Vanneck had comported himself so admirably in the affair of the river. Blue blood, and not afraid to shed it – it was hardly surprising the men regarded him.

Hervey smiled and took off his cap.

'This is Cornet Green.'

Hervey held out his hand, which the cornet took a shade hesitantly.

'How d'you do, sir,' said Green.

The cavalryman's *coup d'œil* was not always faithful when it came to the man rather than the situation. That much Hervey would freely acknowledge. But Green was not of the usual stamp:

that much was impossible not to observe. He looked ungainly, a touch heavy-limbed to be a man at home in the saddle. And his features were a deal less fine than the subalterns prided themselves on. In the few words of his salutation he revealed that he came from the north of England (although that in itself said nothing, for the proud and independent gentry of the northern counties had provided many a son to the regiment during the war). But there was just something . . . *No*, thought Hervey; here indeed was a queer card.

'When did you come?' he asked, with deliberate kindness.

'Three months ago, sir.'

'Did you come via the depot?'

'No, sir.'

Nothing more volunteered than the precise answer – this was going to be heavy.

Vanneck sought to help. 'He has bought two fine chargers, I might say. One of them was that bay of Williams's in the bodyguard.'

Hervey nodded. 'I much approve. I had a mind to buy him myself if ever he came up.'

'Thank you, sir.'

Green's hair was sticking up by his right temple, like a duck's tuft. Hervey found himself staring at it.

Vanneck kept trying. 'Green was just about to go to the adjutant. He's picket-officer today.'

'So I see,' said Hervey, glancing at the cornet's review order.

Green's tunic, and all, looked in themselves immaculate, but even Mr Gieve's best efforts could not make a military coat hang well on a dumpling.

'Very good, Green,' said Hervey, trying hard not to sound dismayed. 'We'll speak at length tomorrow when your duties are done.'

Cornet Green coloured a little, put on his shako (askew, but Hervey thought best to say nothing – the adjutant would correct it soon enough), saluted and took his leave.

When he had gone, Hervey sat down and looked at Vanneck quizzically.

Vanneck sighed. 'I know. But he means well. The others have given him quite a rousting, though. His nickname's "grocer".'

'Green—, I suppose?'

111

Vanneck nodded. 'That, and his father's a tea merchant, in Lincolnshire.' He paused, then added, 'In Stamford,' as if that fact might be of some use.

Hervey smiled ruefully. 'Evidently they drink a lot of tea in Stamford if he can afford Williams's bay.'

'Oh, he's not short of money. On the contrary. The trouble is his ambition is rather in advance of his capability. He's yet to pass out of riding school.'

'Indeed?'

'I did tell him that he might buy a more tractable charger to begin with, but he seemed keen to make a splash.'

'Poor fellow.'

'Yes. And the RM's been sick the while, so the rough-riders have had their fun with him, I'm afraid.'

Hervey laid his cap and whip on the table. 'Can't you help at all, Myles?'

'I'm doing just that, Hervey. I take him out beyond the syces' huts late of an afternoon, where there's no one to see. But I'm not sure he has the hands or legs for it, and I'm pretty sure he hasn't the head.'

'Oh dear. And the drill season about to start.'

'Quite. I'm afraid the dragoons have a poor opinion of him already. He's too stiff about the place.'

'It's hardly surprising from what you tell me. But there have been stiff-necks before; he can overcome that in time. You will keep at him, Myles?'

Vanneck sighed. 'Yes, Hervey. Of course I will. But the others have no such duty as they see it. The trouble is, he has no conversation – and seemingly no interests. At mess the other night even the chaplain gave up on him, and then he fell off his chair quite stupefied.'

'The chaplain?'

'No, Green.'

Hervey smiled again. 'Well, there at least is sign of a kindred spirit, is there not?'

Vanneck smiled too. 'You would think so, but to hear them you'd imagine the cornets had become temperance Methodists.'

'Seems a hopeless case then.'

But Vanneck's sense of propriety took hold again. 'There must have been worse, Hervey. It's perhaps because there's scarce been anything to do these last few months but bear the heat and the rain.'

It was a decent response, and Hervey would not gainsay it, though in truth he could not think of another officer who had made so unpromising a beginning. 'How has Armstrong been, by the way?'

'It would be impossible to praise him excessively.'

'That's as I supposed. How is his family?'

'All well, I understand. Mrs Armstrong is schoolmistress again. There's an ayah for the three babies.'

Hervey faltered – just an instant – at being reminded there were now three. '*Big* babies, two of them '

'Yes They brought the eldest to stables the other evening.'

Hervey made an effort to collect himself. 'Now, we must speak of the state of the troop. I think I had better look at the order books of late, and then perhaps the acquittance rolls.'

But first he would need to see the muster, and Vanneck looked pained as he opened it at the first page, for it seemed there were as many names struck through with red as not.

Hervey stared at it forlornly. He had shaken the hand of every man on attesting. These had been *his* dragoons. The red pen strokes looked every bit as bloody as the sabre's, and not a fraction as glorious.

CHAPTER SEVEN

FAMILY MATTERS

Three days later

Hervey's little Marwari stood motionless, head down to her knees, the fever so great that her neck and flanks ran with sweat as if she had just galloped a mile.

'What do you think, David?'

The veterinary surgeon shook his head as he felt the mare's chest and belly. 'A most violent swelling – malignant, certainly. When did it first come to notice?'

Private Johnson answered. 'Last night, sir, when I came after watch-setting. She'd broken out a bit on 'er neck, an' she'd left 'er feed.'

'What exercise had she had?'

'An hour in the mornin', sir, in hand.'

Sledge stepped back to look at the mare again. 'By common practice I should draw at least two quarts of blood, but I hold with it less and less.' He shook his head. 'If the blood's poisoned it will have some beneficial effect, but otherwise we'll only weaken an already weak animal, and I think she's going to need her strength.'

'I'm content to follow your advice,' said Hervey, sounding

mystified. 'I've not seen a horse looking as she. What do you suppose it is?'

Sledge's brow furrowed more. 'The inflammation – quite possibly it is tumorous. Too early to say, though. It might be a case of the feltoric. I think we had better purge her.'

Hervey nodded, and turned to his groom. 'Johnson?'

'Ay, sir.'

'I can make up the purgative myself if you want,' said Sledge, putting his coat back on.

'We can do that well enough, can't we, Johnson?'

'Sir.'

Sledge turned to Hervey's groom. 'A full quart of hot gruel with four ounces of electuary of senna and double of castor oil. Put in a measure of Glauber's salts, too.'

'Right sir.'

'You shall have to watch her carefully, Johnson. I must know if there's any material change. And the swelled part must be rubbed twice daily with the blistering oils. Come to the dispense and I'll have my assistant give you a good measure.'

'Right sir.'

'And I'll make a fever ball. She may take it at evening stables.'

Johnson nodded again, writing carefully in his notebook.

'Give her only warm water, in small quantities, mind, and the same with mashes. Three or four times in the day. She might be tempted. But she will require every attention.'

'Of course, sir.'

'Good man.'

They left Johnson to begin his ministrations, and walked back along the troop lines. 'You don't think we need move her?' asked Hervey.

Sledge shook his head. 'I see nothing she might transmit. Best keep her be.'

Hervey said nothing.

They walked a few more steps. 'You'll have heard about the RM last night?'

'No.' The rising cadence suggested Hervey was now alerted, however.

'Blind drunk and put to bed by the picket.'

He was not surprised he hadn't heard. It might be a shade

embarrassing for the riding master this morning, but hardly of great moment. 'And?'

'He was ranting against Rose.'

'*Oh.*'

'Yes.'

Hervey thought for a moment. 'How did you come to hear of it?'

'I saw it. I was called out to the colic in B Troop. Broad could be heard the other side of the lines.'

'Then it is known about officially.'

'I don't know for sure, but I think not. I told the picket-corporal to say nothing.'

That was a bold thing to have done for an officer who held no powers of command, thought Hervey. And humane, too. 'Who was it?'

'Someone from A Troop. I forget his name. Did you speak of Broad and Rose with Joynson, by the way?'

When, three days ago, Sledge had told Hervey all he knew, they had talked about it long. And in the end they had decided that Hervey would speak confidentially with the commanding officer. But now he shook his head. 'I had thought to speak first with Rose, as soon as he comes back from his shooting. I think I'd better apprise Joynson now, though. It's not right that we don't warn him if it's come to this.'

'Rather a fine mess in the making, I'd say.'

'Well, it wouldn't be the first time.'

'Hervey, you seem remarkably phlegmatical.'

'You misjudge me if you think I approve. Rose has not acted like a gentleman. There's scarce more to say, is there?'

'Not acted like a gentleman? I doubt Rose would see it that way, since he'd not recognize Broad as one. Just like a bit of foolery with a housemaid, really.'

'Don't be too hard, David. It seems ten times worse here than if we were in Hounslow. And Mrs Broad's a deuced handsome woman.'

Sledge held his peace. Instead he stopped at one of the stalls to look over the new grey that Hervey had bought for his trumpeter. 'The talk in the wet canteen, by the way, is of money changing hands between Barrow and Nirmal Sen.'

Hervey sighed. *Two* of the troop-leaders on the primrose path, and for all to see. He felt sorry for the major. 'Ay, Johnson told me last night. How do these things get abroad? It could hardly have come from Nirmal Sen. He can't very well own to bribing a Company official.'

'So you suppose the talk is accurate?'

'I suppose no such thing. You must not let on, but the major spoke to me of it three days ago. I told him there was no more reason to presume Barrow capable of it than anyone else.'

Sledge stood up having run a hand down each of the grey's legs. 'Very noble. Do you suppose any would agree with you?'

Hervey looked surprised.

'If it were me or Ledley or the paymaster it would be the same,' said Sledge.

'Oh, come. That is a calumny on the regiment. It might have been Towcester's view but that's of the past.'

Sledge raised his eyebrows as if unconvinced. 'I think you chose well, this grey,' he said, nodding to the trumpeter's new pride. 'I think it safe to pay the balance.'

'Even to Nirmal Sen?'

'There's no question but that he's supplying good horses.'

Hervey smiled in a resigned way. 'Shall you come to evening stables?'

'Of course.'

'And shall you dine? I intend doing.'

'Then so shall I.'

Hervey drained his coffee cup and placed it on the major's desk. 'And that is the long and the short of it.'

Major Joynson had taken off his spectacles and begun to polish them. It had become so much his idiosyncrasy that Hervey found himself wondering at what point the polishing would begin, and the length of time and vigorousness of the polishing, for this tended to indicate the process of cogitation and the degree of difficulty presented by the solution. This morning the polishing had been slow and methodical, suggesting that the case of Rose and Broad was not to be treated with summary, and perhaps condign, justice. 'How much of it do you suppose is generally known?'

Hervey raised both eyebrows.

'Yes. You're right,' said Joynson wearily.

'And if it's not known about already then it can be but a matter of time. Broad is a sick man, his wife is unfaithful, and with a brother officer. These things can hardly conduce to tranquillity.'

Still Joynson polished. 'What would you do were you me?'

'What *could* I do? Would I have any option but to require Rose to leave?'

Major Joynson had not hoped for a reply in the interrogative. Nevertheless it gave him an opportunity to exhaust all hope of alternatives. 'Would he have to leave the regiment? Sell out, I mean. Or might he go elsewhere for a time? Somewhere else in India, even. The staff?'

Hervey paused to consider. 'If Broad had been other than riding master or another from the ranks, and had Rose intended marriage with Mrs Broad, then I suppose it might just have been arranged. But very evidently these are not the conditions.'

'And so Rose must sell out?'

Hervey was becoming exasperated at the major's unwillingness to draw the remaining conclusion. 'Neither you nor I make the rules, sir.'

The major sighed. 'If only we were ordered on campaign.'

'There is that, I grant you,' said Hervey. 'But very evidently that is not a condition on which we can count either.'

'I suppose, then, that first I must have Broad before me and ask what he wishes to be done. Or perhaps first I should see Rose?'

Hervey sighed to himself. 'Really, sir, I think it makes no difference whatever. You shall have to see both of them.'

'And Mrs Broad shall have to leave the cantonment at once.'

Hervey hesitated. 'I think she must. But do let us be kind.'

'Yes, yes,' said the major, suddenly increasing the speed of his polishing. 'Oh dear. Poor woman, poor woman. These things in my experience are never quite as the Commandments suggest.'

Hervey was not sure of the major's point, but he judged it of no matter. 'And as for the tattle about Barrow, I'm afraid I can add nothing but that David Sledge has told me it is the talk of the wet canteen. Indeed, I had heard so myself.'

Major Joynson stopped his polishing and replaced his spectacles.

'Very well. I shall summon Nirmal Sen. We had better lance this sore in the same way.'

Hervey got up and took his cap.

The major took off his glasses and unaccountably began polishing again. 'Oh, and Hervey, I am very gratified by your counsel. As you say, neither you nor I make the rules.'

'No, sir.'

'And in that connection I would urge you most earnestly to look to your own arrangements regarding . . . regarding your arrangements. There has been talk, I hear . . . in the drawing rooms.'

That night in the mess there were few officers, and Hervey, more tired than he had supposed after his first full day in uniform, had not been greatly inclined to join them. However, he had been absent from the table for so long that he thought it a positive duty to dine. He had arrived not many minutes before the khansamah announced dinner and found himself at once the senior.

It was the Sixth's custom for the most junior dining officer to sit on the senior's left, with any guest of the mess on the other hand. It was usually an agreeable position to find oneself in, for both senior and junior, but this evening Hervey found that it promised otherwise, for the junior was Cornet Green and the senior of the two guests was the bishop's chaplain, there at the invitation of Seton Canning with whom he had been at school.

'Reverend sir,' said Hervey as they stood by their chairs. 'Would you say grace?'

'Benedic Domine . . .' began the bishop's chaplain solemnly, and continued at some length.

'Per Jesum Christum Dominum Nostrum. Amen,' answered the table, as best they could, when at last he was finished. Strickland made the sign of the cross – evidence, indeed, of Sir Ivo's benevolent dominion. Poor Strickland had almost been forced onto half pay by Lord Towcester's malignance in matters of religion.

Hervey turned to his right as they sat, to begin what he feared must be an unedifying conversation. He had formed no very high opinion of the Bishop of Calcutta, and he supposed his chaplain to be of the same stamp. But from the other side of the table the senior lieutenant addressed him on behalf of the subalterns. 'We

119

were deliberating, sir, on the efficacy of the sabre's point as against the edge, and wondered what was your opinion in the matter.'

Hervey was taken aback somewhat. Indeed, he suspected a prank. It had never been the Sixth's custom to speak of matters of this sort, and Oliver Finucane had certainly shown no previous zeal. He glanced at the other subalterns, each of them showing quite extraordinary attention (except Vanneck, whose eyes were lowered), and wondered what transformation there might have been in the months of his absence. 'I am not rightly sure it is a proper subject to discuss in front of a guest such as Mr Stephenson,' he replied, with a note that implied he would somehow welcome clarification.

'Oh, do not desist for my part,' implored the chaplain. 'These are matters of very evident moment to gentlemen of your calling.'

Hervey would rather have received a less enthusiastic endorsement of the subject, which now commanded the attention of the whole table, and which the serving of soup did nothing to abate. 'It is not reducible to an absolute position. It depends on the nature of the engagement. And opinion would also vary depending whether we spoke of the old- or the new-pattern sabre.'

'But it is so, is it not,' continued Finucane, 'that but three or four inches of the point only is generally sufficient to despatch an adversary, whereas a cut will wound him only – albeit perhaps grievously.'

'True, but if you close with your adversary at speed – which is to what cavalry ought to aim – then it is not easy to draw back the blade after the thrust home. I have known of swords being struck from the hand, or breaking, with the hilt striking a man's breast after the blade had run through his body—'

Hervey did not see Cornet Green's face drain rapidly of its colour – only that he suddenly sprang up with hand clasped to mouth and rushed from the room.

There was much laughter.

Hervey now saw what was the game, and was in two minds about being used in the subalterns' rag. But he could not find it in him to show it. 'Something I said?' he asked, with an expression of forced solemnity.

Seton Canning shook his head in mock despair. Vanneck continued to look down, and the others stifled their sniggers as best they could.

The rest of dinner was a wearying affair, for the chaplain's conversation proved as uninteresting as it was wholesome. He seemed entirely in innocence of what had passed, so that there was little profit in Hervey's trying to explain it, and instead there followed a tedious dialogue on the state of the various missions to Hindoostan. Afterwards, when the port had circulated twice, Hervey led the party back to the ante-room, where a game of primero was got up. He himself stood aloof from it taking his brandy and soda – the married officer's 'nightcap', the sweetener of libatory breath.

Seton Canning came up. 'I fear you've had not so diverting an evening. Stephenson can be earnest, but he's a good man, and he can still thrash me at fives.'

Hervey smiled. 'He must have thought me very dull. I fear I had little by way of conversation. I confess my mind was otherwise engaged.'

'Agreeably, I hope.'

'As it happens, no.'

Harry Seton Canning had joined the Sixth just before Waterloo and had been cornet during the battle when Hervey found himself in command of a troop. Canning had, indeed, brought the troop out of the charge against the French lancers, to the acclaim of many an old hand. But until late he had been Hervey's subordinate, and the two had never become quite as close as officers might who had shared so much. Today, however, they were equals in rank just as they were equals in society. 'Disagreeably on account of Barrow, perhaps?'

Hervey looked surprised at the mention, though he knew it was unreasonable to be. 'As a matter of fact, yes. And other things.'

'What is your opinion?'

'I don't have one, for at present there are no facts as I discern.'

'But are you inclined to think it the smoke and the fire?'

Hervey frowned. 'Harry, I have said; I am not inclined to think anything without facts.'

'But what's to be done about Barrow? There can't be this talk for long. It's not good for any of us.'

'Joynson's to have it out with Nirmal Sen. I think there might have to be a board of officers.'

Seton Canning frowned. 'That would be tricky, in the circumstances.'

'What circumstances are these, exactly, Harry?'

'You know perfectly well. Barrow has never been popular. He's always kept himself to himself. And . . .'

'And what?'

'Well, with this other business . . . Rose, I mean.'

Hervey sighed. There was no doubting that the Rose business would divide opinion in the mess, and a divided mess was not a good place from which to assemble a board of officers. 'Then it would be better to have a board of officers from another regiment. An unhappy day that will be.' He put his empty glass on the khitmagar's tray, declining more. 'I beg you will excuse me, Harry. I want to see my mare before retiring. She's running a high fever. I had thought to see David Sledge at mess this evening, but . . .'

'Yes, of course,' said Seton Canning, taking another glass of port. 'I hope I shall not be long detained myself. Where do you suppose your new cornet is, by the way?' he added, with a wry smile.

David Sledge wore a long smock like a shepherd's, and he was looking grave. 'I'm sorry not to have dined, but Johnson sent word soon after evening stables. He feared she was about to have a seizure. I've been with her since. I thought it best not to trouble you until after mess. I'm afraid I see no alternative to opening up the tumour. She's deteriorated so quickly I wouldn't lay odds on her seeing the morning.'

Hervey simply nodded: there was evidently no alternative to the knife.

The trouble was that Sledge knew little more than Hervey in the matter. He had his manuals for reference, but he had seen nothing the like of these symptoms. 'I must warn you it's a desperate remedy. The blood's in so bad a state it renders it difficult to bring the wounds to a good digestion, and if this is not effected, there'll be a gangrene and mortification.'

Hervey understood. 'Where is Johnson, by the way?'

'I sent him for brandy. I find it has admirable cleansing properties, better than water for digesting dirt and blood. And it will preserve the flesh, too.'

Hervey smiled to himself. How alike seemed the methods of a good surgeon and a veterinarian.

Sledge opened his valise and laid out the tools of his trade on the manger – lancet, probe, scalpels, forceps, clamps, a cautery and two needles with gut already threaded. And a great quantity of lint, and a large bottle of green liquid.

Johnson returned soon afterwards with two flasks of arrack. Sledge took one of them, poured a good measure onto a handful of lint and began swabbing the mare's swollen breast. 'A bit more light, please, Johnson. And then this, if you will.' He handed him the cautery.

Johnson shifted the oil lamps closer, then set about lighting the cautery stove.

Sledge crouched looking at the swelling for some time, touching occasionally to feel for a vein. Then he picked up the lancet. 'Very well, let's try to expunge the malignance.'

He made five incisions in all, using the scalpel to elongate the lancet's work. After each one he expressed a quantity of fluid and blood, wiping the wound gently with arrack before studying it closely with his magnifying glass.

Throughout, the mare remained perfectly still. Her resignation warmed Hervey to her the more. He leaned forward as far as he could to see at close hand the veterinarian's art. 'What do you think, David?'

'I'm tempted to make more incisions. From each there's come a good deal of corruption. But there's a greater risk of mortification each time. No, I think I'll cauterize now, and sew up the two longer incisions. Johnson—'

Johnson handed him the cautery. 'I thought there'd be more blood, sir.'

'Yes, I think I did too. It seems that bad blood was likely not the cause of the inflammation. It was as well we didn't bleed her this morning.'

Johnson's admiration for Sledge these days was as great as it had been for his predecessor, Selden. Selden had elevated the Sixth's veterinary method from farriers' lore to science, and Sledge had confirmed the regiment in that practice.

'I wish she would take a little feed, though. Nothing at all, you say, Johnson?'

'Not a thing since yesterday, sir.'

'And the purgative?'

'Not 'ad a lot of effect, sir.'

'Mm.'

When he had done with cautery and needle, and had dressed the wounds with the green digestive ointment, Sledge turned to Hervey. 'Colic is the immediate concern. I worry about her gut twisting if she's eating nothing. A watch on her all night, and call me at once at any sign of distress.'

Hervey nodded. 'Thank you, David.'

'Ay, sir. Thank you,' added Johnson, moving the lamps back to safety.

Sledge nodded, wiped his instruments clean with lint and arrack, put them in his valise and bid them both goodnight.

'I'll bed down 'ere, then, sir,' said Johnson when he was gone.

'Thank you, yes. I have some matters to attend to first, and then I'll come in the early hours and relieve you.'

'I'd rather tha didn't, sir. I wouldn't want it said I couldn't stag for a night.'

Hervey smiled. 'Very well. I'll come before muster, though. And if you have to send for Mr Sledge then send for me too.'

'Right, sir. 'E's good, Mr Sledge.'

'He is,' said Hervey, gently pulling the mare's ear. 'And as good a man too when *not* wielding a knife.'

There was a light in the bungalow next to his when, an hour after midnight, Hervey walked the cantonment road. He paused for a moment, then turned down the path to the door. The chowkidar, squatting on his haunches at the foot of the verandah steps, stood and made the exaggerated salute which native servants thought correct in acknowledging the soldier-sahibs.

'Good evening, chowkidar. Is the sahib returned home?' said Hervey in confident Bengali.

The chowkidar nodded his head vigorously, gesturing with his night stick towards the door.

Hervey ascended the three steps to the verandah and pulled at the bell rope.

The bearer came quickly, saluting as high as the chowkidar, and admitted him at once. 'Captain Barrow-sahib, Captain

Hervey-sahib is come,' he called as he closed the mosquito door.

Barrow appeared in his shirtsleeves, glass in hand. 'What are you doing up and about at this time, Hervey? You're not captain of the week.'

Hervey smiled as best he could. 'I've been with Sledge. He had to cut up my mare.'

'Oh? What's her problem?' The voice of Birmingham was always that much more pronounced when Barrow had had a drink or two.

'The feltoric, he thinks.'

'Lord. Will you have a peg?'

'Yes; thank you – brandy.' Hervey hoped it would wash away the dispirits as effectively as it had the blood.

'Brandy-pani for Captain Hervey, Ranga.'

The bearer produced glass, decanter and bottle as Hervey settled himself into a chair, and began to pour.

'No, Ranga: chota brandy,' Hervey protested, although his instinct was to take a very large measure indeed.

'A good evening at mess, was it?'

'Yes, though we were few. Only Seton Canning of the captains.'

'I'm not long back from Calcutta – one of the Shitpoor road wallahs. Quite a tamasha, it was. Fine wine – hock and best burgundy. And women.'

Hervey nodded non-committally.

Barrow smiled. 'Or boys, for that matter, I suspect. You know these Bengalis.'

Hervey had been to tamashas at the merchants' houses, in the early days. They were lavish affairs, and the generosity of the hosts could indeed be great. Some of the merchants were undoubtedly men of culture and sensibility – and, he supposed, of honour – who merely enjoyed the company of the sahibs. But all the sahibs knew that the entertainment was in some expectation of pecuniary benefit. Barrow made no secret of his enjoying the hospitality, however much the 'proper' officers might disdain it. He was never entirely at home in the mess, and it was hardly surprising that he found his situation as guest of honour in a merchant's house so agreeable. In any case, it gave Hervey his pretext. 'Whose tamasha was it?'

'The man I bought my last lot of remounts from. And good they were too.'

125

'Nirmal Sen, is that?'

'You know 'im?'

Hervey thought it unworthy of their long acquaintance to dissemble. 'Barrow, I'm sorry to put this to you thus, but tomorrow Joynson will call Nirmal Sen to orderly room and question him about rumours of you and him dealing . . . improperly.'

Barrow looked stunned.

'I'm sorry. It seems the rumours are abroad so much that Joynson feels he has no alternative but to act . . . formally. I understand he will ask to speak with you first in case—'

'In case what?'

'In case, I imagine, that you wish first to say anything.'

Barrow drained his glass. 'And what might there be to say?'

Hervey saw a face he had never before seen. Barrow had looked death in the eye, and defiantly, many a time, yet now he had the look of a fearful man. The eyes spoke of losing all, not simply life. And for the first time Hervey imagined him guilty. What a wreckage he had wrought in but a few seconds. 'I don't know, Ezra. I truly don't.'

'Do you think me capable of a corrupt thing, Hervey? You know me better than most, and longer.'

What was the point in expounding on the doctrine of original sin at such a time? Loyalty demanded that Hervey support him now. 'To me it is inconceivable.'

Barrow stared at him, as if trying to judge his sincerity. 'And what do you suppose the others would answer – Rose and Seton Canning, and Strickland?'

'I cannot say.' He knew it to be false, at least in the one case. 'Why should they answer different from me?'

'You know why, Hervey. You know very well why.'

Barrow's bearer returned to refill their glasses. Hervey wanted no more, but it was not possible to refuse at such a moment.

Barrow drained his new glass at once and held it out again. 'Burra peg, Ranga. And leave the bottle and be off. And tomorrow morning, my best dress.'

'Acha, sahib.' He left, looking anxious.

'*He* knows summat's up,' said Barrow, scarcely waiting for him to leave the room. 'Probably did before you said a word. Before you came, even. Whole cantonment's probably jawing me dead:

"Ezra Barrow, on the *picaro*. What d'ye expect from one as is no better than us?" – or *them* if it's Rose an' 'is like!'

'There's no cause to think that way.'

'Isn't there! Isn't there indeed! Hervey, you think me a fool. I wasn't wanted when Lord George brought me in, but I never flinched from doing what was right on account of popularity.'

'That might go for many a man brought in. But there aren't that many that get field promotion. What does that speak for the regard in which those who mattered held you – *hold* you, indeed?'

'Hervey, you've no idea what it's like to be despised from above *and* below.'

For all their years in arms together, Hervey had no wish to debate with a man in his cups. If he had made a mistake in coming here in the first place, there was little to be gained by staying. And if he had not, then Barrow needed not brandy and commiseration but sleep and a clear head to hold up high in the morning. He stood up. 'Forgive me, Barrow. It's been a long day.'

'Ay, that it has. Home then to your bibi, Captain Hervey. The colonel wouldn't like it, you being a proper officer and all, but it's nothing like the sin of being a ranker.'

Hervey picked up his forage cap. 'Good night, Barrow. I'll come tomorrow morning.'

An hour later, as Hervey lay beside his bibi in the moments before sleep, there was a shot. He knew its cause at once. And the stab in his gut was as if the ball had struck him too.

CHAPTER EIGHT

HALLOWED GROUND

Three days later

The coroner was disobliging. Although Joynson and Hervey had gone to considerable trouble to sow doubt in the minds of the jury, that upright officer of the court had summed up in such a manner as to make that doubt seem unreasonable. Under oath, Hervey had been unable to give any indication that Barrow had wanted to clean his pistols at that time of night, and so the suggestion that he might have could be but speculation. And why, indeed, just the one pistol? It was the greatest pity that the inquest was not held under military jurisdiction. Accident or misadventure was not the probable cause, the jury decided, but death by the officer's own hand.

The verdict presented Joynson with several problems, the most pressing of which was Barrow's funeral and interment. The chaplain, who had turned a blind eye to the rubrics when Private Sisken had hanged himself aboard ship during the regiment's passage east, found himself in some difficulty on this occasion, for the circumstances were known to the entire city, and episcopal supervision was very much closer at hand. However, when it had

128

become known in the canteens that Barrow could not be buried in the consecrated ground that was the regiment's corner of the cantonment cemetery, a deputation had come to the RSM – NCOs and sweats mainly, but not exclusively, from Barrow's troop – to request in no uncertain terms that the captain be laid to rest 'alongside the other poor souls who've succumbed to this place'. Accordingly, and on the recommendation of the RSM, Joynson had summoned the chaplain, adding materially to his troubles by insisting it be done.

The chaplain was tolerated, respected even, to an unusual degree in the Sixth. It was well remembered that he had stood up to Lord Towcester in the matter of Private Hopwood's flogging, so far as he had been able, which was in truth not very far. And there had been Private Sisken's committal at sea, when all who heard his address had been much moved. Indeed, there had been many occasions since when the chaplain's funerary eloquence had been displayed – altogether too many occasions for so small a regiment. But in Barrow's case, the chaplain's solution was, the officers all agreed, worthy of a Jesuit. An hour before the funeral he conducted a ceremony of deconsecration, limited to the ground that had been prepared to receive the coffin, and had then read over Barrow's mortal remains, in the usual way, 'in the sure and certain hope' and all the other ringing phrases that somehow gave succour to usually godless men who stood in ranks fearful that the next time might be theirs.

There was no carouse afterwards, though. The canteen was a dull place that evening, and few officers were at mess. Hervey himself did not dine, an omission that made him feel uncomfortable, for he had berated poor Green for not having the pluck to return to the mess the night he had parted with the contents of his stomach. No one had so much as suggested it was unfortunate that he had called on Barrow that evening, for there was a supposition that the outcome was preordained. And, indeed, Barrow's act had spared the major and those about him the shame of an investigation. Above all, it had spared the regiment the dread board of officers from outside. Barrow's guilt was presumed by the very fact of his noble action, yet Hervey felt his own hand in the business, and he did not rest easy.

Joynson had asked him to be president of the board of

adjustment, which would make an inventory of Barrow's possessions so that those of a personal nature might be sent to his next of kin – when that detail was discovered – and all else sold at regimental auction, as was customary. This Hervey had now done, by himself, and at the expense of dinner in the mess, for it had occupied the entire evening after stables. But that was no matter: it afforded him an alibi.

It had been a thoroughly melancholy job. So much more than he had imagined. Whatever his pleasures on the Chitpore road, Barrow's habits had been sober and moderate, his practice soldierly and prudent. His possessions were few and utilitarian; nothing out of the ordinary, and if he had gained pecuniary advantage in his dealings with Nirmal Sen there was no evidence of its enjoyment here. Barrow's papers were no more elaborate than his other possessions, but there was one letter that indicated to where Joynson might write his condolences – and, indeed, the trouble he would have composing them. The superscription, in a spidery hand, read 'The Almshouses, Yardley', and the signature 'Your ever proud father'.

When he had finished, close to midnight, Hervey bade the bearer secure the bungalow, and left trusting him to the job. What opportunity of thieving could there be, indeed, if he had a list of everything? Anyway, Ranga looked sad, and it could not have been for his own situation, for he had already been offered another. It pleased Hervey to think there was other than a father who had some attachment to Barrow, for although he himself had slowly come to respect the man's capability as a soldier, he had never been able to count him a boon companion.

He walked slowly to his own bungalow. It was a cold night for all that it was not long since the monsoon. The stars were as bright as in the Peninsula – those long, bitter-chill nights when he had learned so much about the heavens. And the air was sweet, perhaps with incense or spices; he could not tell. A barn owl hooted. It seemed strange to think that Ezra Barrow was no longer on this earth when all else remained the same. But things had changed. Tonight would be the last time he enjoyed the companionship of his bibi here. Tomorrow he would set her up in a little haveli outside the cantonments, like so many others. And it really would not be the same.

Next day, the Sixth busied themselves more than usual. Things had to be brought back to good order, and quickly, and nothing helped so much as activity, especially when it was compelled by an RSM of Mr Lincoln's mettle. There were inspections all morning and drill all afternoon. And at colonel's rounds of evening stables, the major, though it was never his bent, made a very passable attempt at what the regiment knew as *jaldi*. At any rate, he managed to roust about the more timid.

At midday, the adjutant had conducted the auction of Barrow's effects. Usually, when a widow was known to the officers, or else the family, it was an occasion for generous over-bidding to provide a gratuity that a grateful government could not find itself able to disburse. In Barrow's case there had always been mixed feelings, although in the end there was a grim admiration for his ultimate gesture of honour. The major, it was agreed, excelled himself, opening the auction by telling the assembled bidders to where the money would be sent, declaring that 'a man is more than his worst error' and that Captain Ezra Barrow had served his king for over thirty years and the Sixth for more than fifteen. At the end of the proceedings, the adjutant announced that the sum of £857 would be sent to Mr Joshua Barrow of the Almshouses, Yardley, near Birmingham. It was a handsome figure, and, in the curious way of these things, it did something to restore the pride of those assembled, for in the last resort they had not let down their erstwhile comrade; and loyalty was nothing if it was easy. Barrow had certainly paid a heavy price himself: a pennyworth of powder had blown away three thousand pounds, at the very least, for on death the value of his commission reverted to the Crown.

That evening Hervey dined with the Somerviles. He was especially glad to do so, for as well as having the ugly circumstances of the past days to put behind him, he had not seen his friends in more than a week. He arrived a little late, however, having gone by way of the horse lines to reassure himself of the progress of his mare. Within a day of the veterinarian's surgery, the little Marwari had begun to eat – at first warm mashes, and now hard feed. The wounds had remained clean, the inflammation was gone, and so was the fever. In so short a time, Hervey thought it a veritable miracle, and he was extolling David Sledge's skill for a full quarter of an hour after arriving at No. 3, Fort William.

'And what so particularly commends him,' he concluded, now well into his second glass of champagne, 'is his devotion to his own greater understanding. His rooms are piled with treatises and papers.'

Somervile was happy to indulge him, and for practical reasons. At the onset of the unhealthy season, confidence in any practitioner, even veterinary, was reassuring. 'Calcutta is as full of quacks as anywhere – fuller, probably. I shall ask him to dine with us,' he said. 'Would it be entirely proper to ask him to look at my stable?'

'I don't see why not. He's not greatly engaged at present, I'm pleased to say.'

Somervile nodded, indicating that the matter was decided.

A khitmagar made to top up Hervey's glass, but he declined. 'Is Emma to join us?'

'Yes, very shortly. I'm sorry to say she has been sick these last few days.'

Hervey supposed that few husbands in Calcutta could be as direct as Somervile. 'I hope nothing—'

'No, no. I shouldn't think so. Calcutta's just a deuced sight unhealthier place than Madras, but Emma has a native constitution. I shouldn't distress yourself.'

He would try not to, difficult though that was with notice of even the slightest illness.

Somervile seemed keen to change the subject. 'I have some intelligence that will interest you.'

'I dare not hope it is of Peto?' replied Hervey, sounding a shade despondent. 'His last letter was a disheartening affair. Said he might as well be commanding a guardship.'

'I regret not. Not even of the war, indeed, for that generally proceeds ill, although there are to be reinforcements – and in good measure – for Rangoon. Campbell ought soon to take the offensive.'

Hervey snorted. 'That was, of course, his purpose in going to Rangoon in the first place!'

Somervile merely raised his eyebrows. 'Well, I am glad to say that my intelligence has at least provided Campbell with the means to do his job. No, the news I was referring to is that Combermere is to replace Paget.'

Hervey sat up. A new commander-in-chief would at any time be ripe news, but now, and the name Combermere – it was the ripest. 'Is this the Governor-General's doing? It would be ill indeed if Paget is to take the blame for things in Ava!'

'Oh no, there's no suggestion of Paget's being relieved. His tenure in command is routinely ended. Indeed, the change – if our intelligence is correct – will not be until next year. But Combermere is a friend of yours, is he not?'

Hervey smiled. 'I could hardly claim that. We have met on occasions, and he has a good memory.'

Somervile smiled broader. 'Then you shall have to meet on more occasions, and place yourself at the *forefront* of his memory!'

Hervey smiled again. But that, indeed, was how it was done. He'd seen it time and again. Perhaps if he had not been so keen to leave the Duke of Wellington's staff he would by now be well placed for advancement instead of, in truth, having marked time a full ten years. And – he hardly dared admit it – with things as they were in the Sixth, what future was there at regimental duty? In Calcutta nothing happened other than death by Nature's hand (or one's own, for every regiment had its Barrow). 'We must see.'

Emma Somervile came in. She looked well enough, thought Hervey, but the rouge did not entirely mask her pallor. She sat next to her husband on a high-backed settee and placed her hand on his. 'And how are you, in the circumstances, Matthew?'

Hervey returned her smile. 'In the circumstances, well, I believe. I am troubled to learn you are not in the best of sorts, however.'

Emma frowned. 'Oh, these things . . . but tell me, what else have you been speaking of?'

'I was telling him the news of Lord Combermere's being appointed to commander-in-chief, my dear.'

Emma brightened again. 'Yes, *good* news for you, Matthew, is it not? Tell me of him.'

'He was at the best of schools.' Hervey smiled just a little wryly.

She at once understood, and turned to her husband with mock solemnity.

'A very long time in advance of me, my dear. And I do not recall his name in academic honours.'

'He was a great man for campaigning,' added Hervey. 'Since the Peninsula, though, he has not been at field duty. There again, neither, indeed, has anyone other than here in India. I confess I don't know how things are in Ireland. He's commander-in-chief there.'

'So I understand too,' said Somervile. 'Well, he is going to need a very fine head upon those fine military shoulders of his to ravel up the mess in Ava. And believe me, there's trouble brewing in Hindoostan too. Every week that we flounder in Rangoon – and Arakan for that matter, since it seems little better there – the malcontents among the country powers grow more impudent. But Amherst won't see it.' He glanced at Emma and shook his head a shade wearily. 'Oh yes, be in no doubt: if Combermere takes the reins here he'll be pitched into the middle of trouble – east *and* west.'

'Shall we go and dine?' said Emma, looking a little anxious, and making to stand. 'Ghulam says we may.'

Somervile was on his feet at once with a hand to Emma's elbow, but she rose unaided.

'I really am in fine health, Eyre,' she insisted, using her fan just a touch. 'I should have returned a little earlier from the assembly, that is all.'

The dining room minded Hervey of home, for whereas the mess and his bungalow were handsome enough, they were wood-built, and the houses at Fort William were stone. And there was a solidity about the place that spoke more of the permanence of the Honourable Company than could the military lines, whose occupants were after all mere birds of passage. The furniture and fittings were mahogany, teak and brass rather than the quartermaster's pine, cane and pewter. And the family portraits, here and not at some English seat, said that the Somerviles were India people – native almost, as Eyre Somervile himself had once said. Emma had been to England, as she always called it, not 'home', but once in the dozen and more years since she had first joined her brother in Madras. Her husband had not been even once.

'How is your groom?' she asked, as a khitmagar began to serve them soup. 'And that corporal of yours – the one who brought you to the ship?'

134

'Wainwright, you mean.' Hervey's face at once registered intense pride. 'Without whom I should not be enjoying your hospitality now. I'm pleased to say he has been advanced to the head of the seniority roll. He may be corporal, full, before the year's out.'

'Bound to be, at this time of year,' said Somervile without looking up from his soup.

Hervey smiled disconcertedly. 'There are other ways, Somervile.'

Somervile continued to give all his ocular attention to his soup. 'Men putting bullets in their brains, you mean?'

'Eyre!'

Somervile at last looked up. Emma's scold was not to be ignored.

'What I meant,' said Hervey, not in the least perturbed, 'is that serjeants leave or are promoted, making vacancies below. Nothing more.'

'I'm glad to hear it,' said Somervile, as if it were well known to be otherwise. 'And when do you suppose it will be the same for officers?'

'In essentials it is,' replied Hervey, sounding cautious.

'Humph! You and I know it's a case of money and little more. How much would a majority cost you?'

Hervey looked rueful. 'Another thousand at least. If we were posted home probably twice as much.'

Somervile smiled. 'Then your toasts should be to a short war but a bloody one.'

'Eyre, I really think this a most unedifying line,' Emma protested.

But Hervey was now smiling. 'No, Emma: that was the toast in the Peninsula. Grim, perhaps, but that is the soldier's way with his humour.' He turned back to Somervile. 'We shouldn't forget the brevet. They're a good deal easier to come by here than in England. There were a fair number in Rangoon, as I recall.'

'What is a brevet?' asked Emma.

'Promotion in the army as a whole, but not in the regiment as such. It's all very well if you want a life on the staff.'

The khitmagars began clearing away the soup, breaking the line of conversation for the moment.

'But how are things otherwise, Matthew?' asked Emma, as the khansamah poured a little claret for her husband to taste. 'We have so missed our visits to the regiment. The officers are well?'

Somervile nodded; a good vintage, predating even Bonaparte.

Hervey inclined his head, as if to say the reply would not be straightforward. 'For the most part I suppose things are pretty good.'

'Oh? No more than "pretty good"? That sounds ill to me.' Emma knew him better than he sometimes remembered.

Hervey braced himself. 'To tell the truth, I fear we shall have another to-do. Hugh Rose . . .'

'Yes?'

'Rose has been dallying with the riding master's wife, and I fear Joynson must have him quit the place.'

Emma raised her eyebrows. 'That is sad, for all. His company is always much sought after.'

'If I were Joynson I'd be looking for some way to keep him,' her husband declared. 'Rose is a good officer from what I see.'

'Indeed he is,' said Hervey, helping himself to a fair portion of beef from the khitmagar's salver. 'And I'll warrant he'd be the hero of any battle. But you know very well what is the principle that Joynson has to abide by.'

Somervile had drained his glass even before the beef came to him, and he now heaped double rations onto his plate. 'Ay, I know well enough. But I'm also of a mind that Joynson's going to need good men about him, and sooner than he supposes.'

Next morning, after exercise, Hervey was called to regimental headquarters. There he found the major in even lower spirits than before. The Barrow affair had been one thing, but Rose and the riding master – and, for that matter the succession of RSMs – was quite another. Whereas with Barrow the course of action was clear (and he trusted he had dealt deftly with it), his other trials required much thought before action. And much thought in these matters lowered the spirits.

'But you declared that Rose would have to leave when last we spoke,' said Hervey, shaking his head. He had no special wish to see Rose go; he shared Somervile's pragmatic view that if the war clouds had actually been gathering something could be done. But manifestly this was not the case.

'Circumstances have changed, Hervey. I'm not sure that I wish to have the captains' ranks so thinned. It will be deuced unsettling.' Joynson took off his spectacles and pulled the silk square from his sleeve.

'Yes, I can see that. But—'

'Rose has asked for leave, and I'm inclined to grant it. Broad must go somewhere a bit healthier for a month or so, too.'

Hervey wondered what was the imperative for Joynson's change of mind, though the major was ever a cautious man. 'In my view, sir, it will merely put off the moment for action – might make it more difficult, indeed. But that is a judgement, and I of course respect yours.'

'That's gratifying at least,' replied Joynson, polishing and frowning. 'And I've settled on Deedes for RSM, though I expect I'll live to regret it.'

Hervey sighed.

'You would have jumped both and taken Hairsine.'

'Yes. That way, at least, you'd be assured of a good RSM. The other consequences you would just have to deal with.'

'Don't imagine I didn't think hard on that solution, but with things as they are I am certain it is better to have as few causes for immediate discord as possible. Incidentally, I have asked Sledge to conduct an enquiry into the Barrow business. I don't regard the matter closed with the universal supposition of his guilt.'

Hervey was surprised. He smiled and nodded.

'I'm glad you're pleased, for I've unwelcome news for you. Assheton-Smith shall have B Troop. I should very much like Vanneck to replace him.'

Hervey's face fell. 'Not Vanneck, not now. Not with that idiot boy as my cornet!'

'I have first to think of the regiment, and Vanneck would make the better adjutant than any other.'

Hervey cast about for the obvious alternative, but soon realized that Joynson's assertion was unchallengeable. 'Shall there be a replacement for Vanneck? I really can't—'

'Assheton-Smith's lieutenancy will be for the buying. I imagine Perry will have it.'

Hervey sighed again. Perry had the makings, for sure, but he'd seen nothing more than a couple of seasons' drill.

'I haven't finished, Hervey. Though this should not be

unwelcome news. I want you to take your troop to Dehli for a month or so.'

Hervey was indeed brightened. 'Dehli? Why?'

'This morning I received word from the brigadier that a troop was to be sent within the week as escort to the resident. I have no other details of the assignment as yet.'

'It is by *no* means unwelcome news – not at all. Though it would be a deal more welcome if I had Vanneck with me and not Green. But are you sure you would not want me to be here . . . in the circumstances?'

'I should prefer that Skinner's Horse did the Dehli duty, but the Governor-General was apparently quite explicit on the matter – *King*'s troops. On the whole I think it right that it should be you. It would seem strange otherwise. You are next senior to Strickland, and his leave is more overdue than anyone's.'

It was true. Not even Strickland could be expected to give up home leave for a month in Dehli. 'Then I suppose I had better make ready at once. Am I at liberty to speak to the engineer?'

'I see no reason why not.'

'Is that all, sir?'

'Yes, Hervey. That is all. Unless . . .'

'Unless what?'

'Would you dine with us this evening?'

'Of course, Joynson. I should be delighted.'

There was even more satisfaction in the major's smile, however (and, had Hervey known it, relief). 'Shall we say seven?'

Hervey nodded, replaced his cap, and took his leave.

There were any number of things he would rather do, especially with only a few nights remaining in Calcutta, for he knew perfectly well why he was bidden to the major's table. But how he might be expected to exert any benign influence in Frances Joynson's direction he could not think. Regimental duty was a queer thing at times.

Only later did Hervey realize that in going at once to Dehli he would miss the RSM's wedding, and it displeased him. It was not just that it was already being spoken of as the best tamasha in Bengal, undoubtedly to be the most notable event in the living memory of the serjeants' mess, rather it was an instinct that he

138

should just be there. He decided at once that he would leave Armstrong behind until after the nuptials, for to do otherwise would have been a deprivation to both his serjeant-major and the RSM – and, indeed, to Caithlin Armstrong, for Lincoln had become a regular guest at their table since their return to the regiment. Armstrong greeted the news exactly like a serjeant-major who knew where his duty lay. 'An' it'll do Collins the power of good to wear a fourth stripe for a while,' he added for good measure.

Myles Vanneck was not so pleased. He had no desire to leave the nominal administrative duties of troop-lieutenant for the weighty ones of adjutant, and he certainly had no need of the modest increase in pay. The adjutant of a cavalry regiment, by long custom, came from the ranks. Often he came from another regiment, as Burrow had done. Assheton-Smith had been the first gentleman-adjutant, as his fellows had soon dubbed him in mock reference to the hyphen in his name (the first not counting Dauntsey, that is, which none of the officers did). The trouble was, he had done so fine a job that it was natural for Joynson to wish to replace him with another of his like. And indeed, Joynson also held the novel notion that an officer might be the better troop-captain – and ultimately even colonel – for having seen the workings of the orderly room. Come what may, all Vanneck's protests were to no avail. By the end of the morning he had handed the various ledgers to Cornet Arthur Perry and taken his seat in regimental headquarters.

Meanwhile, Hervey had been at the garrison engineer's searching for the requisite maps and dak instructions. As the crow flew, Dehli lay in excess of seven hundred miles, and by the dak route nearly eight. With the marching norm for cavalry being twelve leagues a day, it would be a journey of three weeks, and an occasion for sport and other pleasant diversions which could scarcely have come at a better time. He was half disappointed, therefore, when that evening at dinner Joynson declared it his opinion that he should stay for the wedding. 'Give Perry his head a bit,' said the major, with unusual zest. 'They get precious little chance otherwise. You and Armstrong'll be able to catch 'em up in a few days. You should *both* be there.'

*

Joynson's dispensation gave Hervey much cause for pleasure, but it was only next day that he began to learn of the import of his mission. He rode over to the Someriles in the middle of the afternoon for just that purpose, feeling sure that he would learn more useful intelligence there than the commander-in-chief's office was likely to divulge.

Emma was not at home, but her husband was, and deeply engrossed in his book room having come immediately from the council's luncheon table (only the writers and junior officials returned to their offices of an afternoon). He looked up absently as the khansamah announced his visitor. 'Oh, Hervey: you are come very early today. Is there another to-do?'

'Not at all. I'm for Dehli with my troop for a month or so.'

Somervile was transformed in an instant, at once all attention. 'Indeed! I had notice yesterday that Ochterlony had asked for an escort, but I hadn't supposed a decision would be reached so quickly. Indeed I'm surprised: Ochterlony doesn't enjoy the confidence he used to have. Sit you down. Tea, sherbet? Ghulam!'

'Tea, thank you. And some limewater if you have it.'

'*Ji, sahib?*'

'*Bhat, nimbu pani, Ghulam.*'

'*Ji, sahib.*'

'That is the reason I came here, to discover what I could about the assignment. Joynson knows nothing yet.'

'Sit down, sit down,' Somervile insisted, even more attentive. 'There's trouble brewing in that direction.'

Hervey's ears pricked up. He had not supposed the escort wholly ceremonial, but . . .

'Ochterlony's an old man – "Loony Ochter" they're calling him, and not entirely in affection. You must have heard?'

'No, I have not. I know of him of course – everybody does.' There could be no one who needed reminding of his reputation – Major-General Sir David Ochterlony, victor of the Ghoorka war a decade ago.

'Ay, well, he's an old man, as I said. I think Amherst believes him a fool. But I'll say this too: he's one of the few men with any true understanding of the country. He knows when to fight and when to parley. And how to fight, for that matter – but that's not my principal concern.'

Ghulam returned with a khitmagar bearing limewater. Another followed with tea a few minutes later. Somervile waited for them to leave before resuming, and in a voice deliberately lowered.

'I'd wager any amount that what lies behind this is Bhurtpore. There's an unholy tussle for yonder throne coming. The old rajah's not long for this world by all accounts.'

Hervey looked unenlightened. 'And this is the Company's business?'

'It may well become so. You have to be especially careful with sleeping dogs in India. And Ochterlony's backed the rightful heir, the son – invested him with a *khelat*, or some such. Doubtless the old fox wants to parade the escort as a promise of troops from Calcutta if things go against the claim. And you know why Bhurtpore would have the dovecots aflutter here, don't you?'

'We are speaking of the same Bhurtpore, the fortress that Lord Lake failed to take?'

Somervile smiled, but pained. 'The same. Our only defeat in two centuries. When first I came out from England there was still the taunt, "Go take Bhurtpore!" And the truth may well be that we could no more do so now than we could then.'

CHAPTER NINE

A GREAT TAMASHA

Two weeks later

Mr Lincoln further added to regimental lore when the major asked if he would like to be wed as a quartermaster rather than as serjeant-major. He had replied, with absolute decorum went the story, that he would prefer to take the biggest fence first.

The wedding day had been postponed a fortnight on account of Barrow's death. A fortnight's mourning in India was a long time by all but the most fastidious standards, for death was so common-place and sudden that it was neither especially appropriate nor practical to observe the passing of one man, or woman, many days after the committal of their mortal remains. The bereaved or the orphaned went home to England, or else the former began life anew, and as often as not remarried in a short time with someone in their own circumstances. Alternatively a widow might accept a proposal from one of the many all-too-eager bachelor-writers, while a widower might make one to 'a new-arrived angel' from England – a member of what later wags would know as 'the fishing fleet'.

The arrangements for the RSM's wedding were overseen by Mr

Lincoln himself. There were to be upwards of four hundred guests —- all the officers and non-commissioned officers of the regiment, together with a good number of the latter from the other regiments of the garrison, and a surprising number of civilians. *And* the commander-in-chief, for such was Lincoln's reputation in Calcutta.

The marriage service would take place in the garrison church, which, with its double galleries, had just enough space for all of the guests and the regimental band. Its decoration was the only arrangement that Lincoln left entirely in others' hands, for the future Mrs Lincoln was a staunch member of the congregation. On the day itself, she and other members of her Dorcas circle came early, before watering parade, with great boughs of greenery and bunches of vivid orchids in the regiment's colours.

Meanwhile, the regimental quartermaster-serjeant and his working parties were labouring in the garrison gymnasium to work a similar, if secular, transformation – to prepare for what the future Mrs Lincoln delicately referred to as the wedding breakfast, but which all in the Sixth called the tamasha. The RSM came at midday to inspect the work, said not a word as he walked the 'assembly room', as it had become, then astonished the quartermaster-serjeant by saying simply, 'Thank you, Harold' – the first time he had ever addressed him by his Christian name (indeed, the quartermaster-serjeant was astonished to discover that Lincoln even knew it).

At four o'clock, the worst of the heat being past, the first arrivals at the church heard the band strike up its programme of music. The RSM confessed to having an untutored ear, but he had nevertheless scrutinized the programme, striking out the overture to *The Marriage of Figaro* (being uncertain of its propriety) and 'Blow, blow, thou winter wind' (being certain of its ambiguity), and approving more Haydn and Piccini instead.

At twenty past the hour exactly, Mr Lincoln marched up the aisle, eyes front, spurs ringing, as if on parade. He wore review order, shako under his right arm, sword scabbard grasped in his left, leather and metal shining as no one had quite seen either element shine before. Beside him (in truth, half a pace to the rear, for the man could not bring himself to draw level even on such an occasion), was his supporter, Deedes, the senior troop serjeant-major and next RSM. On his left, the same half-pace behind, was his long-serving orderly, who now took from him his shako and gloves and handed him the service sheet. Lincoln made a sharp bow of the head to Sir Edward Paget, the commander-in-chief, and to Joynson sitting in the row behind, and took his place at the end of the front pew. The band then struck up 'Treue Husar'. Herr Hamper had not included it in his submission, for Lincoln would never have approved, but it was a favourite of the Sixth's, and the best part of the congregation believed it exactly apt. The murmur of approval at the end caused the bandmaster to repeat it.

At two minutes to half-past the hour, Herr Hamper and the band embarked on the final 'overture' – *Alceste*, which seemed to compose the congregation perfectly, as indeed the RSM had intended when he chose the piece 'for its dignity and bearing'. The bandmaster particularly approved of the choice because it could be repeated without an obvious break in case of the customary delay in the arrival of the bride.

The future Mrs Lincoln was, however, a soldier's daughter and a soldier's widow, and she had no intention of being, as she put it, 'late on parade'. At exactly the half-hour, Herr Hamper was startled by the signal to curtail the Handel and launch at once into 'Sweet lass of Richmond Hill', to which the bride would process to the chancel. It had been an express choice, for the future Mrs Lincoln hailed from Putney, where her father had been a waterman before enlisting in the artillery train, but Putney was close enough to Richmond to make the choice of music fitting. And in any case, though few knew it, her mother had kept the cows in Richmond Park – together, indeed, with Beau Brummell's mother, as she was proud to relate. She walked up the aisle on the arm of the light infantry's commanding officer, in a blue dress trimmed with yellow and white, which at once won the approval of all in the bridegroom's camp.

'Dearly belovèd,' began the chaplain, managing somehow to overcome the inappropriateness of the salutation, and commanding a respectful silence. 'We are gathered together in the sight of Almighty God . . .'

And so the old, familiar words began to come, like a warm breeze bringing the scent of happy memories. Hervey let them drift over him, savouring a phrase here and there, and with no regrets.

When it came to the homily, seeing the commander-in-chief

sitting attentively not more than a few feet before him, the chaplain's nerve almost failed him. But in glancing at the RSM he was suddenly more afraid of his opinion than the general's, and he managed somehow to fill his lungs with sufficient air. In truth, he need have had no worry, for he had composed what all would agree was a very proper address, by no means too long, at once respectful yet sound in its teaching, combining as it did appropriate adulation for the RSM and all his works, the recognition that in Mrs Lincoln the regiment had gained, in his words (or rather those borrowed from Scripture), 'a pearl of rare price', and last but by no means least God's rightful due in this blessed state of affairs. None of the parties, on earth or in heaven, could have been in the least disappointed.

There followed more singing – Toplady served the mood of temporary exile extraordinarily well – and the signing of the register, on only the second page.

And then, as it were, came the command *stand at ease* (if not quite *stand easy*) as Mr and Mrs Lincoln began their march down the aisle to the band's lusty rendition of 'Young May moon', the regimental quick march. Here and there a brave serjeant clapped a hand on Lincoln's shoulder, wishing him well and 'God bless, sir!'

The troop serjeant-majors had already slipped out of the church to form the guard of honour, sabres in salute at the carry, smiles broad and eyes twinkling. Mr Lincoln took it all in – not least the shine on the leather and the buttons, judging with special satisfaction that Armstrong was better turned out even than Hairsine. Lincoln had never shown a moment's emotion in living memory, and he was not about to do so now, but he could never have imagined such a day, his last as RSM, and he would miss not a detail of it.

Bride and groom left for the gymnasium in a calèche which one of the nabobs had put at their disposal, a gesture that said as much for the RSM's personal standing in Calcutta as the regiment's, and which those from outside the Sixth could not fail to note. The carriage was bedecked with ribbons – blue, yellow and white – with two dragoons posted behind, and driven by the rough-rider serjeant high on the box. It was a turnout fit for Lord Amherst himself, yet none was inclined to think it in the merest degree inflated for Mr Lincoln.

Especially not the private men, who, unknown to the RSM, had lined the road from church to gymnasium in their watering order, having come straight from stables. The cheering could be heard all about the garrison. It broke the rules, of course. Cheering superiors was not approved of. The Duke of Wellington himself had forbidden it – 'for if once you permit them to cheer they may do the opposite when circumstances are not so favourable'. But it was the RSM's last day, and no regulation could adequately apply to that.

In the gymnasium, where the sutler's little army of khitmagars were turned out in their best white, Mr and Mrs Lincoln took post to welcome their guests. On the platform at the other end of the hall, which served usually as a boxing booth, bandsmen were taking their places. The band-serjeant would direct them this time, and the music would be altogether merrier, with the regimental glee club joining them later with glees written for the occasion. The huge punkahs hanging the length of the gymnasium's high ceiling, and strung specially, now began to swing, the punkah-wallahs in the gallery heaving for all they were worth, like ringers first pulling up the bells of a Sunday morning.

The sight which would command greatest admiration, however, was that evidence of the sutler's craft (and the RSM's generosity) which lay on trestles the entire length of one wall. Here was a collation worthy of St James's – sides of beef, mutton, fowls of all kind, fish lying on ice, lentils, rice, pickles and sauces. And on tables down the middle of the hall was the means to quench the thirst of the four hundred: six whole hogsheads of Allsop's pale ale, decanters of Madeira for the officers and their ladies and any others who preferred it, and for those whose taste was neither for beer nor strong wine, punchbowls of *lol shrob*.

When the speeches came they were brisk and brief, the RSM's especially. Mr Lincoln was ever a man of few words. From the band platform he made his thanks to all, paying handsome respects to his wife and her maids, and called for three cheers for the regiment. Serjeant-Major Deedes spoke next. It was considered the form to make some jesting remarks about the bridegroom, revealing past indiscretions perhaps, or some embarrassing aspect of his life off parade. Both Deedes's research and nerve had failed him, however, and he contented himself – and, he hoped, all who heard – with a harmless story of how once, in the middle of a battle in Spain, Lincoln had ridden up to a British and a French officer locked in furious combat and ordered them to stop at once: 'for it is very unseemly, gentlemen!'

There was great laughter and cheering all about the hall, but in truth, any words delivered with a smile would have served this day.

'Ay, it's a fact I did,' declared Lincoln, permitting himself to be a heckler just for once. 'But I made the French officer give up his sword to me there and then!'

There was even greater cheering.

And then Deedes braced himself for the final jest. 'Mrs Lincoln, ma'am. I'm sure I am permitted to say that you are most welcome in the regiment. And doubly so, for tonight you retire with a serjeant major and tomorrow you awake with an officer beside you instead!'

There was now rumbustious, earthy cheering.

'That will touch a raw nerve or two,' said David Sledge to Hervey as they stood together by one of the hogsheads.

'The Broad-minded, you mean?'

Sledge grimaced in mock disapproval. 'I reckon Rose has had a very close shave. A funeral and a wedding to distract attention – I call it very lucky indeed.'

'Well, I for one would not welcome being Paget's quill-driver.'

'Maybe not, Hervey. But then you would not have bedded another man's wife in the first place.'

Hervey blanched. 'David, you take it a little too personally. And there's something in Scripture, is there not, about casting the first stone?'

Sledge was a son of the manse, however, and knew his Scripture rather better than Hervey recalled his. 'That was speaking of punishment, not judgement. Anyway, it's not the same, is it, if the lady's not a lady – not a *real* officer's wife?' He took a long draw on his pot of ale.

'Oh, David, that's unfair. Joynson has the very devil of a job at present.'

'Ay, well, that's as maybe. But a horse that's once kicked over the traces is best shot from the team.'

Hervey was saved by the commander-in-chief. Just when it seemed the speeches and toasts were done, the general ascended the platform.

There were murmurs of surprise, and then silence.

'You tell 'im, sir!' came a voice from the back of the hall, followed by more laughter, and a certain anxiety on Joynson's part that the hogsheads might be emptying too quickly for comfort.

'Mr and Mrs Lincoln, it is an honour to be here,' began Sir Edward Paget in a voice at once commanding and warm. 'Mrs Lincoln would not know that I first met her husband more than fifteen years ago, in Spain. Indeed, it was on a very dark night and it was at a place called Corunna.'

The proverbial pin could now have been dropped. Corunna was a distant memory to just a very few of the bluecoats, but it was second only to Waterloo in the consciousness of the Sixth.

'I, a general officer, was in command of the reserve during that battle, and I and my staff had become lost. I will say no more, but had it not been for the address of a certain serjeant-major the French would have had me in their bag that night.'

There was much approval about the hall, if muted still. This was news indeed.

'As it was' – Sir Edward broke into a broad smile – 'they had me but two years later, I'm sorry to say, else it might have been me and not my brother with you at Waterloo!'

'Yer wouldn't be standing as steady then, sir!' came the voice of another wit from the back of the hall.

And there was cautious laughter about the room from those who understood the reference to Lord Uxbridge's missing leg (while Paget had lost an arm).

'It sounds as though *you're* not standing all that steady either!' returned Sir Edward.

There were hoots of laughter now. There was nothing more entertaining than the heckled putting down the heckler.

'But let me not suspend the celebrations any longer. Except to wish the bride and groom the best of good fortune, and to say that I half think I could send the Sixth east and be finished with the Burmans at once!'

There was now loud and sustained cheering from all quarters. Sir Edward played to the gallery, but he did so perfectly.

Eyre Somervile shook his head. 'A most curious animal, the soldier.'

Emma smiled. They stood apart from the regimentals, and she

was enjoying this intimacy. 'In what way, my dear?'

'He is happier to be thought of as a number in a line, just so long as the line is his own, and with others who belong to it. You saw. There cannot be more than a few dozen who were at Corunna, and yet they all think of it as *their* honour, as though they had all been there, indeed.'

Emma nodded. 'A very proper pride, the sort that comes *not* before a fall.'

'And in men who might otherwise be outside all society.'

'Oh, indeed. They sang well in church, but I have no illusions.'

Her husband took another glass of Madeira. 'And I have observed how they are with their officers, some of whom are as stupid as half those in parliament, yet the little that is good in them is somehow magnified by the connection. And these men' – he nodded to the dozens of chevrons about the place – 'would no doubt be hurling bricks at magistrates were they not in regimentals. Yet here they all are, as if the same family. And those we saw on the road here without chevrons just biding their time until *they're* allowed a bit further under the blanket. I tell you, it's a system that defies reckoning. I've mocked its little absurdities often enough, but I half believe the Company could go anywhere with men like this.'

Emma sighed. 'I hope, therefore, that the Company will remain in ignorance of its treasure.'

Somervile touched her arm, for him a public gesture of unusual warmth.

'Good afternoon Mr Somervile, sir. Good afternoon, ma'am' Armstrong's greeting recalled the two of them.

'Good afternoon, Serjeant-Major – and Mrs Armstrong,' replied Somervile, with a look of genuine pleasure.

Emma smiled as wide. 'Oh, please, don't on my account,' she said to Caithlin as she curtsied. Emma's Indian maids might bow gracefully, but they never curtsied, and, in any case, she could never think of Caithlin Armstrong as of inferior status. 'Especially, my dear, not in your condition.'

Caithlin and her husband glanced with customary pride at the swelling beneath her dress.

'I should say in *our* condition,' added Emma, with the same look of pride.

'Oh, Mrs Somervile,' exclaimed Caithlin, her melodious Cork never stronger. 'How happy I am for you! Is that why Miss Joynson is to be your companion, then, ma'am?'

No fact remained in the possession of but two people in Calcutta for more than a day. 'It is,' said Emma, agreeably. She could not very well add 'ostensibly', although indeed she might. Hervey's suggestion of taking in Frances Joynson for a while had come at a propitious time, though Emma certainly felt in no need of a companion.

Somervile himself was looking rather embarrassed, especially since Armstrong was smiling in a manly, confidential sort of way. There were affairs, indeed, that transcended all barriers. That did not trouble him in the slightest – Somervile was more impatient of the confines of rank than most men – but 'country matters', as he was still wont to call them, he was not at home with.

'What is the news from the east, sir?' asked Armstrong, thinking to save further talk of domestic affairs.

Somervile shook his head. 'Not good, I'm afraid, Serjeant-Major. The business is taking longer than was imagined.' He did not say by whom imagined, nor that there were some who never imagined it otherwise – the commander-in-chief, for one. 'And I fear that our embarrassment there will encourage others to . . .' (he noticed both wives listening intently) 'to . . . become rather impudent.'

Armstrong nodded. 'Well, sir, I for one shall be making in the opposite direction tomorrow with Captain Hervey. And pleased of it, too. I've no partiality for fighting with trees everywhere you turn. That Burma is no place for cavalry.'

The band had struck up a lively jig, and the commander-in-chief had rejoined the major. 'A capital display, Joynson; capital. My compliments to you. But I fear I must return to my desk. The despatches from Rangoon this morning were not at all felicitous.'

'But you still do not think the Sixth will be needed, Sir Edward?'

'No, I think not. If Campbell can break himself out of Rangoon then all should be well, even if takes some weeks more – months, even. And break out he's bound to do at some stage. But the country isn't suitable to develop cavalry operations. I've sent him reinforcements, and if need be, for escorts and the like, I'll send one of the Madras light horse.'

Paget began taking his leave, shaking hands with Mr and Mrs Lincoln, and several others besides, his smile in contrast with the earnestness of his manner with Joynson. As they reached the door he turned again to Joynson, and his former look returned. 'Things are by no means settled among the country powers hereabouts, and our difficulties in the east will only encourage them. I want a handy force here in Bengal if trouble ensues. I have to be able to count on King's cavalry. You'll have the Sixth in best condition, Eustace?'

'I'm sure we understand that, General.'

Sir Edward nodded. 'Hervey will soon be at Dehli, I should imagine?'

'The troop left on Tuesday. Hervey goes tomorrow.'

Sir Edward nodded again. 'A good choice, Hervey. Ochterlony will like him.'

Joynson raised an eyebrow. 'And what's equally to the point, General, Hervey will like Ochterlony!'

Sir Edward smiled. 'Oh, yes, indeed. That is equally important!'

CHAPTER TEN

THE RESIDENT

Dehli, three weeks later

Sir David Ochterlony, the Honourable East India Company's political resident at the court of Shah Mohammed Akbar Rhize Badshah, the Great Mughal, was sixty-six years old. He had entered the Bengal army when he was not yet twenty and had spent his entire service in Hindoostan. He had fought the French, the Marathas and the Nipális, and each time he had added garlands to his reputation as both a soldier and a diplomatist. He had been a major-general since 1814 and resident since 1803. His name was held in the highest esteem – venerated, even – throughout India, although it was the opinion of some members of the Bengal council, and Lord Amherst himself, that his retirement was over-due. Indeed, if any man gave the lie to the oft-heard native lament that a grey hair on the head of a European was never to be seen in India, it was Ochterlony – although, ironically, he had been born and bred in America.

Hervey reported to the residency towards the end of the after-noon, within an hour of entering the great old Mughal capital, but already he had formed the strongest impression of decay and ruin in Dehli – of desolation, even. The city walls, half of stone, half of brick, were in poor repair, tombs and mausoleums were everywhere in dilapidation, grass grew long all about. In places there was a smell of corruption as bad as in Calcutta, and his guide told him there was not a house from where the jackal's cry could not be heard of a night. The centuries of depredations, the sackings and the looting, the sieges and the slaughter had brought the once sumptuous imperial city to little more than a tract of dreary and disconsolate tombs.

'Sahib, here nothing lasts,' said Hervey's guide. 'There is much tribulation and little joy. In years past, the living thought only of reposing after death in splendid sepulchres, and their descendants have thought only of destroying what was intended for eternity.'

And Hervey had half shivered in the chill of that judgement.

But the guide had not been melancholy. He had spoken with the indifferent acceptance of fate that was the mark of his religion. And indeed there was cheer in his judgement, for he told Hervey that things would have been immeasurably worse without Sir David Ochterlony. 'Ochterlony-sahib is greatest man in all of empire after Great Mughal himself, sahib.'

Hervey considered himself well used by now to native blandishments, whether from gholam or pandit. Perhaps, though, in the living memory of Hindoostan – and certainly that of his guide – Sir David Ochterlony had a reasonable claim to greatness. It had been he who had kept Jashwant Rao, the Holkar of Indore, the most powerful of the Maratha chiefs, at bay two decades before, while the Wellesleys made war on the Scindia and the Bhonsla. Greatness, indeed, did not seem too inapt a word as Hervey now contemplated the residency, a classical *palazzo* on Chandnee chouk near the Lahore gate. It spoke of a confident power, for it had nothing to do with the art of the empire of Tamerlane, only that of the Honourable Company.

As he rode up to its gates, the quarter-guard turned out and presented arms. The havildar saluted and stood his ground, so Hervey dismounted and obliged him by inspecting his men – smart Bengali *sipahis*, red-breasted, bare-legged, straps and pouches whitened, muskets burnished. Then a young ensign, very fair-skinned, came. He wore a frock coat and forage hat, as if on picket duty at St James's, and he saluted as sharply, introducing himself and then conducting Hervey to Sir David Ochterlony's quarters. It was, truly, just as if he were arriving at the Horse Guards again.

For weeks Hervey had wondered what he would find at the residency, so many had been the stories. But all he knew for certain was that Sir David was an elderly major-general, and so he composed himself accordingly: the usual military formalities, the stuff of any general headquarters – a brief interview, the presentation of compliments, and so on and so on. But instead of being bidden to wait in an ante-room and then being announced at the door of the resident's office, as he would have expected, the ensign showed him at once into a sitting room furnished in the Mughal style with cushions and divans about the floor, in the middle of which sat a barefoot major-general in a bamboo armchair, wearing a florid silk dressing gown, with a hookah to his mouth.

Hervey rallied quickly enough. 'Good afternoon, Sir David. I am Captain Hervey of the Sixth Light Dragoons.' He had considered the mode of address carefully, concluding that as Sir David Ochterlony was the political resident it was more appropriate to address him by that style rather than as 'General'.

Sir David did not reply at once, nodding as if in a dream.

Hervey stood at attention but removed his cap, uncertain how the interview would proceed. Without doubt, there was here before him what in Calcutta they called a 'mofussil eccentric', one who had been overlong in native India. Any reference to military rank seemed incongruous, and the display of military normality that had attended his arrival only served to make the situation seem more absurd. It was not entirely true to say that his heart sank, but it was not nearly so light as when he had begun his assignment. 'I have the honour to report for duty, three officers and fifty-three dragoons at your service, sir.'

Sir David took the pipe from his mouth and beckoned a khitmagar to bring a chair. 'And a pipe,' he called after him in Urdu, or something very like it, for Hervey grasped its meaning.

'No, thank you, sir. I am, in truth, rather parched.'

'My dear boy, my dear boy!' Sir David took the pipe from his mouth again and bellowed, '*Quai hai!* Sherbet for Captain Hervey-sahib!'

Hervey took his seat and waited to be spoken to, doubts crowding in apace.

The silence continued. Sir David, pipe to his mouth once more, was content to sit and contemplate the new arrival.

At length he seemed satisfied. He took the pipe from his mouth and nodded. 'How are things in Calcutta?'

It was a not unreasonable question, except that Hervey had scarcely moved beyond the confines of the garrison save to the Somerviles' house at Fort William since coming from Rangoon. He trusted that the resident had no more appetite for drawing-room gossip than he. 'In as far as I can say, Sir David, the war with Ava goes badly. There is news, or rumour perhaps would be the better description, that Lord Combermere shall succeed Sir Edward Paget next year. Beyond that I fear there is little I know.'

Sir David's expression of surprise was very pronounced. 'Calcutta has become an exceedingly dull place these late years if that is the extent of your intelligence!'

Hervey sighed inwardly; this was very like keeping company with an ageing parent. He would have to try hard not to become by turns impatient or indulgent. 'In truth, Sir David, I have been laid low these past months, and confined largely to the military lines.'

Sir David looked vexed. 'Laid low? Laid low with what?'

Hervey forced himself to remember that he was speaking to the hero of Nipál. 'I received a ball in my shoulder at Rangoon, Sir David, and thereafter contracted the fever.'

Sir David's mien changed at once. 'Rangoon? Tell me of it.'

It was like the stirring of a sleepy old lion – at first the mere twitch of an eyelid, a flick of the tail, until by degrees the huge beast was on all fours and circling with intermittent grunts and snarls. Hervey spared him nothing. At the end of his account the resident shook his head and sighed. 'That won't do; it won't do at all!'

'I wonder, sir, if I may have more sherbet?'

Sir David scolded the khitmagar for his inattention, as a lion might swipe at an errant cub. 'You will stay to dinner, Hervey, and lodge here. You will no doubt wish to see your troop properly billeted, but your lieutenant may easily exercise command.'

Sir David, for all his eccentric attire, had by now acquired a wholly commanding bearing. Hervey saw no point in protesting. It threw onto Perry an undue burden of society with Green, but that was the way of it: he was captain and he had other concerns. 'I am very obliged, Sir David. But I had better send for my small kit. I have nothing but . . .'

'Oh, we shall not dress,' said Sir David, airily. 'Not in this month. I'll have the khansamah bring you a robe.' He looked at him intently. 'And at dinner I shall tell you of where *our* troubles may lie in the months ahead.'

Hervey bathed and then lay down on the narrow divan in his otherwise ample quarters. All about was marble, like the palace at Chintalpore, but whereas at the Rajah of Chintal's seat the air was full of intrigue and menace, here it was peace, although in the resident's words there was a promise of action. He began looking forward to his commission once more. Dereliction there might be – in so many ways Dehli reminded him of Rome – but he sensed it could fascinate. In any case, it was good to be away from the Calcutta garrison, a station full of left-behinds while hounds were hard at work elsewhere.

Hervey closed his eyes. There was not a sound but for a hoopoe and its mate in the garden beyond his shuttered window. They brought to mind Chintalpore again. How long ago it seemed. Was it seven, eight years? He remembered telling the rajah how he wished one day to entertain him in England. Had he really imagined that he might? Or was it that everything was lived so intensely in India? Could he go back there? It would be easy enough – one of the Calcutta coasters down to the Godavari, thence by budgerow as far as he might up that disobliging river, and on to Chintalpore. Godaji Rao Sundur, Rajah of Chintalpore – Hervey was, after all, one of his *jagirdars*, and his jagir returned a respectable income each year, not all of which was covenanted to the widows of those desperate days' fighting the nizam's guns and the Pindarees. Would the raj kumari be purged of her crimes? Would her father have recalled her from deep in the forest of the Gonds? Or did she scheme and plot still – so reckless a daughter of so sensible a man? Did he really want to see her again? In one respect at least he had no doubt, for even as he lay, her allure had its effect.

At seven, the sun on the horizon and the heat of the afternoon given way to a balmy dusk, Hervey put on the green robe that the bearer had brought him and joined Sir David Ochterlony in his Mughal courtyard. With the resident was a tall, well-made native man, clean-shaven, with sleek hair drawn back and held with a clip. He wore a loose-fitting kurta, white trousers and embroidered slippers, and he spoke freely and easily.

'Hervey, this is Jaswant Sing, my master of horse. And this,' said Sir David, turning to the man, 'is Captain Hervey of His Majesty's Sixth Light Dragoons, who, as of this afternoon, is captain of my escort.'

They both bowed.

'What are your horses, Captain Hervey?' asked Jaswant Sing, with a warm aspect.

'Marwaris, for the most part.'

Jaswant Sing inclined his head in a way that signified approval. 'And you yourself ride the Marwari?'

'I have a charger brought with me from England, but my second is a Marwari, though she is not with me for the present, having been sick.'

'And the Marwari pleases you, Captain Hervey?'

'Oh yes. Yes indeed. I have never seen a better doer' (Hervey checked himself), 'that is, I have never seen a horse that subsisted on so little, and is yet so handy and obliging.' It was too early to volunteer information about the Marwari's endurance in his jungle raid, however.

'The Marwari is from Rajpootana, Captain Hervey, which is my home. If your duties are allowing, I should be very pleased to show you the breeding horses there.'

'If my duties were to allow it, Jaswant Sing sahib, I should like that very much.' He would leave it at that, for he did not imagine Sir David would be inclined to spare him too soon, if at all.

Sir David was attentive, however. 'One of Rajpootana's neighbours gives me considerable cause for worry, Hervey. I am frankly fearful of a struggle over the succession in Bhurtpore.'

Hervey was surprised by such frankness in their present company.

'You will not know of it, I dare say?'

'I know but a very little, Sir David.'

'Nothing much troubles Fort William but the war with Ava, I suppose. Well, the Rajah of Bhurtpore, Baldeo Sing, has long honoured the treaty of friendship with the Company. He is now becoming frail, and his son Balwant is but a boy, and the rajah is fearful that his nephew Durjan Sal has designs on the succession. The old rajah asked that I invest the boy with a *khelat* – a sort of honorary dress – as a sign of our recognition of his rightful claim, and this I did in the early part of the year.'

Sir David beckoned his khansamah and told him that he wished to eat at once.

Hervey decided he would not wait on Sir David's pace. 'And I presume therefore, sir, that you have intelligence that this action has not entirely dissuaded Durjan Sal from his designs?'

'Just so, Hervey,' replied the resident, in an approving tone. 'And everything that we know of him says he is without scruple.'

'Jhauts,' said Jaswant Sing, shaking his head. 'They are stubborn beggars.'

Sir David nodded. 'But when they're not being stubborn, Hervey, they're the most courageous men. In our service they would make fine *sipahis*. I had a mind to visit the rajah now that the cooler season will soon be upon us, for I was not able to invest the *khelat* in person. I judged it appropriate to go with an escort of King's cavalry rather than native, for Durjan Sal would no doubt believe it possible to buy off any native troops, and it would be well to remind him that not all of the Company's forces are engaged with the King of Ava.'

'You mean as a portent, Sir David? I have but fifty dragoons.'

'Yes, just so. Now, let us eat.'

Two weeks passed, during which Hervey saw little of Sir David but much of Jaswant Sing. The resident was sick for several days – he ascribed it to the change of season – and then when he was recovered enough to attend to his papers, was much occupied with the estimates which were overdue for submission to Calcutta. So Hervey found time aplenty to learn the Rajpoot way of horsemanship, and his neglect of the troop – or rather his delegation of day-to-day command to his lieutenant – he was able to justify by these equestrian studies.

'That 'orse got ginger up its backside, sir?' called Private Johnson, standing at the edge of the maidan one morning.

Hervey sat astride a Marwari stallion which was pirouetting and leaping as if being backed for the first time. He managed to collect it, after a fashion, and walked him over to his groom. 'I'll have you know that this animal is trained for war, Johnson. For combat with war elephants indeed!'

'Oh ay, sir?'

'Yes. And very handy he is too, for all the fire you saw in him.' Hervey made to stretch his shoulder, to relieve the ache that had been growing since he took the reins, but he stopped short. He would give no sign, even to Johnson, that he could feel the musket ball's force still.

'And 'ow's 'e fight an elephant then, sir? 'E'd not stand as 'igh as its ear.'

'*He* doesn't do the fighting; the rider does. He gets the horse to leap up and takes the mahout in the flank with his lance. Then he can deal with the howdah.'

Johnson looked sceptical.

'I'll show you what he can do.' Hervey gathered up the reins again, though nothing like as taut as he would normally for proper collection.

Indeed, the reins themselves were unusual. They were stitched double towards the end, and Hervey held this doubled length, close to its fork, in his bridle hand and almost to his chest. It showed a long and graceful length such that his childhood riding master would have admired. But that old *rittmeister* would also have been intrigued, for Hervey was not wearing spurs, nor was he carrying a whip. Johnson could scarcely believe it either.

'The weight of the reins collects him onto the bit,' explained Hervey. 'I don't know how or why, for I've never heard of an animal trained so. In truth, I'd not have been inclined to believe it.'

After circling two or three times at a canter, he put the stallion into a pirouette, then into a reversed pirouette, then into what he knew as '*voltes* on a small compass', stopping on the hocks and turning on them, and from that he had the horse jump into the gallop. Finally, and still at the gallop, he made the animal move obliquely, as Peto would have made headway with a weather helm.

Johnson stood silent but impressed. These were 'tricks' of self-evident utility in the field. It was not difficult to imagine the lance held across the body or out wide, the horse passaging left or right to take the enemy in the flank.

But Hervey had not finished. There were what his old *rittmeister* called the airs above ground. Jaswant Sing had shown him how to perform them, though in truth, as well Hervey knew, all he had done was show him how to sit a horse that knew its airs.

First a *levade*, the horse rising on its hind legs, hocks almost on the ground. Then forward from the levade a *courbette*, with three distinct leaps – or was it four? And finally the *capriole*, the stallion leaping into the air and kicking out long with its hind legs. Jaswant Sing had called it *udaang* – flying.

'You see?' called Hervey, panting almost as much as the horse as he walked him over to where Johnson stood – and rubbing his shoulder now, and more confidently, for he knew that to work like that meant he was all but whole again. 'You see how useful *that* could be!'

There was no doubting it. 'That were a vicious kick all right,' said his groom, shaking his head. 'I've never seen owt like it.'

'You see now how useful for elephant-fighting?'

'Oh ay, sir. Yon 'orse looked as if it would've scrambled up its 'ead.'

'That was the idea,' said Hervey, slipping from the saddle and loosening the girth. 'But all that's over with – elephants and the like. Just a pretty display now. Think how you might turn heads with it in England though, eh?'

CHAPTER ELEVEN

TOWERS OF SILENCE

Bhurtpore, a month later

Hervey sat on the crumbling wall of an old well, in a large straw hat and very unmilitary clothes, sketching.

'Sir David Ochterlony makes but one stipulation,' he had written to Emma's husband, before leaving Dehli:

He would have me do more than merely gawp at the walls of Bhurtpore, he would have me bring back a thorough knowledge of all its defences. And all this, of course, I am to accomplish without for a moment giving cause for anyone to know what I do in that city. To what end this spying may be directed I can little imagine, except that Sir David speaks darkly of the need,
perhaps, of such information in years soon to come. At first I imagined him to mean that he himself, Sir David Ochterlony, might have to do what Lord Lake had been unable to accomplish. But although I believe Sir David to be game for the hardiest adventure still, I am certain he understands the circumstances would be no more favourable now than they were for Lord Lake. I have read much of his lordship's siege, and I cannot imagine that success could be

accomplished with fewer men and guns, and Sir David does not have one half of Lord Lake's force at his own disposal. I believe, therefore, that Sir David would put before the Council in Calcutta a proposal for the stronger reinforcement of his command were it ever to come to a fight, and that meanwhile he is taking all prudent steps to acquire intelligence of any nature. He does not confirm me in this opinion when I ask him, but he does not oppose it either . . .

Hervey was not by any reckoning an artist, but he had been taught to draw, and his practice in field sketching in the Peninsula had made him proficient in the reproduction of landscape with correct proportion and perspective. For several days he had wandered about the city drawing anything he could see which was of no military significance in order to establish his credentials as a travelling antiquarian. No one had shown the slightest interest in him, but he had wanted an alibi – a portfolio of architectural drawings that would serve as evidence of his innocent intent when he began work on the defences.

One sketch he had been especially minded to hide, however. Its subject appalled him – sickened him indeed. He had scarcely been able to keep down his gorge as he drew. And it took him longer to complete than some of the more elaborate works of decorative detail, for he had wanted as faithful an impression as possible; one that might have the same effect on a viewer that the archetype had on him. It had been a repetitive work, a business of drawing skull after skull. He had tried to estimate how many there were: the column was as tall as Trajan's in Rome, and his guide had said it was neither hollow nor filled with sand. Here was no bas-relief of bones, but a solid pillar of Lord Lake's dead. No Christian burial or cremation according to native rites for these men – King's and sepoys alike. The gamekeepers at Longleat would string up their trophies to discourage predators and to impress by their zeal. The Futtah Bourge, the 'bastion of victory', was but the same. How loathsome it stood by comparison with that eloquent commemoration of Trajan's victory, an affront to every decent instinct of a Christian-raised man, and a gesture of contempt for the customs of war. Peaceful Hindoostan might be, but a sight such as this said that peace was an unnatural thing. Hervey considered it well that he concealed his sketch, and thought it best that he hide it from view of his fellows too.

This next stage of his work occupied him a full week. 'The fortress of Bhurtpore is without doubt the largest I have ever seen,' he wrote to Eyre Somervile towards the end of October:

It stands on a plain broken and rugged towards the west but otherwise bare, affording little cover, and I calculate the perimeter to be not very much short of five miles. Any siege force would have to be great indeed to invest the entire fortress. I have now been able to make a very faithful comparison of Lord Lake's dispositions, and it is at once apparent that his insufficiency in men was greater than I had supposed when reading the usual texts, for with the Maratha cavalry harassing him he was obliged to hold ready reserves to deal with them, and he had not thereby the means either to starve out the garrison in the old way or breach the walls in enough places and in sufficient strength to bolt the defenders.

A broad and deep ditch runs the entire length of the perimeter, from the inner edge of which rises a thick and lofty wall of sun-baked clay and stone, flanked by no fewer than thirty-five turreted bastions. I have been able to draw in plan the location of each, though for reasons of economy in time, and so as not to appear excessively interested should I have been accosted, I was minded to draw elevations of only those I judged would command the likely approaches. The citadel itself occupies a natural height, rising above all else in the city, and is itself enclosed by a ditch 150 feet wide and fifty feet deep. And, as if Vauban himself had directed the fortification, there are ravelins and lunettes, flèches and demi lunes the entire length of the walls.

And how blessed are the people of Bhurtpore, too, since the moats and ditches are dry, so they are not plagued by the mosquitoes that thrive on still water, and they may drive their animals wherever they wish. I have learned that water when it is needed to fill the moats comes from a jheel to the north-west of the fortress, a very practical and happy arrangement. This water and these walls would pose the best engineer a test of his science. And when the water and the walls are covered by the guns of thirty-five bastions and countless other outworks, the infantry might very well become so many companies of forlorn hopes unless directed by a general of exceptional address. In the skill of the siege artillery and the field gunners reposes their fate.

163

No fortress is impregnable, we must understand, but it is my decided
opinion that if ever a fortress came close to such a condition it is
Bhurtpore . . .

And then he had confided in his friend the unhappier detail of
his detached duty – unusually, for it touched only on the business
of the Sixth:

I am resolved to have Green out. He daily becomes more awkward in
his dealings with everyone. In truth I can scarcely bear to speak to
him. Every blemish in both his character and appearance seemed
magnified in Dehli, there being no multitude of other
officers to draw away attention. I have therefore written to Joynson
and advised him that he speak severely with him about the
advisability of his remaining in the regiment, for I have concluded
that he could never make an officer, and if ever it comes to a fight the
outcome would be very ill indeed – for himself, principally, for there
could be little enough damage he might do to any of the dragoons,
such is his subsidiary role. Yet were he ever to encounter a half
decent swordsman the result must be disaster.

But, on the other hand, I am pleased to say that Perry is a fine
lieutenant, on whose account I need have had no fears, and I shall
take leave hence, before returning to Dehli, to see the great white
mausoleum at Agra, about which you always spoke so much . . .

These letters he then took with him to Agra, where there were
trusted hircarrahs to carry despatches down the Jumna and thence
to Calcutta, and from where he himself could take a boat back to
Dehli with greater ease. He had indeed grown fond of his licence.
The days were still warm, and at night it was good to sit before a
fire reading or in contemplation. He lacked the company of
English-speakers, Jaswant Sing having now returned to Dehli, but
this gave him opportunity to practise his Urdu with a certain
confidence, and in any case he had never been fretful in his own
company – except at the very end of his stay in Bhurtpore, but the
fever had not developed its full power, and he was abed for no
longer than a day.

Five more he gave himself to see what had once been the proud
Mughal capital, Agra. On the last evening he sat beside the hearth

in a comfortable haveli which Jaswant Sing had arranged for him, below the red walls of the great sandstone fort. The place was strangely peaceful for so teeming a city, and he contemplated its lessons. He laid down his glass of arrack – he had come to rely on it as a faithful aid to digestion, no matter how tempestuous the dinner served him – leaned back in his chair and drew long on the mildest of cheroots. The tobacco smoke mixed agreeably with that of the sandalwood burning in the grate, and he closed his eyes for a moment the better to hear the nightjar – stranger, as a rule, to the haunts of men.

In a while he opened them again, and picked up his journal from the table next to him. It had commanded more time than usual of an evening, for it was his sole entry at Agra:

12th November 1824

The work at Bhurtpore being done – and greatly more of it than I had ever imagined, so immense a place is it – I travelled thence to the Jumna again, under the admirable arrangements of Jaswant Sing, and reposed two nights at the ancient capital of the Moguls. The palace called the Taje Mahl, which means crown palace, is spoken of throughout India as one of unsurpassed beauty, the place of burial of the wife of a great emperor to whom it was erected in praise. I visited it the first day on arriving and was not disappointed. While it is visible in whole from the river, approached from the south through the main gate only its dome and the four minarets, at each corner, of white marble, are to be seen above the circumadjacent trees of a Persian garden, in the way that the dome of the Pope's basilica in Rome can be seen above the crowding buildings of the Borgo. Only when, like the basilica, one comes right upon it can its entire beauty be imagined. I have attempted to sketch it, but it is wholly beyond my skill to render it any justice, and I have instead resolved to find an artist hereabout who will make me a fair likeness. Last night I visited the gardens opposed to it on the other bank of the Jumna, which are in very great disrepair, yet which are called the Moonlight Gardens for here is where, legend has it, the emperor would come at the full moon each month to recall his lost love. It was planted with all manner of herbage that gave off sweet scent by night, and there is still too a night scent, though the place is very

Hervey's journal pretended to nothing more than being well-kept. For the most part it was in note form, serving as a memorandum of movement, acquisition, accomplishment; or occasionally of intention, hindrance or opinion. But never of emotion, not even anger. Had it been his practice to include such feelings he would have filled pages since coming to Agra, for in that moonlight garden he had for a time begun to question the true intensity of his former love. It had been Emma Somervile's suggestion – insistence, indeed – that he visit Agra. There, she said, he would see the perfect expression of a grieving man's love. It had been no mawkish sentiment, for he had spoken with her of raising some memorial to Henrietta, and had done so with perfect calm. Henrietta was not yet dismissed habitually from his mind – thoughts of her, especially of their moments of intimacy, came on him still, and often – but he could now think of her with reason and cool judgement, quite unlike before. And Emma's suggestion had been far from unwelcome, for he had read and heard much of the white marble shrine: it would surely be instructive to see how a man who had grieved and had the means to memorialize that grieving had done so. However, the palace had seemed more and more a rebuke to him. Here stood a memorial as much to the constancy of an emperor's love as to the empress herself. Where was the evidence of his own constancy? In truth, the evidence was to the contrary – his bibi, the letters to and from Lady Katherine Greville, more sportive with each return.

Only later, on leaving Agra, as he read fitfully on the budgerow plying upstream for Dehli, did he learn that in time the emperor had abandoned the city and set up his court in the old Mughal capital – just as he, Hervey, had abandoned England and set up his domain in India. But Mumtaz Mahal had begged her husband not to pine for her, and to remarry. Hervey could not slough off his guilt so easily. And in any case his sins were mingled. He no longer honoured his wife's memory with his body, but neither did he say his prayers with system or regularity, let alone conviction. And he might as well have forgotten the offspring of their union. Somervile had been wont to say that many a man had lost his reason in India as well as his soul. But such men, Hervey supposed, had sought consolation in drink or some other opiate. He relied only on activity. No, he had no fear of losing his reason. But in India colours were brighter and shadows darker. It was not always so easy to judge things faithfully.

A noisy skein of bar-headed geese recalled him to the present. He turned up his collar against the freshening Jumna breeze, and picked up his volume on the Maratha wars again. How had Lord Lake miscalculated so? The walls of Bhurtpore had stood then as they did now. What had been the cause of so fatal a misjudgement? He must have it. And he knew he must then pray that in all his forgetting activity he could himself keep a right judgement in things, civil or military.

PART THREE

THE PRIDE OF HINDOOSTAN

GENERAL ORDER

Fort William
28 July 1825

*The Right Hon. The Governor-General has learned with great
sorrow the demise of Major-General Sir David Ochterlony, resident
in Malwa and Rajpootana. This melancholy event took place on the
morning of the 15th inst. at Meerut, whither he had proceeded for
the benefit of change of air. On the eminent military services of
Major-General Sir David Ochterlony, it would be superfluous to
dilate; they have been acknowledged in terms of the highest praise
by successive Governments; they justly earned a special and
substantial reward from the Hon. East India Company; they have
been recognised with expressions of admiration and applause by the
British Parliament; and they have been honoured with signal marks
of the approbation of his Sovereign . . .*

*. . . The confidence which the government reposed in an individual
gifted with such rare endowments, was evinced by the high and
responsible situations which he successively filled, and the duties
which he discharged with eminent ability and advantage to the*

Public Interests. As an especial testimony of the high respect in which the character and services of Major-General Sir D. Ochterlony are held, and as a public demonstration of sorrow for his demise, the Governor-General in Council is pleased to direct that minute guns to the number of sixty-eight, corresponding with his age, be fired this evening at sunset, from the ramparts of Fort William.

CHAPTER TWELVE

MINUTE GUNS

Calcutta, October 1825

His Excellency General the Right Hon. Stapleton Lord Combermere, GCB, GCH &c., Commander-in-Chief of all the Forces in India, as he was styled, received Hervey warmly but without the same careless ease of their previous acquaintances. They had first met eleven years ago in the field at Toulouse, as Hervey lay painfully under the ministration of a surgeon. The commander of Wellington's cavalry had been all praise and warm regards then for Hervey in that culminating battle of the campaign, in his despatches writing that 'by his bold and independent action he averted what might at the very least have been an embarrassment for the mounted arm'. They had met on three occasions since then, the last being that most diverting evening at Apsley House before Hervey had come out to India, when he had met Lady Katherine Greville.

'I fancy you might care for some coffee, Hervey? It's a damnably cold morning.'

The invitation was to help himself from a pot on a table covered with maps and sketches, at which stood Colonel Macleod, who was to be brigadier of artillery, and Colonel Anburey, who was to be the same of engineers. Hervey acknowledged them both with a brisk bow of the head before pouring some of the strong black liquid into a big cup and adding a good measure of sugar.

'You set us nicely in apposition, Captain Hervey,' said Colonel Anburey, nodding with a grim, if perhaps wry, sort of smile at Colonel Macleod.

Hervey knew exactly what he meant. 'I fear the sappers will have little chance of doing their work without the support of the guns, Colonel, for the approaches to the walls are coverless. And yet the walls are so solid and thick that the guns shall have to come in close, and that can only be done by sapping from outside the range of the fort. Indeed, I wonder that it will not be better to mine one or two of the bastions, for a breach will otherwise be devilish hard.'

Colonel Anburey shook his head. 'I read your opinion, Hervey, but it is out of the question if the country lies as you have drawn it.'

'Too far to tunnel,' explained Lord Combermere.

Hervey looked puzzled.

Colonel Anburey supplied the detail. 'The greatest distance a gallery may be driven is two hundred yards. Beyond that there is insufficient air for a man to breathe, and indeed for the explosive to operate efficiently.'

Hervey was confident he had surveyed the defences accurately. 'That is indeed a pity, Colonel. It will be an affair of heavy pounding therefore.'

And it need not have been, he said to himself later. Six months ago Ochterlony might well have carried the day at a stroke, with that never-failing ally *surprise*, had the Governor-General allowed him to try – even with half the number of men with which Lord Lake had failed. At least he might by now be keeper of the gates in those great walls, thereby shutting out every freebooting Jhaut and brigand who at this very moment was flocking to Durjan Sal's banner.

But the Governor-General had dithered, fatally. Eyre Somervile had told Hervey of how he had gone to Lord Amherst's office the morning Ochterlony's despatch had arrived from Dehli. Amherst had looked alarmed: there was ill news enough already from the east without more from the west.

'You read my earlier minute on the situation in Bhurtpore, Excellency?' Somervile had asked, careful to observe the punctilio of address for once.

Lord Amherst had looked uncertain.

'Three months ago the Rajah of Bhurtpore died, and his infant son succeeded him under the guardianship of his uncle.'

Lord Amherst's face had shown a flicker of recall.

'However, for reasons that should not detain us, the late rajah's nephew, Durjan Sal, has laid claim to the succession.'

'*Why* do you say they should not detain us, Mr Somervile?' Lord Amherst had demanded, his brow furrowed anxiously. 'We are, by your tone, very evidently to be detained by one claim or the other.'

'Durjan Sal disputes the legitimacy of the rightful heir, Balwant Sing. But by all the evidence hitherto before us this is a most villainous claim.'

'Before us? I have not heard anything of it!'

'No, my lord. Matters in this regard have fallen entirely to the resident in Dehli.'

'Ochterlony? Good God: what has he been about?'

Although Somervile shared the general opinion of Sir David Ochterlony – that his best days were long past – he had sufficient regard for his judgement in the rights of things, if not in their consequences. 'Sir David recognized the rightful claim of Balwant Sing twelve months ago by vesting him in a *khelat* —'

'What in heaven's name was he doing? Such a thing is not done without presumptions of obligation. What is Bhurtpore to us? I consider it very rash.'

Somervile had sighed to himself. 'The fact is, my lord, that Sir David has bestowed the Company's recognition on Balwant Sing and —'

'Well, he had better renounce it. We have trouble enough in Ava. Campbell's still stuck in the mud at Rangoon, and his ships gathering weed.' The Governor-General had waved his hand as if the matter was done with.

At whose door might blame lie in that regard, Somervile had been minded to ask. 'I'm afraid it is too late. It seems Durjan Sal moved against Balwant Sing's guardian some weeks ago – and very bloodily – and has proclaimed himself regent—'

'So?'

Somervile had tried hard to hide his irritation at the Governor-General's disregard of the dangers the country powers might pose. 'Sir David has already denounced Durjan Sal as an usurper of supreme authority, by which he means, of course, the Company—'

'I am perfectly well aware what he means, Somervile! He must be told at once to moderate his demands and conclude the affair by diplomacy.'

'I fear it is too late for that. He has called on the Jhauts to rally to him and announced that he will appear at the head of a British force to restore Balwant Sing!'

Lord Amherst had then, by Somervile's account, looked like a man winded by a body blow. His brow had furrowed even more, signalling his utter incomprehension. 'Where is this force to come from, Somervile?'

Somervile had raised his eyebrows. 'By all reckoning he might muster ten thousand men at most, scarcely a thousand of them white.'

Lord Amherst had fallen silent. 'Would that be enough? Sir David was – may yet be – a fine general . . .'

Somervile had put on a most determined expression. 'Opinions vary and differ. The commander-in-chief's is as yet unsettled. His deputy is of the opinion that it would be very far from sufficient. Bhurtpore, you may recall, is the fortress that defied Lord Lake more than twenty years ago, and nothing, I understand, has rendered it any less formidable since then.'

The remaining colour had disappeared from Lord Amherst's face. 'Then the consequences will be very grave. I cannot suffer humiliation in the west, at this time especially.'

Somervile had been much perturbed by the Governor-General's alarm. 'But, Lord Amherst, I understand that the commander-in-chief's opinion tends to reinforcement. If we at once send word to Bombay, and to Madras, we may assemble full three times Sir David's present number, and a proper siege train, and that shall surely be enough to subdue Bhurtpore!'

'No, no, no! We want no second campaign while Ava is un-decided. It is quite impossible!'

Somervile had been taken aback. 'But Lord Amherst, the ultimatum has been given. We cannot withdraw now. The Company would suffer an irreparable humiliation. Every native

176

power the length of India would look at once to take his opportunity. I—'

'Impossible, I say! I cannot be mired in by Ochterlony's intemperate declarations. The only alternative is to let him try with his ten thousand.'

'But Hervey's view is that victory cannot be guaranteed thereby. There must be reinforcements to carry the day if audacity fails!'

'Hervey? Hervey? Who is he?'

Somervile had at once regretted his lapse. 'The captain of Sir David's escort, Lord Amherst. He—'

'Captain of the *escort*? Great heavens, man, have you lost your senses? No, no, it will not serve. Sir David's offensive would be a gamble on his reputation for success. Yes, that is the way it shall be done. I shall send word at once for Ochterlony to withdraw. Indeed, I shall issue immediate orders for the recall of Sir David Ochterlony to an appointment of greater prominence here!'

Somervile had felt obliged to concede defeat. 'Very good, Lord Amherst. But with respect I must give my opinion that none shall see such a recall as anything but the most peremptory reprimand for the resident. Including Sir David himself.'

Colonel Anburey, the engineer, now looked pained at the thought of the heavy pounding that lay ahead, though the same thought seemed to please Colonel Macleod, the gunner. 'You give your opinion very decidedly, sir,' said the former.

'I endeavour always to speak as I find, Colonel,' replied Hervey, with absolute certainty.

'Well, so be it, gentlemen,' said Lord Combermere briskly. 'I shall, of course, make my own reconnaissance, but for the time being I intend proceeding upon Captain Hervey's admirable appreciation. The question then turns on when is launched the – as Hervey has it – *coup de main*. I am prepared to order affairs a great deal in favour of its success. However, there is no profit in seizing these dams if they are only to be recaptured before I am able to send a reinforcement. Quite the opposite, indeed, for the enemy would be at once alerted to our intention and would instantly open the sluice-gates. And yet, if I delay too long we shall anyway have full moats to cross instead of dry ditches.'

The colonels of engineers and artillery looked somehow relieved that their own decisions turned only on what was technically feasible rather than fine judgements of this order.

It was left to Hervey to speak to the commander-in-chief's dilemma. 'I have been considering this, General. The flooding of all the moats would be a great inconvenience to the population. Durjan Sal would not order the dams open until it were strict necessity. We must therefore be circumspect in our concentration. I believe that your lordship would wish to assemble his forces at Agra – and I truly cannot conceive of a better place – but any advance west of there would unquestionably signal to the Jhauts our intention to invest the city, for it is a march of but a few days, and if my own intelligence of the time it would take to inundate the defences is correct, the enemy would be obliged to cut open the bund at once.'

Lord Combermere nodded.

'I fancy that two squadrons of light cavalry with galloper guns might dash from Agra to Bhurtpore in a night, before the garrison were properly alerted. They could seize the bund before dawn, until our engineers came up, and would have the advantage of daylight to beat off the immediate sallies.'

Lord Combermere at once saw the sequence perfectly. 'And the relief to attend on them by dusk.'

'It would be hazardous if they were *not* to be reinforced by then, General. If the enemy did not overwhelm them in the darkness, they would surely mass during the night and do so at first light.'

'Very well,' said Lord Combermere, nodding slowly, as if turning over the facts one more time.

Hervey judged that his services were now done with. He picked up his shako and began making to leave.

'Thank you, Captain Hervey,' said Lord Combermere, looking up. 'Your information has been most valuable. You shall have the honour of leading those two squadrons. And you had better have the rank for the affair, too, once we take to the field.'

Hervey left the commander-in-chief's office with the promise of a local majority. It would give him the authority he needed for his limited command, but in terms of seniority it meant even less than a brevet. He wondered when that recognition might come his way again, if ever. He wondered even more when the next regimental vacancy might occur, though he could not begin to contemplate how he might find the means to buy it. Advancement in times of peace and retrenchment was a snail's gallop – they all knew that – so he had better make the most of his temporary command. He would go at once to the adjutant-general's office to discover for himself the exact order of battle for this, Lord Combermere's first sovereign campaign.

There, he was at once astonished by the scale of the undertaking. The body of cavalry was the largest, it was certain, since Waterloo: a division of two brigades, each comprising a King's regiment, three of the Company's and two troops of horse artillery, the whole under command of Lieutenant-Colonel Sleigh of the 11th Light Dragoons in the rank of brigadier-general. Hervey was content enough with that; Sleigh he knew from Peninsula days, and considered him a good man. But it was the Devil's own luck that Sir Ivo Lankester should have prolonged his furlough, for his seniority would have given him a brigade. And the only reason Sir Ivo had prolonged his stay in England was to coax His Majesty into appointing a royal colonel-in-chief to the Sixth. An expensive adornment *that* would be, mused Hervey, if it cost Sir Ivo the opportunity of the sabre's edge at the head of his regiment.

And the two divisions of infantry were strong ones, too, each of three brigades, with two King's regiments – the 14th and 59th Foot – and the Company's 1st Bengal European Regiment. There were a good many troops of foot artillery, as well as the experimental brigade with their rockets, and strong detachments of the Bengal Sappers and Miners. The strength returns were not yet received in full, said the officiating adjutant-general, but his estimate was that the army would take to the field in excess of twenty thousand combatants.

Hervey scanned the order of battle keenly. The last regiment he came to gave him especial satisfaction, and did as much to assure him of victory as any other. Two rissalahs of Skinner's Irregular Horse would accompany the army, unbrigaded. He resolved at once to enlist them in his independent command.

In the afternoon he sent Corporal Wainwright with a dozen sicca rupees to buy provisions for the budgerow which would – he hoped – soon be taking them back up the Ganges. 'Calcutta will be no place to be these next weeks,' he said, smiling wryly. 'Not for sabres, that's for sure. You haven't seen an army assembling for the field, Corporal Wainwright. It's a grand affair of adjutants and quartermasters and serjeant-majors. Parades, lists, inspections – no end of a business!'

Corporal Wainwright hid his partial disappointment. The oldest sweat in his barrack-room had told him many things when he had first joined, not least that a dragoon should never volunteer for anything. Yet Jobie Wainwright would have liked to see the serjeant-majors and the adjutants and the quartermasters about their business, for he himself wanted one day to fill their boots, and how was he to learn if he did not see? But he was his troop-leader's coverman – *Major* Hervey's coverman, indeed, though he did not yet know it – and he went only where he might parry the cut or the thrust directed at his officer. That next meant to Dehli, or perhaps straight to Agra.

But his officer had a prior duty, one that could not possibly be spoken of between them. When Wainwright left for the bazaar, Hervey went to the Chitpore road.

The whole of native Calcutta, from nabob to bhisti, knew now that the army of Bengal was mobilizing. And every bibi knew like-wise. They also knew that the army's object was what Lord Lake had failed to accomplish, and what had been the shaming cause of Sir David Ochterlony's death. Would John Company rise in triumph this time to the old taunt 'Go take Bhurtpore'? It was the talk of the princely palaces and the havelis of the Chitpore road, debated in the more modest dwellings of the Brahmins and around the bazaars. And in the bibi khanas; *especially* in the bibi khanas, for they knew all about Bhurtpore – 'the Pride of Hindoostan'. Was the fortress not impregnable? Did not the Futtah Bourge, the tower of skulls, stand as reminder to all who would forget it? No, it was impossible that a man should leave for Bhurtpore without visiting his bibi to bid her a proper goodbye, and to receive the soldier's farewell in return, and to assure her of the arrangements he had made for her well-being should he not come back.

Hervey now spoke the words that a bibi needed to hear, but they could never be enough. She loved him. She thought him the world itself. She also understood that in the army's hands lay the Company's honour and prestige, and it made her doubly fearful, for she knew what honour meant to her sahib, and the price he would be ready to pay if it were necessary. She would not say so – it would only distress him – but if his body were brought back to Calcutta she would throw herself into the flames of his funeral pyre in the duty of *suttee*. Except that for her it would not be a duty, rather an end to interminable grief.

She pleaded with her sahib to let her go with him to Bhurtpore; even to walk among the dhoolie-bearers and syces if she could not be with him. But tempted sorely as Hervey was, his soldier's duty stood all too clear: she was not welcome in the cantonment, and she could not be welcome on the campaign.

But leaving her was harder than he had supposed. He did not for one moment imagine he would not return (she would not tell him that she imagined only this) but the necessity of proceeding on that possibility gave their parting a fateful edge that all but overcame him. It was not possible for a man – a man with a soul – to see even native eyes which looked so loving, and not be touched deep. In truth, Hervey had come to love her, too, in a certain way. It was not a love which fulfilled all his needs; their minds, so differently schooled, could never wholly meet, but there was a tenderness that could make him content, for a time. He saw that period of contentment, however, only as time that stood still, not the sharing of life's time.

It was of no consequence, however. He had long known that he could only have shared life's time with Henrietta, and it mattered not how or with whom he shared time that stood still, for it was a wholly different property. As the sun began to sink in the direction to which his duty called, he rose from beside her to bathe. He was certain of one thing: he had not the will, and certainly not the heart, to sever himself from her now. It would take the lawful command of a superior to accomplish that – a return to England, alone or with the regiment. Yet did he have the desire and the will even to comply with such an order? Why should she not accompany him home?

That twisting ache which came in his vitals in such moments of apprehension hauled him back to the truth – that here in Hindoostan he might live largely as he pleased, but that in England (above all in Wiltshire) he must live as he was expected. All the Christian charity of his family combined could not accept an Indian paramour, let alone a wife. And beyond his immediate family – Henrietta's guardians and the gentry of those parts – such a thing could signal only that Hervey had announced his intention to withdraw from all society. He might even come to know what his late friend Shelley had called 'social hatred'.

Would that matter to him? As he lay in her arms he had imagined not. But now, as he sponged the cold water over his shoulders, he knew that he would always hark back – no matter how infrequently – to the earlier, sober days, and that it would begin eating at the heart of the arrangement. And his career? He would have to forgo it. *Any* arrangement with a native girl, except in a native station, was insupportable. Perhaps he might implicate Georgiana, to appoint his bibi as ayah to her? But what passed as a decent and honourable association in India would in England look no better than the slave-owner visiting the cabins of an evening.

As they embraced at their parting, Hervey was in more than half a mind to seek a commission in the Company's forces, to make his home here, to see how long he could make time stand still, until events resolved his troubles.

In the army's hands lay the Company's honour and prestige. If Hervey's bibi understood this, how much more did Somervile. The *King's* honour, indeed, now rested in the balance at Bhurtpore, and there were some in the great houses of Calcutta – those connected with the native powers especially – who would say that the very presence of the British in India was at stake, that in Combermere's hands lay the course of history.

'There is much to speak of, Hervey,' said Somervile, welcoming him at the door of No. 3, Fort William. 'Send for all your necessaries and rest the night here. A good dinner's the very least the council might provide before you go and pay their rent for the next hundred years.'

Hervey needed no inducement to stay with the Somerviles, for besides the unflagging pleasure he took in their company he had no agreeable alternative. He could not return to the bibi khana having said his farewell, the officers' mess was at this moment being readied to lumber in a score of yakhdans and bullock carts in the direction of Agra, and his own bungalow was once again shuttered and draped with dust sheets.

Emma joined them, the ayah with her, babe in arms.

For a moment Hervey saw something – the timeless vision of mother and child, perhaps – that reached deep into his own void. And his godson – a contented baby, swaddled with affection, a child that would grow to manhood sure of its nurture. Mother and child seemed somehow to rebuke him. 'I had a mind to stay here when the Sixth is recalled,' he said, absently.

Emma read that mind, and thought better of questioning it.

Her husband was less nimble. 'Be sure to take six months' home leave beforehand, mark. It would be perilous to chance the marriage stakes on the angels who come out here.'

Serious advice, well-meant as ever – if blunt: Hervey could not take offence. 'Perhaps I shall,' he said, vaguely; and then, in a tone suggesting his true thoughts, 'and I should want to know how my own offspring fares.'

Emma sensed the danger. She nodded to her ayah. '*Mehrbani, Vaneeta.*'

The ayah bowed and smiled back, and took the child to the nursery.

'When do you leave, Matthew?'

Hervey, whose eyes had followed the child from the room, turned attentively to his hostess. 'I, er . . . tomorrow. At first light. By budgerow as far as Agra. Johnson is there with the horses.'

Somervile uncorked a bottle of champagne noisily. 'Damned carriers! They must have trotted every case for a mile and more. I had a bottle blow up in my hand last week.'

Hervey smiled. 'A perilous position you occupy these days, Somervile!'

'I wouldn't trade it for a safer one, I assure you.'

Looking now at the third in council of the Bengal presidency, with his thinning hair and spreading paunch, it was difficult to imagine the defiant defender of the civil lines twenty years ago when the Madras army was in one of its periodic foments, or a decade later the angered collector going at the gallop, pistol in hand, for the Pindaree despoilers of one of 'his' villages. Hervey knew of the first by hearsay, but he had witnessed the latter himself, and he had not the slightest doubt that, after all due allowance for the increasing effects of gravity and claret, there was no one he would rather serve with on campaign than Eyre Somervile. The erstwhile collector looked an unlikely man of action, but man of action he was, at least in his counsels, as well as being a fine judge of men, of horses, of the country, and above all of its people. No, Eyre Somervile did not seek safe billets.

'I am of the opinion that it will not be a safe place inside Bhurtpore. There's a fair battering train and good many sepoys,' said Hervey airily.

'Tell me of it.' Somervile handed him a glass after Emma.

Hervey at once retailed the order of battle, including the line number of the Company's regiments. He had fixed them in his mind as if the printed orders were in front of him – a happy knack, and one he had found could endure indefinitely if he recollected the picture once or twice a day.

Emma, by her eyes, expressed her admiration.

Hervey's exposition lasted the whole of Somervile's glass.

'There was a deal of speculation in the drawing rooms as to his capability when first the news of his appointment reached here,' said the third in council when his friend had finished. 'You know it's tattled what passed when Wellington proposed it to the Duke of York? The grand old man's supposed to have protested Combermere was a fool, to which Wellington's supposed to have replied, "Yes, but he can still take Bhurtpore."'

Hervey frowned.

'You're right, no doubt,' said Somervile, though by no means contrite. 'We all know the respect Combermere's held in from Peninsula days, but now he's no longer subordinate, and it is not for him only to implement the design of the commander-in-chief. The design must now be his own.'

Hervey merely raised an eyebrow.

'So we must trust in Wellington's faith,' continued Somervile blithely. 'And I certainly take it as a mark of Combermere's capability that he should seek out the opinion of a junior officer. How was he, by the way?'

'Cool, thoughtful. He listens very attentively, and reads too, it would seem. He had read all there was about the last siege.'

Somervile nodded with satisfaction. He liked a thoughtful commander. He considered it the prime military as well as manly virtue. But he had his fears still. 'I would wish that he knew something of India, though. The bones of a host of Englishmen and sepoys are piled in those walls, and Lake was a general of much practice. They've stood as succour to every malcontent and freebooter who thought he could tweak the tail of the Company or chew off a bit of the bone – look at how the Jhauts have rallied to that murdering usurper just because he dares hoist his colours in the place! There must be no possibility of defeat this time, Hervey. If Combermere does not take Bhurtpore, then we may as well recall Campbell and his army from Ava and hand in the keys to Fort William!'

Hervey sipped at his champagne, judging that no answer was required.

'By my reckoning there are not so many engineers,' said Somervile suddenly, and looking puzzled. 'I should have thought the requirement in a siege was for more of these, even at the expense of your own gallant arm.'

Hervey sat up again. 'I had thought the same. But it seems the engineers can't drive tunnels far enough. And Durjan Sal will have a host of cavalry to hold at bay.'

'Has Combermere good interpreters? He must have someone who is fluent in Persian as well as others for the native languages.'

It was a detail Hervey had not missed, for the officer was an old friend. 'Captain Macan, from the Sixteenth Lancers. Do you know him?'

Somervile nodded contentedly. 'Yes indeed. A most able linguist.'

'Then I regret the position appears filled.'

Somervile saw the tease. 'Believe me, Hervey, if I thought it was safe to leave Calcutta for one hour without Amherst changing his mind about this enterprise then I should take to the field at once. But you will see me there as soon as you take the place. After your gallant comrades have reduced Bhurtpore and put Durjan Sal in a cage there will be a good deal of political work to do, and quickly. The new resident will need all the help he can get in the first months, and I for one would not stand on ceremony on that account.'

Sir Charles Metcalfe's name – Ochterlony's successor – was rarely absent from any conversation in Calcutta these days. Hervey wondered he had never heard of him before, so prominent a place he now took in the counsels of state. 'I hope I shall meet him, then.'

'I think he would hope that too, for he knows your work.'
'How so?'
Somervile took the champagne bottle from its cooler and refilled their glasses. 'I shall tell you.'

It had been in July, the evening of the Ochterlony minute guns, that Somervile had declared his opinion to Emma, who had understood him at once, as she always did. 'They would do better to take yonder guns and go finish what he began at Bhurtpore,' he rasped, flinging down a sheaf of his home papers. 'This defiance by the Jhauts cannot stand!'

No one but Emma knew how much Somervile had striven those past months to conclude a satisfactory outcome to the usurpation. He had come to regard it as a rebellion against the Company rather than solely as a source of humiliation, and his object had been its crushing. 'What does Lord Amherst say? Does he feel Ochterlony's death in any measure?' Emma had asked.

'Amherst's no fool. He knows well enough that in repudiating Ochterlony's proclamation he as good as put a bullet in his head. He was decidedly ill at ease in council today, and he railed against me beforehand as if the affair was somehow of my making. He's afeard that this will play ill in London.'

'What's to be done, Eyre?' Emma had enquired in the simple certainty that her husband would know.

And, indeed, he had already weighed the options. His position in council was sometimes tenuous, but he had no desire to hold on to it through mere compliance. 'Metcalfe's here tomorrow from Haidarabad. I doubt he'll need much persuading, and Amherst'll be too fearful of going against his advice, for his stock has always stood high with the directors.'

Though Somervile would scarce admit it, Emma knew that none but her husband's stock might stand so high in council if only he would take pains to promote it a little more. She knew his manner was not best calculated to win their affection, but not a member could be in doubt of his understanding. The Governor-General had readily taken his counsel in the appointment of a successor at Dehli: as soon as Sir David Ochterlony had tendered his resignation Somervile had pressed on Lord Amherst the claims of Sir Charles Metcalfe, though perhaps that was an easy victory, for

Metcalfe had held the appointment until five years before, and his judgement had been amply tested of late as resident in the nizam's capital.

And so, next morning, he had called on Sir Charles before there was opportunity for subornation at Fort William. 'You have got to make Amherst see sense in this matter, Metcalfe. Had that place been reduced twenty years ago—'

'You forget I was Lord Lake's political officer at that time,' Sir Charles had replied, frowning. 'It is a great wonder his army achieved half of what it did. Bhurtpore was never within his grasp.'

'Let us not debate it. Now the whole of India will believe it without *our* grasp.'

'It may be so. It may well *be* without our grasp. In which case we ought not to make it an objective to grasp it.'

Somervile had relied on cool relentless logic, however. 'Nothing that is made beyond the Company's territories ought to be without the Company's grasp. It is surely the knowledge that, were the Company to will it, any country power might be subdued that secures our peace. And occasionally that will must, most regrettably, be put to the test.'

'But what say the soldiers, Somervile? What was Paget's opinion?'

'We shall never rightly know, for he's been gone these several months. All we may now do is wait on Lord Combermere. He's due here ere too long. Meanwhile I should as soon ask his deputy to play the violin as ask his opinion on the matter. The man is an ass.'

'That is a very decided opinion, Somervile. Is it much shared?'

Somervile had looked astonished. 'I have never thought to enquire! I come to my own judgement in such matters.'

Sir Charles Metcalfe had shaken his head slowly from side to side. 'Then the Governor-General, and by extension you, are without sound military counsel?'

Again, Somervile had looked surprised. '*I* am not. I have had very good counsel, and from the seat of the trouble.'

'Indeed? And are we to know whose is this counsel?'

'A dragoon captain formerly on Ochterlony's staff.'

Sir Charles Metcalfe had looked dismayed. 'A captain? Are you quite well, Somervile? There are generals and colonels here, and you put your trust in a captain of dragoons!'

187

'I do.' The tone had been less defiant than emphatic, as though he would have pit his judgement in this against all comers.

Sir Charles had laughed. 'Then I should very much like to see this man.'

'You shall, you shall. And in the breaches of that place, I hope. He's studied the Bhurtpore defences and drawn plans.'

Somervile now had the khitmagar open a second bottle. 'So you see, Hervey, Sir Charles was apprised of your observations, and I might say that they materially informed his judgement.'

Hervey raised an eyebrow. 'And what transpired?'

'What transpired is that Sir Charles studied the question for a full week and then gave his opinion in council.'

Emma smiled. 'And it was, Matthew, the most eloquent opinion you might ever hear. Even Eyre was much moved.'

Her husband nodded. 'I confess I was, my dear. I can read it aloud, too, for I have all the proceedings here at hand.'

Hervey did not object.

Somervile rummaged among some papers on a side table, then returned to his chair with a look of triumph. 'Hear this, Hervey:

> *'Your lordship, Gentlemen, we have by degrees become the paramount state of India. Although we exercised the powers of this supremacy in many instances before 1817, we have used and asserted them more generally since the existence of our influence by the events of that and the following year.'*

He glanced first at Hervey and then at Emma at the mention of 1817. They had each been so embroiled in events leading to the Pindaree war, a war which, as Sir Charles Metcalfe here made clear, had changed for ever the Company's status both north and south of the Sutlej.

> *'It then became an established principle of our policy to maintain tranquillity among all the states of India, and to prevent the anarchy and misrule which were likely to disturb the general peace. Sir John Malcolm's proceedings in Malwa were governed by this principle, as well as those of Sir David Ochterlony. In the case of succession to a principality, it seems clearly incumbent upon us, with reference to that principle, to refuse to acknowledge any but the law-*

ful successor, as otherwise we should throw the weight of our power into the scale of usurpation and injustice. Our influence is too pervading to admit of neutrality, and sufferance could operate as support. We are bound not by any positive engagement to the Bhurtpoor state, nor by any claim on her part, but by our duty as supreme guardians of general tranquillity, law, and right, to maintain the right of Rajah Balwant Sing to the raj of Bhurtpore, and we cannot acknowledge any other pretender.

'This duty seems to me to be so imperative that I do not attach any peculiar importance to the late investiture of the young rajah in the presence of Sir David Ochterlony. We should have been equally bound without that ceremony, which, if we had not been under a pre-existing obligation to maintain the rightful succession, would not have pledged us to anything beyond acknowledgement. With regard to the brothers Durjan Sal and Madhoo Sing, the competing claimants for the office of regent, I am not of the opinion that any final decision is yet required, but my present conviction is as
follows. We are not called upon to support either brother, and if we must act by force it would seem to be desirable to banish both.

'Negotiation might yet prove effectual, but if recourse to arms should become necessary, there would not be wanting of sources of consolation, since I am convinced that a display and rigorous exercise of our power, if rendered necessary, would be likely to bring back men's minds in that quarter to a proper tone, and the capture of Bhurtpoor, if effected in a glorious manner, would do us more honour throughout India, by the removal of the hitherto unfaded impressions caused by our former failure, than any other event that can be conceived.

'And then Sir Charles bowed and sat down,' said Somervile. 'And many were the sheepish looks about the place, and the oyster eyes at the memory of Ochterlony's ill-treatment.'

'In a glorious manner!' Hervey nodded, content.

'Eyre?'

'My dear?'

'You must tell what was Lord Amherst's reply.'

'Ah, yes, indeed.' He rifled through the papers in his lap. 'Here I have it – it is but brief, and rather a handsome testimony I do think. Hear this, Hervey:

*'I have hitherto entertained the opinion that our interference with
other states should be limited to cases of positive injury to the
honourable Company, or of immediate danger thereof. In that
opinion I have reason to believe that I am not supported by the
servants of the honourable Company most competent to judge of its
interests, and best acquainted with the circumstances of this
country. I should therefore have hesitated in acting upon my own
judgement in opposition to others; but I am further free to confess
that my own opinion has undergone some change, and that I am disposed to think that a system of non-interference, which appears to
have been tried and to have failed in 1806, would be tried with less
probability of success, and would be exposed to more signal failure,
after the events which have occurred, and the policy which has been
pursued during the last nineteen or twenty years. A much greater
degree of interference than was formerly called for, appears to have
resulted from the situation in which we were placed by the pacifica-
tion of 1818. It might be a hazardous experiment to relax in the
exercise of that paramount authority which our extended influence
in Malwah and Rajpootana specially has imposed upon us. Applying
these general principles to the particular cases before us, and believing that without direct
interference on our part, there is a probability of very extended dis-
turbances in the Upper provinces, I am prepared, in the first place,
to maintain, by force of arms if necessary, the succession of
Balwant Sing to the raj of Bhurtpoor.*

'And so decided did the opinion sound that the chamber was silent
for a full minute,' added Somervile, putting the papers back in
order. 'And then Amherst said simply, "I perceive that no one
would gainsay. I shall today cause instructions to be drawn up for
the commander-in-chief to begin preparations to restore Balwant
Sing to the raj of Bhurtpore." '

'In a glorious manner,' said Hervey again, shaking his head and
smiling grimly. 'We must hope for more glory than Rangoon has
seen. What a prospect – war on two fronts when we can scarce
make war on one!'

CHAPTER THIRTEEN

IN A GLORIOUS MANNER

Agra, 1 December

Not since the first Mughal emperor, Zahir ud din Mohamed – *Babur* (the tiger) – had Agra seen such a host of men under arms. Three hundred years ago almost to the day, having taken Punjab with great but economical bloodshed, Babur had come down the Jumna from his new capital at Dehli to confront the Rajpoot federation. His army had been small by comparison with theirs, as it had been small compared with that of Ibrahim Lodi in Punjab, but Babur knew how to manoeuvre them to advantage. The martial Rajpoots, two hundred thousand and more, learned defeat at Kanwaha near Fatehpur Sikri, where Babur's grandson, Akbar the Great, would in time build a new Mughal capital. After the battle, Babur, rejoicing at becoming a *ghazi*, a killer of infidels, had made great mounds of the bodies of the slain, and pillars of their heads – models to be copied at Bhurtpore centuries later with Lord Lake's men.

Lord Combermere's army knew its history. The sepoys spoke among themselves of the Futtah Bourge, the 'bastion of victory', the great tower of skulls that stood as affront to both their caste

191

and their calling. The private men of the King's regiments, their information learned more recently but with no less indignation, likewise spoke of the insult to be effaced – and, it must be certain, the retribution to be exacted on the defenders of Bhurtpore. That the Jhauts who now stood defiantly on the walls of the city were not the same enemy as Lord Lake's was of no moment. They were of the same country, and they dared to oppose John Company and the King.

Red was the colour that predominated in the camps, but a vivid red, scarlet, the colour of blood, not the mellow red of the great sandstone fort nearby, nor the rich deep red of the silks that clothed men and women alike in the *chaupars* and bazaars of this old imperial city. The Company's native infantry regiments were as regular in their appearance as Lord Combermere had known the duke's in Spain, save that the sepoys' legs were bare. The cavalry, too, had all the appearance of his own command at that time, except that in the hands of some was a weapon that hitherto he had seen only in the hands of the enemy – the lance, its pennants now fluttering in the ranks of His Majesty's Sixteenth Lancers, who aped their models in this part by wearing the *schapska* of Bonaparte's Polish lancers instead of the shako. Hervey could not look at their scarlet bibs without a fraction of distaste, for blue had been the colour of all who did not fight in lines, and he thought it needless show. Show in both senses, for scouting and outpost work was hard enough at the best of times without robin-redbreast display.

Hervey had been busy on his own account with matters of uniform. For some time now he had become convinced that for field service their own coats should be modified in the same way as had their horses' bridles. Early on in the Peninsula the regiment had doubled the leather browband with chain so that a sword could not cut it and make the bridle fall from the animal's head. He had listened to accounts of Maratha and Rajpoot swordsmanship and learned that a favoured device was the passing cut at the shoulder, and he had concluded that chain on the shoulder – as of old – would serve them well. Major Joynson had been persuaded, and the metalworkers of Calcutta had been engaged to fashion six inches of mail, three inches wide, for each dragoon's shoulder. Lord Combermere saw it when he inspected his troops at Agra, and much approved. And when, three days later, he went by dawk upstream to Muttra to inspect the other half of his army, and there found Hervey and his troop, he remarked on it favourably, so that Hervey was in no doubt that Lord Combermere's estimation of him was truly of the highest order.

'I intend beginning a general advance on Bhurtpore three days hence, on the ninth,' the commander-in-chief told him as he turned his horse away. 'I shall make all appearances of wanting to parley, so that they do not take steps to inundate the defences, but I shall want you to break from the force at last light and move to seize the bund. Then at dawn next day I shall send with all despatch a force to relieve you.'

It was exactly as Hervey had urged at Fort William. 'Very good, General'

'Two squadrons, you said.'

'Yes, sir. One of the Eleventh's, and a rissalah from Skinner's Horse, they with their galloper guns. The horse artillery would only impede us.'

Combermere nodded, but slowly, as if considering. 'The Eleventh, yes – and your own troop, I should suppose.'

Hervey nodded his confirmation.

'But the irregular horse . . . are they to be so relied upon?'

Hervey smiled assuringly. 'I may say with utter certainty, your lordship, that one could do no better in trusting them with one's very life. Three years ago, in Burma, I had proof of it myself.'

Combermere nodded again, this time more definitely. 'Very well, then, I shall have Colonel Watson write the orders at once. Is there any more you would have me do?'

'No, sir. Except, of course, that our orders should not be made general.'

'Of course.'

Hervey knew he had suggested the obvious, but he had his reasons. Combermere rode high in his estimation from all that had gone before in Portugal and Spain, but this was India.

'Cap'n 'Ervey, sir, if yon farrier's sick another day I'm gooin' to 'ave to ask one 'o' t'Eleventh's to do Gilbert. Them corns are gettin' bad.'

Gilbert's shoes were a problem that Hervey could do without. It wasn't just Gilbert, either, for although Corporal Brennan's assistants were capable of admirable cold-shoeing by replacing worn iron with the stock shoes carried by each dragoon, they were not yet proficient enough to make a therapeutic set, and there were half a dozen troopers needing that attention. 'I'll speak to their colonel, then,' replied Hervey, still wondering when he might have the orders which would give him authority to address his mission.

Johnson was content. 'Lord Combermere looked 'appy enough this mornin'. I were tellin' all them green'eads that fancies themselves as dragoons about 'im at T'loose.'

Hervey looked pained. 'Not anything in connection with General Slade, I hope.'

'Of course it were about Slade. That were t'story!'

Indeed it was a story. Lord Combermere's timely appearance at Toulouse had made General Slade drop his prey – and Hervey had raced back to the regiment a free man again. But Combermere, as far as Hervey could tell, had never known how providential had been his arrival. He had known only the eagerness of the wounded cornet to be back in action. There was a time, however – and certainly at Toulouse – when Hervey would have been truly perturbed, believing that the disparaging of a senior officer, even one such as Slade, would have been inimical to discipline. Now he cared not at all. The canteen was entitled to its views, as long as it held them in private, so to speak. And if they could disparage Slade they could extol Combermere, as it seemed they might. Johnson did the commander-in-chief a service therefore; Hervey ought to commend him, indeed. There were always difficulties attendant on commending Johnson, though. 'That reminds me—'

But Johnson was not finished. 'Word is in t'canteen that them walls is fifty feet thick, and made of bones and solid rock.'

Hervey raised an eyebrow. 'How do the intelligence agents of the canteen believe solid rock and bones are mixed together?'

Johnson did not consider it an impossible notion. 'They didn't say, only that the walls is so thick it'd take a month o' Sundays just to scratch 'em.'

Hervey frowned. 'They're thick, Johnson, I grant you that, but not fifty feet, and not solid rock. They'll withstand some battering, but they're bound to be breached at some point, and then it will be the bayonet in the old way.'

'Let's 'ope so, sir,' said Johnson matter-of-factly, taking the reins of Hervey's second charger as Hervey himself began picking up each of the little Marwari's feet to check for stones. ''Ave yer 'eard there've been some deserters an' all?'

'There are always deserters, Johnson,' replied Hervey, just as matter-of-fact, picking out a pebble from the off-fore.

'Ay, but they reckon these've gone over to t'Jhauts.'

'Who reckons? How do they know?'

'Corporal McCarthy 'eard. 'E always 'ears everything if they're Irish.'

Hervey continued checking his mare's feet (they looked in good shape). 'And who are they from, these men?'

'T'artillery.'

Hervey looked up. 'The *artillery*?'

'Ay, and supposed to be good gunners an' all.'

Hervey tutted. He was not disposed to think that they could have gone over to the enemy, for he could see no inducement ... except that as experienced gunners their services would be keenly sought, and therefore, he supposed, well rewarded. But surely they would not—'

'An' one of 'em was at Waterloo, even!'

That concluded it. 'Tattle, Johnson. I should sooner imagine the sar'nt-major a preacher!'

But Johnson was unmoved. 'Well, that's what they're saying, Cap'n 'Ervey. Is there owt else?'

Hervey shook his head. 'No, I believe we may offsaddle and give them some hay.' There was only grass, but hay was what they called it still. 'And we can take our ease too for an hour or so. Call me if Mr Sledge comes in. He said he might come up from Agra today. Oh, and ... see if you can find out any more about these deserters, will you?'

There was much to do, even had he not had the assignment at the Bhurtpore jheels. The camp was beginning to look like a bestiary come alive, with every manner of creature to provide milk or flesh for the army, or muscle or a strong back. His own troop might occupy him every minute, though for the most part they were not without experience. It was strange that they had seen action – fierce action – but had not yet been 'shot over', as the saying went.

195

The affair at the river three years before had turned them into veterans overnight, and it had been long enough past to give them the taste for more of it now. Yet there were things he must check for himself – the firelocks especially, since he expected that what would come first against them at the jheels was better seen off with the carbine than the sabre. It was not something he could leave to his subalterns. Or rather, *would* leave. It was out of the question in any case to give the duty to Green, still as ineffectual as ever. Indeed, he would not even have passed the duty to Seton Canning, had he been with him still, for certain things were properly his particular responsibility.

In the afternoon, he received copies of general and field general orders. He was keen to see the appointments to both the staff and to commands of brigades and divisions, for there had been endless speculation and not a little wagering, and he retired to the relative peace of his tent to peruse them with as much leisure as seemed apt:

GENERAL ORDERS

Head-Quarters, Agra, 3rd Dec. 1825
The following officers are appointed Brigadier-Generals from 1st inst., subject to the confirmation of the Right Hon. The Governor-General in Council:

Brevet-Col. J. M'Combe, 14th Foot. Brevet-Col. J. W. Sleigh, C.B. 11th Dragoons. Col. W. J. Edwards, 14th Foot. Lieut.-Col. Childers to be Brigadier. Capt. Hervey to be Loc.-Major. Lieut. Maxwell to be Aide-de-Camp to Brigadier-General Sleigh.

Division of Cavalry. – Brigadier-General J. W. Sleigh, C.B. to Command.

1st Cavalry Brigade. – Brigadier Murray, C.B. 16th Lancers, to Command. Capt. W. Harris, 16th Lancers, Major of Brigade. – To consist of H.M. 6th Lt. Dragoons, 16th Lancers, 6th, 8th, and 9th Regiments of Light Cavalry.

2nd Cavalry Brigade. – Brigadier M. Childers, 11th Dragoons, to Command. Lieutenant G. Williamson to be Major of Brigade. – To consist of H.M. 11th Dragoons, 3rd, 4th and 10th Regiments of Light Cavalry. – N.B. The Brigade of Irregular Cavalry, consisting of the 1st Local Horse, under Col. James Skinner. Troop 6th Lt.

Dragoons under Maj. M. P. Hervey.
1st Division of Infantry . . .

On went the list, specifying each and every non-permanent appointment. 'Baggage-Master of the Army', as onerous a position as any might be, was to be filled by Lieut. J. M'Dermot, H.M. 14th Foot. And 'Brigadier-Gen. Sleigh, C.B., will be pleased to select, and send in the names of three smart, active, and intelligent Non-commissioned Officers of Dragoons, for appointments as Assistant Baggage Master of Divisions.' Hervey thought he had better have someone in mind lest the general devolve one of the number on his troop. Stray would be best, of course, except that he was not from his troop. Neither was he by any standard smart.

And then, enclosed with these orders, there were others – a long exhortation, and in a style he knew from many a time in the Peninsula and France. The duke's own, indeed:

FIELD GENERAL ORDERS

Head-Quarters, Camp, Agra, Dec. 2, 1825
The Army now assembling for Service on the Agra and Muttra Frontier, being about to advance, His Excellency the Commander-in-Chief requests, that Officers commanding Regiments will impress upon their Officers, &c. the imperious necessity which exists, for each individual reducing the number of his servants to the lowest scale, and taking the Field as little encumbered with Baggage as possible; and desires that they will use their utmost endeavours to prevent superfluous individuals
following the Bazaars of their respective Corps. All superfluous Baggage will be left at Muttra and Agra respectively, in the first instance, by Divisions, on advancing.

The March about to commence being through the Territory of an Ally of the British Government, and not that of an enemy, His Excellency prohibits in the strictest manner, all marauding or plundering; and desires that Officers commanding Divisions and Brigades will cause it to be three times proclaimed to their respective Corps, that the Provost-Marshal has received peremptory orders to seize, and inflict summary punishment of Death, on any individual or individuals caught in the act of plundering. In thus

197

*publicly promulgating the decided measures to be resorted to in sup-
port of discipline, His Excellency feels assured, from the correct
habits of the European and Native Troops under his command, that,
as far as they are concerned, the warning above given is unnecessary; but as the followers of Bazaars of Corps might avail
themselves of opportunities to
plunder the inhabitants of the country and others, the Commander-
in-Chief deems it necessary to promulgate thus publicly the
retribution which will await such conduct.*

It was a handsome confidence, thought Hervey, if ill-disguised in
its attempt to avoid besmirching the soldiers of the Line. It could
scarcely be otherwise, this latter, though. His own troop he might
vouch for, the NCOs certainly, but the arousal of baser instincts
was something he had seen all too often to be so sure he would not
see the same again, for there was nothing saintly about the men of
E Troop. Better to tell them straight, perhaps with the excuse that
one man might lose his wits in the noise of battle, and that Hervey's
warning to him now might thereby save him his neck.

He read through half a dozen more routine orders and calls for
returns, alternately relishing his independent command and ruing
it, depending on the requirements of the paper. Just as he was
nearing the end, a despatch rider from the Cavalry Staff Corps
rode into the lines. Hervey watched keenly as the red-jacketed
dragoon reported to the regimental orderly tent, whence the
corporal of the day emerged at once to bring him to Hervey's.

Hervey was obliged to sign a receipt for the contents of the staff
dragoon's sabretache. 'More, evidently, than just a call for
returns,' he said as he did so.

'Sir,' replied the man, giving nothing away, though he hoped it
was indeed more than a routine despatch. He had just risked his
neck in a gallop from Lord Combermere's headquarters, and he
would prefer to return there with something more than a list.

The corporal of the day watched and listened keenly for any
indication of what the despatch contained. His standing in the
canteen would be raised immeasurably if he brought news in
advance of actual orders.

Hervey took the despatch, broke the headquarters seal and read
quickly, but silently:

FIELD SPECIAL ORDER

Head-Quarters, Muttra, Dec. 6, 1825
Major Hervey, 6th Lt. Dragoons, is required to form a mounted
party for a special task, consisting of one squadron H.M. 11th Lt.
Dragoons, and one rissalah 1st Local Horse. The party is to be
ready at once to undertake the task on orders emanating directly
from H.E. the Commander-in-Chief, along the lines already
communicated. The object and design may not be
communicated to any man, however, until approval by H.E.
By Order of His Excellency the Right Hon. The Commander-in-
Chief,

(Signed) W. N. WATSON
Adjutant-General.

It was no more or less than he needed. 'Thank you, staff dragoon.
Please return the following reply.'

The man had his pocketbook and pencil ready. 'Sir.'

'Major Hervey acknowledges receipt of the special order, and
comprehends it.'

'Sir.'

The corporal of the day looked disappointed. He would have to
embellish his account to the canteen considerably.

'That is all,' said Hervey, when the staff dragoon looked up
again.

The man slipped his pocketbook back inside his jacket.

'Up!' said the corporal of the day.

The two right hands shot, as one, to shako peaks, and Hervey
nodded to acknowledge. As the two men left, he called the troop
orderly corporal waiting outside. 'Have Mr Perry come, please,
Rudd.' He then mastered himself fully: 'And Mr Green. And the
sar'nt-major of course.'

'Sir!'

Hervey was glad it was Rudd. Rudd was an honorary pal – more
than honorary, since the original pals were now but two. And
there was something that nurture in that corner of the Great Plain
did by way of making comrades across the ranks. 'Corporal
Rudd?'

'Sir?'

'How handy were you about your mother's shop?'

'*Sir?*' Corporal Rudd was glad there were no witnesses to this exchange; he did not like being reminded of the millinery.

'I mean, how well are you with needle and thread?'

'As good as any, sir. Have you something to be mended?'

'No. Johnson could do that. I need a more skilled needle. Embroidery.'

Rudd looked puzzled. 'I can do that, sir, if it's not too knotty. What is it you have in mind, sir?'

'I need something that passes for a major's star on these epaulettes.'

Rudd was all pleasure at the prospect.

'But you shall have to unpick it when the siege is done. Local rank only, I fear.'

'Very good, sir. But rank is rank, isn't it, sir?'

'Thank you, Rudd. You are the first to hear.'

'You mean not even Johnson, sir?'

'Not even Johnson. Go to it, then – the officers and sar'nt-major. Oh, and say nothing to Johnson.'

Rudd smiled. 'Ay, sir.'

Hervey lost no time that afternoon. He told his officers and serjeant-major the contents of the several orders, and added his own. He wanted the troop to ride at light scales, with no bat-horses (he would long remember the dismay on Cornet Green's face) save with the serjeant-major for extra powder and ball. The baggage he wanted dividing into two: field stores and other necessaries – that which could be carried by pack-animal – to be put in charge of the quartermaster-serjeant and to move with the rest of the brigade; the remainder – camp stores and general comforts – to stand ready under Corporal Stray with the bullock carts here at Muttra awaiting opportunity to rejoin them, which, he believed, there would soon be once the siege was under way. 'But it shall have to be judged right,' he said. 'I don't want the Jhaut cavalry cutting them up, which is why I want Stray with them.'

Serjeant-Major Armstrong smiled. Corporal Stray was the fattest man in the regiment. The order 'light scales' had at once precluded his riding in the first echelon, for Stray was generally now to be found on the box rather than in the saddle. And yet there was not a man in the Sixth who was more at home in the field than Corporal Stray. His economy with stores was celebrated, he could fashion any necessary from the most unpromising raw materials, and quickly too, and he was utterly imperturbable in the face of enemy and superiors alike. Once, in Paris after Waterloo, he had been posted as lone sentry on a bridge that the Prussians were intent on blowing up for solely retributive reasons. The explosive in place, the officer of engineers had asked him to quit the span and seek cover, to which the then Private Stray had replied, 'Not until properly relieved by the corporal, sir.' The Prussians had lit the fuses, but still Stray would not budge, standing on-guard with the bayonet when they tried to remove him bodily, so that in the end the engineers had had to rush about frantically pulling the fuses from the barrels of gunpowder. Corporal Stray was not a man to have in the front rank at a review, but he was without doubt a man to have at hand on campaign, and Hervey was pleased for having the promise of him for a time.

After doing what he needed with his own troop, Hervey had addressed himself to the matter of the other corps. The commanding officer, the senior major, proved difficult at first, demanding to know what was the object of the special task despite the clear injunction in the written order. At length he had given way, however, naming the captain to do duty with his squadron, and had acceded at once to Hervey's request for a farrier. The regiments of the yellow circle, as the cavalry knew themselves, could have their difficulties with each other, but these remained within the circle and were fiercely guarded. Perhaps it was the fellowship of the horse, the common essential of their arm, for the horse took no side for himself in a fight, instead submitting humbly but nobly to the bit in whichever cavalry had impressed him. Sometimes, his rider unseated, he ran away, terror-stricken, but for the most part he remained dutiful, despite all privation. Hervey looked about at the Eleventh's troopers as he left the lines. They were as mixed a bunch as any in Hindoostan, but bigger than his own in the main by a good half-hand. If they bore the field well, they would be formidable indeed when it came to closing with the Jhaut cavalry – more so than his own, he had to admit, for size told when it came to a clash.

Next he had gone to Skinner's Horse, and if he had anticipated vexations with the Eleventh, he was positively certain that they would be legion with the irregulars since Colonel Skinner was in personal command. He had never met James Skinner, he had only heard of him. Indeed, there had been times since coming to India when he had heard nothing but of Skinner and his silladar horse. Three regiments there were of these singular cavalrymen, of which the second was commanded by James's brother Robert, and the third, hastily raised for service in East Bengal five years before, had without doubt saved his own troop in the affair of the Chittagong river. The Sixth Light Dragoons, or Hervey's troop at least, regarded them as special friends. They admired their skill as horsemen, and with the lance; they admired their boldness and proud independence; and they admired their determination to see things through. Skinner's was not native horse in the sense the canteen would understand it – serviceable but inferior: Skinner's was a corps apart.

Their camp was a vivid, lively place, noisier by half than any King's regiment's, with much music and singing. It might have been Tamerlane's own, the canvas and caparisons, the silks and the streamers, and all of the richest colours. As Hervey rode towards the guard tent, the sowars of the picket began falling in under their daffadar, lance pennants picking up the merest breath of wind, men and lances otherwise like statuary.

A syce ran forward to hold Gilbert's bridle as Hervey dismounted. The daffadar saluted. Hervey turned, to find a jemadar beaming at him. 'This way, please, sahib.'

Hervey followed to the tent of the woordi-major, who explained that both the second in command and the adjutant were at exercise. Then a bearer came into the tent, and, after an exchange of words, the woordi-major said that Colonel Skinner himself would see him. Hervey put his forage cap back on and walked with him across the maidan to a yellow-striped pavilion set to one side nearest the river. The sentry came to attention as the two began walking the line of whitened stones. As they reached the beaded entrance a voice called from inside. 'You are most welcome, Major Hervey!'

Hervey noted with appreciation how nimble must be the regiment's hircarrahs. He pushed aside the strings of beads and paid his compliments.

'I know very well who you are, Major Hervey. I have naturally heard all there is of the affair of the Chittagong river. I stand in admiration, sir,' said James Skinner, designated commandant of what was officially the 1st Local Horse. He held out his hand.

Hervey took it, and acknowledged the accolade with a bow of the head. 'But it is I who stand in admiration, Colonel Skinner.'

'Well, well, let not either of us stand long. Take a seat. You will have some whisky?'

It was a moment or so before Hervey could judge whether he was speaking to a British or a native officer. One half of Colonel Skinner was Scotch, his father's half. His voice was that of a British officer, perhaps a shade fastidious, but without all the music of the native voice, the *hanji-banji* as Somervile called it. But it was the Rajpoot half, his mother noble-born, that presented itself in appearance most. James Skinner was forty-seven years old, his hair was silvering, and his face, though benign, spoke of many years' campaigning, and for several masters (only in Lord Lake's day had he thrown in with the Company). He had raised and trained the corps himself. He had given it its creed, and thence its uniform, and had led it to victory after victory against any that would oppose those 'sworn to die'. His wealth from booty was said to be prodigious, he had three wives – one Mahomedan, one Hindoo, one Christian – yet he was no dissolute nabob. He was as much a scholar as Babur had been, speaking and writing flawless Persian, and knowledgeable in the history and art of all of Hindoostan. His men worshipped him. But why was he here, in the field, in person? Hervey wondered. He was three years older than the duke had been at Waterloo. He might easily have devolved command on an executive officer. The share in any booty, such that it might be in a campaign made in the territory of an ally, would anyway go to him as the colonel of the corps – even if London (Hervey understood) would not officially recognize his rank. Did Colonel Skinner, who could have taken his ease in Dehli or on his jagirs nearby, crave still the sword and the saddle for their own sake? There were such men, and Hervey saluted them. Indeed, he took more pleasure in Skinner's chair and his whisky at that moment than if they had been those of the duke himself.

'Jaswant Sing tells me you have a promising seat. He says you were quick to the Rajpoot way of riding.'

Hervey was gratified, and smiled obligingly, though puzzled that Skinner should know of it. 'But I fear I had the best of attention and horses. I could not imitate those airs when later I tried them on my own horses.'

Colonel Skinner nodded slowly as if he understood. 'Woordi-major, you may go to your ledgers or you may stay and drink whisky, as you please. Which is it to be?'

The woordi-major answered in English. 'Huzoor, I have many papers to return for the Lord Combermere.'

'Very well, my friend. There will be time for us to drink whisky when we have taken Bhurtpore.'

'*Ji, huzoor,*' and he continued in Urdu, though too quickly for Hervey to catch more than the odd word.

Colonel Skinner took it up, but Hervey managed to catch even less. They seemed to be turning over an idea – about horses, he thought, but the idiom was beyond him.

When the woordi-major had gone, Colonel Skinner poured more whisky. 'Now, Major Hervey, what is it that His Excellency has in mind?'

Hervey was surprised at the connection Colonel Skinner made, but he judged it of no matter; it was just the way of things in India. 'I beg you would read this, Colonel,' he said, handing him the order.

Colonel Skinner took longer to read it than Hervey expected. At length, the commandant looked up and said, thoughtfully, 'The jheels?'

Hervey saw little point in protesting. 'May I ask how you knew, Colonel?'

'It is evident, from the size and composition of the party, that the object is detached from the fortress, for otherwise it would be futile. There can be but one such object if one has read the accounts of Lord Lake's endeavours.'

'Do you know the bund, Colonel?'

'Of course.'

'I am of the opinion that such a force as mine could hold them until relieved – within the twenty-four hours following. We should rely greatly on your galloper guns, of course.'

Colonel Skinner nodded. 'I am of this opinion, too. I cannot suppose the Jhauts will garrison the jheels until they perceive the

204

army is moving on them. There is much industry in the Jhauts, but little imagination. They will work most fiercely to eject you once you have them, however. Who is to lead the relief?'

'General Sleigh, or perhaps even General Reynell, as I understand.'

'Good. Combermere sees its importance then.' The commandant drained his glass. 'You will stay and dine with us, Major Hervey?'

Hervey saw his duty done. 'I thank you, yes. My corporal . . .'

'He will be the guest of my daffadars.'

When dinner was finished, more hours later than Hervey had thought possible, Colonel Skinner accompanied him to the picket to see him on his way. It was a fresh night, not cold, with a full moon. Torches blazed about the camp, and beyond in the city and the many other camps about it. As they came upon the picket, Corporal Wainwright led up Gilbert. Beside him, a naik led another horse, smaller but with twice the blood.

'Marwari, Major Hervey, of very choice breeding and schooled in our classical manner. I hope you will accept him.'

Hervey was all but dumbstruck. In hand was as fine a stallion as he had seen in Hindoostan – black, with a white face and massive neck. 'Sir, I . . .'

'He is called Chetak. Do you know the legend of Chetak, Major Hervey?'

'Indeed I do, Colonel. I know it was Chetak's leap that let the Maharana Pratap kill Man Singh's mahout.'

'And much more, Major Hervey.'

'Indeed, Colonel. Much more.'

'But the Maharana's Chetak was a grey, Major Hervey. And I would not have you ride *two* greys. So we make you a gift of one of our best bloods, and one, needless to say, who is well schooled in the Rajpoot airs.'

Hervey was a long time in his leave-taking. He had met a man among men, and he had known the regal hospitality of the Rajpoots. These things were to be savoured and honoured, even at times like this. Especially at times like this. There was no place for a stallion in his troop, but what a saddle-horse he would make when they were returned to Calcutta. And what a sire, too.

That night, though very late, he wrote to Somervile:

I am very glad of your letter (numbered 7), and especially its intelligence of Peto. How pleased he will be to slip anchor and be up the Irawadi at last! Let us hope, as you say the gossip has it, that a treaty is near.

What a camp this is! How I wish you could see it! Each fighting man with us has more than one follower, and a large bazaar accompanies the camp besides. We carry the men's tents on elephants, and each elephant has two men, four bhistis to each troop, a cook to every 16 men, every horse has a man to cut grass for him, the men have six camels and two men per troop to carry their beds. Then come the gram grinders, tailors, bakers, butchers, calasseys, or men for pitching tents, and many others. Each hospital has six men, and of these there are 40, making 240, and there are 50 dhoolies for a regiment. I should say that for 560 officers and men we must have 5,600 followers, this counting in the bazaar and officers' servants. I have in my own service 14 men, 5 camels, and a hackery, five horses and two ponies, and this for a mere captain of dragoons. Although this night I have received the gift of a magnificent Marwari stallion of Colonel Skinner of the Native Horse. It is tempting to ponder on the nature of the battle to come, and whether we shall see the single combat again that was the purpose of these great brutes. I trust not. I think there is a more glorious manner in which to take Bhurtpore, and it must be with art and powder in very large measure rather than with the breasts of brave men and horses . . .

Hervey completed another page of observations, then laid down his pen. He knew full well that many a brave man's breast would be torn open, sepoy's and King's man's alike. And he trusted it would be sepoy and King's man in fair measure, since it did not do for the King's men to be preserved, like Bonaparte's *Garde*, while the legionary Company regiments were expended. But he knew, also, that the butcher's bill would be determined in large measure by his own aptness – and audacity – in executing the special order. The affair of the jheels would be decided by a few, but the price of failure paid by the many.

CHAPTER FOURTEEN

L'AUDACE!

The early hours of 10 December

The order had come by semaphore from Agra at first light the day before. The divisions were to advance on Bhurtpore before dawn on the 10th, the cavalry brigades leading. It was not a difficult movement. Bhurtpore, Agra and Muttra formed an almost equal-sided triangle, with Muttra at the apex, and the object of operations at the base, left. The roads, the sides of the triangle (although the base itself was not straight) were good and wide, permitting easy movement of formed bodies of men. The rains had gone and there was no rutting to speak of. The country either side was more flat than not, and not too jungled, so that if the divisions found the roads blocked it would be no very great impediment to progress, even for wheels. Not that opposition was expected. Each day the divisional commanders had sent patrols as far as three or four leagues, without sign of a Jhaut picket, and a cloud of spies, in exchange for quite modest amounts of silver, had daily brought assurances that the roads beyond, all the way to the walls of the city itself, were open and empty of troops. Indeed, the only obstacle to movement would be the sacred cows that ambled with perfect liberty along the old Mughal highways, for Krishna himself had been born in Muttra, and so the sacred cows wandered on sacred ground.

The distance they had to march was no great trial to either shoe or boot – or even to the bare feet of the sepoy. From Muttra it was but eight leagues, at a cavalry trot no more than three hours. Even at the sepoys' steady rate of three miles an hour it was only a matter of eight – an easy day's business. The light companies of King's regiments could do it by forced march in a morning (the road from Agra was a little longer, winding through Fatehpur Sikri and the battlefield of Kanwaha, but not by much more than two hours or so). And Lord Combermere's orders were clear in respect of not encumbering the columns with excess baggage, so that by Hervey's estimation there could be no doubting their relief at the jheels by last light. His only worry was the reliefs finding him. The jheels were not especially difficult to find, but they lay to the north-west of the fortress, and were therefore masked to the advance. There was always the chance that the Jhauts would cut the road nearest the fortress once the game was up, and so the relief force would have to be strong enough to force the road or else find the long way round via the south-west, through water-logged pasture. Hervey, conferring with Brigadier-General Sleigh, had therefore decided to send back guides as soon as he had taken the bund.

The previous day had been all bustle throughout the camps at Muttra and, he imagined, at Agra too. His own troop, forewarned, had had an easier time of it, and the unprotesting Corporal Stray had received a steady flow of camp comforts into his makeshift depot. In the afternoon, Hervey had received orders by hand of one of Lord Combermere's aides-de-camp that he was to seize the bund as soon as was possible after dawn the following morning, with the limitation that he must not leave Muttra before midnight. He had at once sent word to the Eleventh and to Skinner's Horse, and their two squadrons had assembled at the Krishna Ghat a little before midnight, their captains – or jemadar in the case of the Skinner's rissalah – having spent an hour and more with him beforehand to agree the conduct of the affair.

'What is the parole, Johnson?' he asked, as he took Gilbert's reins from him. He had not asked him that in ten years. It had been their ritual – their game, almost – before any affair began. It had started in Spain when his groom had drawn the fire of the regiment's outlying picket early one morning having searched all night like the good shepherd himself, but to bring in a lost horse. His habitual reply to any sentry's challenge to state the password was 'Sheffield', to which the equally invariable response was not 'Pass, friend' but 'Pass, Johnson.' Except that that night in Spain he had stumbled on the horse-artillery picket, and since then Johnson had had a healthy respect for the daily parole.

'Dehli,' he replied, a trifle gruffly, feeling the effects of a long day. 'What a lark *this* is. Do we get t'first pick o' t'pudding?'

Even in India, where dragoons fed like princes compared with home, Johnson's metaphors were still principally of the table. Nevertheless, Hervey thought to continue with it for a while. 'There will be no pudding, certainly not one with plums. Lord Combermere made it clear: we are putting down rebels; the country is not the enemy. Durjan Sal will lose his possessions, as well as his head, but that's not likely to amount to more than a measure of grog for every sepoy.'

Johnson muttered his disappointment. He would have to rely on his own resources rather than the prize agents'. So be it. He had always had a good nose. And he always knew how to draw the line between honest booty and plain loot. He had been as condemnatory as the officers when he heard of the Fifty-ninth's men in Agra stealing across the river in the night to prise gemstones from the walls of the Taje Mahale. No, Johnson's speciality was military, things that an officer might want for his own service or souvenir, or else liquids and perishables, which might sell at an inflated price before the sutlers arrived with their stocks.

Hervey sprang into the saddle with almost the same ease as he had at first riding school. The thought pleased him, though he knew he favoured his left shoulder still, as much by instinct as real necessity; the twinges had now grown much less painful, and greatly fewer. He gathered up the reins and shortened his stirrups one hole – which vexed Johnson greatly, for he had ridden at that length since leaving Dehli. Hervey looked about him. The moon, the torches and the campfires lit up the ghat as if it were almost day. His only regret was that, in leaving so far in advance of the main body, he would not see the division drawn up, for this was an affair in the old way and he might not see its like in another ten years. He wondered for the moment if the prospect displeased him, but he could not dwell on it since he had a mind to be off at the very instant he had given his own orders to advance – as the minute hand of his watch reached twelve. They would have six more hours of pitch dark, then one of twilight until, at seven, there would be no more dark to conceal them within hearing distance of a sentry.

The luminescent face of Daniel Coates's gift-hunter told him he had but four minutes to wait. There was light enough to see even the plain face of his own bought watch, but in a couple more hours, when the moon had set, he would be glad of Mr Prior's clever work. Four minutes only – perhaps he ought to make a start? They all knew Bonaparte's lament that anything could be bought but time. Very well. He would pay them back their four minutes when the Motee Bund was theirs. No trumpets, though. They were Lord Combermere's picked men; they had no need of fanfares.

'Column, walk-march!'

He had thought very carefully about the order of march. It was not the first time he had ridden with lancers, but their handiness at night was uncertain. He would lead with his own men, therefore. The trouble was, he didn't have a cornet, for Green he considered not worthy of the name, and he wished now he had asked Eustace Joynson to find him some billet in Agra. He had even thought of leaving him with Corporal Stray, with the other useless baggage, except that it might have been an affront that demeaned the whole troop. So Serjeant Collins would command the advance guard, and command it well too. And Corporal McCarthy would take Collins's place at the rear of the first division. Next would come the Eleventh, and then Skinner's with their two galloper guns. Riding with Hervey himself would be a galloper from each squadron, and a lieutenant of engineers. No man who had served in the Peninsula could have aught but regard for the sappers and pioneers. They had breached and mined, and built and bridged for the army from Lisbon to Toulouse, in baking sun and freezing rain, shot over as they worked, even as the line took cover. Hervey, for sure, had that regard in highest measure. If only they could ride, though. Then he would have been able to take a whole company of them instead of just their officer, relying on the unskilled labour of the dragoons.

Eight leagues: they would cover them all mounted – no leading – as if it were just a long point in Leicestershire. They could trot for the first hour, for the Eleventh's patrols had had orders in the afternoon to picket that night at the two-league point. Thereafter they could proceed at a walk, which would give the advance guard time to scout properly. Hervey did not know how many of his command had ridden an Indian road by night. It was not so bad at this time of year, when days were cooler, but the traffic could be greater even than by day – mounted men and pedestrians alike escaping from the sun's heat, hackeries and elephants, palanquins and dongas. And always the sacred cow of the Hindoo, couching, utterly unmoved by all he heard and saw.

But the country people of this corner of Rajpootana knew that John Company was about (they sold him all they could in Agra and Muttra), though at night they took care to keep themselves scarce, for no one knew what the sahibs would do when the time came, or even Durjan Sal and his Jhauts if they dared leave the fastness of Bhurtpore. And why, indeed, should the Jhauts do that? Bhurtpore had stood against the *gora log* before. Against Lord Lake, even – he who had dealt the mighty Marathas such a blow. Was not Bhurtpore impregnable? Let John Company try if he dare, they said among themselves – as he tried in vain at Rangoon – and here he would meet the same as there. Only let us not be about the roads when he does try, they said. Let us not run or ride to Bhurtpore to warn Durjan Sal. He has his own spies for that. Let us secure ourselves at night in our villages, with fires burning to ward off marauders, and trust in the boy Krishna, our neighbour from Muttra become a god – and all the other gods that would protect us poor country people from armies of any colour.

They made the Eleventh's distant picket at ten minutes to two. Fires burned bright, but the two dozen dragoons were all alert and anxious for their own off. They even raised a cheer as Hervey led the column past at the walk.

'Nothing to report,' called the officer, standing wrapped in his cloak by a lantern. 'Your scouts went by not five minutes ago.'

Hervey thanked Providence it was Collins in front of him. There were but three men in the regiment he could trust so. Four, properly, for there could be no doubting RSM Lincoln – or rather Quartermaster Lincoln now – even though Hervey had never patrolled with him. A year or so more and there would be another two or three: Wainwright had the makings, certainly – he wanted only experience atop his courage – and Myles Vanneck. But for the present it could only be Collins, or Armstrong, or Seton Canning. The task was straightforward enough: judge, clear the route, report. But it wasn't easy. At night the ablest of men lost their capacity to do what they did by day. They imagined too much, or else too little, they lost command of their dragoons, they failed to observe and forgot what to report. No, Hervey had formed the opinion over long years that scouting at night tested a man more than did the worst trials of the day. He cursed that Cornet Green was so worthless. He wished the man had stayed in the pretty sort of shop that his father must one time have kept. Even though he had no need of him, Collins was entitled to have an officer share the danger. He ought, indeed, to have all of Green's pay.

Hervey's orders to Collins had been few, because they were unnecessary. All that Collins needed to know was the route and rate of advance. Certain of each, he now proved the way with the surest touch. Here and there he had to make a sleeping hackery driver pull his team off the road, but otherwise his progress towards the great fortress was unchecked. For almost five hours without pause, until just before seven o'clock, at the very first intimation of the dawn, he led the Company's troops into the territory of Bhurtpore, and Hervey had not a moment's hesitation in following.

Then, as arranged, only a quarter of an hour later than Hervey had predicted, the advance guard halted at the last village before the road opened onto the plain of the fortress city, and sent word back to him. He was not many minutes coming up, and fewer still at the halt. He had his telescope out at once and made a sweep of the plain.

Nothing, not even the outline of the distant walls. That was good. He risked a great deal in cutting things so fine, but without the help of a bit of daylight he couldn't find the jheels, let alone the bund. He was counting on poor camp discipline among the Jhauts; it was, he knew from experience, a peculiarly British

212

rule for troops to be stood-to with arms for the dawn watch. He counted here on there being but a few sentries, tired after a long night, alert only to their relief at daybreak.

He would take over the lead himself now, for they must soon leave the obliging road. He remembered clearly that it curved in a full right angle north towards the fortress, but a curve at night, especially a shallow one, was not easy to gauge. It would all have been so much easier with a guide. That, however, he had judged impossible without somehow giving away the intention, or else having a man who happened to live in Agra or Muttra and professed a knowledge of the jheels. Either way, it was scarcely a requisite they could advertise. Instead Hervey would have to trust his compass. God bless Daniel Coates, he said to himself, as he thought to check it again – finest of men and best of old soldiers. Who would have imagined there could be so small a thing as this piece of brass and whatever, and yet so serviceable to the hour? Clever Dan Coates, an ancient who sought the innovating as keenly as any lettered man. First the percussion lock, then the watch to read by night, and now the compass to make a man see in the dark – what a testimony to him, once a trumpeter, who had learned and risen by his own exertions alone. Hervey took the compass from its case on the saddle and noted the direction of the needle. 'Very well then,' he said, squeezing his legs the merest touch to put Gilbert into a walk.

Five minutes and the needle was backing very definitely. Hervey waited five minutes more, until the needle had moved a full quarter, and then turned right off the road to make for the stream which would lead them north of the fortress and on to the jheel bund. Gilbert, his feet now on pasture, at once sensed the change of purpose and began to throw his head, hopeful of a gallop. Trumpeter Storrs's grey, the only other in the troop, began whickering. Hervey winced. If the others took it up they would soon alert the doziest of sentries. There was nothing he could do, though, and he had worries enough finding the stream. It must be there; only if he had judged the needle so badly as to be almost doubling back would they not be able to find it. Navigating by night – the officer's constant trial. And yet he had the advantage on any in Hindoostan with Coates's 'contraption', as Johnson called it. Hervey could picture Coates now (omitting to make allowance for the difference of time), rising as always before it was light to beat about the bounds of his prosperous farm, as he had risen every day before dawn as a dragoon in America, and Flanders, and a dozen other places, and then as labourer and shepherd, and now as magistrate and man of consequence in West Wiltshire. Daniel Coates would now be—

Gilbert squealed and ran to the side. Hervey pulled him back onto the bit. 'Snake,' he said to Storrs, as matter-of-fact as he could having almost dropped the compass. 'I fear we'll have more of 'em if we're near water.' He would gladly put up with the inconvenience were it the price of finding the stream. He could never fathom the horse's ability to detect the proximity of a snake. Was it by smell or by sight? It could hardly be the latter at night, and yet it was curious what a horse could see in the dark when it had a mind. Gilbert had once shied at a basking krait thirty yards away, and yet the troop had lost two others, grazing, to kraits in the last year alone. Jessye had almost died from the same, when first he had gone to India, although that had been in the black of night.

The grass was now taller. Hervey raised his hand for Storrs to halt, and pressed Gilbert on gingerly. At last he was on it – the stream. He reined about and then motioned to Storrs to follow again as he turned right and north more, sighing with relief. The rest ought to be easy enough, even if it meant the point of the sword.

Serjeant Collins, a dozen yards behind, saw Hervey turn. Rather, he saw Gilbert turn, for a few white hairs made all the difference in the forewarning of daylight. Collins knew that Hervey was onto his line. He never doubted he would be, though he too knew how tricky the simplest of things were when night and the enemy were about. And he knew that everything would change in the next half-hour. The day came on faster in these parts than ever it managed in Spain. In half an hour they would be revealed even to a sentry on the walls of the distant fortress – intruders, murderous, like the snakes in the grass. The blow would surely be swift, as it must be against a snake lest it bite the hand that strikes. Collins had no illusions as to how desperate would be their position in the hours ahead.

The column was now in a trot, an uneven one, as the ground

itself was uneven, but more than double the pace of the walk nevertheless. The noise was greater too, bits jingling and scabbards clanking. It sounded like a wagonload of tinkers on the move. Could that be what any who heard it thought it was? Some hope, thought Hervey. Bullocks didn't snort and whinny. He pressed Gilbert for more speed: get it over with, get in among whoever was between them and the Motee Jheel, cut and slice through them and get to the bund. The commander-in-chief was depending on him, countless lives were waiting to be spared by his success.

The ground was with them for a while. Between the stream and the walls, half a league distant, was a rise which hid them from all but an observer on their side of it. And it was still too dark to see further than earshot. He could remember seeing a great many hovels when he had sketched here, but they had come across none so far. They were on the common pasture, after all, and he wouldn't expect to see even a grass-cutter abroad at this time. They were trotting even faster now – Gilbert stumbled once or twice until Hervey took a proper hold and lifted him onto the bit. He reckoned there would be light enough to canter in ten more minutes. Then they could sprint for the jheel bund and be done with it.

Another three hundred yards: the sun seemed to be racing them. Hervey could now see huts all along the rise. He would risk it – no words of command, just press to the canter and let the rest follow. Gilbert struck off eagerly with his off-fore, as he always favoured, Hervey peering intently ahead, praying that a cut or a bund would not suddenly check them. Four hundred horses pounding the till – if they could not be heard, then the earth must surely be shaking enough to rouse the dead. He thought he saw the odd figure on the ridge – with luck, terrified villagers.

Now there was light enough to make out the walls, but still in the dim distance barely more than a silhouette. They had the grass and the reeds as a backdrop, the advantage yet. Would the guns on the walls be trained on the approaches to the jheel bund, shotted and run out ready? Hervey knew they ought to be. Would they have the range? A thousand yards, he had estimated, perhaps a bit more. He had heard all manner of stories about the Bhurtpore guns, massive affairs, immovable, which could send an eight-inch ball of iron with great velocity over the outworks and beyond. Such a gun, well-served, could visit terrible destruction on a battery or a sap. This was Colonel Anburey's fear, that his sappers and miners would be too exposed to develop their work, but it could be no less a concern for Colonel Macleod, who had to expose his guns to some extent in order that they might fire at all. There was bound to be ground less dominated by the bigger guns, but the whole art of fortification was the facility to rake any approach and demolish any siege device. Hervey did not envy the engineers as they dug their saps and tunnels, nor the artillerymen, who heaved shot and powder and made themselves senseless and deaf – nor, indeed, the infantry who would have to sit patiently waiting for a breach and then storm it. And all these men relying on him now.

The sun broached the jungled horizon to his right, a brilliant torch which at last signalled an end to the night watch and to stealthy manoeuvre. It was day, the time for fighting.

And fighting they would have – directly ahead, a quarter of a mile (no more), a cavalry camp come hastily to life. He could see men rushing for their horses, and others already mounted forming up. How many they were he could have no true notion. It might be the entire Jhaut host beyond them, and these a picket only. Even so, they barred his way as effectively as any earthwork.

'Left wheel into line!' he called, checking the pace to a trot to allow them the manoeuvre time.

Trumpeter Storrs blew the call perfectly: just the four notes, and a simple fifth interval – easy enough with the bugle, even at a bounce.

Hervey's own troop wheeled effortlessly, an evolution they might do in their sleep so often had they practised it. The Eleventh, behind, had a harder time of it, with more ground to make up and two ranks to form, not one. Hervey wished he were leading with lances: they were not much use to him at the rear, and the sight of them lowered might well send the enemy packing. As they stood, he could only let them pursue once the dragoons had broken the Jhauts up. He cursed himself.

He looked rear again to see if the Eleventh were close enough yet for support. His jaw dropped. Up on the rise was a line of lances and yellow kurtas. He could scarcely believe their celerity and address. Skinner's sowars had taken post as flankers, and on the commanding ground, and without a word from him.

'Draw swords!'

Out rasped two hundred blades.

Four hundred yards now, and the ground ahead was even. He put Gilbert back into a canter, glancing over his shoulder again. There was Wainwright, covering, and Perry, upright and assured. He saw Green struggling with both hands to hold his mare. This was the best time, the troop in hand, every man intent on his next word of command. In another two hundred yards or so, when he shouted 'Charge!' he would relinquish all control for a frenzied few minutes, as each man fought his own battle, self-reliant instead of, as now, knee to knee.

He glanced left. The rissalah was pulling ahead – good! They would cut off any flight to the fortress, pin the enemy against the stream. Hervey lengthened the stride to a hand-gallop. How would the Jhauts meet them? They were still standing. Would it be with the flintlock? Surely not! Yet they showed no sign of movement. Why didn't they counter-charge? It was their only hope . . .

Then the Jhauts turned.

'They're breaking!' shouted Hervey, waving his sabre their way. 'Charge!'

Four hundred cavalry at the gallop, lances couched, but swords held high. Only infantry and guns saw the sabre's point; fleeing horsemen felt its edge.

Hervey fixed on a distant tree on the centre line and pressed Gilbert for all he was worth. In seconds they were among them. There was no need of his blade at first: the Jhauts were over-matched. Skinner's sowars were doing good execution, and his own dragoons were drawing blood. Yet an unseated man, sword in hand still, received his point cleanly at the throat – foolish or deter-mined was he? It did not matter.

He tried to estimate how many they had bolted – two, three hundred at least. Gone like chaff in a puff of wind – no need to sound recall. He could see his objective clearly now. The lone thicket of *jhow* marked it unmistakably – the bund. Another half a mile at most. Come back to a canter, he told himself – but press on. Trust the squadrons to rally and conform.

Now he had to pray the bund was intact, the moats not yet

inundated. Was that why the Jhauts had run – their job done, the bund breached, nothing more to cover?

There was a thunderous eruption of smoke and flame from the north-east bastion, the same distance away to his left. Shot whistled overhead – miles too high, he sneered. Had their gunners no art? Had they not ranged in their idle moments? Could this truly be the fortress that had defeated Lord Lake?

He could see no movement at the *jhow*. Was this really to be so easy an affair, or were they too late? More guns fired their way from the smaller bastions and redoubts as they bore on, but with no greater effect. He felt only contempt for the Jhauts' perfunctory opposition, even if they *were* safe behind their water-filled ditches.

He pressed Gilbert to a final effort.

Then they were at the *jhow*. His heart sank as he saw water in the channel. He could see the breach – not large. He needed his engineer. 'Mr Irvine!'

CHAPTER FIFTEEN

SIEGE

---

10 December

To Major W. S. Beatson,
Deputy Adjutant-General

Before Bhurtpore, 10 Dec. 1825

Sir,

*I have the honor to report, for the information of His Excellency
the Commander-in-Chief, that, in obedience to his command, I proceeded to make a reconnaissance on the Fortress of Bhurtpore with
the object of intercepting the means of inundation of its defences at
what is known as the Mottee Jheel, with under my command one
troop 6th Light Dragoons, one squadron 11th Light Dragoons under
the direct command of Captain Rotton, and a detachment of
Colonel Skinner's Horse, under Major Fraser. On advancing in the
vicinity of the Bund at first light, I encountered an encampment of
the enemy's cavalry, which was at once attacked and the enemy driven off without loss. The body of Colonel Skinner's Horse, acting
on the initiative of Major Fraser, made a flank movement; by which
they intercepted and cut up more than five hundred of the Enemy's*

cavalry, before they could reach an outwork in which the greater proportion of them took refuge. At this time the guns of the Fortress opened a moderate fire upon the force, but without damage.

After the affair of the Enemy's cavalry, I proceeded at once for the Bund which was found to be cut in two places, though the breaches had not been quite completed. A moderate amount of water, only, was judged to have entered the channels, and this was later confirmed by reconnaissance, the ditches of all the outworks being dry. Work was begun at once, under Lt. Irvine of the Engineers, to repair the breaches, and this was accomplished by late morning. The Enemy mounted two attacks on the Bund during this time, but they were heartless affairs and easily beaten off. At thirty minutes past midday, the relieving party under the command of Brig.-General Sleigh took possession of the Jheel Bund, and, as instructed to do so, I relinquished my responsibilities in this regard.

I beg I may be allowed to express my approbation of the intelligence and zeal of Major Fraser and Lt. Irvine, and that the conduct of the body of Colonel Skinner's Horse was exemplary.

> *I have the Honor to be,*
> *&c. &c. &c.*
> *M. P. Hervey, Major*

Hervey led his troop into the Sixth's lines late that afternoon, his command now dispersed, but their feat of arms already the talk of the army. Edmonds had turned the regiment out in their honour, mounted ranks with swords drawn, and the quarter-guard with carbines at the present. Local rank Hervey's majority might be, but it entitled him to arms presented rather than a mere butt salute, and Edmonds would have the regiment know what a day in its annals this would surely become.

Hervey could scarce believe the material for the siege now assembling – the ordnance, the tentage, camp stores, provisions, transport; the livestock, somehow driven from Agra and Muttra with as much ease, it would appear, as a Wiltshire shepherd might press his flock along a downland drove. And the regiments, King's and sepoy, battling for good order and military discipline as they began their routine of the siege – proud, colourful, cheery, possessed of self-confidence in limitless quantity. Hervey knew that he and his men had saved them blood, and he was glad of it also because the mounted arm would after all be able to look the infantry in the eye in this affair of digging and then the bayonet.

What a scene it was. In Agra and Muttra he had known its individual elements, but only now did it appear to him as a whole. It was a scene from many a picture he had thrilled to in his youth – the Crusades, the Hundred Years' War, Cromwell and the King, the Peninsula. It mattered not where, for the principle was the same: the paraphernalia of the siege, the methodical, patient, painful marshalling of resources, and then their remorseless application, until the besieged struck their colours or had them torn down, or else the besieger, his resources exhausted, struck camp and stole away. Only the detail of the brown-skinned servants and camp followers – the sutlers, dhobi-men, sweepers, bhistis, syces, Lascars and countless others – gave the scene its place.

Hervey nodded modestly to the salutes and well-wishers. His troop were less restrained in their acknowledgements. Enjoy it for the moment, he thought; the monotony of the siege will soon dull the remembrance. But, oh indeed, it had been a very fine affair at the Motee Jheel, and nothing could take from them the rightful sense of victory, if only as local as their leader's rank.

But two days later it seemed that the monotony of the siege would have them all exchange places with any man elsewhere than at Bhurtpore. Major Joynson read the day's general orders to the captains and staff assembled in his orderly-room tent, a well-made affair the size of a tennis court, twelve feet high and lined with vivid yellow cotton – though the smoke of a wood stove and a dozen cigars rendered the lining not as striking as once it had been:

FIELD GENERAL ORDERS.

Camp Before Bhurtpore, 13th Dec. 1825

Parole – FUTTYGHUR

Officiating Assist. Surgeon, J. Douglas, 14th N. Infantry, proceeding to join the army, is, on his arrival in camp, to be attached to the Field Hospital.

A working party of the following strength, from each of the Infantry divisions, to be sent to the Engineer Park to-morrow morn-

ing, and to be in attendance there at daybreak, or as soon after as possible – 100 Europeans, 250 Sepoys.

A Detachment, consisting of one and a half Company, to be furnished immediately from the 2nd Infantry Division, for the protection of the Engineer Park, and to provide small Escorts with cattle sent out for materials. The Officer commanding the party, to place himself under the orders of Brigadier Anburey, C.B.

Lieut. G. E. Smyth, 3rd Light Cavalry, Major of Brigade Western Division, is directed to join and do duty with his regiment on service with the Army on the Agra and Muttra Frontier.

Officers in Command of Posts and Piquets, are peremptorily required to detain all persons coming out of the Fort at the Piquets or Posts, reporting the circumstance immediately to the Field-officer of the Piquet, or to the Quarter-Master-General, and not to send them, as hitherto has been the practice, into the interior of their Camp, unless desired to do so by competent authority. Individuals also who may be bearers of Letters or Despatches from the Fort, are not to be permitted to pass the Piquets, but to be detained there, and their Despatches to be forwarded to the Quarter-Master-General, for Lord Combermere's information.

Officers commanding Corps and Departments, to which public or hired camels are attached, are directed to prohibit in the strongest terms, the owners or attendants, when going out with their cattle for forage, from advancing too far into the Jungle in the direction of the Fort, or from proceeding too great a distance from the Camp, as they are liable to fall in with scattered parties of the Enemy's horsemen.

'It's all working parties and foraging, I'm afraid,' Joynson concluded. 'And we have received orders to strengthen patrols and escorts. Dull work, but better than labouring for the sappers.'

The troop-captains nodded.

'I have made a roll of the duties. The adjutant is having them copied as we speak. That is the long and the short of it. Are there any questions, gentlemen?'

There were none.

'Very well, that is all. But let us see if we can dine together promptly at seven tonight. Hervey, stay a while longer if you please.'

Major Joynson sounded confident enough, if a shade tired. When he had said, 'I have made a roll of the duties,' Hervey knew full well the major would have done just that – himself, and in every detail, rather than delegating the task to the adjutant. That was what Eustace Joynson did best, better than anyone, indeed, and such was his conscientiousness that he could not allow a task to be performed any less well than was possible. Throughout Lord Towcester's diabolical time in command, Joynson had tried his best in these regards, but all too often he had counted himself a failure – including for his part in the events that culminated in Henrietta Hervey's death. Not that Hervey himself would apportion one ounce of blame to the major, whom he had grown to respect on account of both his conscientiousness and his doggedness in the face of the most wretched personal circumstances. And there was no doubt, too, that the painstaking attention to detail occupied Joynson's mind admirably. Daily he fretted about Frances, for despite everyone's best efforts his daughter had lately become engaged to an officer of native infantry, a penniless and stupid one at that. The responsibility of allowing his daughter to embark on an unsuitable marriage weighed heavily with him. Yet he simply did not have the strength of mind to forbid her.

'Lord Combermere's express orders are that you keep the rank of major, Hervey, *pro tempore*. I should be much obliged if you would act therefore as second in command.'

Hervey was not disposed to agreeing without some qualification, for besides aught else he would have no job to do if Joynson continued to attend to every detail. 'Of course, but I must keep command of my troop.'

Joynson nodded blankly. If Hervey thought himself capable of both then who was he to gainsay him? 'I gather Combermere asked that you join his staff.'

Hervey smiled. 'A nice gesture, but a siege is a dull enough thing to be engaged in without having to watch it from headquarters!'

'No gesture, I heard. It was to be General Whittingham's deputy.'

'Yes, but an affair of paper all the same.'

'Sooner or later, Hervey, you'll have to submit to such a regime. Armies aren't run from the saddle, as well you know.'

Hervey smiled again. Joynson's paternalism was endearing, if not always deft; he was no Edmonds – not in his sureness of touch, that is. 'I know, but I would wish for the time being that it were later rather than sooner. This affair will not be at all easy.'

Joynson looked troubled. 'You doubt we will prevail?'

Hervey considered his words. 'Nothing is certain. It would be well to remember it. The engineers say they can't tunnel; they can only sap the guns forward, and General Edwards says he can't guarantee a breach of walls so thick, even with his twenty-four-pounders. The train begins arriving today, by all accounts.'

'You are well informed. Is there word of how long the engineers will need?'

'Upwards of ten days before they get the first battery into position, according to Brigadier Anburey's major.'

'I think we shall be much occupied, then, with our little escorts and the like. I've agreed with the Eleventh that we shall patrol alternate nights throughout our allotted sectors. Without a natural feature as our boundary it's too chancy to have patrols from both beating about the place. They will take duty tonight.'

(Five days later)

FIELD GENERAL ORDERS.

Camp Before Bhurtpore, 19th Dec. 1825

Parole – GAZEEPORE

A working party from each of the Infantry Divisions, of the same strength as yesterday, to be sent to-morrow at day-break to the Engineer Park. The Quarter-Master's Establishments, and public cattle, to be sent there as usual. A Carpenter is also directed to be furnished from each of the Corps in the 1st and 2nd Divisions of Infantry.

A Detachment, consisting of five Companies from the 1st Infantry Division, will march to-morrow morning, and take charge of 300 Hackeries proceeding from the Artillery Park, for ammunition and stores, to Agra.

With reference to an Act of Parliament, 54th and 86th Geo. III. On the subject of Prize Property Agents, and claims thereto, the Field General Orders of the 16th Instant, appointing a Prize

*Committee, and directing Prize Agents to be nominated by ballot
for each of the Divisions of the Army, and by the General Staff, is
hereby cancelled; and it is now ordered, in conformity with the provision of the said Act, that two Agents only be appointed for the
Army.*

*His Excellency the Commander-in-Chief and the Field Officers
will nominate one Agent, and the other to be appointed by the
Captains and Subaltern Officers with the Army. The Prize Agents
will be furnished with the required letters of attorney appointing
them Agents for the Army; and they will be prepared on their part,
to give security in the sum of £2000 sterling each. The Prize Agents,
on all points of duty connected with their Agency, will be guided by
the spirit and letter of the Act of Parliament before cited, and which
is to be found in Carroll's Code of Regulations, Chap. 59.*

*That part of the Field General Orders of 16th Instant, which
directs that all property captured from the Enemy by any individual
of the Army, be forthwith delivered up to the Prize Agents, and
imposes the forfeiture of all claim to share, besides other penalties,
on individuals who may be discovered secreting or detaining property, knowing it to be a Prize – and further requires the Agents to
demand all Prize Property, wherever it may be discovered – remains
in full force.*

Major Joynson took off his spectacles as he concluded. 'Well,
gentlemen, from the first part it would seem that the sappers are
making good progress if powder is to be brought forward.' The
same assembly, his troop-captains and staff, heard the day's orders
each afternoon before evening stables, and this was indeed the first
intimation of true progress. 'As to the enemy,' continued Joynson,
now polishing his spectacles, 'I had expected them to be more
active by day and by night, yet it appears they will do no
more than beat up a few grass-cutters now and then, and they
surely won't venture out at night, it seems. That being said, we
cannot afford to lapse in any vigilance.' He looked at each of the
captains as sternly as he could, a game effort. 'As to the last, on
the subject of prize money, I cannot imagine that it will amount to
much, this Durjan Sal's army being scarcely well-equipped, but we
had better attend to the election of these agents. I shall ask the
adjutant to canvass all officers. But let it be rightly understood:

whatever prize is taken is first the prize of the regiment. If it is a worthy trophy I intend that it is kept by us.'

'Then let us hope we intercept the treasury as it makes its escape!' said Hugh Rose, smiling and blowing a great deal of smoke into the air from his cigar.

Hervey contemplated Rose's raffish mien. He thought it a not altogether helpful pose with Riding-Master Broad, his dupe (there was no avoiding the word), sitting in the rear rank. Hugh Rose's appearance betrayed nothing of the conditions they were living in – comfortable enough, but undeniably reduced – and his thick black hair and fine features, which won him the easy admiration of his dragoons as well as their women, looked the picture of grooming, as if for a drawing room at Fort William. His remark on the pecuniary spoils of war, albeit no doubt intended in some levity, required a rebuke.

'A happy thought indeed, Rose,' said Joynson, however, inclined more to punctilious attention to regulations than to scruple. 'But on that I fear we should have to follow General Orders. And in any case, any treasure in Bhurtpore must belong rightfully to the deposed rajah. That is why I said I do not suppose the prize money will amount to much.'

The captains feigned disappointment.

'Are there any questions? No? Very well, then, dinner at eight.'

When the others were gone, Hervey spoke his mind. 'I think we might propose some more active duty. The men are restless.'

'Yes, I know it. What activity do you imagine?'

'Well, we could make an effort to root out these cavalry who pick off the working parties, instead of merely trying to guard everyone and everything. They're not sallying from the fort, that much we know, and they can't be coming from the east, or north across the jheels. If both brigades put up a squadron, or better still all of Skinner's Horse, to beat all the cover to the west, and stood-to every man during daylight for three days, say, we might bring them to battle.'

'I can suggest it to Childers tomorrow. It has merit enough, even were the men not restless.'

'It would have to be done soon, however. There's a danger that once the artillery begins they may bolt Durjan Sal. He may not have the stomach for a siege. From what I heard yesterday of Sir Charles Metcalfe's treaties with him he never imagined it would come to this.'

Joynson nodded. 'Very well.'

'There is one more thing I would speak of.'

'Green?'

'Not this time. He has had his warning. *Deedes.*'

'Oh. I feared it would come.'

'He's the most blusterous serjeant-major I've seen. There've been all manner of confusions these past ten days.'

Joynson was silent for some time. 'Sir Ivo will be back in but a few weeks. He will know what to do.'

'Sir, *you* know what to do,' said Hervey, in a tone meant to be encouraging, though the words themselves accused the major of evading his duty.

Joynson shook his head slowly. 'I had hoped not to have this sort of trouble.'

Hervey sympathized, for trouble it would be. The major did, however, have the advantage of being in the field. It was a far easier place in which to dismiss a man than the barracks. 'A word with the brigadier tomorrow?'

Joynson sighed. 'O the pleasure of the plains!'

Hervey looked at him blankly.

'Very well. But you know, it will look very ill with the other regiments.'

Hervey knew that too. But he knew it would look even more ill were the regimental serjeant-major to falter at a time less propitious. He said nothing, but picked up his cap and made to leave.

'Thank you, Hervey,' said Joynson, wearily. 'I knew well enough that Deedes was incapable, but I kept telling myself it was only by comparison with Mr Lincoln.'

The tone was a shade too despairing. Hervey turned full back. 'Sir, I know I speak for the regiment when I say that all ranks hold your stewardship in high regard. This is but trying detail, and the corrective is at hand. Sir Ivo ought to be very well pleased with what he finds.'

Joynson looked genuinely surprised.

In the event, it was very easily done. The major called for the RSM soon after first parade next day and told him that, with regret, it was his decision to relieve him of his duties. He was to report as soon as was practicable to the depot at Agra pending a further decision as to his employment thereafter. When Joynson recounted the interview to Hervey later that morning it was with surprise, still, at Deedes's reaction. 'You know, he seemed almost . . . pleased, relieved. He said he had always done his best – which I fear is true. He said he wished to serve on in some other position if it were possible. I don't know; there may be something in Calcutta . . .'

'Well, I am all astonishment. I imagined he would bluster as ever.'

'And he left camp with some dignity, too. I called in Hairsine and told him he was to be acting serjeant-major, and Deedes treated him very decently by all accounts.'

Hervey nodded, though he had not a moment's doubt that Deedes's dismissal had been necessary. 'Well, he must have had some quality otherwise he would never have been advanced in the first instance. I imagine he felt some loyalty too, even in his exigent position.'

'That was to have been my method if it had come to it: calling on his better self to accept things for the good of the regiment. Still, it is done now.' Joynson appeared to take no satisfaction in it, however, even with Hairsine making a difference already at orderly room.

'Who is to take C Troop?'

'I've told Strickland to make his senior serjeant do duty until there's time for a proper regimental board. By then Sir Ivo should be back. I'm deuced glad Strickland postponed his leave.'

Hervey saw no reason why a board should not be held at once, but he saw no likelihood of convincing Joynson. C Troop's man would do well enough; Strickland would not have it, otherwise. 'Did the brigadier express an opinion about taking the offensive?'

'He said he would speak with Sleigh. But it seems the guns will be going in soon and Combermere's likely to want a strong cavalry presence.'

'We shall all say amen to that. It's well time the fort's guns were answered.'

The guns of two bastions in particular had caused annoyance and casualties since the army had first appeared before Bhurtpore, yet could not be answered with any effect at the extreme range of the field artillery, nor even, indeed, with the long guns of the siege train yet. Only when the engineers had sapped their way to within a thousand yards or so, and built up redoubts, could the gunners try to dislodge the enemy's cannon. And dislodge them they must, for the siege guns could not pound away with the bastions commanding the ground so. A siege was an occasion when Adye's general injunction against counter-battery fire did not hold.

'I await orders on this keenly, too, said Joynson. 'Shall we take a ride to look at the ground?'

Hervey had never before ridden ground with the major, and he was eager to do so. He wanted to learn how good was his eye for country compared with that for administration, for in spite of the banter of the camp at Agra, he was certain that the cavalry must be more active in this siege than the textbooks allowed. He had studied the accounts of Lord Lake's failure. He was certain that if the cavalry became a mere arm of the commissary then the siege would go the same way as Lord Lake's.

They rode with only their covermen, Hervey marked by Corporal Wainwright, Joynson by the senior corporal. The major was not one for panoply, and in any case he scarcely expected trouble within the ring of scarlet around the fortress.

Everywhere was purposeful activity. Hervey could not remember scenes the like since San Sebastian, perhaps Badajoz, even. Columns of sepoys tramped to and from great breastworks thrown up in a matter of days like molehills on greensward. Guns and ammunition wagons lumbered forward continuously, and empty wagons passed them on their way back from dumping powder, shot and shell at the batteries in anticipation of the great pounding to come. And the engineers, the sappers and miners, who opened the way for the infantry, whether by bridge or breach, worked oblivious to their surroundings, and to the enemy's guns which periodically sent hissing spheres of iron arching into the sky, then to throw up fountains of earth where they struck before bowling along the ground to knock down men and horses like skittles if they didn't look sharp.

Hervey had observed the same curious detachment in the Peninsula, the sappers working as calmly as if they were navigators at an English cut. It was a cool courage, theirs, not one fired by dash or steadied by the touch of cloth. He wondered if it could endure as the guns began to take their toll. Sapping to the foot of the walls would be hot work indeed.

'Do you think Durjan Sal doubts the outcome, seeing all this, Hervey?' asked the major suddenly. They had ridden for ten minutes and more in silence.

Hervey was unsure what he had heard. 'You mean will he ask for terms?'

'No. I mean, does he consider those walls impregnable? Does he believe we shall just go away? You could scarce call firing from those walls much of a counter-action.'

'I confess to being surprised,' replied Hervey, watching warily as another ball arched from a distant bastion towards them.

Joynson watched it too. It hit an outcrop of solid rock a hundred yards ahead of them, sending a shower of deadly shards in all directions.

'But he must think those walls solid enough. And, in truth, he might be right. I've not seen their like before, I think.'

'Do you know why it is the engineers can't tunnel?' Joynson supposed only that the ground was too hard.

'The distance, pure and simple, is my understanding. They can't get close enough to begin a gallery.'

'I can't say as I understand. If they can sap forward, why can't they then tunnel?'

'Because after two hundred yards there isn't air enough to breathe, or to make for a good explosion.'

They rode on a further half-mile in silence, or rather without a word, for Durjan Sal's guns were now speaking continually. Three of them fired at once from the long-necked bastion, the report so loud that both men looked its way. Hervey saw the homing shot first – low and straight, not plunging like the others. 'She comes our way,' he said warily.

Neither man moved a muscle more than had they been on parade. It was as unthinkable as it was pointless.

Eighteen pounds of iron grazed the rocky outcrop fifty yards to their right then ricocheted half a right angle, but chippings the size of musket balls shot their way, drawing blood from Hervey's hand and his mare's shoulder.

Joynson, on his nearside, but half a length in front, cursed as his shako was all but knocked from his head, the silver cross beneath the oilskin having stopped a stone bullet. He didn't see his mare's wound at first, looking about her legs and flanks for marks. 'Oh, God!' he cried suddenly, jumping from the saddle.

Blood spurted from her breast as if from a stirrup pump. Joynson took off his silk stock and pressed it to the wound – a neat slice like the sabre's work. 'An artery, Hervey, for sure,' he groaned.

If it were an artery there was nothing that they – or even David Sledge – could do. But Hervey got down and took the bandages from his valise.

Corporal Wainwright did likewise, and Joynson's coverman the same. But Joynson's sleeves were soaked through, and the pool of blood at the mare's feet was spreading rapidly.

'It's no good, Eustace.' But Hervey knew the major had bought the mare for his wife years ago. Conceding would be a doubly painful business.

'Give me a pistol!'

Hervey took one of the flintlocks from his saddle holster, already loaded, tamped. He held it out to him. 'Shall I do it while you steady her?'

'No, Hervey. It wouldn't do,' said Joynson simply, taking the pistol and letting go the silk stock.

Nevertheless, Hervey took out his second pistol and made ready. He had no idea if the major had ever shot a horse. It was the Devil's own job even without sentiment.

'Offsaddle her, will you, Hervey,' said Joynson resolutely.

When it was done, the major wiped his hands on his overalls, rubbed the little mare's nose, cocked the pistol and put the muzzle gently but firmly into the fossa above her left eye, angling it so as to aim at the bottom of her right ear.

He pulled the trigger. The mare's forelegs folded, and she fell to the ground without so much as a grunt.

Hervey was impressed – a businesslike despatch, as neat as any he'd seen. It had not been two minutes since the stone had done its worst. 'She was a fine animal,' he said, with real admiration.

Tears welled in Joynson's eyes, which he did nothing to hide.

'She was. And I should have left her with Frances.' And then, with an almost bitter note, 'except that I couldn't have trusted her to see to her rightly.'

Hervey thought to say nothing.

Joynson knelt and cut off a lock of the mane. 'The last of Anne Joynson, then . . . save for Frances herself.'

Hervey still thought it best to stay silent. Indeed, he had begun wondering how they might decently dispose of the carcass.

Joynson's coverman was already resigned to walking back to the lines. 'I'd swear them guns was trying to do that, sir,' he said, making ready to hand the reins to the major.

'So would I, sir,' added Wainwright. 'Somebody in that fort knows how to shoot. That's for sure.'

Hervey frowned and shook his head. 'The way that shot ran level, the gun must be a giant. It couldn't be retrained quickly enough to aim. Anyway, I doubt they can even make us out from that distance. No, a lucky shot I'll warrant.'

That evening, however, the camp was abuzz with rumour about the accuracy of the Jhaut guns. It was confidently asserted that the gunners were Frenchmen or Italians, as there had been in native service throughout the Maratha wars. And there were wilder stories, too – that the deserters from His Majesty's artillery were directing the fire. The direst retribution was sworn for any who had changed sides, nor was it clear where a Frenchman would stand in this reckoning. Hervey did his rounds that evening well pleased with the evidence of the Sixth's fighting spirit. Even the grocer – a name that Hervey found himself thinking of increasingly, if not actually uttering – seemed more animated at dinner. Joynson, certainly, had an edge not usually apparent. It had been a dozen years and more since he had been shot over. The sudden taste of gunfire that afternoon seemed to have been an exceptional tonic.

Hervey turned in just before midnight after walking the horse lines. They had been quiet, with nothing but an occasional whicker and grunt from the animals themselves, or an 'evenin', sir' from a sentry of the inlying picket. And although it was the picket-officer's job to check that the running lines were taut, he had inspected each of the troops' in turn. He had known enough times in Spain where a loose line had ended in runaways and broken legs. And he had checked, too, that the sentries knew the parole and how they were to be relieved. The men were alert, and it had given him much satisfaction to go to his tent knowing that the Sixth were as keen in their field discipline as they were in their fighting intent. He was afraid the former would be tested far longer than the latter, for what he had seen of the siege that day did not lead him to suppose there would be anything but cannonading and sapping for a month or more – save, perhaps, an obliging sortie by Durjan Sal's cavalry.

But now he was pleased for his campaign bed, and that it was the Sixteenth – Daniel Coates's old regiment – who stood sentinel. He could rest assured. Private Johnson had placed a bowl of hot water on one of the chests, but it was now only lukewarm. Hervey undressed, put on his nightshirt, washed his hands and set to work with sponge and tooth powder. Then he unmade his bed in the nightly routine of shaking out anything that might have crawled there during the time his groom had been gone, and, satisfied at last of his safety, lay down between white cotton sheets beneath two thick woollen blankets. He took care to double them and fold the edges under, for he knew he would need their warmth on so starry a night. The pillow was soft, and he had no desire to read or to contemplate anything. He turned down the lamp to the merest glow, and closed his eyes.

CHAPTER SIXTEEN

RUMOURS OF WAR

The early hours

From the depths of sleep, Hervey was called rudely to arms. To awake to the 'alarm' – the bugle's repeated C and E, unmistakable, and easy enough for the most frightened trumpeter to blow – had been a thrill in his cornet days, but now it meant only anxiety in the knowledge that there had been some failure. Perhaps his own? There was firing, too, distant but near enough to take account of. He turned up the lamp and began hauling on his overalls as Private Johnson, breathless, pulled back the tent flap.

'Major 'Ervey, sir!'

Hervey had no idea why his groom was already abroad and dressed.

'They 'ad me up cos thi mare's got a bit o' colic. All 'ell's broke loose over where t'Sixteenth are.'

'Very well. You'd better saddle up Gilbert if you will.' He began wondering who had given the order to sound the alarm.

'Bring 'im 'ere, sir?'

'No. Just where we stand to.' This was no time to be making things complicated.

Johnson picked up Hervey's boots and shook them.

'Thank you, Johnson. Now away.'

It took him but a minute more to finish dressing, fastening on the swordbelt last and picking up his pistols from beside the bed. He put on his shako as he ducked out of his tent, straining his eyes in the darkness, which fires and torches made all the darker in the unlit places. Men were hastening all about him, but with order and purpose. All they did, indeed, was the same as for stand-to before first light every day, except that it was at the double and in the expectation of action rather than merely the possibility. When he reached E Troop's line, the chargers to the right, he found Johnson with Gilbert under saddle, fastening up the bridle. He put both pistols into the holsters then made to tighten the girth and surcingle.

'Right, sir,' said Johnson, taking away the head collar rather than spending any more time looping the straps.

Hervey was not yet ready to mount, though. 'Mr Perry! Mr Green!' he called. There was a good deal of calling all around, and he was not about to enter into a competition with the corporals; but he wanted to know his officers were at their posts.

Serjeant-Major Armstrong came up with a lantern. 'Mr Perry's reporting to the adjutant, sir.'

Of course he was. Hervey had forgotten for the moment that Perry was next for picket-officer. 'And Mr Green?'

'Haven't seen him, sir. Both sections'll be ready in not many minutes more. They were quick out of their pits, I'll say that for 'em. Mind you, Collins was on picket.'

Corporal Wainwright now came up, leading his trooper. 'Sir.'

'Where is Mr Green?'

'I don't know, sir. I'll find 'is groom.'

'No. Let it be, for the moment. Come with me to the major.'

'Ay, sir. He's by the picket tent.'

'Very well. Johnson!'

'Sir?'

'Get someone to find where Mr Green is.' He turned to Armstrong. 'Carry on, then. Not to mount without the order, though.'

'Right, sir.'

Hervey strode off with Corporal Wainwright down the flanks of the horse lines, noting the state of each troop as he passed – so far as the darkness allowed him. Only A Troop looked unready. He found Joynson and the adjutant at the picket tent, the RSM standing with his notebook poised, the picket-officer just taking his leave. There was still firing from the Sixteenth's lines, but no sign of a galloper from brigade.

'Well, Hervey?' said Joynson, a touch wearily.

'Have we sent anyone to make contact?'

'No. And I'm not inclined to risk it,' replied Joynson firmly. 'Finding what's happening would be the very devil of a job. If there's a real reverse we shall hear of it soon enough.'

'Then I believe we should move up to support the Sixteenth without orders.'

'Why?' The major's tone did not so much challenge as request elaboration.

'Because – unlikely as it may seem – it might just be the sortie in strength that we were speaking of.'

'Why have we not had orders to that effect from brigade, then? I've sent Perry there, by the way.'

'Well, the brigadier will be no more certain than we are, in all likelihood.'

Joynson was clearly troubled. 'Yes, but the general must be given the opportunity to exercise a proper command, must he not?'

Hervey was becoming exasperated. This was the Joynson of past years, not of late months: the Joynson cowed by Towcester, sick headaches and the like. 'Eustace, since when did cavalry have to await an order to close with the enemy?'

There was no answer to this. The major turned to the adjutant. 'Very well, then. Have the regiment mount.'

The adjutant turned to the trumpet-major. 'Troops to mount, please.'

'Sir!' The trumpet-major put his bugle to his lips and sounded the regimental call followed by the octave leap of 'prepare to mount', then the simpler repeated Cs and Gs of the executive.

'I'd like you next to me, Hervey,' said Joynson, perfectly composed. 'It'll be a deuced tricky business in this light. Perry can look after E Troop. They can ride under second squadron.'

'With respect, sir. It might be better to keep the troop in hand. You never know—'

'Very well, very well. If you are content with that then I have no objection. Perry's able enough to have them on his own.'

Hervey would say nothing more, but he was hardly content, for the troop would be under command of the grocer until Perry returned from his galloping. Assuming, that was, that Green would actually find them. However, there were Armstrong and Collins, and he could always take the lead again before they were committed. He turned to Corporal Wainwright, who nodded his understanding and made off at once to E Troop.

Hervey had greater concerns, however. The handling of a regiment of light dragoons in troop ranks was, even by day, a testing undertaking. When the ground was unbroken, as on a review, it could pass off at the trot tolerably well, though anything beyond a couple of hundred yards led to bunching and bulging of the line to such an extent that it was difficult to recover proper dressing without coming back to a walk. When it was dark, however, and the ground broken as here, the undertaking verged on the reckless. He took out his telescope, stepped the other side of the picket tent's fire, and tried to see what was happening in the Sixteenth's lines.

Meanwhile the troop orderly serjeants were reporting to the RSM. It was only another minute or so before Mr Hairsine could report to the adjutant that the regiment was ready. Johnson had brought Gilbert up, and Hervey now pulled down the stirrups and mounted.

'Skirmishers out?' said Joynson as Hervey closed up to his side.

'I would think it better to advance with a clear front,' replied Hervey.

'Very well. "Advance", please, trumpet-major.'

That Joynson asked for such an opinion did not in the least diminish his standing in Hervey's eyes. That he accepted it only increased it, too. Seeking support for a decision already made was the true sign of the weak-spirited.

'If it is a sortie, they might just be intent on mischief,' said Hervey, having to raise his voice against the jingle and clamour behind him (it took a fair few yards, always, before the NCOs got the dressing passable in close order). 'But it sounds a determined affair. They might be making for the guns.'

'I take my hat off to them if they are,' said Joynson, matter-of-factly.

'They know the ground better than do we.'

'But it would be a desperate affair nevertheless.'

The adjective struck Hervey forcefully. Perhaps a night sortie was indeed the act of a desperate man. Had Durjan Sal already concluded that his fortress could not withstand a determined siege? He would have known why Lord Lake's had failed – not just for the want of heavy guns but because of the attacks by the Maratha cavalry on his siege forces. How many cavalry could Durjan Sal dispose on such a night? There was no telling, and neither was there telling the damage a resolute force could do if ever panic seized hold in the camps. 'We might have to make a wide front if they're really intent on breaking through to the guns. It will hardly be enough but it might check them for a while. I hope there's a general stand-to by now.'

Lieutenant Perry rode across the front of A Troop to report. His horse was blowing hard, for he had had him in a gallop, and Hervey was pleased with this evidence of boldness. Perry saluted as he came up to the major. 'Sir, brigadier's compliments, and would you be so good as to place the regiment in a position to support the Sixteenth. They were attacked by a large force of cavalry and their object is not clear. The Sixteenth have one troop only under saddle, and the rest are standing ground with the carbine.'

'Where will the brigadier be?' asked Joynson.

'He did not say, sir, but I presumed he intended remaining with the reserve.'

Joynson did not reply.

'It's no good presuming, Arthur. We have to know where the brigadier is!' snapped Hervey. Galloping was no use without a clear head.

Perry said nothing.

'Well,' said Joynson emolliently, 'it is the brigadier's duty to make his post known. Thank you, Mr Perry.'

'Take post with the troop, then,' said Hervey. 'They're not to answer but to the regiment.'

'Sir,' replied Perry, saluting and turning, trying hard not to sound cast-down. Joynson's thanks were welcome, but Hervey's reproof was deserved.

'A little sharp, Hervey,' said Joynson when he was gone. 'He did well to get orders so quickly.'

238

Hervey did not reply at once; an increase in firing in the direction of the Sixteenth's camp, though two furlongs away and more, commanded their attention. 'I think we had soon better extend, sir,' he said finally, the fusillade having gone on a full minute. 'It can't be long now before they break through.'

'I think we had,' said Joynson assuredly. 'Mr Vanneck, Second Squadron to extend to the left, please. I want them to cover as much ground as they can.'

The adjutant wheeled right and put his horse into a trot. There was no trumpet call by which the order could have been conveyed, for trumpet calls by and large regulated activity rather than conveyed changes in design. Joynson put his own horse into a lateral trot so as to be at the junction of the two squadrons.

Strickland brought Second Squadron quickly into line by the simple expedient of halting them for a time so that First Squadron cleared enough ground ahead to allow Second to trot up with the merest incline left. Once his right marker was level with First Squadron's flanker, he ordered them back to the walk and called 'dress by the right', which brought the left flank wheeling smartly round. 'Ready, Major Joynson!' he shouted.

Joynson replied at once: 'Draw swords!'

Four hundred sabres came rasping from their scabbards. A regiment drawing swords was ever a sound to thrill, more so even than a battalion fixing bayonets. Hervey smiled to himself: it was the first he had heard it in earnest in ten years. He could even forget the blunting of the edges, steel on steel.

What sight daylight would present him with this instant he could not be certain. C and A Troops were in good order in front. He could only trust that D and B were keeping both space and station in the support line, and likewise E to the rear of them. It was truly no bad thing to have a third line of sabres, a second reserve, in circumstances such as these – even if no more than a troop's worth. He would just have to trust Perry to have them in hand.

Eyes were getting used to the darkness by now, especially since there were no campfires to dazzle them any more. They could see well enough to trot, thought Joynson. But if they did they would not see the enemy until they were on top of him. Did that matter? What method in the fight could there be but a strong arm and a sharp blade?

239

'Trumpet-major, "trot" if you please!'

The next minute was a free-for-all of stumbling and cursing. Hervey was near to using the flat of his sword a dozen times, so bad was the barging. And then they were into a good rhythm. And just in time, for the first clash with the Jhauts came sooner than expected – on the left, so that at once there was a bending of the line and a loss of direction in C Troop. Not that Joynson, or even Strickland, could see it, for the one was too far away and the other was busy with his sabre. D Troop ran into the rear of the mêlée with no idea of what was happening, but Perry sensed the trouble and took E Troop at once into the breach opening with First Squadron, himself closing with the major.

'Hold hard, sir!' he shouted. 'The left flank's engaged.'

'Halt!' bawled Joynson, heaving on his reins for all he was worth.

But the whole line was now run up against the Jhaut cavalry. With both sides in no more than a trot, the collision was gentle enough, but the shock was great nevertheless.

Joynson's sabre flew from his hand as a tulwar sliced out of the dark. His coverman, stirrup to stirrup with him, lunged forward with his sabre and fended off the follow-through. Hervey could make out nothing. He lowered his head and thrust his sabre forward in the guard. Something hit the blade, not too hard. Corporal Wainwright, beside him, reins looped over his left arm, thrust forward with a pistol and fired. Joynson, his sabre hanging loose from his wrist by the sword knot, pulled a pistol from its holster and fired just as a huge Jhaut raised an axe to his charger's head. The man somersaulted backwards like a dolly at a fair.

Joynson pulled out the other pistol and fired at a man crossing left to right, but missed, leaving his coverman to finish the job with an arm's-length shot. Firing increased the length of the line as dragoon after dragoon managed to disengage his sabre long enough to draw a pistol. It seemed to gain them the initiative, for there was no shooting by return.

Joynson began shouting – bellowing – '*Forward!*' They had saved themselves with steel, and turned the tables with shot. Now they would press home the advantage with the leg.

It was not long in the doing. Suddenly there was a great shout and then the drumming of hooves, and the Sixth knew they were speeding the Jhauts from the field. 'Follow, sir?' came voices from left and right.

But Joynson would not pursue in the dark. Even before Hervey could urge him not to give chase he was shouting, 'Re-form!' He intended closing on the Sixteenth's lines in good order and standing to until they could take stock at first light.

'I'm going to my troop, sir,' called Hervey, certain he was not needed in the van any longer.

'Very well, Hervey. My compliments to Mr Perry. His action was sharp.'

Hervey smiled. It was so very like Joynson to be thinking thus. The men might consider him an old woman at heart, but they would always like him and therefore do his bidding willingly.

'And have your troop look for any wounded, if you please.'

'Sir.' It went without saying that the reserve troop picked up the wounded. It would be a dangerous affair, though. A moon would be a kindness to both sides. He would send for lanterns. 'Mr Perry,' he called, as he tried to make his way through the confusion of men and horses at the rear.

Eventually he found him. 'All accounted for, Hervey, save Green.'

'Green?' Hervey sounded as worried as he was astonished.

'And his groom.'

'How? Where was he?'

'I don't think he was ever with us. I don't think he mustered. No one has seen him.'

'Good God! Where's his coverman?'

'In his place.'

'Well, he'd better go back and bring him. And he can fetch some lanterns. We're to search the field.'

'Very well, sir.'

Hervey shook his head angrily, but swallowed hard. 'That was smart work bringing up the troop as you did. The major is well pleased.'

'Thank you, sir.'

But one man's address did not make up for the lack of it in another. Hervey continued to seethe at Green's absence as they set about searching for any who had fallen from the saddle.

*

241

At first light E Troop stood to their horses in the rear of the other four troops, fifty yards short of the Sixteenth's firing line – the line they had held since their own stand-to-arms in the middle of the night. Their search had rendered up one dragoon killed – by a ball in the back of the neck, which had very probably come from a fellow dragoon's pistol in the black confusion of the fight – and three others with sword or spear wounds, none of them too likely to be fatal. They found eight Jhauts dead or dying, but any who had been less severely injured seemed one way or another to have crawled to further cover. There were a good many dragoons riding-wounded, patched up where they stood by the surgeon's assistants, Sledge himself having beat about the ground with Hervey. Of one man, or rather two, there was no sign, however. Cornet Green was nowhere to be found. Hervey was now almost beside himself with anger. Never had an officer of the Sixth absented himself so. The word, indeed, was desertion. And in the face of the enemy.

When the light of day let them see to the range of the telescope, Joynson stood-down the regiment and issued orders to return to camp. Hervey told him of Green.

'His groom as well? That is most strange,' said the major, bruised by the day's cannonade and weary from the night's exertions – and yet disinclined to see the worst in the report.

'I can't see what else to make of it,' said Hervey sharply. 'The man's unfit to command a picket, even.'

But when they returned to camp Hervey was obliged to consider making something else of it, for into the lines soon afterwards rode Green and his groom, both of them in field order. Propriety required that he held his anger in check; reproving an officer in front of the ranks did no one credit as a rule. But the tone perfectly conveyed his state of mind. 'Well, Mr Green?'

'Sir, I am afraid I became lost.'

Hervey's mouth fell open. 'Lost? Lost, Mr Green?'

'I regret so, sir.'

Dragoons were trying their best to watch without being caught too obviously doing so.

'Mr Green, you had better attend at once on the adjutant.'

'Sir, if I might explain—'

Lieutenant Perry cut him short. 'You may explain first to me,

Mr Green,' he said, glancing at Hervey and hoping for his leave. 'Report at once to my tent.'

Green saluted.

'And do not ride your charger through the lines, sir!'

Green dismounted sheepishly.

Hervey looked at Perry and nodded. It was the right thing to do. There might conceivably be an explanation that rendered his offence a lesser one than a regimental court martial would dispose of – though he could not imagine it.

'Private Needham, a word with you,' said the serjeant-major to the cornet's groom. Armstrong's Tyneside conveyed an unnerving degree of affability, which fooled no one within its hearing.

Hervey concluded that his best course was to repair to his own tent to shave.

Half an hour later, as he drank one of Johnson's fortified brews from regimental china, Perry and Armstrong came to his tent. They had first compared accounts of the night's wanderings and found them in essentials to be the same. 'Green admits to failing to rise at once to the alarm,' said Perry. 'He went back to sleep until Needham rousted him out, and then he had to prime his pistols.'

'Why were they not primed at evening stand-to?' said Hervey.

'Because he's an indolent officer,' said Perry decidedly. 'But he appears at least to tell the truth.'

'That, or he's very calculating in his confidences.'

Perry sighed. It wasn't the sort of remark that one officer should make of another, but Green had exhausted everyone's patience an age ago. 'By the time he was ready, it seems the regiment had moved off.'

'And he spent the whole night trying in vain to find us?' The incredulity in Hervey's voice was marked.

'He said he thought we would have ridden in the direction opposite to that from which the fire was coming, on account of wanting to fall back on the guns.'

Hervey paused to consider the notion. 'Astonishing. Why might he believe that?'

'Hervey, he is, as I said, an indolent and ineffectual officer. While you or I or any other would have ridden towards the sound of the firing, he it seems works with a different instinct. But it would be difficult to say that that instinct was any more than feeble. There is nothing to prove that he was . . . well, running away.'

Hervey thought for a while again. 'Sar'nt-Major?'

Armstrong inclined his head ever so slightly and raised an eyebrow. 'It's not for me, sir, to make comment on an officer's capability. All I can say is Needham's not a bad man. He says he kept saying to Mr Green that it seemed strange they were finding no sign of us, and saying they ought to make for the firing, but Mr Green was certain of himself. And then he says Mr Green seemed to lose his notion of where they were, so they stopped for an hour or two, and it was only at dawn that Mr Green could see which direction was camp.'

Hervey sighed. An entirely plausible story. And yet he was not inclined to believe it. He didn't doubt Needham. Nothing that he knew of him suggested he would run from a fight. The opposite, perhaps. And Corporal Wainwright messed with him regularly; that was surely recommendation as to character. 'I just can't see how an officer could think in the way Green did!'

Green was no boon companion of Perry's, but the lieutenant was scrupulously fair. 'If every officer's instinct were the same, sir, there would be no occasion for surprise.'

'That might be so, but I can't believe it exculpates Green. There must be something wrong with the logic, but I haven't the time to look for it,' replied Hervey, his irritation increasing.

Armstrong could see no other conclusion either. 'Sir, with respect, if Mr Green had been a corporal we couldn't bring any charge as would stick – save failing to turn out for "alarm".'

Hervey shook his head. 'But he's not a corporal, Sar'nt-Major.'

'No, sir, of course he's not,' replied Armstrong, looking sideways at Perry. 'But the same evidence would apply if charges were brought. That's all I'm saying.'

Hervey was silent a while. Then he got up. 'Mr Green had better pay a good sum to the widows' fund, then. And you had better put him on his guard, Arthur. I do truly believe we have a wrong 'un here; and I say thus saving your presence, Sar'nt-Major.'

Armstrong said nothing. It was a confidence he would rather

244

never have heard, but they had been together too long for Hervey to withhold even so infamous an opinion.

Hervey looked at him sternly. Armstrong was worth a hundred Greens. No, more than that, for a worthless thing did not gain in worth by mere increase in numbers. Come what may, Armstrong and his like would never have their just desserts; no more than would Green. Hervey put down the teacup. What a powerful thing was this drink: it brought the nation to fight in Hindoostan and it paid for Green to play the gentleman. Yet Armstrong's pension, if he were to have one, would scarcely keep his family in it. But this was no time for philosophy. He nodded emphatically: 'Very well, then, gentlemen. Boot and saddle at ten.'

CHAPTER SEVENTEEN

SAPPERS AND MINERS

Two days later

FIELD GENERAL ORDERS.

Camp before Bhurtpore, 21 Dec. 1825

Parole – LUCKNOW

The nature of the operations upon which the Army is about to be employed, requiring that the Infantry Regiments should have as few calls upon them for Guards as possible, the Right Hon. The Commander-in-Chief is pleased to direct, that the following Detail only be furnished; all other Guards not included in this statement, are forthwith to be withdrawn . . .

Hervey passed the statements to Armstrong. 'They do not directly bear on us, but it's as well to know the comings and goings.'

Armstrong, sitting in a chair in front of him, with Lieutenant Perry to Hervey's right, took the papers and looked quickly over them.

Private Johnson emerged from Hervey's tent with a coffee pot. 'Any more, sir?'

Hervey gestured to the others first, then let his cup be filled with the blackest liquid he had seen in many a year. Johnson would never throw away the unexpended portion of the day's coffee ration, and so each morning he boiled up the same liquid and the same beans, throwing in more in random measure. With the addition of copious quantities of sugar, and warm buffalo milk, it was a fortifying and nourishing drink, even if only very distantly related to any that could be had in the coffee houses of London.

'But the infantry will have a longer wait than they think, by all accounts,' said Hervey, still stirring his cup. 'The Jhaut gunners have found their mark on a good number of saps.'

Armstrong looked puzzled. 'They are tunnelling, though, aren't they?'

'It seems not. They can't get close enough.'

Armstrong looked incredulous.

So did Perry, but for a different reason. 'I don't understand, Hervey.'

'They have to dig ventilation shafts once the tunnel exceeds a certain distance, which would rather give away the game.' Hervey took a sip of his coffee. 'And they're no fools behind those walls. There are counter-tunnels ready dug. I saw some of them myself. So I think we may safely say there will be no assault this side of the new year.'

The Sixth had been in worse places at Christmas. Here at least it was warm when the sun was up, they were dry, there was fire wood aplenty, and the supply of rations and powder was regular. Armstrong's expression changed to a smile. 'Corporal Stray'll be here today, sir, and a full load of rum.'

Hervey smiled too. The officers' mess was well stocked with excellent claret, but rum was so versatile an additive. He was almost of the opinion that he would exchange it bottle for bottle. 'Very well, then. There are no further orders. Interior economy today, make and mend. And I am brigade field officer, you'll recall.'

Perry and Armstrong rose. 'If it's all right with you, sir, I'd like to ride over and see them sappers working later on,' said the serjeant-major.

'By all means. Don't be *too* hard on them, though,' replied Hervey, smiling still.

'No indeed, sir. But I'd like to see how many of them would make colliers.'

Hervey reported to the headquarters of the First Brigade of Cavalry at ten o'clock. There was no telling what the duty might entail. Last night had been quiet, and the siege proceeded, as they were all informed, in the usual methodical if painfully slow manner. But activity was the nature of staff work, and he could therefore expect anything. Certainly the headquarters looked well-shod. The brigade tent had yellow pennants at each end of the ridge pole, and a lance-guard at the entrance. There was no doubting that this was the post of Colonel Murray, a man fervent in holding to the cavalry opinion that everything mattered, from the patent shine on a pair of levee hessians to the edge on a troop man's sabre.

The major of brigade, Captain Harris – of the 16th Lancers like Murray himself – received him with a smile. 'Well, Hervey, we have at least seen how it is done!'

They had indeed, thought Hervey – many a time in the Peninsula. Siege after siege, it seemed in that campaign. 'I wonder if the Jhauts have.'

'I don't know what to make of their sortie the other night, that's for sure,' said the brigade-major.

'I thought perhaps they intended disturbing our sleep every night, but it seems not.'

'Thirty and more dead: they could not long afford that price.' He looked disturbed suddenly. 'I've offered you no refreshment. Where *is* that bearer?

But the bearer was alert to Hervey's arrival, and he now came into the big marquee that was the brigade orderly room with a tray of coffee and limewater.

'Shukria,' said Harris, and then turned to the staff orderly. 'Inform the brigadier that Major Hervey is come, if you will.'

'Colonel Murray wishes to see me?' asked Hervey, taking both coffee and limewater.

Harris nodded. 'He's not long back from General Sleigh's conference. The news wasn't good.'

'Oh?'

But before Harris could make much of a beginning, the officer commanding the First Cavalry Brigade came into the marquee looking far from his usual cheery self.

Hervey and Harris stood up as one. 'Good morning, sir,' said the former.

'Good morning, Hervey.' He turned to the bearer. 'I'll have some of that coffee, if you please, Manesh.' Then he sank heavily into a leather armchair.

Hervey and Harris sat down again and waited for the brigadier to begin. They were not kept waiting long.

'How does being an infantryman appeal to you?'

Hervey could see no sense in the question, but his recollection of the late events at Rangoon provided a prompt response. 'It does not especially appeal, sir,' he said plainly, and looking bemused. 'But we are part dragoons by name, so if there were compelling reason . . .'

'Combermere is so troubled lest he has not enough infantry for the attack that he's contemplating unhorsing the division, leaving just Skinner's for patrol and escort work.'

Hervey would agree that that was a compelling reason, albeit a desperate one. 'The trick, though, would be to judge the moment to dismount. We have no true idea how strong is the Jhaut cavalry, and they won't have lost their appetite for sorties completely.'

'Just so,' agreed the brigadier. 'And Combermere's worried too about the breaching. The sappers are having a deuced hot time of it. But they reckon they'll have the first parallel open in a day or so, and then they can get some of the siege train in close. We're expected to demonstrate up and down the place, to draw attention from the real activity, but it'll be a damned tedious business. And if this Durjan Sal knows his siegecraft it will not fool him.'

Hervey knew the siege design well enough, for all the field officers had been apprised of it. The principal object of the engineers' work was to dig parallels in front of each of the four most prominent bastions. The most troublesome was the one they had called the long-necked bastion, its height being such as to give the clearest view of any approach within half a mile. Sapping was a hazardous enough task at the best of times, but commanded by the guns of the long-necked bastion it was nearly suicidal. 'That would be the time for a bold sortie. Better for Durjan Sal not to let the guns come into action than to take them on in a duel, no matter how commanding a position his own may have. Nothing is certain in these things, as well we know, sir.'

'Quite. It's on this that I wanted to speak with you.' He held out his cup for more coffee. 'I have an idea we could tempt his cavalry out in strength, and if we lay the trap carefully enough we could despatch the lot of them very surely.'

Hervey said nothing for the moment. A grand fight of cavalry, on the scale of Waterloo – he had never imagined such a thing again. But he was unsure of more than just how they would tempt Durjan Sal out. 'It's a fair prospect indeed, sir. But I'm afraid I do not see its purpose, except to employ the cavalry actively – and I am all in favour of that.'

The brigadier smiled in a satisfied sort of way. 'I'm glad you don't immediately see the purpose, for that means Durjan Sal likely as not shan't.' He sipped at his coffee, clearly relishing the ingeniousness of his plan. 'Do you think that Durjan Sal is a man who would prefer to fight to the death rather than strike his colours?'

Hervey furrowed his brow. 'On that I have no true insight. I should judge, perhaps, that since he is a usurper he is at heart a hazarder, and therefore unlikely to stick.'

'Just so. And for as long as he has his cavalry he will know – or rather believe – that if the fortress were to fall he could make good his own escape.'

Hervey nodded. 'I would imagine that, yes.'

'Then what would be the purpose in destroying his cavalry?'

A smile crept across Hervey's face.

The brigade-major was not yet certain of his own comprehension. 'Do you mean, sir, that Durjan Sal would be obliged to seek terms rather than risk a fight over the walls?'

'I mean exactly that, Harris. We might never *need* a breach.' He turned back to Hervey. 'Now, you have ridden the whole of the ground, and seen inside the walls. *Guns*: where might our decoy be best placed to tempt him out?'

Hervey's brow furrowed again. 'I should need a little time to consider that, sir. I made some plans and sketches—'

'Good, good! I want you to consider it carefully and let me have your opinion. But your best estimate today, if you please. And by all means go and consult your sketches. But keep the notion to yourself, Hervey. Loose tongues would be the death of it.'

When he returned to the Sixth's camp that evening, Hervey found that the officers had already dined. Private Johnson was therefore despatched to bring food to his tent – hot food, for there was a distinct chill in the air already and the brazier was only just lit.

'Serjeant-major says 'e'd like a word when tha were back,' Johnson remembered, as he pulled open the tent flap.

'Well, you may tell him I'm at home. Did Corporal Stray arrive with rum, by the way?'

'Oh ay, sir. T'quartermaster made an issue after stables.'

'Good. He was also meant to be bringing some bottled fruit for the mess. You might see if any has survived.'

'Ah, so tha did know about it then?'

'The fruit? Why shouldn't I?'

'No, I mean ... it sounded as though th'd 'eard what'd 'appened.'

'Happened?'

'Ay, to Corporal Stray.'

'For heaven's sake, man!'

'Corporal Stray got attacked on 'is way 'ere. They killed t'bullocks pullin' 'is cart.'

Hervey looked almost alarmed. 'And is he all right?'

'Oh ay. T'two that were wi' 'im said 'e just stood on t'box like 'e were at sword exercise. Better than Collins they said 'e were. 'E killed 'alf a dozen of 'em an' then they ran off. T'Jhauts, I mean.'

Hervey smiled. He was not in the least surprised. Corporal Stray's resolute immobility atop the hackery box might have been in part the product of his great bulk, but it was in equal part the action of an old soldier. 'The hero of the wet canteen. I hope he gets a serjeancy for it.'

'I'll be gooin', then.'

'I'd be obliged.'

A few minutes later, Serjeant-Major Armstrong came to the tent.

'Come in, Geordie; sit down. There's nothing to eat but I can offer you some good Bordoo,' said Hervey, smiling again. 'Though I gather rum is the celebratory drink tonight.'

'You heard, then? Stray? I'd 'ave given aught to see it. The big fat bugger!'

Hervey laughed. 'When was he last on parade, do you think?'

'Mounted? Lord knows. He'd never have lasted if old Soggy hadn't been quartermaster.'

Hervey poured two glasses of claret and took his seat again. 'Otherwise a quiet day, I gather?'

'Ay, sir. Farriers have been busy, and the saddlers too.'

'Well, here's to Stray and all the stout hearts like him.'

Armstrong raised his glass. 'To stout hearts.'

Hervey refilled it at once, and his own. 'Johnson seemed to think there was something in particular you had?'

Armstrong frowned and nodded. 'Ay, there is. I went to see the sappers this morning, as I said. This business of not being able to dig out a tunnel – they're not doing it right.'

'Oh?' Hervey looked sceptical, even allowing for Armstrong's aptness in all field matters.

'I talked to the artificer for a fair while and he said they'd wanted to drive tunnels under the main bastions, but they couldn't go more than two hundred yards without ventilating shafts. Then the captain came – a grand man, he were, not in the least bit bothered talking to me – and he said they'd started to drive one under the west bastion but the Jhauts had spied the venting shaft and driven it in.'

'I fear it's the same the whole way round. The Jhauts will be very wary of mining. The trouble is, the sappers can't begin close enough anywhere. And as soon as it's known they're digging, they'll blow the tunnels in by countermines. The galleries are already made. I've seen them.'

Armstrong nodded. 'Ay, but these engineers aren't miners. We drove some long galleries in Hebburn pit and got the air in. Longer than two hundred yards – a *lot* longer.'

Hervey looked even more sceptical. 'But that would have been with steam pumps, surely?'

'Not when we were digging. We got a draught going with a furnace. Anyway, I told the captain all about it, and he said he'd think on it.'

Hervey was still doubtful. 'But how much further do you think they could go, then?'

'Well, twice as far as they reckon they can now.'

'*Twice* as far?' Hervey's disbelief was clear.

But it did not dismay Armstrong. 'Ay, at least.'

Hervey said nothing, seeming rapt in thought.

'Look, sir, why not let me lend a hand to them? The sappers, I mean. There's nothing that Collins can't do with the troop as things stand. It's nowt but working parties and escorts. It'd be good for him to have some practice.'

Hervey was not easily persuaded, though he agreed Collins was more than up to the job, especially on what seemed increasingly like garrison duties but in the field. 'I seem to recall you believed colliery a sight more dangerous than life in regimentals.'

Armstrong pulled a face. 'Aw, come on sir. I no more ran from being a collier than I have from anything.'

Hervey winced at his own crassness. It was the loss of father and brothers – and indirectly his mother – that had sent young Armstrong to the recruiting serjeant. 'No, I hadn't meant to—'

'And in any case, there's no firedamp here in 'Indoostan.'

That, too, was true. 'Very well,' said Hervey, with a smile that spoke volumes for his admiration of his old friend's spirit. 'I'll speak to the major, and if he agrees I'll speak then to the sappers.'

Later that morning, after watering, an orderly arrived at the Sixth's headquarters with a most imperative request from Brigadier Anburey, the chief engineer. Joynson at once sent for Hervey.

'What is E Troop about now, Hervey?' The major's tone was just a fraction weary, but a request from a senior officer, even of engineers, was not a thing to be brushed off lightly.

'I'm sorry, sir. I had meant to speak with you about it at orders today, but it seems Armstrong's assistance is more pressing than I'd thought.'

'Just so. You'd better sit down and tell me of it.'

Hervey hardly thought it a long enough story to require comfort, but he obliged the major nevertheless. Then he told him all he knew.

Joynson listened with especial attention, removing and polishing his spectacles several times in the brief course of the explanation – a sure sign of his interest, as well, perhaps, of his anxiety. 'Well,' he said at length, firmly placing the spectacles high on the bridge of his nose. 'Anburey wants to speak to Armstrong in person. You'd better go with him.' His tone was as incredulous as had been Hervey's earlier.

'I think I should.'

Joynson nodded several times, slowly, as if contemplating something of real moment. 'You know, if Armstrong's little scheme works, we should think about making him . . .'

Hervey's ears pricked. He looked keenly at Joynson, now polishing his spectacles for the third time.

'There again,' said the major, now shaking his head from side to side, and as slowly as before. 'Tunnels and powder and the like . . . it's not the thing I myself would choose. I imagine there to be a great degree of hazard?'

Hervey nodded, but grimly. 'I fear so. But Armstrong *will* have it.'

When they reached Brigadier Anburey's headquarters, a mile or so from the Sixth's lines, Hervey and Armstrong found a dozen engineer officers in hot debate. They saluted as they entered the marquee, and Anburey shook them both by the hand. The faces of some of the officers, however, indicated a distinct disdain; perhaps a collier in their midst was not something easily to be borne. But Armstrong was sure of his ground, even though it had not been his for twenty years. He ought indeed to be sure of it: his father and his brothers had died in a split second for the want of good method in Hebburn pit.

'Serjeant-Major, Captain Cowie has told me of the system by which you say that a tunnel may be dug beyond the normal distance without recourse to ventilating shafts. To five hundred feet, you say?'

'Ay, sir. But as I recall, there was no saying a tunnel couldn't go even further. It's just a matter of keeping the draught strong.'

Heads were shaking disbelievingly, though not Anburey's. 'If it were possible to dig such a tunnel here, the question would be whether there would be sufficient combustive air for an explosion,' he said. Then he paused, appearing to think on it the more. 'But that is not a matter to trouble you with, Serjeant-Major. Now, the officers here are all engineers skilled in surveying, bridge-building, the development of the siege and such like. None of us have practical experience of underground working comparable with yours. I want you therefore to explain in as great a detail as possible the system which you have witnessed, and then we shall decide if there is justification to put that system into effect here.'

Armstrong looked not in the slightest degree perturbed as he took the stick of chalk from the brigadier and advanced to the blackboard. Hervey wondered what recognition his scheme would bring, for it was certain that Armstrong's name would come to the attention of the commander-in-chief. He could only pray that it should not come before Combermere for *posthumous* honour.

The mood at the major's orders, two days later, was beginning to reflect the coming season. The Sixth had always looked to stand down on the day itself, and for all ranks to share a good dinner, even in the late French war – although more than once they had found themselves horsed, with sabres drawn. But here the siege was well settled into its routine, the chance of alarms diminished; and supply, on short lines from Agra, was for once excellent. There was every prospect of a good Christmas dinner and sport.

Joynson, allowing himself a cheroot, most unusually, now came to General Orders. 'And today there's rather a good story, gentlemen:

'Head-Quarters, Camp before Bhurtpore, 23rd Dec. 1825.

'The Commander-in-Chief has received with much pleasure, the report of the excellent conduct of a Jemadar of the 4th Light Cavalry, Sheik Rangaun Ally, who was sent out with twenty Troopers to protect the Foraging Party on the 19th instant, and who, by his steady soldier-like example, and the judicious arrangement of his small force, kept off a very large body of the Enemy's Horse, saved the Foragers he was sent to protect, and brought off his Detachment in the face of the Enemy for a considerable distance, with no other loss than two men and three horses wounded. His Lordship, in consideration of the foregoing ser-vice, as well as of the high character borne by this Native Officer, is pleased to promote Jemadar Sheik Rangaun Ally to the rank of Subadar. His Lordship further directs, that his approbation may be communicated to the whole of the Party, for their steady conduct on this occasion. Officers will perceive from this

255

Joynson looked over his spectacles at the assembled officers. 'Well, gentlemen, as I said, a good story. And I think the latter point is clear enough, too.'

It could hardly have been made more heavily, thought Hervey.

'I wonder if Stray will be promoted jemadar?' said Rose, blowing a great deal of cigar smoke towards the roof of the marquee.

There was an equal deal of laughter.

Joynson looked wryly over his spectacles. 'Well, the Eleventh are ruing their distance from camp these past couple of days. They were cut about in the outlying picket the day before last. No one killed, but the Jhauts drove them in. *Not good.*'

'I just wish the beggars would come out and face us instead of all this chopping at foraging parties and pickets, and feinting on our part.'

'So that we can send them all to hell, Rose?' said Joynson, peering over his spectacles again. 'And why should Durjan Sal be so obliging when he's got solid walls between him and us?'

'By the way, sir,' said Hervey, wanting to bring the conference back to its muttons. 'Armstrong is to begin today.'

Joynson looked grateful. 'Indeed, yes. Gentlemen, for those who do not know, Sar'nt-Major Armstrong is attached forthwith to the engineers to render assistance in their excavations.'

Hervey noted the final noun. It was entirely accurate without giving away the precise nature of the work.

'Serjeant Collins shall stand in his place, and E Troop shall stand ready to provide assistance as required. Oh, and Corporal Stray is forthwith posted to E Troop.'

Nicely done, thought Hervey. No one would be likely to deduce anything. Indeed, the odd smile and coarse comment suggested that the others pitied E Troop as having been made a fatigue party.

Joynson pressed on, modulating his voice just sufficiently to suggest that what he now relayed was unconnected with what had gone before. 'I am very glad to report that last night, it seems, there was an operation, entirely successful, to take the gardens before the long-necked bastion – known on our maps as Buldeo

Singh's garden – and the nearby village of Kuddum Kundee. The heavy cannonade we heard this morning was directed on the two prizes, but, I am given to understand, to little effect. The engineers will now begin the planned parallel, and this will materially assist the sapping operations in that direction.'

There followed more routine information, lists of escorts and patrols, and orders for the night's pickets.

'Does anyone have a question?' asked Joynson finally.

No one admitted to it.

'Very well, gentlemen. I think there will soon be rapid progress. You know what is his lordship's general design; you must act on your own cognizance when it is called for.'

The assembly began to break up.

'Oh, and I have some further excellent news, gentlemen. Sir Ivo is proceeding at this time from Calcutta to rejoin us. He is expected, *Deo volente*, within the seven days following.'

This latter news displaced all else. Hervey was full of admiration for the obvious ploy – and not a little disappointed for Joynson, who would thereby be deprived of the honour of command in the hour of victory. But that was the way of things.

Corporal Stray was a practical man, and as such he was not inclined to nod to something until convinced. 'See thee, Sar'nt-Major sir,' he replied, pushing his undersized forage cap back and scratching his head. 'I can't see that owt I can make'll do t'job.' The accent was not nearly as pronounced as Johnson's, but it was marked nevertheless. 'When I were prenticed at 'Untsman's—'

'Corporal Stray, I couldn't give a fart about Huntsman's. Just do as you're told. I want a wooden duct, six-inch-square, that can be extended as we dig. As simple as that.'

Stray scratched his head again. 'All right, Serjeant-Major.'

'It'd better be. And later on I'll want a burlap partition the size of the tunnel.'

'Where do I get t'wood, sir?'

Armstrong checked himself. It was, looked at from one angle, a reasonable enough question. 'Corporal Stray, the engineers' entire field park is at your disposal. Just go to the artificer over there and give him your requirements.'

'Right, Serjeant-Major.'

'But Mick, ask him nicely.'

Armstrong shook his head as Corporal Stray shuffled off.

Hervey smiled. Time and place were all the same to Corporal Stray. 'How long will it take to dig?'

'If we don't hit any rock, it shouldn't take us more than five days round the clock.'

Hervey looked again at the ground. Three hundred yards they proposed to dig. 'Geordie, seven or eight feet every hour? How are you going to keep that up? How are you going to bring out all the spoil?'

Armstrong looked assured. 'That's them engineers' worry. It'd be the same if they were sapping rather than mining. A good gang of colliers'd clear that in a ten-hour shift.'

'What is it exactly that you'll do?'

Armstrong shrugged his shoulders. 'There's no need of me at all, sir. It's just that some of the officers don't believe it'll work, and Brigadier Anburey wants me to make certain it does.' He gestured to where, covered from view by half a dozen tamarisk trees, the sappers were beginning the drift down to the level at which they would drive the tunnel to the bastion's foundations. 'See, they know what they're about right enough.'

Hervey thought they looked as though they did. 'The major's asked that I keep an eye on things, but there's no use my being here, not to begin with anyway. I'll come each morning and evening. Where will you sleep – here?'

'Ay, sir. Stray's going to need a hand too. I'd like Harkness an' all if I can. He were a cooper, if I remember right. He'll be handy with hammer and nails. And a couple of others in a day or so.'

It was a growing bill, but better, thought Hervey, than the endless fatigues and working parties. He told Armstrong he could have Harkness, and any other he thought had a particular skill. It seemed the least he could do when the regiment were otherwise so cosily set up, and safely, in their distant lines. Then he set off back through the workings to find Gilbert, and quickly, for he had arranged with Johnson for his bath to be drawn by seven. He had to watch his step, though: the paraphernalia of the sappers' siege park – and the activity, so different from that of cavalry lines, could be hazardous for an outsider.

*

He slept little and fitfully that night. Both sides had kept up a harassing artillery fire well into the early hours, and soon after midnight there had been an alarm which saw them stood to their horses until two o'clock. It was the routine of the siege he had first come to know a dozen years before, first standing on the defensive at Torres Vedras, and then, the boot on the other foot, at Ciudad Rodrigo. Long days of boredom, occasional danger, with little opportunity for action – only the tumultuous climax, the breaching of the walls and the rushing-in of brave men bent on promotion, the 'forlorn hope', more often than not aptly named, and then the fight through the streets until the heart of the fortress struck and its flag was hauled down. It was the business of the artillery, the engineers and the infantry, the cavalry at best on lookers, at worst an appendage of the wagon train. It was true that volunteers were called for throughout the army for the forlorn hopes – and if Combermere did indeed want to dismount the cavalry they might all be in red coats soon – but as a rule a dragoon might as well be astride a screw as a blood. They had been luckier this time for sure, with the dash for the Motee Jheel and the skirmishes with Durjan Sal's cavalry, but it had been momentary and, in the greater scheme of the siege, would be quickly forgotten. Only the brigadier's *ruse de guerre* offered them sport, the chance of fighting en masse from the saddle in the old way.

After stand-down, Hervey shaved in plentiful hot water and then breakfasted on eggs and bacon, and very good toast. The coffee, too, was quite excellent, hot and without bitterness. There were even newspapers. They were out of range of cannon fire and it was as if they were at camp for the winter manoeuvres. It was the sole advantage of the siege over a campaign of movement, he considered. The only vexing aspect of these otherwise most congenial arrangements was the presence of Cornet Green. Hervey could barely bring himself to speak civilly to him, if at all. Besides his constant maladroitness with the dragoons, and – present to Hervey's mind still – the abominable affair of the night battle, the cornet's bearing in the mess was chafing him more and more. Green seemed unable to enter the marquee with any ease, usually bumping into something or stammering to a khitmagar. And his table manners ... Once he had picked up his knife and fork he seemed unable to lay them down again until his plate was empty. It was perhaps of no great hazard to good order and military discipline (Green was hardly likely to be seated next to the Governor-General, ever), but for some reason this morning it gave Hervey increasing distress.

'Mr Green!' he said suddenly, making the unfortunate cornet cough up a part of his breakfast. 'I shall want you to do duty with the sar'nt-major today.'

'Yes, Hervey,' replied Green, his face the colour of a beetroot, though whether by way of the coughing or because of his troop-leader's attention was uncertain.

Strickland lowered his copy of the *Calcutta Journal* and looked Hervey in the eye. The transaction of any sort of business in the mess was distasteful, most certainly at the breakfast table. But that was not entirely the purpose of the gesture.

Hervey cleared his throat. 'Is there anything of interest in the *Journal?*' he asked, as matter-of-fact as he could manage.

Strickland took a sip of his coffee. 'The bishop has given a party to the ladies left behind.'

'That is very good of him,' said Hervey, in a mildly ironic tone.

'He writes very fine hymns, Hervey. Even I would concede that.'

Hervey merely frowned.

By now, Cornet Green had finished his breakfast – or rather, had finished his attempt at it – and had quit the mess, leaving just the two of them.

'Something must be done about Green,' said Strickland, folding his paper and laying it down. 'I feel half sorry for him.'

'I'm afraid I find not a single redeeming feature,' said Hervey decidedly.

'Can he not be persuaded to exchange? He's not short of money, and he can hardly be happy.'

'I imagine the subalterns have tried. I can't think for the life of me why he chose to come here.'

'Perhaps that is his single redeeming feature, then?'

Hervey raised his eyebrows. 'Strickland, I'm sorry to say but I think he's gun-shy.' He related once more the night affair.

'So you want him shot over in the trenches with Armstrong?'

'That's the idea.'

'Then you had better have a care yourself. I gather the brigadier has something in mind for us.'

Hervey looked at him keenly, but he had no intention of quizzing him on where he had got his intelligence. It seemed next to impossible to keep secret even an idea.

When Hervey got to the tunnel workings, about eleven, he found Armstrong begrimed and resting, with an empty bottle of pale ale by his side. The lines that now permanently grooved his forehead seemed to have been conduits for the sweat which, even on so cold a day, had evidently run freely, so that from brow to the faintly receding line of his black hair was like veined marble – and the eyes, closed, like chips in the surface exposing the creamy un-polished stone beneath. His jaw looked squarer, even if the chin were a little fuller than in years past. His shoulders, broad yet compact like a bull terrier's, their strength outlined in the sodden shirt which clung to them as he lay, looked more powerful than ever. Once, the morning of Waterloo indeed, Hervey had told Armstrong that he believed him to be indestructible. And he half believed it still. He certainly prayed it was, for Armstrong's loss would be intolerable, and not only to Caithlin.

'He has not stopped for more than ten minutes since you left yesterday,' said the engineer major. 'Even my artificer turned in for a couple of hours. And he is famous for not sleeping until the job is done.'

The exchange was punctuated by three mighty explosions a hundred yards or so the other side of the clump of tamarisk trees, as the siege battery hurled a hundred pounds of iron at the long-necked bastion. Cornet Green flinched, but no more than would any man who had not expected it.

The major shook his head. 'They may as well throw pebbles at a shuttered window. There's scarcely a mark on those walls. We'll have to get them closer.'

'You don't think mining will breach them, then?'

'Oh yes, indeed. If we can get to the foundations we can have it down. I've no doubt that if there's enough air for a man to dig with there's enough for combustion. And once packed in we could always open a ventilator shaft by night when it was too late to do anything about it. It's just the time it will take, and if the Jhauts don't find us first.'

Armstrong opened his eyes. 'Sorry, sir, I didn't know you were come,' he said, getting to his feet and fastening the neck of his tunic.

'I'm sorry to disturb you, Sar'nt-Major. You've been working all night, I understand?'

'Ay, sir. I'll give it to these little brown beggars: they can dig.'

'How far have you got?'

'Just behind the battery. We opened the venting shaft just an hour ago.'

Hervey looked astonished. They had dug the drift down ten feet and driven a tunnel four feet high and as many wide for the better part of a hundred yards. 'May I see?'

'I wouldn't, if I were you, sir. You'd only get in the way. Leave it till we've driven a bit further and got the burlap in.'

Hervey was disappointed, but he was not going to ignore the advice. 'I'll go and have a look at the battery, then. How is Corporal Stray faring, by the way?'

'He's doing a good job, sir, him and 'Arkness. They've made fifty yards of ducting, and they'll be quicker once they get the extra timber.'

'Good. I take it he's not expected to go into the tunnel with it?'

Armstrong returned the smile. 'No, he's not. The idea's for the air to flow, not block it with Stray's great arse!'

The trench was full of men from the light company of the 14th (Buckinghamshire) Regiment, their green plumes bobbing as they shuffled forward at the crouch. An ensign explained they were going up to form a skirmishing line in front of the guns; it seemed the Jhaut sharpshooters had been getting bolder in their sorties.

Hervey turned to the covermen. 'Go fetch our carbines!'

Even in the few minutes it now took him to get to the battery parallel, a dozen roundshot from the bastion flew over with the characteristic buzz of the bigger-calibre guns. The ensign smiled. 'I am pleased to hear that at last, sir! All the serjeants ever talk about is the queer noise of the shot at Waterloo. I never thought I might hear it for myself.'

Hervey resisted the temptation to look behind at what Cornet Green's face revealed. 'I should very much like to know why it's flying so high. They surely have the range by now.'

The answer came soon enough. Just as they debouched into the parallel a ball plunged into the breastworks where stood artillerymen enjoying the spectacle of the overshoots. It threw up a great fountain of earth and bodies, spreading the ordure of a dozen men about the battery.

Hervey and the ensign's men rushed at once to begin digging out the others. 'Bastards!' he cursed. 'They baited the trap good and proper.'

Two more roundshot ploughed ineffectually into the breastworks, empty now of spectators, though earth rained down in the trench again. The ensign burrowed with his bare hands for all he was worth, as did his men. Hervey searched for the battery's captain. He found him with half his head blown away, the clever Woolwich-trained grey matter exposed like brains in a butcher's shop. But he was breathing, with an eerie sucking noise. Hervey reached for his pistol, but before he need use it the man gave up the ghost.

Earth gushed high above them again like a geyser. 'Christ!' cursed Hervey, realizing what more it might be. The Jhauts had not yet sortied, and it was now that they ought. 'Ensign, get your men up ready!'

The boy – Hervey thought him not eighteen – knew at once what was wanted. In an instant he and his serjeant had a dozen men in a firing line.

Wainwright and Needham came up the sap with the carbines, followed by Johnson. Wainwright blanched at the carnage and looked about anxiously until he saw Hervey.

'Where's Mr Green, sir?' asked Private Needham, no less anxiously; a coverman should never lose sight of his officer (the rebuke from the night affair stung his ears still).

'I don't know,' said Hervey, trying to take stock of the damage, and looking for an artillery officer on his feet. 'He was behind me in the sap.'

Johnson pushed his way past the confusion. 'Sir, is thee 'ead all right? Tha's covered in blood.'

'Yes, it's all right, Johnson,' replied Hervey, gruffly. 'Not a drop of it's my own. Why have you come up?'

'Corporal Wainwright said we was doin' a bit o' shooting.'

Hervey wondered why he had asked. 'Ensign, can you see anything?' he called.

'No, not a thing, sir.'

Hervey clambered over the debris of the revetments to stand next to him. 'What is your name?'

'Leveson-Gower, sir.'

'Is it, indeed? Your father is not, by any chance, Dean of Wells?'

'He is, sir. Do you know him?'

'I've heard tell a good deal of him. Now, do you think you can get your men out of this trench and up to that bit of a hillock yonder?' He indicated a long, shallow rise two hundred yards to their front.

A gun on the long-necked bastion belched yellow flame. Hervey spied the shot almost at once. 'Coming our way, I think, Mr Leveson-Gower. Down, men!'

They slid to the bottom of the trench, and a second or so later the big iron ball clipped the forward edge, grazed the bottom and drove itself, hissing, into the earth wall behind.

'As I was saying . . .'

'Yes, sir. Of course we can. At once.' The ensign turned to look for his serjeant. 'Detail half a dozen men to stay here until the wounded are dealt with, Sarn't Docherty. Remainder in extended line prepared to advance.'

'Sor!'

There followed a deal of shouting, incomprehensible to any but the Fourteenth, as the men fell in.

'I intend joining you as soon as I'm able,' said Hervey. 'But first I want to see the gunners recovered. Who gave you your orders?'

'The captain, sir. He's picketing the rest of the company and then he's coming here.'

'Good. Go to it, then.'

The ensign saluted, climbed out of the trench and drew his sword. 'Detachment will advance!'

As quickly as red coats were scrambling out of the trench, blue ones were coming in from the sap – drivers and ammunition numbers keen to dig. A lieutenant looked horrified.

'You are in command now, I fear,' said Hervey, briskly. 'Your captain's over there, under the blanket. There's a skirmish line out two hundred yards in front, and the bastion's got the range.'

Private Needham came into the trench, with Cornet Green behind him.

Hervey's brow furrowed deeply. 'Where in hell's name have you been, Mr Green?'

'I'm sorry, sir. I forgot my telescope.'

'Mr Green, you have a servant!'

'Yes, sir, I—'

Corporal McCarthy now appeared, breathless. 'Sor, the major's compliments, sor, and please would you return at once. There's orders from the general, sor.'

Hervey bit his lip. 'We'll speak later, Mr Green.'

When Hervey got back to the Sixth's camp he was expecting to hear orders for the brigadier's ruse, but instead he found the entire regiment standing to their horses.

'Durjan Sal's making a sortie, it seems,' said Joynson as Hervey took his place beside him. 'Or going to.'

Hervey wondered if the business at the battery was connected. 'What are the orders?'

'Childers' brigade's going clockwise about, and we're going the other way. The horse artillery will stage behind us and signal with rockets if there's a sortie when we've passed.'

'A straightforward enough drive,' said Hervey, disappointed by his conclusion that they were about to embark on a wild-goose chase. 'I wonder if our birds will leave their covert, though?'

'Well, someone has the wind up. How is Armstrong, by the way?'

'He's doing well.'

'Let's hope he continues doing well, then. Combermere's in the dumps well and truly, if this morning's anything to go by. He rode through and said the artillery had made not the slightest impression on the walls to date.'

'That much was evident to a telescope in the garden just now. And the Jhauts have some deuced big guns in that bastion.'

'Thirty-two-pounders, says Combermere.' Joynson nodded to his front. 'Well, that looks like the Sixteenth off. Trumpet-Major, regiment will advance!'

But the day went as Hervey feared. Round the fortress they rode – ten miles without sight or sign of the enemy save the odd impudent ball that flew their way. None fell within a hundred yards of them, but they signalled nevertheless the defender's constant surveillance of their progress. Why would anyone oblige Combermere with a sortie when his men paraded before Bhurtpore in such strength? The Jhauts had their walls, and these were serving them very well indeed. Why should they leave their shelter?

When the Sixth rode back into camp, it was a tired and frustrated Hervey who dismounted and handed the reins of an equally weary Gilbert to his groom.

'I said I would go see the sar'nt-major, but it's too late. We'll go tomorrow morning.' He took the pistols from the holsters on the saddle as Johnson drew up the stirrups. 'At least *they* are getting closer by the hour. *We* may as well be at Brighton for all the good we do. And I think by today's display we have put paid to Murray's ruse having the slightest chance of success.'

'Ay, sir.' Johnson had not the least idea what was this ruse, but evidently his ignorance was of no moment now. 'A merry Christmas, then, sir. See thee at gunfire?'

Hervey smiled. 'Gunfire – yes, indeed.'

CHAPTER EIGHTEEN

THE SINEWS OF WAR

Next day

FIELD GENERAL ORDERS.

Head-Quarters, Camp before Bhurtpore, 24th Dec. 1825.

Parole – SECRORA

General for the Day to-morrow Brigadier Whitehead
Field Officer, Lieutenant-Colonel Cooper.
Major of Brigade, 2nd Infantry Division.
Adjutant, H.M. 59th Regiment.

The Advanced Posts of Buldeo Singh's Garden and Kuddum Kundee to be relieved this afternoon at three o'clock, by parties of similar strength in Infantry as directed in yesterday's Orders, from the 1st and 2nd Divisions respectively. H.M. 11th Dragoons, and 4th Light Cavalry, will relieve the two Troops at present on duty at the Posts; and the Officers commanding them, to consider themselves placed under the immediate orders of the General of the Day, to whom they will report accordingly.
The remaining Guns of the Light Field Battery (from which a

267

*portion has already been attached) on duty at the Advanced Posts,
are to be ordered down to join this afternoon, and to be considered
as placed under the orders of the General of the Day.*

*One hundred Sepoys (Goorkas) from the Sirmoor Detachment,
with a proportion of Native Officers, to be sent to Buldeo Singh's
Garden at three p.m.; and the Officer in Command is instructed to
report himself to the General of the Day.*

*Working parties for the Trenches will parade in front of H.M.'s
14th and 59th Regiments, this afternoon at four o'clock, and to be
furnished as follows: by the 1st Division, for the Posts of Buldeo
Singh's Garden, 200 Europeans, and 450 sepoys; by the 2nd
Division, for the Post of Kuddum Kundee, 100 Europeans, and 400
Sepoys. An Engineer Officer to attend at the hour appointed.*

*Officers proceeding in charge of working parties, are to be strictly
cautioned to pay particular attention to the conduct of the men
under their command, whilst employed on working duties, and to
prevent fires being lighted in the Trenches, and any
unnecessary noise being made . . .*

*. . . The Hon. Lieut.-Col. Finch, Military Secretary to the
Commander in Chief, is appointed Prize-Agent for His Excellency
and the Field-Officers of the Army.*

*The second Agent, authorized to be nominated by the Captains
and Subalterns, is to be selected from the Hon. Company's Service,
and may be an officer of any rank.*

*The General Officers commanding Divisions, and Commandants
of Departments, are requested to collect, without delay, the Votes
for a Prize-Agent from the Captains and Subalterns of their
Divisions and Commands respectively,and will transmit them to the
Adjutant-General.*

*It is to be proclaimed through the several Suddur Bazaars in
Camp, and Bazaars of Corps, that any person bringing in cannon-
shot or shell, delivering them into the Park, to the Commissary or
Deputy-Commissary of Ordnance, will be entitled to rewards, as follows:*

For every 24lb. Shot	. . .	*12 annas.*
———— *8 & 12 ditto*	. . .	*6 ditto.*
———— *6 ditto*	. . .	*4 ditto.*

Joynson took off his spectacles. 'Well, Gentlemen, the orders are eminently clear, if late in the arriving. The adjutant will collect votes for prize agent at evening stables. By the by, who is field officer of the day?'

'I am,' said Rose.

'The outlying picket, only, under saddle today please.'

Rose nodded.

'I conclude, then, by extending my own good wishes for the day. The chaplain will say prayers at eleven. That is all.'

Joynson had called them together earlier than usual. Since the officers had taken gunfire to every man at reveille he had thought it best to capitalize on their wakefulness by holding his conference immediately after stand-down. The sun was now well up and taking the chill off the air, which even the braziers in the marquee had not managed to do when they first assembled, and the prospects for the festive day looked good.

Hervey stayed seated as the others left.

'I believe I may guess your thoughts,' said the major.

'It were better not to,' replied Hervey. 'Not all of them at any rate. I was wondering earlier what we might do to tempt out Durjan Sal's cavalry.'

'And what did you conclude?'

'That we couldn't.'

Joynson looked blank. 'Really, Hervey, what profit had you supposed lay in such a line of thought?'

'When I was brigade field officer the day before yesterday, Murray told me he had conceived a stratagem by which all the Jhaut cavalry could be lured from the fortress and then destroyed, which would mean that Durjan Sal, having no means to escape if the fortress fell, could not dare risk a storming and would have to sue for peace at once.'

Joynson nodded. 'That is artful. I wonder you didn't tell me of it.'

'Murray said to speak to no one. He asked my opinion as to where a demonstration would have greatest effect, and I concluded the Agra gate. But thinking the more, I believe now that nothing would tempt him out, for he can risk losing his cavalry even less than losing the fortress. And it would be folly to suppose he has not made that inference for himself. Perhaps General Sleigh thinks the same and does not approve it, therefore.'

'Mm.' Joynson nodded again, but slower. 'You're a very clever fellow, Hervey. You ought by rights to be on Combermere's staff.'

Hervey smiled, acknowledging the tease.

'You know,' he continued, putting his spectacles in their case in such a way as to suggest a conclusion. 'I've seen little enough field service, but what I've seen and read leads me to believe that there's rarely a clever way to things. Better to do well what's to be done.'

It would have been too easy to dismiss Joynson as a plodder, suited only to organizing supply for the fixed defences of the Sussex coast – which had been his former extra-regimental service. Hervey would not. Indeed, he had come to respect 'Daddy' Joynson as a man who knew his limitations to an uncommon degree, and acknowledged them. 'That would appear to be what Combermere is about, is it not – doing well what's to be done?'

'I hope so. I hope he's listening to Anburey rather than Murray. I can't see that this business will be settled other than by powder and the bayonet. You know, I've a mind to leave things here for a while and go see Armstrong and his cohort. I've a mind that Armstrong's shovel will be a deal more serviceable in this than the whole of Murray's brigade. You'll come with me?'

As they rode into the extensive earthworks that Buldeo Singh's garden had become, the battery at Kuddum Kundee, a furlong away, fired in unison – eight of the artillery's biggest siege guns laid painstakingly on the same point of the long-necked bastion, 250 pounds of iron hurled with a velocity which vastly multiplied that weight on impact. Hervey pressed Gilbert to the top of one of the earth ramparts just in time to observe the effect – a column of dust higher than the walls of the fortress itself. Were there troops ready to assault the breach?

As the dust cleared, he saw there was no need of a breaching party, nor even a sign of the gunners' work. The long-necked bastion stood as before, prominent and defiant. He frowned and turned Gilbert back down the bank, muttering about Joshua and his trumpets.

'God in heaven!' cursed Joynson, climbing from the saddle. His mare looked as if she had taken root, her legs splayed, immovable.

'It was enough to startle a seasoned trooper, Eustace. She's very green, still.' Joynson's luck with horses was evidently not great, thought Hervey. 'Give her a lead?'

Joynson shook his head crossly. 'No, no I'll walk in, damn it! Serjeant Lightfoot!'

The major's covering-serjeant took the reins. Hervey dismounted and handed his to Private Johnson.

They set off through the tamarisk grove with Joynson still tutting about his second charger.

'It's as well we approach on foot, anyway,' said Hervey, leading. 'The place is getting tight-packed with limbers.'

They picked their way through the siege park like sightseers at a fair. There were piles of shot, powder kegs in dugout bays, explosive shell in others, all manner of engineer stores neatly piled, sacks of corn for the horses, tubs of salt beef, dripping, biscuit, heaps of black bread, barrels of water, firewood and quartermaster stores, and the surgeon's dressing post, empty now, though at the same hour yesterday it was a sorry butcher's shop. It all spoke of the effort and patience a siege required, the organization. *Someone* at least knew his job, thought Hervey. And it was as well, given the impotence of the eighteen-pounders that had just been demonstrated.

'Steady, man!' bawled Joynson suddenly, as Private Harkness all but ran into him.

'Sir! We need the surgeon sir! It's the serjeant-major!'

'What?'

'He's in the tunnel, sir. The roof's tumbled in!'

Joynson pointed to the surgeon's tent, then set off after Hervey, running for the first time in years.

At the foot of the drift, where the tunnel began, an artificer

271

stopped them. 'There're too many in there, sir. It's too narrow.'

'Stay here, Eustace,' said Hervey, unfastening his swordbelt and taking off his shako. 'No use in two of us going.'

'My orders, sir,' said the artificer.

'My sar'nt-major, though,' said Hervey, pushing him aside.

The tunnel was well lit by oil lamps, but silent. Hervey moved as fast he could, neither quite walking nor running, ducking lower still every few yards to avoid a roof support. It took him a while to reach the airlock.

'Who's that?' said the crouching figure at the burlap partition.

'Armstrong's officer. What's to do?'

'Oh, Major Hervey, sir; it's Irvine. I'm officer of the day. The roof's fallen about fifty yards in. There are two of your men and Brigadier Anburey digging the sar'nt-major out.'

Hervey pulled aside the burlap.

'Sir, it's awfully tight in there.'

'Yes, thank you, Irvine.'

It was not so well lit the other side of the burlap. Hervey could see the flicker of lamps ahead, and hear voices. He crouched lower still, and pushed on as best he could again.

'Who's that? Surgeon?' came a voice.

'No, sir. It's Hervey, Armstrong's officer.' Hervey could just make out Shepherd Stent on his knees beyond Anburey, shovelling earth to one side. 'Who's with you, Stent?'

'Corporal Stray, sir.'

Hervey pushed past them both. Earth was flying back as fast as Stent could clear it, like a terrier digging out a badger. He could now make out Corporal Stray's great bulk, seeming to fill the remaining space. But it was Stray's shovel that worked like a machine.

'How long has he been buried?'

'A good ten minutes, sir,' said Stent, not checking in his own shovel work. 'The engineers had just put in another support and the serjeant-major was taking a turn at digging. And suddenly the roof just fell in.'

'I had only just arrived myself,' said Brigadier Anburey.

Buried ten minutes. Hervey bit his lip. How did they know the roof-fall they were clearing would not be replaced at once by more? Had the tunnel wholly collapsed, with a hollow in the ground above them? Should they not be digging from there too?

'I've got 'is feet, Shep!' called Stray.

'Major Hervey's here, Mick.'

'Major 'Ervey, sir, I've got 'is feet. And they're movin'!'

Hervey crawled past Shepherd Stent and laid a hand on Armstrong's boot. It was moving, very definitely moving.

'Can we pull 'im out, d'ye think, sir?'

'I don't know,' said Hervey, clawing away more earth around the foot. 'He must somehow have air under this lot. If we start to pull him out we might disturb it. How long would it take?'

Corporal Stray, breathing heavily, didn't know either. 'Even if 'e's got a bit of air, sir, it might run out soon. It can't be owt much. What else can we do? It'll take an hour to shift this lot.'

Hervey felt the desperation welling. 'We'll pull him! Keep digging while I get ropes.'

'Right, sir,' said Stray, relieved not to be the one to make the decision, and pleased to have the digging to occupy him.

'I'll get them,' said Anburey.

'Colonel, I'd be obliged if you would stay here. I am not a technical.'

Anburey nodded, and Hervey took off back down the tunnel like a bolting rabbit.

Joynson had not been idle, either. There were props, lamps, picks, shovels, all manner of stores piled at the bottom of the drift – and rope. Hervey quickly explained his intention then set off back into the tunnel with the end of a coil, Corporal Wainwright playing it out and Serjeant Lightfoot attaching other lengths with deft reef knots.

'Relay my orders, if you please, Irvine,' said Hervey as he pushed aside the burlap.

Corporal Stray had cleared to Armstrong's calves, but earth slid his way as fast as he could move it.

'There's a good fifteen feet of tunnel forward,' said Brigadier Anburey. 'It's that spoil which is falling back. I don't think the whole working has collapsed.'

'He knows we're 'ere at least, sir,' said Stray, sounding as though he was taking as much comfort by it as Armstrong himself.

The brigadier's assessment was cheering. At least they wouldn't be pulling against the weight of a dozen feet of earth. Hervey

273

looped the rope around Armstrong's feet, binding them together tight. He thought of removing the boots, but judged it better to leave them for protection. 'Keep digging, Corporal Stray,' he said, once he had made the final hitch. 'Irvine, pull away!'

A second or so and the rope tautened. Then it began to inch back. Then more obviously. In a minute they saw the back of Armstrong's knees.

'Thank Christ, sir!' said Stray, digging for all he was worth.

'It's taking too long,' said Hervey. 'He'll soon have no air.' He started clawing away at the earth with his bare hands. 'Pull harder, Irvine!'

It was working, just. Inch by inch Armstrong's body emerged from the roof-fall, but the minutes ticked by. How in God's name could anyone go that long without air?

In five more they saw his waist. And then he was out in one, like a cork pulling evenly from a bottle.

'Stop!' bellowed Hervey down the tunnel.

The rope slackened at once.

He turned over the uncharacteristically motionless frame, desperate for some sign of life. He saw only the earth-caked shell of a man he'd once believed was indestructible – limp, like a rag doll thrown down in the mud.

'Surgeon!' He cursed himself; he ought to have called him up before.

Armstrong's mouth fell open, and then his eyes, the lids flickering perceptibly.

Hervey gasped, and Stray knew they'd done it. But it was too much like the brush with death in America, when Armstrong, alone, had taken on the war party – then, as now, beyond, *well* beyond, the call of duty. The thought of that devotion, and its fruitless and terrible outcome in America, was too much for Hervey, and tears began welling.

It was left to Corporal Stray to restore matters. 'Yer gave us a right scare there, Serjeant-Major, sir,' he said, in the cheeky understatement which only a corporal of his standing was allowed.

Armstrong spat, but weakly, and closed his eyes again. 'And it won't be the last, Corporal Stray,' he croaked, barely audible. 'Be sure of it.'

CHAPTER NINETEEN

FORLORN HOPES

Three days later

FIELD GENERAL ORDERS.

Head-quarters, Camp before Bhurtpore, 28 Dec., 1825.

Parole – BOMBAY

The Commander-in-Chief is pleased to appoint Brevet-Captain Hake, of H.M. 16th Lancers, to the superintendence of the Field Telegraph. An establishment of one European Non-commissioned Staff, one Lascar, and three coolies, is authorized to be attached to each Field Telegraph in use. The above appointment to have effect from the 22nd instant.

The three Senior Field Officers of Infantry without Brigades, viz. Lieut.-Col. Commandant Fagan, Lieut.-Cols. Nation and Price, are brought on the Roster of Generals of the Day, until further orders.

The Advanced Posts to be relieved this afternoon at three o'clock . . .

A working party of 100 men from . . .

A relief working party of a complete Regiment of Native Infantry . . .

The Infantry Piquets to mount, till further orders, at five P.M.
and to be withdrawn from their position at day-break; and
permitted to return to their tents. The Infantry Piquets to remain in
readiness to turn out at the shortest notice, as directed.

A Foraging Party of the usual strength in Cavalry and
Infantry . . .

The Commander-in-Chief has received with much pleasure, the
report of the excellent conduct of a serjeant-major of the 6th Light
Dragoons, John Armstrong, who was engaged in work in the field
defences at Buldeo Singh's garden in most hazardous
circumstances, and who suffered burial for half an hour following
the collapse of his trench, whereupon he was brought out upon the
exertions of his fellow Dragoons, notably Corporal Stray of that
Regiment, and after the shortest period for recovery and
examination by the Surgeon, returned to his post to continue with
the same hazardous work as before. His Lordship, in consideration of
the foregoing service, as well as of the high character borne by this
Non-commissioned Officer, is pleased to advance Serjeant-Major
Armstrong one year in Service and Seniority, and likewise Corporal
Stray to be advanced six months in Service and Seniority. His
Lordship further directs, that his approbation may be communicated
to the whole of the Party, for their steady
conduct on this occasion.

'Well, gentlemen, a handsome testimonial, if necessarily somewhat recondite in its description of events.' Major Joynson laid down his copy of the orders beside him and rubbed his hands together. 'By God, it's cold today. Are there any questions?'

'You were going to tell us of progress,' said Strickland helpfully.

'Indeed, I shall,' replied Joynson.

'Where does the telegraph run?' asked Rose.

'Agra and the two divisions of infantry.'

There were no further questions.

'Very well, the siege,' said Joynson, cupping his hands together and blowing into them. 'There is nothing I may say about the progress of the saps and mines. Indeed, there is nothing I *can* say, for that intelligence is very properly kept privy to the divisional commanders. We do, of course, know that Armstrong's tunnel has now reached almost to the long-necked bastion – further, so I understand, than the engineers have ever known a gallery driven in such circumstances. There are others being driven now from the third parallels, but they are highly susceptible to countermines. One indeed has already been blown in.'

'Have the guns made a breach anywhere?' asked Strickland.

'Not that I'm aware of.'

'I'm beginning to wonder if powder is going to have any effect if solid shot hasn't.'

'Well,' said Joynson, not entirely unsympathetic with the proposition, but mindful of the need not to show it, 'I should imagine that if the foundations are attacked . . .'

There was a degree of nodding. It seemed a sound enough observation. None of them was an engineer, after all.

Rose, who had managed at last to relight his cigar, blew his habitual cloud of smoke towards the roof of the marquee. 'Pigs are the answer.'

There were smiles all round, save from Joynson. 'Not now, Hugh!'

'I don't think I'm entirely jesting,' replied A Troop's wounded buck. 'Our seat is in Kent, close to Rochester.'

Hervey had some distant recollection now. One or two others looked as though they might. But Joynson did not. 'I am none the wiser. You had better spell it out.'

'When King John laid siege to the castle there they tunnelled under the keep and then packed it full of brushwood and fat pigs and it was like the burning fiery furnace. It brought down a whole corner of the place.' He blew another cloud of smoke upwards as if to illustrate the feat.

Joynson smiled. 'And yet, Hugh, I am not minded to ask the chief engineer what is the relative combustive value of pigs and powder.'

They all enjoyed the diversion. Things had become very tedious.

'But I may tell you this,' he continued, taking off his spectacles and placing them in their case. 'The commander-in-chief does not intend that any part of the cavalry dismount, save of its own volition.'

Smiling faces turned puzzled-looking.

'I mean simply that his lordship is calling for volunteers for the storming parties.'

277

All were at once energized.

'We shall do it in the old way,' said Joynson, holding up his hand. 'And a ballot.'

The hubbub continued. 'Useless to ask when we shall be needed?' said Rose.

'Yes,' replied Joynson.

The adjutant cleared his throat in such a way as to bring the conference to order.

'One more thing, gentlemen. This shall be my last with you in command. Sir Ivo will be here this evening. Thank you for your forbearance this past year. That will be all.'

There was silence, and then a buzz that somehow managed to combine the keen anticipation of the lieutenant-colonel's return with genuine regret at Joynson's supersession. There was scarce a man who would not say that the major had grown comfortably into the habit of command.

When the others had left, Hervey stood up and put on his forage cap. 'Sir, I speak for myself, but I don't doubt that were I not here any of the other captains would say the same. It has been—'

'Yes, yes, Hervey. Likely so, but we have much to be about. There are loose ends I would tie up before Sir Ivo arrives. It wouldn't do for the regiment to appear to any degree careless.'

Hervey smiled. 'Eustace, I hardly think—'

But Joynson would have no compliments. 'And you shall be able to return your attention wholly to your troop.'

That, of course, was a blessing. 'Do you want me to do anything preparatory to Sir Ivo's arriving?'

'I think not. But I should like you to be here when he does arrive. He will need to be apprised of things, and yours is the greatest knowledge of what went before.'

Lieutenant-Colonel Sir Ivo Lankester, Bt, had returned to the executive command of His Majesty's 6th Light Dragoons from his post-nuptial leave amid several thousand acres of Hertfordshire by way of Calcutta, where his bride, the second daughter of Sir Delaval Rumsey, a man of greater acres even than Lankester himself, had been hastily lodged with the Governor-General. To Hervey he looked not a day older, very content (but then, he had always appeared so), and keen to gather up the reins.

'Eustace, I heard a great deal of the regiment even in the short time I was in Calcutta, and all of it the highest praise. I really cannot thank you enough, especially since my furlough was longer, in the event, than anticipated.'

'You have our congratulations on that account, Colonel,' replied Joynson.

And at dinner Sir Ivo would see those sentiments in tangible form, for the officers would present him with a fine silver statuette of a mounted officer of the regiment, a wedding present executed by one of the best native silversmiths in Hindoostan.

'Thank you, Eustace. Thank you very much indeed.' He nodded to his orderly, who advanced on him with a small box. 'And I should like you to have this, just a little token of my gratitude.'

A silver-mounted horn snuff mull – Joynson looked genuinely abashed. 'It is very handsome, Colonel. Thank you.'

'Well then. I will tell you what I know – which is only that which the brigadier has told me – and you may then tell me how little I know.'

They all smiled. And then Sir Ivo began.

It was more than an hour by the time Joynson had related the signal occurrences, incidents and events of the past year. Here and there Hervey added some detail or opinion, but it was largely the major's occasion, and one which admirably suited his eye for detail.

Sir Ivo was well pleased both by what he heard (on the whole) and by how Joynson related it. At length he smiled again, expressed himself ready to reassume command, and called for wine. 'One thing more I would hear about, though it is a curious interest only: how did Armstrong survive his entombment?'

Hervey inclined his head and raised an eyebrow as if to acknowledge the singularity of the ordeal. 'There was a duct which conveyed air to the end of the tunnel – which was itself of Armstrong's doing – and it seems that this was somehow close enough to ensure a sufficient quantity of air, even amid the debris of the roof. But how there remained sufficient air once we began to pull him free is unclear. Certainly, Armstrong has no recollection.'

279

'Well, let us not speculate on the science of it. But I am intrigued to know of his design.'

'The principle appears very simple, Colonel. The duct extends the length of the working, and about eighty yards in, just behind one of the siege battery earthworks, there is a narrow ventilation shaft – masked from the enemy, of course – and the tunnel is sealed by canvas, but which the duct passes through, just to the rear of the shaft. There is a fire at the foot of the shaft which draws air from the tunnel, and this in turn draws fresh air along the duct.'

'Most ingenious,' said Sir Ivo. 'I wonder the engineers didn't think of it themselves.'

'Oh, Colonel Anburey, their brigadier, is full of praise for Armstrong,' said Joynson. 'And Combermere's made special mention in his orders.'

'Capital! Now, leave us, if you will, Hervey. I have one or two matters I would discuss with Eustace in private. And do be assured that I am most especially obliged for all you have done, too, in my absence.'

Hervey was gratified, if, like Joynson, a shade abashed. 'Honoured, Colonel.' He saluted and left them to the privacy of the orderly room.

'In truth I should have been lost without him on any number of occasions,' said Joynson when he was gone.

Sir Ivo nodded. 'I saw Combermere on the way up. He said he would have him for his staff. I think we might contemplate that when we return to Calcutta. It would be greatly to his advantage.'

'I agree.'

'Very well. Now, the storming parties you spoke of – the volunteers.'

Joynson smiled. 'A very full manger.'

'And you'll draw the names in the usual fashion?'

Joynson hesitated. 'I have had two representations.'

'Indeed?'

'Well, three indirectly. Rose for one, for obvious reasons.'

'I should be very much inclined to accept that, Eustace. He will feel it keenly that he should restore his honour in the breaches. It could only serve the regiment's *esprit de corps*.'

'The other is Hervey and his cornet, Green, who really is a most execrable tick. Hervey believes him to have shown cowardice on two occasions, which he cannot of course substantiate, and wants to determine his mettle.'

Sir Ivo's benign expression changed. 'Good God! Never did I think to hear we should have a coward in the mess again.'

'I fear so.'

'Then I am inclined to accept Green's bid. The fact that he's made one would indicate there might be some doubt as to his infamy.'

Joynson raised an eyebrow. 'We must hope so. However – I do not know this, officially, of course – but Hervey gave him no practicable option.'

'How so?'

'Better you do not know, Colonel.'

Sir Ivo sighed. 'Why does Hervey have to go too? To bear witness, I suppose?'

Joynson nodded.

'Very well. And there is a fourth representation, Eustace.'

'Indeed, Colonel?'

'Yes. *I* shall join one of the parties. I think it only proper, my having been absent so long.'

'No, Colonel, I protest. That would be most irregular. The brigadier would surely not allow it.'

Sir Ivo smiled. 'I've spoken with him already. Oh, I'm not going to play the subaltern thrusting for promotion. I'm happy to let Green or whoever else lead. I think it right, though, that I go into the trenches and watch, at least. And you can sit in front of the regiment, where you deserve to be.' He smiled again. 'In any case, Murray says there'll not be a thing for the brigade to do!'

After boot and saddle next day, Hervey rode to Buldeo Singh's garden. He could only marvel at the difference between the Sixth's lines, with their comfortable order, and, not a mile away, the ant-like activity of the siege park, battery and earthworks. Indeed, it reminded him of nothing so much as a schoolboy's picture again – the building of the pyramids – so many were the brown-skinned labourers and so endless seemed the task.

He imagined that his purpose in going there was, however, an utterly vain thing. He had tried to persuade Armstrong that, his method proved, there was no purpose to his remaining there. To which Armstrong had replied that he was remaining for precisely the reason that Hervey himself would have stayed had the latter found himself in the same circumstances. Hervey had even spoken with Brigadier Anburey, but the chief engineer had only reinforced Armstrong's request, applauding the serjeant-major's sentiment but, further, stating that Armstrong was of the utmost material assistance. Hervey had reluctantly conceded, therefore, but hoped this morning to hear when his serjeant-major's work might eventually be at an end.

'Collins is standing your duties well,' Hervey now assured Armstrong, as they sat drinking what Johnson called a bad-mashing of tea – a drink which in any circumstances but those they now found themselves in, with periodic explosions from the siege guns and the returning cannonade whistling and buzzing overhead, would have been undrinkable.

'Are they about much?'

'No. For the last week there's been only one troop at a time under saddle. We had to have bending yesterday to keep them keen. Sir Ivo has decided to inspect the entire regiment. That at least will be something for them to work to.'

'Ay. Not a bad move.'

'He intends coming down here.'

'He's been missing the smell of powder, has he?'

'I suspect so. He's going with one of the storming parties into the trenches.'

Armstrong's face showed surprise.

'And so am I.'

'Good. I've cause to be there, too, then. I'd like to see what this 'ere tunnel does.'

'That's the reason I'm here now – to say that as soon as it's finished I want you back with the troop. The only reason I shall be in the trenches is Cornet Green, as you might imagine. There's no call for anyone else. All it will take is one lucky shell and we'll both be under the surgeon's knife. I'm not having you risk more than you have already.'

'Aw, there's not likely to be a shell – any more than anywhere else.'

Hervey smiled wryly. 'Geordie, I am not going to be the one

who has to explain to Caithlin why you're peppered with shrapnel after being buried alive. Have some compassion!'

Armstrong took another gulp of the tea, grimaced, and started rummaging in his small pack. 'Lord knows I've no ache for rum at this time of a morning, but . . .' He poured some into Hervey's mug and then his own. 'Just as you say, sir.'

Hervey did not like the tone, for it suggested the matter was not concluded, though he knew there was little enough point pressing it. 'How much further have you to dig?'

'It's gone slower than I thought since the collapse; fifty or sixty yards – three days, four at the most. Do you know when Lord Combermere's planning on an assault?'

'No, I don't. But we all know it can't be long. There's a full muster any day now, I hear.'

'Brigadier Anburey was saying the guns have brought down the major part of yon bastion's facing, but the heart of it's too solid an affair. He reckons they must have weakened it, though. He intends putting ten thousand pounds of powder under it.'

'Great God!'

'That's why I'd a mind to see it. But believe you me, sir, I've no intention of feeling it!'

The week following passed in a curious mix of tedium and fever for the army of Bhurtpore. The tunnel – or rather Armstrong's tunnel, for a second was now being driven into the north-east curtain from the sap under the great ditch, an unexpected opportunity as yet unchallenged by the enemy – made steady but slow progress, unknown to all but a few. The divisional musters, though they signalled to every man that the assault must truly be near, were nevertheless thorough affairs of inspection and repair which occupied all ranks for days before and afterwards. The names for the storming parties had been forwarded to the respective headquarters, but no choice had yet been made, or at least communicated, by the general officers commanding. Daily orders were scrutinized and discussed endlessly with a view to what they revealed of the keenly awaited date. On the second day of the new year, they announced that a lack hospital would form immediately, to the charge of which Assistant-Surgeon Murray of His Majesty's Sixteenth Lancers was appointed, and this was taken by the sweats to be proof positive of assault within the week. However, there seemed only the same requirements for working and foraging parties, for guards, pickets and advanced posts – 'of the usual strength in Cavalry and Infantry' – so that by the seventh of this first month of the new year there was an edgy listlessness to the camps.

That night, at Sir Ivo Lankester's invitation, Lord Combermere dined with the officers. He arrived at seven, just as it was dark and the night pickets had been posted, ate heartily, drank sociably and remained late. He appeared wholly content, as if events were entirely within his command. General George Stapleton Cotton, Baron Combermere, looked not unlike the Duke of Wellington himself – as Hervey had once observed in more exigent circumstances – except that the hooked nose and spare features never quite took on the duke's hawklike countenance, never quite gained the ruthless look that Hervey had noted as the hallmark of the best Peninsular generals. Yet Combermere had undoubtedly proved himself in Spain and Portugal, and indeed in Flanders and Mysore before that. And even if, as he well knew, the drawing rooms had it that his intellect did not fit him for the highest commands, were Combermere to take Bhurtpore then his name would go down in history as greater than Lake's.

Hervey studied him long this evening. He could reach no firm conclusion, however, unlike his most decided, and approving, opinion in the Peninsula. But there, of course, he had been but a cornet. Too much had passed since then for him to be whole-hearted about a man he could not know more intimately. He was past hero-worship; long past. What did his opinion matter anyway, local major of King's line cavalry?

'Are you able to tell us, General, how things proceed?' asked Sir Ivo as he removed the stopper from a decanter of best port.

They were twenty at table, and though Sir Ivo's question had not been posed any louder than his conversation hitherto, his fellow diners fell silent in keen anticipation of a substantive reply.

Lord Combermere lit his cigar and leaned back in his chair. 'I am among friends, Ivo. I think I may tell you a little of how things have gone.'

There was now an almost tangible hush.

'Five days ago I concluded that the batteries were not

sufficiently effectual to breach the walls, and so a mine was commenced in the escarp of the ditch on the northern face. The engineers, however, fearing a discovery should they continue their operations during the day, sprung it at daylight on the following morning when not sufficiently advanced to have any material effect on the wall. This unfortunately alerted the enemy to our designs, as I had always feared, and so when a second attempt was made our miners were countermined from the interior before they had entered many feet. We were, of course, alert in general terms to the possibility of countermines thanks to the work beforehand of Major Hervey.' He nodded in Hervey's direction across the table.

'I'm obliged, General,' said Hervey, bowing in return.

'So this second gallery was at once blown in by us,' Combermere continued. 'I was compelled therefore to delay the assault, waiting upon the result of two mines which the admirable Brigadier Anburey is now driving into the curtain from the sap and under the ditch. Much as I regret this unexpected delay, I feel a consolation in the hope that the place will be eventually stormed with comparative facility to the troops.'

The diners all nodded in agreement.

'I have not spoken, of course, of all our activities in these respects, for to do so would be – even among friends as here – an unpardonable indiscipline. But I may tell you that I have today sent Durjan Sal a letter laying out the general extent of our preparations, the hopelessness, therefore, of his position, and calling on his surrender of the fortress – upon generous terms, I might add, to his own person. But if he should refuse the terms – and I do not believe, gentlemen, that he will – I have laid upon him other wholly reasonable terms for the *laisser aller* of the women and children of the fortress, who must otherwise, I fear, suffer grievously soon from our mortars and when the assault itself begins.'

'Hear, hear!' said Sir Ivo, tapping the table with his palm.

With the third tap there was a huge, distant explosion. Combermere looked puzzled rather than troubled. Hervey felt a wrench at his gut, which might not have been as great had he been forward, as Armstrong. He made to rise. 'If you would excuse me, my lord . . .'

He did not wait for a reply. In any case, he was field officer of the day. He left the marquee, straining for his night vision, but it was not necessary. Flames and more explosions from the direction of Buldeo Singh's garden confirmed the worst. He raced to the charger lines, stumbling two or three times, and called out for saddle and bridle. Much fumbling and cursing followed before he was able to mount and leave camp – alone and at greater speed than any would have thought prudent in the direst of alarms. But it still took him a quarter of an hour to reach the garden.

As he neared the earthworks behind the engineer park, he could see quite clearly, for it looked as though everything combustible was alight, and blazing with a great noise punctuated by more explosions. It was at once obvious what had happened. There had been a single explosion – occasioned how, it did not matter – and then the fires had spread like ripples in a pond as successive explosions sent burning residue on a search for something else to ignite – charges for the guns, torpedoes, carcasses, rockets. And that initial explosion, massive as it was, could have been only one thing: ten thousand pounds of corned powder.

Gilbert stood the explosions well, neither did he shy from the flames. But Hervey would not take him any closer. He looked round for a horse-holder. Men were running everywhere, white and sepoy, equally dazed, but he could see no one into whose hands he could place the reins, and there was nowhere to tie a horse. He wished he'd a spancel, or even something to fashion one with. Instead, he knotted the reins and slid from the saddle, patted Gilbert's shoulder and said, 'Stay there' – as hopeless an arrangement as it was a command.

He ran through the park and into the zigzag, but he couldn't get through for sepoys carrying out the wounded. He climbed out of the trench and over the breastworks, but he couldn't see beyond the battery for there was so much flame. And all the time the noise – like a roaring wind and cannonade.

He turned back to go to the mouth of the tunnel. There was yet another explosion and he felt the air punched out of him as surely as if he had been struck by a pug. He hit the ground hard. His forage cap was gone, and his crossbelt was round his neck. He cursed loud and long, but he was not hurt.

He picked himself up, gave up the search for his cap and climbed back down into the trench. The flow was now against him again, as sappers in good order doubled through towards the battery. He flattened himself against the trench wall to let them pass, then rushed through the zigzag and out through the park to find the other way into the tunnel workings. Gilbert was standing where he had left him, head up.

''Ello, sir,' said Corporal Stray, changing hands with the reins in order to salute.

'Where's the sar'nt-major?'

''E's gone lookin' for yer, sir,' said Stray, as if the affair was nothing more than a night in the feringhee bazaar. 'We came across yer 'orse. T'serjeant-major were worried.'

'*He* was worried! It sounded as if an arsenal had blown up in camp. Was it the tunnel?'

'I don't think so, sir.'

'So you weren't in it at the time?'

'Oh ay, sir, we were in it. On us way out. But I don't think it were that.'

Corporal Stray's phlegmatic disposition – indeed, his utter and habitual indifference to all about him – was a byword throughout the regiment. Even so, Hervey found it difficult to credit with a siege battery and an engineer park blowing themselves to oblivion close by. Yet so relieved was he at learning that Armstrong was alive that he smiled and shook his head.

'Would yer like a wet, sir?' said Stray, holding out a flask.

Hervey had had more than his fill of champagne and claret – and port – but he felt a powerful need of the medicinal properties of Stray's flask. He took a good draw. 'This fell from the back of your hackery, I suppose?' He smiled again.

'Ullage, sir, we calls it in the trade.'

'There were no bloody ullage in *my* establishment, Corporal Stray!' came the serjeant-major's voice. 'Good evening, sir,' he added, throwing up a sharp salute. 'I heard the officers were dining with Lord Combermere?'

'*I* heard the sound of ten thousand pounds of powder, Sar'nt-Major. I think we should have a word.' He handed the flask back to Stray. 'Hold on to him a little longer, if you please, Corporal,' he said portentously, and then led Armstrong into the shadows.

'I know what you're going to say,' said Armstrong once they were out of earshot.

'Well then?'

'I can't slip the lead-rope now. Not just as they're coming to the end.'

'It seems to me that's a very good reason. Are you telling me they can't complete the tunnel without you?'

'No, I wouldn't say that. I just think they'll do it better if I'm there. And I want to see it through an' all.'

Hervey sighed. 'Look, Geordie; you're exposing yourself to unnecessary hazard. You've already had one very lucky escape, and tonight looks like a second.'

'Aw, come on sir! What are we supposed to be about, then?'

That was not the point, Hervey knew, but it was the point on which Armstrong was going to dig in his heels. 'I could say that you were E Troop's serjeant-major for one thing.'

'And you'd know that I knew that Collins were doing it fine. And good for him to do it, too.' He put a hand on Hervey's shoulder. 'Sir, I know what this is all about, and I'm grateful. But I'd rather stay, and I'm sure you wouldn't just resort to *ordering* me to leave!'

'I ought to, Sar'nt-Major. I really ought to.'

'No you oughtn't, sir. And you oughtn't to concern yourself another minute. Jack Armstrong's not going to 'ave 'is 'ead blown off by owt in *these* kegs,' he insisted, gesturing with a thumb to the engineer park behind. 'Yon Stray's kegs'll be a sight more trouble to me when we're done!'

CHAPTER TWENTY

THE STORM

Ten days later

Camp before Bhurtpore 17th January 1826

My Dear Somervile,
You will forgive me for having left these several weeks empty of any communication, and it is not as if by that you might rightly infer that I have been so engaged as to exclude aught else, for the last weeks especially, though not without incident, have been but a trial of labouring and waiting. Rather, I hesitated in placing on paper anything which, were it not to reach you, might be of material advantage to the enemies of the Company and its officers.
    All the preparations are now made for the storming of The Pride of Hindoostan. And in this I must tell you of the part which our Corps has played of late, for besides the seizing of the jheels, whose possession has kept the ditches dry before us, it has fallen to no less a man than Sjt. Major Armstrong, together with a detachment of dragoons, to drive a gallery at great length – greater, indeed, than the Engineers had thought feasible – under the strongest part of the enemy's citadel, and this is now tight-packed with not less than ten

*thousand pounds of powder. It shall be sprung at Eight o'clock in
the morning, tomorrow, and shall be the signal for the storming of
the fortress in as many as six places. Armstrong's exertions, and his
devotion to duty, have been without equal. He has been so near
killed these past weeks that I begged him to quit so exposed a place
when the gallery was dug, but he would not.*

*And so tomorrow we shall be through and over those infernal
walls and be done with Durjan Sal and his usurping band. There
shall be two breaches, if all is carried off, and two storming
parties are formed of volunteers, in which the Cavalry shall play a
distinguished part, I am glad to say. Lord Combermere had at first
thought to dismount a large part of the Cavalry, but the arrival of
the 1st Europeans lately had rendered that exigency unnecessary. I
shall be with the party that storms the main breach, at the Cavalier,
along with our Lieutenant Colonel, Sir Ivo Lankester, who rejoined
but a fortnight ago and is full of ardour, and Hugh Rose and others.*

*Then let me tell you now of the particulars of His Lordship's
design for battle . . .*

Hervey penned two pages more on the vellum foolscap which he
reserved for correspondence that would travel a good distance
inland, then put down his pen, picked up the last sheet and began
to wave it about gently. The air was cold, with not an atom of
moisture: it would not take many minutes for the ink to dry. He
took up the first page meanwhile and began to read.

When he was done, he picked up his pen again and reached
for a fourth sheet. He did not imagine anything, but on the eve of
such a battle – in which the Company must prevail, whatever the
cost – there were certain 'arrangements' he felt obliged to mention,
arrangements which, though the regimental agents in Calcutta and
London were perfectly able to expedite them, needed the supervision of someone of sensibility, sensibility of Hervey's own
situation.

These things now occupied a good three-quarters of the page –
nine or so inches of Hervey's small, neat hand to arrange the future
for his daughter, sister, parents . . . and bibi. On this latter he was
doubly insistent:

You who know so much of these things, of my own circumstances as

well as the travails that might come to a destitute bibi, will appreci-
ate my imperative wish that no scruple should stand in the way of
my will in this regard.

And now, if you will forgive my overlong trespass into sentiment,
I must say how it has been my very great pleasure in knowing you
both, and in the friendship you have unfailingly shown to me. I am
proud to be godfather to the offspring of your perfect union, which
duty, I most fervently trust, I may discharge to its ultimate purpose.

> *Believe me,*
> *your ever grateful friend,*

> *Matthew Hervey.*

*

The sap was quiet, voices hushed, no lights. It was a little before eight, with the merest hints of daylight in the sky behind them. Hervey had not slept. On finishing the letter he had left his comfortable, warm tent and walked the troop lines and then the picket – 'the little touch of Hervey in the night' – before setting off on foot with Green and the others to the place from which they would storm the long-necked bastion. There was a deal of time to wait still, for as they slipped into the trenches in the early hours the word was passed that the mine would be sprung not at eight but at half-past. In order, they were told, to have just a little more light to carry the breach with.

Hervey thought he would rather have a half-hour of dark than of light for such an enterprise, but then he was not an infantry-man. If that was Major-General Reynell's wish he personally was to direct the storming of the main breach – then be it according to his will.

There were so many senior officers in the sap that Hervey wondered if they might yet see Lord Combermere himself. There was General Reynell, commanding the first division of infantry, a fine, whiskered foot soldier who had seen more campaigning than most men in his thirty years with the colours, and whose appetite for the fight was no less diminished by it. There was Brigadier-General McCombe of the 14th Foot commanding the first brigade, and Brigadier Paton of the 18th Native Infantry commanding the fifth. There was said to be a wager between them as to who would be out of the trench first.

And there was Sir Ivo Lankester, wearing his pelisse coat still, feeling the chill a little but as determined as McCombe and Paton to be out of the trench at once when the mine was sprung. He exchanged a few words with Hervey and Hugh Rose when they were settled, waiting, and then said he would see if he could get a few more yards forward to be next to the brigade commanders for a better view of the explosion.

'He's a spanker all right, sir,' said Armstrong.

The consolation in letting Armstrong remain with the sappers was that E Troop and his serjeant-major now stood side by side at the point where must come the decision in this battle. 'I wish *we* might have a better view of it,' complained Hervey. 'I'd no idea the sap was going to be this deep.'

'We'll be grateful of it when yon mine's sprung, sir. I never saw so much powder in my life. They only got the last keg in just before midnight.'

'We must hope for a good pile of stones to scramble up,' said Hugh Rose. 'It'll be the very devil if all it does is rearrange the wall.'

Hervey raised his eyebrows. It would not be the first time if that happened. 'Yes, indeed.' He turned and looked over his shoulder. 'Mr Green?'

'Sir?'

'The lieutenant-colonel has gone up the trench to be with General Reynell. You had better go up and be with him in case he has any orders.'

'Yes sir. Which way is "up"?'

Hervey was momentarily speechless.

'This way, Mr Green, sir,' said Armstrong equably, making to lead him past Hervey and Rose.

Johnson now wholly recovered the situation, whether intentionally or not. 'Tea, Mr 'Ervey?'

Hervey smiled – though it was still too dark for any to see. 'Do you think it is why I got a ball in the shoulder at Rangoon, Johnson? Because I'd not had your tea at daybreak?'

'Ay, 'appen tha did, sir,' replied Johnson, uncorking his patent warming flask. 'And for you, sir?' he added, directing the question at Rose, having a care to use the less familiar second person.

'Mindful of its possible properties, I should indeed. Thank you,' drawled Rose. 'Do you think we might smoke, Hervey?'

Hervey smiled again. 'I rather think not, Hugh.'

There were a dozen or so of the Sixth in the trench. Their function, along with the fifty other volunteers, was straightforward – to rush the breach as soon as it was made and to hold on to it until the infantry could come up in proper order. It was ever a precarious enterprise. By rights, if the engineers and artillery did their work, it was but a headlong dash into a devastated space and then a few exchanges of fire with those of the garrison not too stunned to raise a musket. The work of carrying the fortress was then the business of the assault columns. But if the breach was feeble or incomplete it was theirs still to take it. And then they might face disciplined volleys, or the raking fire of guns not over-turned in the blast. It was vulgarly called 'the forlorn hope', but no one really knew why. One or two were always killed, subalterns usually, well in the van and hoping for the reward of field promotion. But for the rank and file it was not a bad gamble: a good breach was worth a year's reckoning of service.

Not that Hervey or Rose would be in the van. Command of the party was the prerogative of an ensign, always, and today it fell to one of the Fourteenth's, the senior regiment of foot in the army before Bhurtpore. It was Ensign Daly's eighteenth birthday, and he had shaken hands with each man of the storming party, as was customary, before taking his place next to General McCombe at the head of the sap, together with Lieutenant Irvine of the Engineers and, just behind, Sir Ivo Lankester and Cornet Green.

There was more method in Hervey's sending Green forward than merely to give Sir Ivo a galloper. If Green showed a moment's hesitation in leaving the trench then the lieutenant-colonel would see it for himself, and all would be up. But Hervey was not entirely closed to the notion of redemption. He thought it possible that Green, with so many brave men about him, and his blood heated by the occasion, would find after all that he had the resource to do his duty, and that once it was done he would then have appetite for it in the future. However, he had determined one thing: if Green did hesitate to leave the trench – if he were still not out when he himself came up – then he would have him out at the point of the sword.

'A bit confused, I'd say, Mr Green, sir,' whispered Armstrong to

Hervey as he rejoined them.

Hervey sighed. 'Well, Sar'nt-Major, there'll be no doubting which way to advance once the mine's sprung, so that's one thing he needn't concern himself over.'

'No, that's true. But I gave him some wadding to put in his ears, and told him to cover them if he got a chance. I've known sound enough men become a mite addled in a thunderstorm.'

Elsewhere about the fortress were other storming parties braced for the assault. But all would take their cue from the springing of the cavalier mine, or what was now known in the Sixth – the secret at last out – as the cavalry mine, or even 'Armstrong's mine'. What Hervey had written to Somervile the evening before was as much as he knew, and a good deal at that, for Lord Combermere's staff had been generous in their information in the final waiting days. But he supposed that only Combermere himself had in his mind a complete picture of the assault, the commander-in-chief having appointed no deputy, the major-generals being with the assaulting divisions. If he should fall, it would likely as not be his quarter-master-general, the veteran cavalryman Sir Sam Whittingham, to whom the reins would pass and in due course the laurels be given. But Hervey hoped that when the fortress was taken, Armstrong's part would receive its due recognition – more so, even, than it had already. And, of course, that of Brigadier Anburey, for it had been he who had directed the preparations for the assault and had ordered the cavalier mine to be driven under Armstrong's supervision.

And even now Anburey courted oblivion by attending the mine like an anxious midwife with her charge. He had assembled ten thousand pounds of the coarsest-grained powder – 'corned' powder, as it was known, as opposed to the fine 'mealed' sort – which, because of the air between the bigger grains, burned faster and therefore produced an explosion of greater force. But he did not know if this depended on a normal supply of air in the atmosphere in which the powder burned. The only way that he could be sure there would *be* an explosion was to have air at the end of the tunnel, and this required Armstrong's fire to be lit and Stray's duct to function. He would not, of course, ask either man to see to the work. He would not even ask one of his own. He did it himself –

lighting the fire and then crawling to the end of the tunnel to be sure that air was being drawn through the duct.

And so he stood now at the mouth of the gallery in the knowledge that all he could do he had done, yet still uncertain that it was enough. The lives of so many men depended on that powder. He had emptied the Company's arsenals in Hindoostan of the coarsest, and he had put bellows into the middle of the pile of kegs – *and* he had doubled the quantity first calculated in order to make up for any slowness in the burn, whether through damp or poor air. But he remained as fearful in his way as the ensign in command of the storming party.

He looked at his watch. It was time to seek cover. He had lit the quick match fifteen minutes ago and it was timed for twenty. Its accuracy he was in no doubt of, for he had made it himself, sending to Calcutta for isinglass, and he had tested two others in the tunnel before they had brought in the powder.

In the sap, Hervey looked at his watch too – the luminescent hunter that Daniel Coates had given him. It said the time was past eight-thirty, but no watch or clock agreed with any other to within five minutes, except when the noon guns fired, and so he could not know if the mine was live or not. The sky was rapidly lightening. Now would be best, while they could still cross the hundred yards to the walls without the defenders seeing all. He made to draw his sword, but the sap was too tight-packed. He pulled the pistol from his belt instead.

'Sar'nt-Major, do you think—'

The mine went off like the crack of doom. The earth shook as if the trench sides would fall in, splinters of stone whistled overhead like bullets, rocks showered into the sap. A dragoon standing only two feet behind Johnson was felled dead instantly. Ahead there was shouting and moans. Hervey began to push forward, but he could not get past the men in front waiting to debouch from the end of the sap. The artillery had opened fire, on the signal, making it difficult to communicate any sense of what was happening. But it was clear the mine had somehow gone off ill.

'Help me up!' he barked, raising his hands to the side of the trench.

Armstrong and Johnson hoisted him high, then scrambled out

295

themselves, followed by Rose and the covermen. He ran only a dozen yards before coming on Sir Ivo. The sap was all but blown in and covered with debris from the bastion. 'Christ!' he groaned, seeing his lieutenant-colonel a mass of blood. 'Johnson!'

One of the surgeons got to him first. The assault was nothing if not well provided for. 'I have him. On you go!' rasped the Glasgow voice.

'Stay with him, Johnson,' said Hervey, firmly.

He got up, only to see Cornet Green a few yards away, and in a worse state. 'Christ almighty!' he spat, kneeling by his head. But it did not take a practised surgeon to know there was no life whatever there.

He now saw General McCombe lying almost as bad, and Brigadier Paton. And Irvine, the faithful lieutenant of engineers. A few yards further on was Ensign Daly sitting upright, as if in a stupor. His right leg was unrecognizable as a limb, attached only by the thinnest thread of flesh and bone. 'Jesus!'

Up came Colonel Nation, commanding the 23rd Native Infantry. He took in all with one glance, drew his sword and shouted 'Forward!'

Then came General Reynell, shouting, 'Go to it, Fourteenth!' and running on with them.

Hervey cursed worse than he might remember, drew his sabre and followed.

There should have been cheering; that was the old way. But there wasn't. Or perhaps he just couldn't hear it, for his ears rang like the bells on Easter Day. He glanced behind – just a mass of men running at the crouch, mainly red-jacketed. Wainwright was with him, and Rose, and he could just make out Corporal McCarthy.

Now they were clambering over fallen masonry, the bastion no more – a great hole in the side of the Pride of Hindoostan. He looked up and saw Colonel Nation in the breach, and then he saw him fall – to what, he couldn't tell, for the artillery fire of both sides was drowning all.

The storming party was now thoroughly mixed up with the Fourteenth's assault columns. He saw their two majors urging them on. Everard knew how, thought Hervey: he'd led the forlorn hope at Monte Video. And Bisshop – he'd been at Badajoz.

He saw the first bodies of the defenders – bits of them, rather, the primitive butchery of the mine. An arm stuck out from the debris; a private of the Fourteenth, huffing and puffing as he struggled up the broken ramparts with a scaling ladder on his shoulder, took the hand and shook it before plodding on.

At the top an ensign was triumphantly planting the Fourteenth's colours. But the regiment was not intent on consolidation. Without seeming to check, a company set off at once along the wall to the left, and two more under Major Bisshop to the right. And Bisshop's were almost at once hurling themselves at a bastion whose guns the Jhauts were desperately trying to re-lay for enfilade instead of sweeping the ramparts.

Hervey glanced left and right as if trying to choose, but Major Everard was even now mustering the rest of the regiment to press into the fortress. Hervey looked about him to rally any of the Sixth who had made it to the top: Rose looked game, Armstrong was with him, and Wainwright; McCarthy, his instincts still a foot soldier's, had picked up a musket.

They set off after Everard's men, half-tumbling down the shattered ramparts. Bodies and pieces of bodies lay thicker than before, scattered like winnowed chaff, the harvest of Armstrong's method. Even as they slid and stumbled over rock and flesh, brick and bone, Hervey hoped the army would indeed remember its debt.

Now there was the rattle of musketry, and to the smell of powder which had hung in their nostrils since the springing of the mine came that other stench of battle, of ordure and evisceration. Always it nauseated some men and excited others.

Soon they were doubling. There seemed no resistance despite the musketry. They were soon into the streets of the town, mean though it was. Hervey had his bearings now: the citadel lay straight ahead. An easy affair this was, his pistol and sabre as clean as a whistle.

They debouched suddenly into the maidan before the citadel. Hervey at last got a clear view ahead as the Fourteenth's companies spread left and right. He saw the great gates swinging closed, and he groaned. What an opportunity was gone!

Then he saw what the gates had also shut out – hundreds, four or five perhaps, of Durjan Sal's legionaries, who now turned back in desperation.

Everard had his men ready in the space of two words of command: '*Extend! Present!*'

One hundred muskets levelled at the host not fifty yards in front. '*Fire!*'

The citadel and all before it was at once masked by a wall of black smoke.

'*On guard! Charge!*'

It was not his fight, this, but Hervey would not hold back – not when the citadel itself stood within their grasp. He raced forward, barging ahead of the bayonets even, sabre thrust out like a lance.

He saw only a mass of limbs and faces in the seconds before they clashed – no 'pick your man, recover sabre, ride through, rally'. The infantry had their science too, but it didn't amount to much when it came to steel on steel. Only brute strength and will atop a certain skill. He felt the sabre jump in his hand as the point found a mark. But his grip was tight, and in deep went the blade. Then up came the pistol, the flash and the smoke, and the ball striking the same chest as the sabre, point-blank, throwing the man from off it, freeing the sabre to begin its proper work – the cutting and slicing and blooding of its razor edge. In seconds, red ran the length of the blade.

He was gasping for breath. There were only bodies now within reach of him. Wainwright closed to his side, Armstrong was already reloading a pistol next to him, McCarthy stood on-guard with the bayonet. Only Rose was still fighting, determined to force his way past friend and foe alike to get to the citadel gates. 'Hold hard,' said Hervey to the three of them. It made no sense to press forward when there were formed ranks of redcoats doing their work so efficiently.

At first it had been a fight. Now it was merely slaughter. The Jhauts who had not fallen to the Fourteenth's volley had stood their ground until the first clash, but without order they had soon collapsed, while those in the ranks behind sought in vain to escape. There had been no time for quarter, either to beg it or to give it. The Fourteenth – and the Sixth's men – had gone at their quarry with brute strength and a will. Some of the Fourteenth's bayonets had run two men through at once, and some had broken with their wielders' ardour. Not a Jhaut was spared in the maidan that hour. Not one.

Hervey had not stood back, but he was ever thankful for the infantry's skill at execution. These men were now so heated they could surely escalade the walls of the citadel! But that was asking too much, for there was increasing musketry from the high walls, and they had but a few scaling ladders, and those inadequate. Instead, Major Edwards coolly retired with his company to the cover of the havelis across the maidan and sent word back to General Reynell for the engineers to bring up longer ladders, and powder to blow in the gates.

Rose now rejoined them. He agreed it was an affair of redcoats, with little they themselves could do. Instead they would explore: if the other breaches and escalades had been successful, there ought now to be attempts on the stronghold from a number of directions.

'South, I think, towards the Agra gate,' said Hervey. 'That's where General Adams's brigade should enter.'

Armstrong shouted for McCarthy and a couple of the volunteers from B Troop to join them, and they slipped away down one of the narrow streets running parallel to the citadel, not quite at the double, but breaking into a jog-trot here and there when it seemed right.

They saw no one at first, either alive or dead. The havelis must be empty, thought Hervey – and thank God, too, knowing what might happen. And then, round a corner, they ran into the pitiful flotsam of any siege. Half a dozen women, children in hand, some with babes in arm, were evidently trying to flee the place that had sheltered them during the bombardment. They were young women girls, some of them – handsome, dressed well. Their fate in even the best-regulated siege would be uncertain.

'Christ!' spluttered Hervey. 'What in God's name do they think they're doing? Get inside!' he shouted, gesturing with his sword.

They were now terror-struck.

Armstrong and McCarthy ran forward, taking off their shakos and making a show of courtesy. It seemed to work. The party started back indoors. Armstrong made a sign to them to draw the bolts and hide themselves.

Hervey saw their chowkidar trying to slink away, and tried to make the same reassuring gestures as Armstrong. Then he had a suspicion – just something in the man's look. He took a step towards him and the man turned to run. He followed – not long –

and then it was out. There was the Khombeer gate, and before it was Durjan Sal – there could be no doubt. He had just paused long enough to collect his zenana, and now he would make his escape. Hervey could have spat with contempt as he thought of the men left to fight and die, ignorant of their prince's craven course.

One of the spearmen turned his horse and ran at him. Hervey raised his pistol and waited for the certainty of hitting, but a shot from behind brought his adversary down instead. He glanced round, to see Corporal Wainwright already reloading his carbine. And there were Armstrong, McCarthy and the two B-Troop men.

The carbines brought down three more before the gates swung open and Durjan Sal and his coterie – it looked like fifty – dashed for their freedom.

Hervey rushed for the nearest horse, a stallion that defied its gender by standing still. He sheathed his sabre and vaulted into the saddle, turned quickly to see how many would be with him, then kicked hard, for he wore no spurs.

The guards were too slow. They tried to close the gates and bring him down, but two well-aimed shots from the B-Troop men set them to ground, while Armstrong and Wainwright began a struggle to unseat two of the rearguard.

Hervey met a ragged fusillade outside, which stopped as quickly as it began, and then cheering as the sepoy picket realized their mistake.

He kicked on for all he was worth, the stallion flattening into an easy gallop.

He glanced behind as he began to narrow the lead. Armstrong was following, half a furlong, and he guessed the other was Wainwright.

He kicked and kicked. The stallion lengthened more and was fair eating the ground. Hervey's only thought now was to finish the business of Bhurtpore once and for all, to take the usurper himself and put an end to his insolence. But Durjan Sal had fifty horsemen about him – more, perhaps, for some were joining him from the little jungled patches that dotted this side of the plain. Hervey knew he could not overpower so many, even with Armstrong and Wainwright at his side. What *could* he do?

Now they changed direction, to make for the scrubby dhak half a mile in front of the Anah gate. He would lose them there, and all hope of ending the affair decisively.

The sepoy picket before the gate volleyed as best they could, but the target was hopelessly beyond range. Durjan Sal's ardour was checked, though. The party slowed just a little, seeming to hesitate over direction, before deciding to make for the dhak after all. But half a dozen of the escort now detached themselves to form front against their pursuer.

Hervey saw he could not evade them. He glanced back again: Armstrong and Wainwright would be up with him in less than a minute. But he couldn't wait that long: Durjan Sal would escape into the dhak, and—

Three of the Jhauts sprang to a gallop and made straight for him. He drew his sabre and brought it up to the guard: he wanted nothing so much as to get by them and on to the others – Armstrong and Wainwright could deal with them as they turned after him.

As they closed, Hervey flattened, and screwed up his face waiting for the passing cut. The three Jhauts lost nerve, however, opened too far to let him through, and the nearest misjudged the timing of the backwards cut.

Missed by a mile, thought Hervey. Would his luck hold?

There were four now, barring his way. Another hundred yards – what would they do? Then he saw their pistols rise as one.

At a dozen lengths they volleyed. He felt the ball strike. The stallion squealed but hardly checked before Hervey himself reined him in. He couldn't afford to stumble at that speed.

Two tulwars met him, fearsome-looking blades and wielded skilfully, the other two fallen back in echelon behind. These were men who could fight as a team. Hervey knew he had but an instant to judge his manoeuvre.

He put the stallion in a line for the further two, to pass just right of the nearer pair – a desperate evasion, since they would be on him at once from the rear as the second pair engaged him. But a few strides short he pulled the reins up and left, but loose, across the stallion's neck, in the Rajpoot manner, and pressed his right leg as firmly as he could behind the girth. The native saddle, with neither tree nor flaps, gave him more leg than usual, in closer contact with the horse's flank as if riding bareback, and the stallion responded at once, passaging left extravagantly to career into the closer Jhaut's nearside.

The tulwar came too late into the guard, and instead the man took the point of Hervey's blade in the shoulder. The Jhaut's horse turned on its quarters in response to the unintentional rein and collided with the second horse, giving Hervey precious seconds to deal with the other pair.

He loosed the reins and squeezed with his legs, and the stallion leapt forward like a cat to meet the first opponent on the nearside again, the other man masked on the off. The Jhaut, surprised by the length and direction of the leap, failed to get his guard in place quickly enough, and 'Cut One' all but severed his bridle arm.

Hervey pressed the stallion on, but the horse faltered, then stumbled, throwing him forward. He swung his sabre left and rear instinctively to 'Bridle Arm Protect'. The Jhaut cut too soon, and the tulwar struck the sabre with only a few inches of blade; but his horse had more impulsion, and the tulwar carried down from the sabre onto Hervey's shoulder. He felt the blow, but the mail stopped the blade, and he was able to slice the back of the Jhaut's neck with Cut Two as the man overran.

Then his stallion stumbled a second time, the forelegs folding, and fell dead, throwing him hard to the ground, but clear. He heard a shot – Armstrong serving notice with his pistol at a hundred yards – and scrambled for the protection of his downed horse.

He searched the distance for his real quarry, and cursed: now Durjan Sal would make good his escape. Where was the cavalry cordon?

Armstrong and Wainwright were at last bearing down. One of the Jhauts had already made off, the two wounded had fallen from the saddle, and the fourth now threw down his tulwar. Corporal Wainwright, pulling up hard, unclipped his carbine and began reloading calmly. Eight seconds – no more – and he raised it to the aim. The Jhaut was a hundred yards away, but the ball struck him square in the back and he fell dead before his horse could cover another ten. Hervey smiled grimly.

But it made no difference, Durjan Sal would give them the slip and—

'Why ay, sir, look at that!' called Armstrong suddenly, pointing. 'I thought those black buggers must be in their charpoys still. Why weren't they standing this side of the cover?'

Hervey all but gasped. He could even see who they were – the 8th Light Cavalry; the blue and the white of their Company uniforms could have been the Sixth's own. More and more of them appeared from the dhak, extending line so rapidly that it was impossible to evade them.

Durjan Sal saw it was thus, too. In a minute more the usurper of Bhurtpore, his most favoured wife and jewels, and his worst henchmen, would be prisoners.

Hervey wished he had his telescope to see the moment. Durjan Sal was as good as bagged, though – that was what mattered.

But Durjan Sal would not be put in a bag by brown faces from Calcutta! He was a Jhaut. He did not submit to effete Bengalis. He turned back and began trotting instead towards the King's men, sword held high in both hands as a gesture of submission.

Hervey took the reins of the loose horse which Armstrong now led up, sheathed his sabre and sprang into the saddle. He would receive Durjan Sal's sword with proper ceremony. But he could not trust him, even now – even with two hundred of the Company's best cavalry trotting up fast behind. Wainwright took post left and rear, his carbine cradled, loaded ready. Armstrong drew and sloped his sabre, taking post on the right.

Durjan Sal, his tulwar now sheathed, and those of his followers, brought his horse to the walk and then to a halt in front of them. He bowed his head – not submissively, but in acknowledgement that he was beaten – drew his sword again and held it out in both palms. Wainwright brought his carbine to the port, lest the usurper have second thoughts. Armstrong took the tulwar – a fine, jewelled piece – and handed it to Hervey. The two dozen followers could wait for the Eighth to close.

Hervey looked Durjan Sal in the eye, searching for a clue. He saw only a mean-featured man, who could not hold a candle to those who had fought so senselessly for him on the maidan just now – and who were dying still, no doubt, in the citadel. He looked at his charger, a sleek Marwari stallion, blood about its mouth and flanks from its rider's hard hands and ruthless spurs. He would have this horse, in the old fashion. He would ride it, as victorious generals had their adversaries', and show the usurper what it was to defy the King's authority. He looked at the favourite wife, a beauty by more even than Jhaut measures. There was a time when she would have been his too, to submit like the charger to the victor's will. He had the urge to revive the custom now. He had the *greatest* urge to revive it.

'Take the lady Durjan Sal into protection, Serjeant-Major,' he said. 'Corporal Wainwright, have the prisoner ride another, and take possession of his mount!'

CHAPTER TWENTY-ONE

REGIMENTAL MOURNING

Three days later

Despite the laurels that had daily come the regiment's way since the fall of the fortress, there was a distinct air of discouragement about the Sixth. The death of Sir Ivo Lankester had gone hard with all ranks. Not surprisingly though, for despite his absence of a year and more, and his return only very lately, there had been something about Sir Ivo that seemed to win the absolute trust of a subordinate. It was perhaps the same easy, patrician manner with which he went about his command – nothing in the least dilatory, yet breathing a calm assurance that said all would be well. Hervey thought him superior even to his brother, and Sir Edward Lankester had been a paragon. Sir Ivo, though he had come late to the regiment – direct to the lieutenant-colonelcy, indeed – had been an officer in the true Sixth mould nevertheless: he did not flog, he spent his money generously but unostentatiously, and he gave his time as unstintingly. He did not have to come to India in the first place. He was rich enough to have sold out and bought command of another regiment more agreeably posted, as many did. And he had died because hefelt he had not shared enough of his regiment's perils.

And to all this was added a curious and entirely illogical sense of failure: the regiment had lost its commanding officer – by some dereliction it had brought about his death. Even Joynson, who of all men knew the circumstances of Sir Ivo's being in the trenches, could not escape the mood.

With Hervey discouragement was made worse by apprehensiveness. It was uncertain what the succession of command would be, and it seemed only yesterday, still, that the regiment was made unhappy by the imposition of an unworthy lieutenant-colonel. Combermere had been quick to give Joynson a brevet, but that would not do with the Horse Guards for long. But for now there was little business to be about but that of a garrison – and little enough of that, since the occupation was the business of the infantry.

'I wish that budgerow could have been but half a mile faster in the hour,' said Eyre Somervile, picking his way carefully over the loose masonry of the citadel's walls. 'It's a poor business to hear accounts only.'

Hervey unfastened his pelisse coat a little. The sun was warm, and the wind that had shaken the Sixth's camp so much the day before had gone.

'And Amherst had particularly wanted that I accompany Sir Charles Metcalfe when he installed Bulwant Sing,' continued Somervile, himself wrapped in thick woollens.

'Well,' said Hervey, sympathetically, 'I can see that he might have thought the siege would go longer. But you were right to be elsewhere in the hours after the citadel struck. I'm afraid it was the old rules of war for many, and the sepoys the worst. The officers were not nearly active enough. I do believe that many of them were so intent themselves on loot that – do you know I once had to put a bullet in a man in Spain? He was in such a craze of lust and murder. They get their blood heated in a storming, and it takes a time to cool, especially if it's full of drink. That's when an ensign shows his mettle, in my view.'

'I heard something about men from the artillery, gone over to the Jhaut side.'

'Oh, yes – two, and able gunners they were.'

'They are to be executed, I imagine. Is their reason known?'

Hervey smiled grimly. 'They were hanged at once for all to see – from the walls.'

Somervile looked surprised. 'Was that lawful?'

Hervey shrugged. 'I suppose it was justice. They danced a full two minutes.'

They walked on in silence another fifty yards.

'I should so much have liked to see the assault,' declared Somervile, now having come to terms with its aftermath. 'You know, Bhurtpore has been a name to me since first I came to India.'

'Well, it is better that you come now than a month hence. The engineers say there'll be not a thing to see by February. They blew up the Futtah Bourge two days ago. You really should have seen it – the most monstrous heathen edifice! Though I'm half agreed with those who say we should erect one of our own.' He gestured to where the column had once stood. 'But what an affair it was. You know, we took the place in the end with remarkably little loss compared with these things in the Peninsula. It was all done very scientifically. I'm daily more of a mind that there's so much that could be done to better the business of campaigning. We went to this business, you know, with the same weapons of a hundred years ago.'

Somervile nodded gravely. 'But in the end, it is the breasts of brave men that win the day, is it not?'

'In the end, yes,' said Hervey, reluctantly. 'Though the end has too often been close to the beginning. And for want of imagination by those whose design the battle is. Of that we had ample evidence in Rangoon. But I'm glad to observe also that it was officers' breasts in higher proportion here. General Edwards is killed, and a good many brigadiers and field officers wounded.'

'I am truly sorry in Lankester's regard,' said Somervile, stopping and shaking his head. 'You know I believed him a most admirable fellow.'

'The best,' replied Hervey, simply.

'And I'm sorry that events did not prove you wrong about your cornet.'

'Green, yes. I confess I feel no remorse at having placed him in the position whence he met his death, but I heartily regret the circumstances, for his mettle was not truly determined. But then perhaps it was the best way. If he had dishonoured himself and the regiment, what would follow now? No, it's better, surely, that the regiment believes he died doing his duty, having volunteered for the hottest place. And there's the letter, of course. I've no notion of Green's father, a tea merchant in Lincolnshire as I understand it, but he has lost a son, and it will doubtless go heavily with him.'

'And I imagine,' said Somervile, helpfully, 'that having invested so much of his provincial fortune in making a gentleman of him, he would want to be able to tell his family and friends that he had died like one. It is ironic, is it not, that the profits of tea should send a man to die in the very place the profits originate?'

Hervey sighed.

'What of Rose, by the way? I did not see him this morning.'

Hervey brightened. 'Oh, Rose. I confess I was wrong there. He's been the very best of troop-leaders. He was in the storming party. He fought like a wildcat. "Death, or honour restored" I think his motto was.'

'I am pleased to hear it. A regiment cannot afford to cast aside a talent for battle at such times – even a flawed one as Rose's might be.'

'No, indeed. And the further question in this regard is what shall be Armstrong's reward.'

Somervile nodded. 'Ah yes. Just so. His doings are, by your account, wholly exceptional.'

Hervey smiled. 'Not for Armstrong. But, yes, they are singular for a man whose schooling and obligation are so limited.'

'Then I trust he shall have a prize.'

Hervey frowned. 'Prizes. Now there is a matter for attention.' He reached inside his coat and took out a package of papers. 'General orders; listen: "Officers commanding Corps and Detachments, are directed to have it particularly explained to the men under their command, and also have it proclaimed in their Regimental Bazaars by beat of Tom Tom, that the Prize Property of every description, taken within the Walls of Bhurtpore, is immediately to be sent and delivered over to Lieut.-Col. The Hon. J. Finch, Prize Agent; and any person found secreting or detaining Prize Property, will be placed in confinement, and punished accordingly."'

Somervile looked puzzled; it was but the usual way with prize money.

'The point is, there has been far too great an expectation of prize money in the army. Durjan Sal's property isn't likely to amount to much, nor his instruments of war either. The real wealth of the place is Bulwant Sing's.'

'Indeed so,' said Somervile, still looking puzzled. 'I am presuming that the agent will determine what is for restitution.'

Hervey looked doubtful. 'That is not my sense of it. The order makes quite explicit that anything taken is, by that fact, *prize* property. But perhaps that was not the intention. Perhaps the order was written with too pressing a haste.'

'Is there anything else?'

Hervey turned to another of the sheets. 'Indeed there is. The commander-in-chief's thanks to the army.' He began scanning it for the titbits. '"The arrangements which fell to the share of Brigadier-Gen. Sleigh, C. B., Commanding the Cavalry, not only during the Assault, but from the commencement of the investiture of Bhurtpore, are to be appreciated by the fact, that none of the Enemy escaped from the Fort but on the conditions of surrender; and that the Capture of the Usurper Durjan Sal, with his Family, and almost every person of rank or authority under him, has been effected through the vigilance and gallantry of the several Corps employed under his command."'

'Handsome, indeed,' said Somervile. Then his brow furrowed. 'You know, Hervey, we had a very particular fear for you. Emma and I, I mean.'

'Oh . . . I should not—'

'I mean that your name at the head of any casualty list would have gone hard with us. There are too many senior officers on that list for it not to be perfectly apparent how the fight went.'

Hervey nodded. 'Indeed,' he said quietly. 'And thank you for those sentiments. It is appreciated, I do assure you.'

'And speaking of senior officers,' added Somervile, brightly, 'you say that Anburey is perfectly well?'

Hervey shrugged and smiled. 'Not a mark on him. He is much grieved, however, by how the mine went. He blames himself for the excess of powder.'

'Not for long, I hope,' said Somervile, his usual cool detachment returned. 'It sounded like science of the most experimental nature, from all you've told me.'

'Indeed it was. And I hope Anburey is duly fêted for it.'

Somervile narrowed his eyes a little. 'And what, might I ask, shall Local-Major Hervey expect for *his* address?'

Hervey shrugged matter-of-factly. 'A brevet, I would hope. Combermere's as good as said so. He wants me to join his staff in Calcutta.'

'You will say yes, of course?'

'I'm very much inclined to, but there's a deal to resolve in the regiment first. There'll be promotion without payment if Joynson gets Sir Ivo's half-colonelcy, but besides Strickland there are two who are senior to me serving on the staff in England, so that will not be mine.'

'It seems unfair since you were the one in harm's way.'

'It is the system.'

CHAPTER TWENTY-TWO

PRIZES

Calcutta

GENERAL ORDERS
BY THE RIGHT HON. THE GOVERNOR-GENERAL
IN COUNCIL

Fort-William, 29th Jan. 1826

A Royal Salute, and Three Vollies of Musketry, to be fired at all the Stations of the Land Forces serving in the East Indies, in honor of the Capture, by Assault, of the Fortified City of Bhurtpore, on the morning of the 18th instant, by the Army under the Personal Command of His Excellency the Right Hon. Lord Combermere, Commander-in-Chief, and the Unconditional Surrender of the Citadel of Bhurtpore, on the same day.

By Command of the Right Hon. The Governor-General in
Council,
GEO SWINTON
Secretary to the Government.

A month after the salute was fired at Fort William, Hervey and the Sixth returned to Calcutta. It was a good homecoming. Europeans and natives alike welcomed them, and 'Lo, see the conquering hero come' was played so frequently that it began to pall. Hervey, as Joynson's second in command once again, confined himself to the regimental lines and the voluminous administrative detail that accompanied the end of a protracted period in the field. In addition, there was the matter of the church parade for Sir Ivo Lankester. His remains lay with the others who had died in the assault – interred close where they had fallen, with the simplest of ceremonies and yet to be memorialized in marble – but his memory had still to be hallowed in the regimental fashion. To Hervey fell the duty of making the arrangements, and not least in accordance with the sensibilities of Lankester's widow.

On the third evening he dined with the Somerviles. Eyre Somervile had told his wife everything of Bhurtpore when he had returned a week earlier, and she had read, too, Lord Combermere's despatch to the Governor-General. Emma was as much apprised of events as any woman in Calcutta; there were but a few details awaiting Hervey's personal explanation. And she had, with great delicacy, attended on Lady Lankester several times in order to supply answers to such questions as the widow could conceive, she knowing so little of affairs in India. Besides the obvious pleasure in their reunion, therefore, both Emma and Hervey expected the evening to be of material advantage in the question of regimental mourning.

'I am to call on her tomorrow,' said Hervey, nodding his thanks to the khitmagar who held his chair for him as they sat down to dinner. 'With Joynson and the troop-captains. I hope then to gain her general approval for the form of service. It's a pity the bishop is off on one of his peregrinations. Our chaplain shall just have to rise to the occasion.'

'You will find her very composed, Matthew. That, I think, I can assure you. She was very grateful for your and Colonel Joynson's letters especially.'

'Joynson is trying to discover what her intentions are with regards to a passage home. Has she said anything?'

'Only that she did not intend travelling at once.'

'I am surprised.'

'She will have her reasons, I'm sure, which doubtless will become apparent with time.'

'Indeed, my dear,' said Somervile, anxious to begin their dinner. Emma nodded to the khansamah for the soup to be brought.

'Now,' continued Somervile, draining his first glass of hock faster than Emma's glance suggested approval of. 'Laying this matter to one side for the moment, what have you decided about the appointment to Combermere's staff?'

Hervey raised his eyebrows. 'I am offered a brevet – a lieutenant-colonel's brevet, I mean. I can hardly decline the promotion.'

'Excellent!'

Emma smiled too. 'And my congratulations, Matthew! Lieutenant-colonel – it sounds exactly *comme il faut*, and very deserving, I'm sure.'

'Thank you. Thank you both,' said Hervey smiling, but not as fully.

'You have some reservations?' asked Emma.

He did not answer. Indeed he did have reservations, though they were not easily put. He was thirty-five years old (his birthday had been but a few days ago, unobserved except in the bibi khana, to where he had escaped for a few hours of forgetfulness) and the proprietor of a troop. Who would salute his prospects if he did not take the brevet? And yet . . .

'Matthew?'

'Oh, I . . . the regiment is recalled to England, don't you know. We learned it only today.'

'Ah, I see.' Emma glanced at her husband. The news seemed not to disappoint them both as much as it might.

'I, too,' replied Somervile, half-emptying his refilled glass. 'Not recalled as such . . .'

'Eyre has been invited to join the Court of Directors,' Emma explained.

Hervey did now smile without reserve. 'That is capital news, is it not? My congratulations to you too!'

Somervile nodded. 'Capital indeed. And yet I am in two minds. I have spent so long in the Indies.'

'I think, Matthew,' said Emma, glancing at her husband again, 'that Eyre believes that if you take the position here with Lord Combermere, his own choice will be the easier.'

Somervile said nothing.

'A really very agreeable thought,' replied Hervey, much heartened. 'Though I fail to see how my being Lord Combermere's military secretary should facilitate your business with the Governor-General and the council.'

Hervey's reply presumed which decision it would be, but Somervile was not minded to observe on it. 'Just wait until you have seen the workings of Fort William, my good friend. Then you will understand.'

The prospect sounded not altogether inviting.

'So you see, Matthew,' said Emma, laying a hand on his. 'You shall make the choice between you.'

Next day at ten o'clock, Brevet-Lieutenant-Colonel Joynson, Brevet-Major Hervey and Captains Strickland and Rose stepped down from the regimental calèche at the residence of the Governor-General. They wore levee dress and together presented a picture of the utmost smartness, as was their intention in order to display their greatest respects.

Lord Amherst's major-domo showed them into a sitting room hung with bright Indian silks, and Sir Ivo's widow entered soon afterwards with a female companion some years her senior. The officers bowed, as one, and Lady Lankester curtsied.

'Permit me to introduce myself, Lady Lankester,' said Joynson stepping forward. 'I am Eustace Joynson, your late husband's major. May I present, also, Major Hervey, Captains Strickland and Rose.'

Each nodded in turn.

'Gentlemen,' she said by reply, softly.

Hervey observed a beautiful woman, for all her mourning weeds. Neither did the pain of her loss line her face excessively, so that she appeared no older than the twenty-five years which Emma Somervile had asserted. But the reason for her delaying passage home was easily apparent. To a skilled observer her complexion told, and to one less so the swelling at her skirts. Hervey had known of it, through Emma, and had told the others. Nevertheless, the appearance of widow with child was more a trial than any of them had expected. Lady Lankester was now, if not before, 'on the strength'.

Three weeks later, on a bright, hopeful spring morning, Emma Somervile walked the Sixth's lines with Hervey, probing him for some intimation of his decision on the appointment to Combermere's staff.

'I think Joynson is of a mind to quit India sooner than I thought,' he said at length, as if it had some special bearing.

'I believe I may know why.'

'Oh?'

'Frances. I spoke with Eyre about her only a little time before you all returned. I do believe she will very soon make a spectacle of herself. *More*, for she has in truth made herself so on several occasions. It was a blessing when the army left for Bhurtpore.'

'I feel very sorry for him. There's no word yet from the Horse Guards about whether the regiment can be his.'

'And your own decision will be consequent on learning it?'

'I'm bound to say that it could. I'm being pressed almost daily by Lord Combermere's military secretary for an answer.'

'You surely cannot turn down promotion, Matthew?'

He smiled. 'Do you want me to say "yes" so that Eyre might take his post in London with ease?'

Emma squeezed his arm. 'I confess I do not know what would be the right course for Eyre. I myself have no very great inclination to return to England, and Eyre is so very suffused by all that there is in this land that I fear he might decline in spirits. You know, Matthew, he prizes your society greatly. I do believe that whatever your decision now, his would be to do likewise.' She laid a hand to his arm. 'And I should be very happy too if that were so.'

Hervey was greatly touched by the continuing evidence of his friends' affection. But he was as yet unable to give any undertaking. 'Well, I may tell you that I must give an answer to the military secretary within the week. But I tell you, Emma, I have scarcely ever found a decision so troublesome.'

Emma simply raised an eyebrow and inclined her head, a gesture to say she understood perfectly but could be of no help.

'But how is Somervile today?' asked Hervey, determined now to be bright. 'In good spirits, I trust. Shall he dine with us in mess, as we arranged?'

Emma brightened too. 'Oh, he is in excellent spirits, though he is angered by the commander-in-chief.'

'Combermere? How so?'

'He had a letter this morning from Sir Charles Metcalfe, who complains that the prize agents are appropriating property by rights the rajah's. He says it's little better than outright theft.'

Hervey sighed. He had imagined it might be so, though he supposed it was nothing entirely new. 'And the bulk of it, I fear, will find its way down the throat, though the widows will be glad of their share.'

Serjeant-Major Armstrong stepped from the forage store as they drew parallel. He saluted and hailed them in a model combination of propriety and familiarity.

'Mr Armstrong, I am sorry we have not met since your return,' said Emma, beaming wide. 'Let me shake your hand. I am all admiration for your exploits. The whole of Calcutta is!'

Armstrong glanced at Hervey, who nodded. 'Ah, *them* exploits, ma'am!'

'I believe Mrs Armstrong may have told me of the others, Serjeant-Major,' replied Emma, with just the right note of mystery.

'Well, ma'am, it felt queer to be on me hands and knees again after all these years, but it worked in the end.'

'And I hope it is rightly esteemed.' Emma looked at Hervey.

Armstrong had no doubt of it, however. 'It is indeed, ma'am. Advanced in seniority and service by three years no less. As I was saying to Mr Hairsine, I'm only a molehill from being RSM.'

Emma smiled again, and turned to her companion. 'Are there moles in India, do you know, Major Hervey?'

On the Saturday morning following, after the customary weekly parade, Hervey sat down at his desk in regimental headquarters and began at last to compose his letter to Lord Combermere's military secretary: 'Sir, I have the honour to . . .'

The clerk had lit a fire, but Hervey did not expect the letter would take him many minutes to draft.

He was scarcely begun when a red-faced Joynson marched in and began angrily waving a sheet of paper in front of him. 'Look! Unspeakable! Infamous!'

Hervey could not suppose what on earth might bring so equable a man to such a rage. He stood up, took the sheet and began to read. There were a good many words, and figures, before he came to the offending ones. 'I cannot believe it!'

'Hah! My thoughts too. Read on!'

Hervey continued to the second page. 'I am astonished. Wholly dismayed,' he said, shaking his head, still half incredulous.

'Is this what we were about at Bhurtpore, then?' Joynson sounded like a man betrayed. 'Is this what Armstrong risked making a widow with three orphans for? And Lankester?'

On the other side of the door to the orderly room, Private Johnson's ear was pressed as close to the keyhole as it could get. 'What's it about, Smithy?' he said quietly, turning to the clerk behind him.

The clerk frowned. 'It's about the prize money. An order's come. It says what the Company will pay us.'

''Ow much do we get?'

'You and me get forty siccas.'

'It's better than nowt. What's wrong wi' Major 'Ervey and t'colonel?'

'I think it's because it says Lord Combermere's going to take all his share.'

'That's not right. Everybody knows that's not right! 'E ought to give 'alf of it to us!'

Private Johnson pressed his ear to the door again, straining hard to make out what else was to come.

Brevet-Lieutenant-Colonel Joynson took up the order and began looking at the figures again. 'It's plunder, Hervey – plunder, pure and simple. As I recall, Cornwallis gave away half his share after Seringapatam. That's the *way*.'

'*All* of it,' Hervey corrected. 'He gave away every last rupee.'

Joynson threw down the orders contemptuously. 'I have a mind to make protest. Do you suppose there is anyone with honour left in Calcutta to take note?'

Hervey shook his head slowly, without a word. Then he picked up his sheet of writing paper and tore it in half. 'Eustace, my mind is now made up. I stay with the regiment.'

THE END

HISTORICAL AFTERNOTE

The Burmese war dragged on until the end of February 1826, with Campbell's force getting within fifty miles of Ava before King Bagyidaw conceded defeat. Of the 3,500 British troops who originally landed at Rangoon, only a couple of hundred survived the campaign. All but 150 or so died from disease and sickness rather than by the enemy's hand. The sepoys fared little better, twelve thousand of the twenty-seven thousand who eventually landed at Rangoon failing to return. It was, simply, the worst-managed campaign in the long history of the British army.

Maha Bundula deserves further mention. He was, even allowing for the generally atrocious quality of his peers, a very fine commander. His feats of forced marching through jungle and swamp in the midst of the monsoon were remarkable. He had a shrewd mind too. He early came to the conclusion that the British could not be beaten: they could deploy more troops in both Arakan and Burma itself then he could possibly counter, and he was quick to recognize their technical superiority as well. On first encountering the explosive shell he is said to have gone into deep meditation for a whole day. When he realized that Bagyidaw would not sue for peace, he put himself in the front line and openly courted death. He was killed by a rocket in April 1825, and from then on both Bagyidaw's and the army's spirit seem to have ebbed.

The controversy over the Bhurtpore prize money was very real. Lord Combermere was held in high regard for his Peninsular record and for his determined conduct of the siege – he had to be physically restrained from taking part in the final assault – but there was first a widespread belief that the army had looted Bhurtpore rather than merely taking the legitimate spoils of war. And then the news that Combermere would retain all his share – close on £60,000 – provoked almost universal disgust when a private soldier received £4 and a sepoy half of that.

The haul of ordnance at Bhurtpore was great too: 133 guns, and a further 301 'wall pieces' firing a one-pound ball. One of the biggest guns can be seen today at the eastern end of the parade ground at the Royal Artillery barracks, Woolwich.

The battle was the first time the lance was used in action by British cavalry, and the first time that Gurkhas fought on the British side.

Of the great fortress itself, 'the pride of Hindoostan', nothing remains but a small and derelict part of the citadel. The walls were blown up or pulled down almost at once, and the jheels are now a spectacular bird sanctuary.

Bhurtpore fell to mines and the bayonet as my narrative recounts, but Serjeant-Major Armstrong's innovation was in truth that of a slightly later military generation – and in America. The credit must go to the splendid men of the 48th Pennsylvania Infantry, recruited from the coal-mining districts of Schuykill County, who achieved devastating surprise over the Confederate defenders in the siege of Petersburg, 1865, prelude to the famed 'battle of the crater'.

The medal inscribed 'To the Army of India', perhaps the most romantic of all, bears last among its twenty-four clasps that for 'Bhurtpur'. The cavalry received especial praise from Lord Combermere, in marked contrast to the, at best, grudging recognition that the Duke of Wellington had usually bestowed, since 'none of the Enemy escaped from the Fort but on the conditions of surrender'. Of Skinner's Irregular Horse, Combermere said that 'nothing could exceed the devotion and bravery of this valuable class of soldiery'; and James Skinner was granted an honorary King's commission as a lieutenant-colonel and appointed Companion of the Order of the Bath.